BEYOND THE

GATE

Henry Kelly

Contents

CHAPTER 1

F aye Caldwell was falling.

The wind whipped her hair around her face, devouring her, as she continued her treacherous decent toward the ground. She searched frantically for something to hold on to, to halt the fall. But there was nothing. Nothing to protect her from the harsh blows from the wind, nothing to protect her from the pain as her hair bit her skin, nothing to protect her from her imminent death below.

Faye opened her mouth to scream, but nothing came out. Her voice was lost in the wind, the sky, the atmosphere. She herself was lost. She could feel herself losing hope, the will to survive. The only thing that kept her going was fear. The fear of her body colliding with the ground. The fear of closing her eyes and never waking up. The fear of everything ending.

"Faye."

Faye searched fervently for the source of the voice. She could feel panicked tears drip from her eyes, flying upwards on her face due to her position. The tears flicked her forehead painfully. She wanted to call out the person yelling to her, but she couldn't. Her voice was gone.

"Faye!" the voice shrieked.

It was then that Faye realized who the voice belonged to: her sister, her best friend that was related to her. Terra Caldwell.

"Faye, please!" Terra cried.

And then, like emerging from out of water, Terra appeared, her expression the definition of worry. Faye reached out, scrambling to catch her sister's hand as she tumbled through the air. Dread pierced her as she fell away from Terra, away from any hope of making it out alive.

Thunder rumbled. Lightning flashed through the darkened clouds. Freezing rain poured, soaking her entire body. Her clothes stuck to her like glue, only adding to her discomfort. But Faye didn't care. All she cared about was finding her sister, finding the only hope she had left.

"Faye, look out!"

Faye barely had time to take in the sudden horror of the ground before the impact came. She braced herself, ready to feel fire course through her veins and pain filled her entire being. She closed her eyes, waiting for the end to come.

But that's not what happened.

Faye opened her eyes. She was standing, her legs full of strength despite the long fall she'd just endured. She shivered. How had she survived such a horrendous fall? Why hadn't her spine broken? Why hadn't she snapped like a twig off a tree branch? Faye sighed shakily, turning her gaze to the rocky terrain below her.

And screamed.

Faye's wails become utterly audible as she stared down at Terra. Her body was twisted, deformed beyond repair. Her neck was broken, her eyes wide and her mouth agape. Her palms lay outstretched before her as though she were praying. The sight was gut-wrenching. Faye fell forward, collapsing on all fours before hurling onto the gravel.

But even with her eyes scrunched closed she couldn't escape the image of her sister, lying dead, on the ground.

Faye opened her eyes, staring at Terra despite her yearn to turn away. Something about the disgusting sight consumed her. All she could see was the deformed body of the one she loved. All she could see was Terra.

Suddenly Terra blinked. Faye shrieked, falling back on her butt and scrambling back quickly. She breathed deeply, her eyes never leaving her sister's body. Terra's head turned, twisting around on her neck. Faye stared in a shocked, terrified silence as Terra began to scream.

"You're next! You're next!"

Faye screeched, bolting up in her bed. Cool sweat dripped down her face, getting into her eyes. Faye swatted it away with her hand, giving a deep sigh. Again with the dream. The dream of her sister's death. Terra Caldwell had fallen to her death after throwing herself off a cliff. No one could ever figure out why Terra had done what she did. This is what haunted Faye despite that Terra killed herself seven years ago. Faye was supposed to be the one that Terra trusted with everything. Faye was supposed to be the one that Terra turned to when she needed help.

But Terra didn't turn to her that time.

Plucking the remote from the bedside table, Faye clicked on the television set that sat, kitty-cornered, at the far end of her room. She leaned back into her pillows, taking deep breaths in order to slow her breathing. Despite the amount of times she'd dreamed the recurring dream many times before, the result was always the same: she woke up screaming and sweating, alone in her despair.

"It has been reported that Prita Bancs was spotted trespassing into the Gate's territory this evening."

Her dream forgotten, Faye's attention snapped to the television. The news reporter of channel six, Diana Han, stood in front of Central Park, looking out of place while mothers played with their children in the grass. She did this for effect of course. Just behind Central Park was the forest. And within the forest was where the Gate resided, cutting everyone off from the rest of the world.

"Now, Miss Bancs will be receiving a life sentence in the Government's prison wards," Diana continued, gripping her microphone, trying her best to look professional and informative.

Faye's eyes widened at the news. A life sentence? How close had the woman gotten?

"She will have an hour or so to say goodbye to her closest family members. Nothing else is said on this latest case, but I'm sure it will turn out just like all the rest. Kate?"

Faye glanced out her bedroom window as Kate Ide appeared on the screen, reporting on a fire that consumed a two-floored home an hour or so away from where Faye lived. According to the police it was arson, and people were to inform them if they had any information what-so-ever. With a roll of the eyes, Faye shut off her television set and settled back into her blankets.

Her mind immediately drifted off to the latest rebellious case. The Government never let an arrest go untelevised. It was their way of saying that no matter how many times people attempted to cross into the Gate's territory, they were never going to get over to the other side. The Government would catch you, and they would convict you. It was as simple as that.

No one knew what was beyond the Gate's borders. When Faye was a young girl she always feared that a beast would jump over the Gate and turn on the cities and the women who resided there. Faye used to have nightmares, waking up in tears. Her mother or Terra would comfort her, saying that it was only a nightmare and that everyone was safe. The Government had seen to that. Nothing was going to harm them.

After Terra died the nightmares of the Gate's monsters disappeared, transformed into equally—if not worse—terrifying dreams. Every time it was the same: Faye would fall, her sister would appear, and then she would hit the ground only to find that it was her sister that was dead, not her. Faye wished the dreams would stop, but they wouldn't. They haunted her like a poltergeist. They wouldn't leave her alone.

A loud, high-pitched beeping noise screeched through the night. Faye shrieked, jumping in her bed. After recovering from the shock of the beep, her eyes turned to the television. The screen turned white, enveloping Faye's room in shadows. But, despite Faye's fear for the shadows, her eyes remained trained on the screen.

Her bedroom door opened and her younger sister, Kat Caldwell, appeared. Her dirty-blond hair pulled back into a messy bun. Faye could just imagine Kat tumbling out of bed, awakened by the noise. She'd probably hurried to make her hair presentable before running into Faye's room, not wanting her bed-hair to show. Kat's baby blue eyes were wide as she bounded into the room, hopping onto Faye's bed. Faye scooted over to make more room.

It wasn't long before their mother appeared. Her brunette hair was everywhere. Evidently Mary Caldwell didn't care about what she looked like at five-thirty in the morning like her child did. Faye smiled slightly, gesturing for Kat to make room as their mother stepped forward, entering the threshold.

They sat there, waiting.

A moment later the screen turned static, blacks and white colliding into one. And then the head official of the Government appeared. Courtnie Featherstrom smiled, her magnificently white teeth flashing. She was suit, her hair cascading down over her shoulders. She managed to look laid back yet professional at the same time. "Hello, my wonderful people of Cesve," she began, her voice seeming to boom through the television set. "For generations we have lived at peace, the Government and its people. The people followed the laws given out, and the Government saw that the people were happy. Though, now, that doesn't seem to be the case."

Courtnie's eyes grew dark. "My lovely people of Cesve, the people that I care the most about in the world, are disobeying the simple rule of staying away from the Gate's borders. To keep the rebels at bay, the punishments have grown harsher. Anyone within a one mile radius of the Gate's borders will be convicted and put into prison. We cannot have anyone near the Gate's borders.

"Please understand that the Government is only trying to protect you from what is on the other side. It is all for the greater good."

The screen went black.

Faye glanced at her family members. The weight of Courtnie's words hung through the air. Despite the fact that this new Law didn't really affect their lives at all, it seemed like everything had changed for the worse. Faye couldn't understand why. Maybe it was because it made the issue with the rebels seem so much more real. Maybe it was because it seemed like the Government was simply oppressing them even more. Maybe it was both.

"I'm going back to bed," Kat grumbled finally, standing up and dragging herself out of the room, looking like the walking dead.

Faye turned to her mother who was staring out the window absently. Mary turned after a moment, her eyes meeting Faye's. Mary smiled slightly before letting her mouth fall. "Is everything going to be all right with the Campout?" she murmured.

The Campout was an famous event within the high school's walls. Every year sixteen girls ages thirteen and up camped out in the woods, telling ghost stories. Every year Errika told the same story: The Legend of the Gate. The Campout was a way of getting away from the expectations and the Laws from the real world. It was a way to get away, to have fun.

Faye nodded, dismissing Mary's question with the wave of her hand. "Errika will figure something out."

Mary nodded before standing up and sauntering toward the doorway. She turned, flashing her daughter a smile. "You might just want to stay up and get ready for school," she said softly. "You'll be awfully tired if you go back to sleep now."

Faye nodded. She knew her mother was right. She felt awake now, anyhow. How could she feel tired after her nightmare and then the sudden announcement from the Government? "All right."

Her mother disappeared behind Faye's closing bedroom door and Faye stood up. She made her way to the far end of the room, bracing herself as she flipped on her bedroom light. The light burned her eyes for a moment, but as Faye blinked fiercely, her room became visible.

Faye flopped onto her bed, staring at herself in the body mirror leaning against the wall on the opposite side of the room. Her hair was like fire with its reds, oranges, and yellows all collaged into one single colored. Girls around Eve High had asked if she dyed it numerous times, but she hadn't. Her hair was natural, as we her vibrant green eyes. She smiled slightly at her reflection in the mirror before standing up and trotting over to her bureau.

She paused before opening one of the drawers, picking the picture of Terra up from the wooden surface. Her sister looked exactly how Faye had always wanted to look: beautifully tan with dark locks of curly hair and big, wide brown eyes. While Faye was short, Terra was tall. While Terra was stunning, Faye blended in with the crowd. Faye couldn't remember one moment where she hadn't wished she was like Terra. That was, until, Terra ended her life. Now all Faye saw when she looked at the photograph of her sister smiling brightly while she held her soccer ball within her hands was a mangled body.

Faye sighed shakily, dropping the photograph onto the bureau. She shook her head. She couldn't be getting herself upset right before school started. Errika would have none of that. After a moment of collecting her thoughts, Faye knelt down, pulling a drawer out to choose her outfit for the day.

"A mile, really?"

Errika flicked her wrist defiantly, removing some stray strands of hair from her face. Faye couldn't help but smile at her friend's irritation. Errika was never one to enjoy change, and the fact that it was a last minute change must have overwhelmed her. "It's not that bad," Faye reasoned, fixing her backpack's strap on her shoulder. "We'll just have to stay a mile away."

Errika huffed. "I'd already marked a tree so that we wouldn't go further than we were supposed to," she complained, scowling. "Great, that's one more thing that I have to do. Sign-ups are still going, and nobody's told me what they're bringing." She sighed in irritation. "Sometimes I really hate doing this, you know?"

Faye nodded understandingly. Year after year she watched her friend stress out, feeling guilty that there was no way to help her. When she had attempted to aid her friend, Errika had assured her that she could do it by herself. Though, by the looks of it, she really couldn't. "You sure you don't want any help?" Faye asked slowly, knowing the answer even before Errika spoke.

"Yeah, I'm sure." Errika flashed her a grateful smile. "Everything will turn out fine. I'll just go out tomorrow and mark off the tree so that we don't go too far, and I'll e-mail everyone tonight demanding to know what they're bringing. If they don't reply I'm taking them off the list and opening up a spot." Errika nodded to herself. "Yes, that's exactly what I'll do."

Faye glanced around at the people around her. They'd just arrived onto Eve High's grounds, twenty minutes before they had to get to class. Errika liked to be early so that she could stash away unneeded things into her locker. Faye never put anything in her locker out of fear that a girl would steal something.

They were about to enter the school building when a short, blond, freckle-faced girl flounced in front of them. "Hey, Errika," she breathed. "Can I talk to you for a minute?"

Errika eyed the girl up and down a moment before nodding. "You have two minutes."

Faye's lips pricked up into a smile. Of the two girls, Errika was the one who had the backbone, the one who wouldn't accept anything before it went her way. Faye may have been brave when it came to dealing with her sister, but when it came to anyone else her mouth was clamped shut. If it weren't for Errika, Faye would have lost so many battles in her lifetime.

"You still have openings for the Campout, right?" the girl squeaked, her eyes wide with anticipation.

Errika nodded. "Yes."

"Is it possible for me to join?"

"That depends," Errika drawled dramatically, eyeing her finger-nails. "You thirteen or older?"

"Yes."

"You gonna bring something from the Items Needed list?"

The girl nodded vigorously. "Of course!"

Errika looked the girl over once more before sighing. She glanced at Faye and winked before turning her attention back to the girl. "All right," she said slowly. "Give me your name, e-mail, and phone number on a piece of paper. You have thirty seconds."

Faye shook her head in amusement as the girl rushed to scrounge up a scrap piece of paper and a pen from her backpack. Of course Errika wouldn't really revoke the privilege of going to the Campout just for being slow when giving contact information, but anyone other than Faye wouldn't know that. Errika was known for being tough around the school. No one dared to mess with her.

"Thank you," Errika chirped as she took the paper with the girl's information on it. "Be prepared to get an e-mail tonight. If you don't respond, your spot will be revoked and handed to someone else."

The girl nodded before rushing away, running straight to her small group of friends at the opposite end of the school yard. They talked animatedly, their arms flying around as they spoke. Faye tilted her head to the side. She couldn't fathom why everyone got so worked up over going to the Campout. Though, she reasoned, that might have been because she had the privilege of going every year.

Being best friends with the host really did have its perks.

"Faye, stop staring at people," Errika muttered, grabbing Faye's arm and tugging her toward the school's front door. "It's rude."

Faye rolled her eyes, knocking her friend's shoulder playfully. "Oh, please. It's not like you don't have the habit of staring at people."

Errika responded by staring at her. Faye struggled to contain her laughter as they headed up a stairwell. Errika kept eye contact with her the whole way, her big blue eyes never blinking. Errika's eyes went well with her hair, Faye couldn't help but notice. Dark brown, so dark that it could almost be considered black. Faye had always been jealous of her friend's hair; it was so long and thick, and while Errika always managed to keep her hair looking like a super model's, Faye had to use assorted hair products to keep the frizz at bay.

"Okay, quit it," Faye said, exasperatedly pushing Errika's face away. "You're going to trip, fall, and then die."

Errika wriggled her eyebrows. "And what would you do if that did happen?"

"Stare, laugh, and then maybe loot your pockets for loose change."

Errika stared at Faye for a long time before bursting into fits of giggles. She clutched the railing for support, pointing at Faye as she laughed. "That was good," she complimented once her laughter receded. "That was very good."

Faye laughed along with her friend for a moment before sighing. "I had the dream again."

Errika eyed her sympathetically. "Again?" She brought her arm around Faye's shoulders. "I'm so sorry, babes."

Faye nodded slightly. "I just . . . I keep waiting for the dreams to stop, but they don't. I don't know what to do."

Errika sighed. "Have you talked to your mom about this?"

"No." Faye shook her head. "I don't want to bring the memory of Terra to her when she seems to finally be pulling herself together."

Mary was a sweet woman, and Faye couldn't bear to see her in pain. It hurt to watch such a kind, loving woman sink into a deep depression after her daughter took her own life. For a long while Faye had been angry at Terra, wondering why she would do such a thing to her family. They hadn't done anything to deserve it. Terra had been everything to her mother and Faye.

"True." Errika nodded. "And you don't need Kat getting all upset because Terra dying was the reason why she could be delivered to the house."

The limit of children in Cesve was two per household. Once a child reached the age of eighteen or, like in Terra's case, died another child was able to be delivered to the house. Once a month Government officials came around, delivering ordered children. Though, there were some cases where no one chose to take some of the children available and they were sent to an orphanage near the outskirts of town. It was there that Faye's mother had received Kat.

"Definitely," Faye agreed, nodding. "That was horrible the last time. It was like she'd lost Terra herself even though she's never met the girl before."

Errika sighed, turning and blocking Faye's way from the rest of the stairwell. Faye tried to dodge her, but Errika simply shifted so that the path was blocked again. "Let's not talk about death and depression today, shall we?" Errika said, her tone final. "I don't want you going through that again, all right?"

Faye nodded, biting her lip. "All right."

"Now!" Errika said, her voice becoming animated once again. "What are you going to bring to the Campout? Let me assure you, just because you're my best friend does not mean that I won't revoke your invite."

Faye smiled. Let the day begin.

CHAPTER 2

The wind blew through Kole Frost's hair, making him shiver.

He was sitting on his hill, the place he always went to brood unfortunate events within his mind. He'd gone there when his older brother, Alex Frost, had broken his leg when protecting Kole from an oncoming vehicle. He'd gone there when his best friend, Terence Favel, had pissed him off after getting drunk at a club. And now he was there because the father of his close friend, Zander Khadel, had been convicted and arrested for crossing into the Gate's territory.

Kole scowled. From his hill you could see the forest that led to the Gate's borders, the place where Zander's father had thrown his life away. Kole couldn't fathom why people would destroy their lives for the sole reason of being curious. Why try and cross into a place that they were obviously being protected from? It just didn't make sense.

"He's been take away, Kole," Zander had said when he called earlier that evening. "He's been taken away."

There had been no sign of a disturbance when Zander had arrived home from school that day. There was no note, not explanation for why his father had done what he did. The only sign of something terrible happening was Zander's five-year-old brother, Zachary Khadel, weeping on the living room couch. And just like that Zander had transformed from a regular teenage boy to a guardian.

Kole's hands clenched into fists. He was angry. Angry that people in the world were stupid. Angry that the Government wouldn't just tell them what was behind the Gate. Angry at everything and everyone.

He tried to imagine what his friend was going through. Walking into his house thinking that everything was normal just to find out that his life had been altered forever. Becoming practically an orphan just because of a father's stupidity. Kole couldn't do it.

"What are you doing?"

Kole jumped, spinning around and glaring. Terence stood before him, his dark hair blowing in the wind as he glared. He crossed his arms over his chest menacingly, scowling at Kole fiercely, his bright blue eyes flashing. Kole sighed, closing his eyes for a moment before standing up. "What are you doing here?"

Terence's scowl deepened. "I believe I told you that you were going to Xia with us tonight."

It was Kole's turned to scowl now. Xia was the only club in town that allowed minors through its doors. Kole hated everything about Xia. Its bright lights flashing through the building, the drunkards acting like complete fools, the rowdy dancing on the dance floor. All that came with events like that was chaos. Kole wasn't one for chaos; he never had been. He was the type of person who liked to sit at home and read or play video games on his X-box.

But, apparently, that wasn't enough.

"I believe I told you I wasn't," Kole retorted, shoving his hands into his sweatshirt's pockets.

"Yeah, well, no one cares what you say." Terence grinned, grabbing Kole's arm and tugging it in the direction of the road. "Come on, Kole. You need to have some fun once and a while."

Kole resisted his friend's grip, shaking his head. "Xia isn't fun. It's a bunch of drunk people getting their asses kicked."

"Yeah, but isn't watching it fun?" Terence wriggled his eyebrows. "I promise I won't get that drunk, okay?"

Kole scoffed, shaking his head again. He didn't trust Terence's words for even a second. He and Terence both knew that the second they entered Xia, he was going straight to the bar. Xia didn't allow minors to drink, but that didn't stop anyone from trying. Terence himself had a fake I.D. saying that he was twenty-one years old; in reality he was seventeen. "Yeah, okay," he muttered, shaking Terence's hand off his arm.

"Come on, man!" Terence was practically begging now. "Even Zander is going."

Kole hesitated. Zander was going? What about his brother? Kole couldn't believe that Zander was actually going to a club the day his father got arrested. "Seriously?" he asked incredulously.

Terence nodded. "Yeah, though Seth had to do some major convincing. After like two hours he finally agreed to go."

Kole sighed deeply. Why his friends couldn't let Zander stay home with his distraught brother, Kole didn't know. Seth and Terence liked to party, and they always felt the need to drag everyone else down with them when they did. "Whatever," he said, giving in. "But if you get drunk, I'm going to kick you in the ass."

"I'm going to get drunk," he said bluntly, waving away Kole's threat with a wave of the hand. "I'm just not going to get wasted. There's a difference."

Kole scoffed. "Whatever."

Terence rolled his eyes, grabbing Kole's arm and practically dragging him down the hill. Kole didn't bother resisting his friend's grip, finding it pointless to waist his energy when he'd only need it later. Someone, if not Terence, was going to get wasted tonight and he was the one who was going to need to take care of it. Sometimes Kole wondered if that was why he got dragged along. To supply help when needed. It wouldn't shock him if that were the reason.

"Hey, watch it!" Kole hissed as Terence shoved him toward the passenger door. "I don't need to break something before we get to Xia."

Terence smirked, saying nothing as he opened up the door on his side and plopping in. After a moment's hesitation, Kole got in also, struggling to get comfortable in the passenger seat. Terence's car always smelt odd, like a mixture of pine, alcohol, cigarettes, and vomit. It was the definition of a partier's smell. The little pine tree hanging from the small mirror over the dashboard showed off the minor attempt to help out the smell in the vehicle. But there was no helping it. The car was forever doomed to smell like shit.

"How about you try not to piss off the bartender tonight?" Kole advised as they drove down the road. Since there was no point in telling Terence not to drink, he'd made it his duty to play the "parent" role, telling him off for every little thing he did.

"How 'bout we not play the 'daddy' role tonight?" Terence mocked, rolling his eyes.

"How 'bout I just stay home tonight?" Kole challenged, crossing his arms over his chest.

Terence's eyebrows rose, and his lips pricked up in amusement. "Nice try," he congratulated, laughing shortly.

Kole sighed in defeat. Well, it had been worth a shot.

For the most part, the rest of the ride to Xia was silent. Kole leaned his head against the window struggling not to drown himself in his thoughts. That would only cause him to become even more irritated than he already was, and nobody needed that. Kole could become vicious when he was irritated—or so people told him.

Terence turned on the radio and tapped his fingers on the steering wheel to the beat. Kole swallowed down his irritation, not wanting to get in a fight with Terence while he was all pumped up. That would be as stupid as him picking a fight with him when Terence was drunk.

"This is ten percent luck, twenty percent skill!" Terence roared out along with Fort Minor. "Fifteen percent concentrated power of will."

Kole resisted the urge to plug his ears. His friend couldn't sing well, no matter how many times he tried to show everyone that he had talent. He didn't seem to understand that he lacked skill. Even when Zander had duct-taped his mouth shut, telling him to "shut the hell up," he refused to relent.

"Five percent pleasure, fifty percent pain and a hundred percent reason to remember the name." Terence whooped, pumping his fist in the air. "Terence Favel! Remember that name!"

Kole rolled his eyes, shaking his head. "We're not even at the club yet, and you're driving like you're drunk," he muttered as Terence danced around in his seat. "You're going to get us killed, you know."

"You're a fuddy-duddy," Terence said, ignoring Kole's warnings. "You need to get out more, man."

"I don't like getting out. It's full of alcohol poisoning, idiots, and smelly breath."

"Said like a true poet," Terence teased.

Terence pulled over on the side of the street and unbuckled. They were across the street from Xia, the line so long that it curled around the other side of the building. Kole inwardly groaned at the prospect of waiting in line for over an hour just to watch his friends destroy themselves by consuming alcohol. Terence didn't look to excited either, for when he turned to Kole as Kole forced himself out of the car he was scowling. "This never would have happened if you'd agreed to come in the first place."

Kole shrugged, shoving his hands into his jean pockets. "I'm pretty sure the line would still be here even if we'd gotten here earlier."

"Yeah," Terence snapped, "but we'd be at the front of the line."

Kole sighed deeply, deciding not to take the conversation any further than where it was obviously escalating to. He sauntered into the road after checking twice to see if cars were coming, heading toward the ever-growing crowd. He turned, ready to head toward the end of the line. But, right as he lifted his foot in that direction, a recognizable voice rang out.

"Kole, over here!"

It was Seth. Seth Baye always reminded Kole of a hawk with his pinched and angular facial features. His shaggy light brown hair was usually brushed forward, making it looked windswept. That had been Seth's hair style ever since Kole met him in their early years of school.

Kole waved, signaling that he'd heard his friend before turning to Terence. "They saved us spots."

Terence nodded, a smile breaking out on his face. "I forgive you, Frost."

Kole scoffed. "Honored, Favel."

Terence punched Kole's shoulder playfully before scurrying across the street, making his way toward the front of the line where Seth and Zander waited. Kole braced himself before following.

"Where've you two been?" Seth demanded, scowling as the two boys reached them. "The doors are about to open."

"Kole wasn't cooperating," Terence replied, shooting Kole a pointed look.

Kole shrugged, turning his attention to Zander. Zander, unlike the rest of the boys, was tan. Everyone always called him out on it, saying that he was probably a deformed being from the other side of the Gate. Kole envied Zander's pigment of skin, though. He'd always wanted to be tan. Though, he didn't want Zander's ink black hair. As much as he liked the color black, having it as a hair color was not something Kole yearned for. "Why did you come?" he wondered, tilting his head to the side.

Zander shrugged. "Seth practically shoved me out the door, so I decided to come for a couple hours."

"What about your brother?"

An emotion Kole couldn't place flashed across Zander's face. He brought a hand through his hair, sighing. "He's with a sitter."

Kole was about to reply, but at that moment the bouncer pushed open Xia's doors and stepped outside in front of the small rope keeping people away. He undid the rope, gesturing for Terence to come forward. Terence obliged, holding his arms out. Kole watched with bored eyes as the bouncer patted Terence's shirt, working down all the way to his feet. It was like a police officer checking for weapons on a suspect.

Terence was deemed access to the club and disappeared inside. Kole stepped up next, holding his arms out while swallowing down a sigh. He wasn't looking forward to going inside, nor was he looking forward to staying inside for the next two hours or so. In that short period of time he would manage to get a headache and his friends would manage to get themselves drunk beyond understanding.

After the bouncer finished with what he needed to do, Kole dragged himself into the club, biting his lip as his ears made contact with the music roaring from the speakers. He couldn't recognize the band or the song, nor did he like the band or the song. He just wished everything would be quiet.

A moment later Zander was next to him, guiding him to the bar to buy a couple of sodas. Seth and Terence screamed and danced over the music, acting like they'd downed a minimum of three beers despite being sober. Kole cringed, thinking about how much worse they were going to be once they were drunk.

"Here," Zander hollered over the music, passing Kole his drink.

"Thanks," Kole replied, sipping at his soda. "Let's go find a seat, yeah?"

Zander nodded, and the two of them immediately turned toward the seating area. It was a semi-circle surrounding the dance floor, filled with tables, couches, and chairs alike. Every time Kole was dragged to Xia, he'd always sat there and did absolutely nothing despite his friends' pleas to join them in the fun.

There was nothing fun about this place.

They passed a group of boys scrambling to finish their home-work, shouting answers to each other as they struggled to block out the music blaring around them. Kole couldn't understand why they bothered coming to a club if they were only going to do homework. What was the point? They were only going to get distracted, and they probably weren't going to get a single thing done.

"Here's a good one," Zander said, plopping down at one of the free tables. He set his drink down, looking out at the dance floor blankly.

Kole set his drink down as well, rubbing his eyes with the back of his hand. "If I thought that Seth and Terence could afford to have us leave, I'd suggest us sneaking out and heading back to your house."

Zander smiled. "Too bad they always get wasted."

It wasn't like Zander wasn't guilty of getting wasted every once and a while; he was. But, unlike Terence and Seth, Zander didn't choose to do that every single time he came. Sometimes he drank, sometimes he didn't. It really depended on his mood.

"Yeah," Kole muttered, shaking his head.

Zander sighed, rubbing his eyes. He looked so worn out, so exhausted. And who could blame him? He'd just lost his father, he'd just gained the total responsibility of a person. If Kole had to go through that, he'd be exhausted too. "I can't believe my dad did that!" he exclaimed finally, his hands falling and his eyes fierce with rage. "He left us. Why would he do that?"

Kole stared at Zander for a long time before answering. "I don't know, Zander. Some people just don't have their priorities straight."

"You've got that right," Zander mumbled, letting his head fall in his hands. "Now, if I screw up even once, Zachary is going to be taken away from me. And it's all his fault."

"You're not going to screw up," Kole said with a dismissive wave of the hand. "You were pretty much taking care of him to begin with, right?"

Zander nodded, sighing again. "Yeah, but at least he was still there some of the time. He was there to cook dinner; he was there to read Zander a nighttime story. But now that's all up to me. And you know I can't cook."

It was true. The last time Zander had attempted to cook on the stove, he'd almost burned Kole's house down. His father hadn't really appreciated that. "You're not in this alone," Kole assured, tossing his friend a smile. "You have me, Terence, and Seth here with you."

Zander laughed. "Yeah, that's true."

Kole was about to reply, but it was cut short by a huge crash, so loud that it could be heard over the music. Kole turned in his seat, his eyes immediately finding the source of the commotion: two boys had taken the ice box used for cooling drinks and had dumped it over the bartenders head. He watched as they whooped and hollered, spinning the now-empty ice box around their heads. The boys' triumph didn't last long. One of the boys slipped off the counter in which they were standing on, dragging the other boy down with them, leaving them in a pile of drunk guffaws.

"Idiots," Kole muttered, shaking his head as the bouncer picked the boys up by their shirts and dragged them out of the club.

"Morons."

Kole glanced out on the dance floor. Boys were jumping up and down, dancing horribly to the beat of the music. Most of the boys just couldn't dance. And, though Kole couldn't put his finger on it, there was something off about the way people danced. It was like something was ... missing. Every time this crossed Kole's mind he struggled to figure out what was wrong with the dancing, but he could never figure it out.

"What the hell is Terence doing?"

Kole followed Zander's gaze, biting his lip to keep from laughing when he saw Terence doing the chicken dance. Normally that wouldn't be as funny, but he happened to be in the middle of a dance-off with a more professional dancer. While the other dancer was doing flips and spinning around, Terence was flapping invisible wings. Kole mentally face-palmed. His friend was so stupid.

"He must be hammered," Zander mused.

"Yeah," Kole agreed. "And if he's hammered, there's no hope for Seth."

Seth was the worst drinker of them all. In all honesty, Kole was surprised that he hadn't died from alcohol poisoning yet. The amount he consumed here was ridiculous.

"Seth the Llama is here for buuusineess," came a slurred voice from behind them. "Oh, hey, guuuuys!"

Kole sighed mentally before turning. Seth stood there, smiling goofily as he struggled to keep himself from falling. He was drunker than Kole would have thought—seeing how it was so early in the night. "I see you found the bar," he muttered.

"That bartender and I have a lovely friendship that goes way back to the fish ages," Seth announced, waving to the bartender. The bartender, happening to catch Seth's wave, waved awkwardly back before continuing to hand out drinks.

"The fish ages?" Zander questioned, amused. "And what is that?"

"The age where the world was filled with donkeys, duuuuh," Seth exclaimed, waving his arms in the air. "The fish ages were epic. Epic, man!"

"And I'm sure the donkeys ate the fish?"

"What? There were no fish." Seth shook his head. "Man, you're so stupid sometimes."

"Yeah, I'm stupid," Zander muttered under his breath. Kole laughed, holding his fist out. Zander knocked it, laughing along with him.

"Oh yeah," Seth slurred, leaning back on the table. "Call me stupid, guys. Real nice. But, here me when I say: the turtles will rule the world again someday!"

"All right, whatever you say."

"I do say!" Seth hollered. He began laughing uncontrollably, curling forward and laughing into his chest.

Zander and Kole watched him silently. Kole sighed, imagining how unpleasant Seth was going to be the next day. Seth in a hangover was never fun. Kole always made sure he was busy that day so he wouldn't get snapped at every time he opened his mouth.

Seth abruptly snapped up and twisted toward the table. With the goofy smile still on his face, he snatched Zander's drink from the table and splashed it in Zander's face. The Coke dripped down Zander's emotionless face slowly, seeming to fall in eerie slow-motion.

Kole watched as emotion finally appeared on Zander's face. He stood up, his face pinched with rage. He slowly brought his hand up to his face, wiping off the remaining liquid. "That is it," he snapped venomously. "We're leaving. Now."

"Come on, man!" Seth whined as Zander grabbed his arm and dragged him toward the door. "It was only a joke!"

"Kole, go get Terence," Zander ordered, ignoring Seth's pleas to let him go. "We're going home."

Kole nodded, hurrying off toward the dance floor. He struggled to find Terence through the crowd, annoyed that everyone was getting in his way. "Terence!" he shouted. "Terence come on, we're leaving!"

After a few moments of searching, he found Terence still doing a horrible impression of the chicken dance, balking like he was actually apart of the species. When Terence saw Kole walking towards, he whooped, his dancing coming to an end. "Kole is finally coming to party!" he hollered.

Kole shook his head, grabbing Terence's arm. "No, we're leaving."

"But, I don't want to." Terence shook his head, ripping his arm from Kole's grip. "You leave, I'll stay a little longer."

"Terence, you are in no condition to drive. Your designated driver is leaving. Let's go."

"You'll have to drag me out before I agree—hey!"

Kole grabbed Terence roughly by the shoulder, dragging him away from the dance floor. Terence attempted to smack his hand away, but Kole refused to relent. Zander was probably having difficulty getting Seth into his car, and the sooner he got Terence safely into his own vehicle, the sooner Kole could go help.

"Ah, it smells nice out here," Terence mused as Kole threw open Xia's door.

"If you think pot smells nice, then yeah," Kole muttered, rolling his eyes.

Terence guffawed, finding Kole's comment to be the most hilarious thing in the world. Kole sighed deeply, trying not get annoyed at his friend's stupidity. He hated it when his friends got drunk—or anyone for that matter. What was the point of losing yourself? Not only were you going to regret it later, but it made people lose respect for you.

"Get in the car," Kole ordered once they finally made it across the street. He opened the passenger door and gestured for Terence to sit. "Let's go, we don't have all night."

"We would have all night if you weren't such a party pooper," Terence muttered, the slur obvious in his voice. He plopped into the passenger seat, kicking his feet up onto the dashboard. "Let's go," he mocked, grinning like the idiot he was.

Kole slammed the door shut and rounded to the driver's seat. He took the car keys from Terence's outstretched hand and jammed the keys into the ignition before pulling out onto the street. Zander appeared behind him a moment later, and then they were off.

They stopped at Seth's house first. They travelled together so that once they reached Terence's house Kole could have a ride home instead of having to walk the whole way. As they pulled up to Seth's driveway Kole unbuckled his seat, bracing himself for the fight Seth was about to put up. He was a terrible drunk, he really was.

"He puked in the back seat!" Zander exclaimed as Kole made his way toward him. "Uck, this is so gross."

Kole's face scrunched in sympathy. "I'll help you clean it up later," he reassured, opening the back seat door. Let's just get him out of here."

"He passed out," Zander said as Kole peered into the back.

Zander was right. Seth was sprawled out in the back, his arm barely missing the pile of puke on the floor. His mouth was open, loud, obnoxious snores roaring from the gap. Kole scoffed, grabbing his legs and pulling him not-so-gently out of the vehicle. "You grab his arms," he ordered.

Zander nodded, quickly grabbing Seth's arms as they came into view. Together they carried Seth toward his porch, struggling not to drop him as they did.

"Damn, he's so heavy!" Zander exclaimed.

"We're almost to the porch," Kole struggled out. "We'll just ring the doorbell and leave him there."

Zander nodded slightly, beginning the journey up the porch steps. Kole adjusted his grip on Seth, following him up slowly. Every step took time and strength, leaving Kole exhausted. He was tempted to drop him and leave him to wake up on the steps. But, being the good friend he was, decided that would be too harsh—even if he did dump Zander's drink all over him and puked in his car.

After was seemed like forever, they finally reached the front door. Kole and Zander immediately dropped him, stretching their arms out to regain their strength. Then, after counting to three, Zander pressed the doorbell.

"Run!" Zander exclaimed in a whisper, pelting it down the porch, toward his car.

Kole didn't have to be told twice. He ran towards the car, throwing himself into the driver's seat and slamming his foot into the gas. Seth's father wasn't going to be very happy when he saw a drunk Seth on the doorstep. The last time he'd outright slapped Seth across the face and then threatened to call Zander's and Kole's fathers. Ever since then they'd made sure that they weren't around when his father came out.

"Woo!" Terence yelled excitedly as they zoomed down the road. "It's like we're on the run from the cops, man!"

Kole barely cast his friend a glance as he pulled over before making a U-turn. From the rearview mirror he could see that Zander was copying, turning around slowly. Terence lived a few miles past Kole's hill, in a small neighborhood near the edge of town. Kole wished that he was on his hill right now, left in peace to think of whatever he wanted to.

"Man, have you ever wondered what was behind the Gate?" Terence mumbled as they neared Kole's hill. "I think I wanna find out."

"No you don't," Kole said, shaking his head. "Stop being stupid."

The hill was in view now. Terence sat up, letting his feet fall from the dashboard. "Yes I do," he argued, his eyes bright with determination. "And I'm gonna. Right now."

Before Kole had any time to react, Terence unbuckled his seat-belt and threw the car door open. He turned, tossing Kole a foolish grin before jumping out of the car, rolling on the tar until he came to a stop.

"Holy shit!" Kole screeched, slamming on his breaks. He struggled to unbuckle his seatbelt as Terence ran up Kole's hill, straight toward the hill.

Kole cursed under his breath, throwing the seatbelt off of him and hurrying out of the car. He paused for only a moment, trying to find Terence before running after his friend, right into the forest.

CHAPTER 3

"What the hell happened?" Courtnie Featherstrom shrieked frantically as she threw open the security room's doors.

Fifty heads turned to look at her as she entered. She glared around at everyone, placing her hands on her hips. Everyone was sitting in front of a computer, each set to monitor a camera placed in the forest. Anyone caught in the camera's lens was immediately arrested, no questions asked.

"The—the computers have stopped monitoring," a nervous security worker squeaked.

Courtnie's attention snapped to the woman. She was shrinking back in her seat, her dark eyes wide with fear of what Courtnie would do to her. Courtnie almost laughed at how pitiful the girl looked. She was small, shorter and skinnier than the average worker in the security room. She couldn't have been more than nineteen years old. "Very good," she said slowly, almost sarcastically. "Care to tell me how they came to stop monitoring?"

Fifty heads began shaking simultaneously. "No one knows, ma'am," a more brave worker in the back called out. "It might be a virus, someone may have sabotaged it. It could be anything."

Courtnie's eyes widened. "Sabotage, you say?" She looked up, blinking. "Excuse me."

Before anyone could react, she stormed out of the room, slamming the door behind her. Courtnie's hands clenched into fists as she stomped down the long, dark hallway. The Government's building may have been large, but she knew how to navigate her way around. And now, with her anger to guide her swiftly through the halls, she was headed straight for the prison wards.

Courtnie cursed under her breath viciously. She couldn't believe her ears when Fortis told her the news, that the cameras on both sides of the Gate had stopped monitoring. She just couldn't fathom how perfectly good cameras and computers could randomly malfunction like that.

That was, unless someone purposely infected them.

She could think of only one person who would do something so vile, one person who relentlessly tried to meddle in with the Government's plans. And even though they'd caught her long ago and locked her up, she still managed to be the bane of Courtnie's existence.

Digging through her pockets, Courtnie pulled out a ring set of keys. Every key to every door in the building was placed onto this ring, giving her access to anything she wanted. Since she was the one in charge, she was the proud owner of the ring, making sure that everyone knew that she was the one who controlled everything.

Courtnie felt herself smile as she rifled through the keys, looking for the correct one. Every key was hand labeled so that she wouldn't be standing around all day guessing which key was which. "Dammit, where is it?" she muttered to herself, becoming flustered as time ticked on. "Aha!" She smiled thinly as she tugged onto a rather large key labeled Prison Wards Entrance. Finally.

She roughly shoved the key into the key hole, twisting it impatiently. She heard a faint click and then pulled the key back out. After dropping the keys back into her pocket, she pulled open the door and stepped inside.

The door locked automatically after she closed the door behind her. Courtnie looked around, taking in the familiar sight of the metal hallway, before hurrying through. Her footsteps echoed as she walked, incredibly loud in the silence. Courtnie smiled. She could only imagine how threatening this must have sounded to everyone on the other side.

She turned down another hallway, elated to hear the shrieks and cries of the woman trapped there. Something about the woeful, helpless cries that amused her. She smiled, waving at every cell as she passed, ignoring the hateful glares she received in return.

Her smile slowly faded as she neared the last cell. She was there, breathing despite Courtnie's wishes just to put an end to it. She begged Fortis to let her kill her, to stop this nonsense, but Fortis continuously told her no. But, that never stopped her from imagining what it would be like to watch the light leave her eyes, to watch as her breathing came to a final stop.

Too bad dreams weren't reality.

Courtnie stepped up to her cell, and slammed her hands into the bars, "You," she spat.

She barely moved. Courtnie watched as she shifted on her cot, her eyes meeting hers with burning hatred. "What do you want, Courtnie?" she spat back.

"I know what you did to the computers," Courtnie snapped venomously. "You infected them with something, didn't you?"

She laughed bitterly. "Oh, but Courtnie, how could I ever do such a thing? I'm trapped in here all the time." She waved her hands around. "A lovely place, might I say. Would you like to join me?"

"You did something," Courtnie insisted angrily. "You did something, and I'm going to find out exactly what." She paused dramatically. "And when I do, let me tell you this: Fortis won't be able to stop me from slitting your throat."

With that, she let her hands fall away from the bars, and she stormed out, hurrying away from her cell and the prison wards in all entirety.

"You all know what's said to be beyond the Gate, right?"

Faye bit her lip to keep from laughing as she looked around at all the girls in the tent. They were all leaning forward, clutching their pillows tightly as they stared Errika down with wide eyes. This was how it always was during The Legend of the Gate. Every year girls hung on to every word, looking at Errika like she knew all things. This thoroughly amused Faye for many reasons. Though, this main one would have to be because most girls came more than one year and had heard the story before.

"What is it?" a young girl, probably thirteen, squeaked. This was her first year to the campout, Faye observed. She didn't recognize her.

"Well, Janie," Errika murmured slowly, dragging every word out to be dramatic, "it is said that there is a foul beast residing just beyond the Gate's borders." She smiled maliciously. "It's also said that before the Gate was brought to be, the beast roamed free, eating every innocent woman in sight."

Some girls shrieked, their grips tightening on their pillows. Faye couldn't understand what they thought was so scary about what Errika was saying. She was being casual about it, as though she was simply giving you a lesson in history. Though, Faye mused, eyeing her friend in amusement, that may have been why it got to the girls so much. Because it sounded like something read in a history book.

"As centuries past, the people of Cesve began to lose hope," Errika said woefully. "But, then, a great ruler emerged from the ashes of the dead and repaired what was lost."

A girl who looked no older than fourteen murmured, "Was it . . . ?"

Errika nodded, smiling magnificently. "Yes, Rey, it was the great Fria, the creator of peace. She had her people create the Gate, telling them that in order to save womankind from such a horrible fate, that the creature had to be locked up. The workers honored her so much that they built a gate so long that it traced along the whole border of Cesve, cutting the beast off from ever entering again.

"But, it is said that someday the beast will overcome the Gate's incredible power. As time goes on, the beast becomes stronger and stronger feeding off those who dare to near its home. Someday, maybe soon, the beast's malice will be unleashed once more."

Faye smiled as the girls eyed each other fearfully. A couple of the girls were as old as she and Errika were—seventeen. She couldn't understand how people could still believe in such stories as fake as those. It seemed highly unlikely that a creature would live as long as it did, steal seeking vengeance for being locked behind a gate. And if it were so powerful, wouldn't it have broken through by now?

Though, what were they supposed to think was behind the Gate? The Government gave no hint, no clue as to what was hidden there. This didn't used to bother Faye. She used to think it was for the greater good—like Courtnie had always assured them. But, as she grew older, she began to doubt. Wouldn't people be more likely to listen to the Government's words if they knew what was behind there? Surely the Government didn't think that fear of the unknown was going to stop everyone.

Well, apparently, they did.

"Lights out!" Errika called suddenly, shutting off the only lantern supplying light within the tent.

A minimum of half the girls screeched out in dismay as the tent was covered in darkness. Errika did this to torture the girls. She liked having them go to bed right after she told The Legend of the Gate, enjoyed hearing them wail about being frightened of every little noise. Errika was demented in that sense, Faye had always thought. But, if she admitted it to herself, she found it amusing too.

"Faye," Errika whispered in her ear suddenly.

"What?" she whispered back.

"On my count, scratch the tent as fast as you can."

Faye struggled to contain her laughter as she dragged herself closer toward the edge of the tent. They did this every so often, just to keep the girls on their toes. When Errika was in the mood she would announce she planned on scaring the Campouters even more, and Faye was eager to oblige. There was something about the girls screaming at something so simple that amused her greatly.

"One," Errika murmured under her breath. The girls were still complaining about being frightened, so there was no danger of being heard.

Faye got into position, her hands poised to start scratching.

"Two."

Faye cast her friend a glance, smiling when she saw Errika was in the same stance.

"Three!"

Faye's fingertips collided with the tent. She laughed silently as she scratched as swiftly as she possibly could, creating a terrible sound. She never liked the sound, but the result was always worthwhile.

"It's come to eat us!" a girl shrieked.

"It's right outside the tent!"

"Errika! Help us!"

Faye and Errika shared a look. Errika nodded before letting her hands fall and hurrying back to the lantern. Faye rushed back to her sleeping bag, trying to pull off a convincing frightened look. A moment later the lantern came on. Errika stared, wide-eyed, pulling off a great frantic look. "What the hell was that?" she shrieked.

"It's the beast!" a girl wept. "We're all going to die."

Errika shook her head, holding up a finger as she listened dramatically. Faye stared at her intently with everyone else, feeling the rush of the joke flow within her. Sometimes she really loved being in Errika's little tag team. "Well, whatever it was," Errika murmured, sounding perfectly relieved, "it's gone now."

"I'm never going to fall asleep now!" a girl Faye recognized whined.

"Yeah, well, try." Errika rolled her eyes. "And no, the lantern is not staying on all night."

And then the lantern was off, enveloping the tent into complete darkness.

"Terence!" Kole yelled, searching frantically as he jogged through the woods. He'd been looking for hours, long after the sun had been replaced by the moon and the stars. With each passing moment he became more worried, fearful that the Government had taken him away for trespassing into the Gate's territory. In the back of his mind, Kole was scared that he was now trespassing onto the Gate's territory.

"Terence, come on, this isn't funny!"

A branch snapped, and Kole whipped around. He sucked in a sigh of relief when he saw that it was only a squirrel scampering around, chasing nothing. He paused a moment to shake off the scare before continuing on.

Faye closed her eyes, taking in the cool breeze of the night. She shivered, frightened when she saw her sister's face, distorted in agony. In an instant, her eyes reopened, and the forest appeared before her.

Again with the dream. She'd hoped that since she'd had a great day that her nightmares would leave her, give her a break. She'd barely thought of Terra or her death at all that day, which was a great improvement. But it seemed as though her mind thought otherwise.

Faye rubbed her eyes with the back of her hand, trying rid herself of the exhaustion holding her hostage. She didn't want to go back to sleep, to relive the horrible moments of her sister's death. She wanted to stay awake where nightmares were only nightmares, not reality. She wanted to stay awake and be happy. Not horrified, mortified, and crushed.

She had to walk this off. If she just stood there, consumed in her thoughts, she was going to drown. She had to keep moving, to keep her mind on her surroundings, not her sub-consciousness. Faye sighed deeply, feeling her feet move her through the forest. In the back of her mind she knew she was doing something incredibly stupid, that she could end up in the Gate's territory, but now that she'd started she couldn't bring herself to stop.

She walked for what felt like hours. The forest was dark, frightening with the moon casting shadows over everything. Her nerves were on edge. She was conflicted on whether she liked the distraction or not. Sure, she wasn't thinking of her nightmare anymore, but was this really better? Either way she was terrified.

A snap.

Faye whipped around, her eyes searching for the source of the noise. Was it the Government coming to take her away to the prison wards? Had whatever been hidden behind the Gate been freed, and she was going to be the first victim? She searched, dread and anxiety filling her when she found nothing.

Another snap.

Wait, the sound wasn't coming from behind her. It was coming from in front of her, sounding as though it was drawing closer. Faye's insides froze, her mind playing horrible games with her. It was the beast; it had escaped. With her death playing her head over and over again, she moved forward, stepping further into the forest.

What are you doing? her mind screamed. You're walking straight toward your death!

Faye knew full well that what she was doing was completely idiotic. But she couldn't stop walking. She was on autopilot, her feet continuing to move even though she begged them to stop. It was as though they knew something she didn't, a hidden secret that even her mind couldn't grasp.

And then, all at once, her feet stopped.

Faye looked around frantically, hoping that her life wasn't about to end horrendously. She looked straight forward, her eyes latching on to a pair of bushes. There was something odd about them, something behind them that seemed off. Her eyebrows crinkled together. What was that?

She rushed forward, pushing her way past the bushes. Her hands collided with metal.

Faye screeched, backing up. Her eyes shot up, and then she realized: she was standing right in front of the Gate.

CHAPTER 4

Faye backed away slightly, covering her mouth with her hand. She hadn't expected the Gate to be so intimidating, towering over her like a bully towered over its victim. She stared at it, amazed and terrified at the same time. How had she managed to make it all the way to the Gate without being caught by the Government? Why hadn't she been arrested?

Faye knew she should have been running. Running away from the Gate, back to the safety of her friends sleeping soundly in the tent. But she couldn't. All she could do was stare. And even though her mind screamed at her, she felt herself move forward, her fingers curling around the metal of the Gate. It was cool to the touch, and she almost yanked her hand back in surprise. But, as she kept a firm grip on the Gate, she became used to its lack of heat.

"Wow," she murmured, unable to accept the fact that she was standing in front of the one thing she was forbidden to ever look at, to walk up to, to touch. She just couldn't believe where she was, what she was doing.

Another snap pulled her from her reverie. Faye's hand flew from the Gate, and she took a step back. For just a moment she'd forgotten the terror of the beast on the other side, the terror of being consumed whole. Maybe no one ever got arrested. Maybe they all got eaten and the Government covered it up. Faye shook her head. No, those were silly thoughts of course. She'd seen those convicted being pulled away in Government's vehicles.

She felt herself stop breathing as movement became visible on the other side of the Gate. She stood there, frozen as bushes began to move, and a silhouette appeared in the darkness. Faye's insides went cold. She opened her mouth to scream, but nothing came out.

A figure appeared. Faye's eyes widened and she slapped a hand to her mouth to keep a cry of fear from escaping her lips. She took a step back. And another. The figure didn't seem to notice her yet, for it was looking around frantically as though it was searching for something. It's looking for me, Faye thought in a verge of panic. And once it finds me, it's going to eat me.

Faye felt herself stop moving as the figure stopped in its tracks. Its eyes landed on her. The dread moving through her, she stared the strange creature down. But, as she examined it, she realized that it didn't look strange at all.

It looked exactly like her.

Well, not exactly. The hair on the creature was much shorter, and unlike the girls of Cesve, this creature did not have curved hips or breasts. It was wearing clothes, but its clothes were much different than the ones she was used to seeing. Something about them, though she couldn't figure out what, was just . . . different.

The creature took a step forward, as though assessing if she was going to attack or not. Faye couldn't fathom why it would think she would attack. It was the beast, was it not? And then, as Faye continued to gape at the creature in front of her, it spoke. "W-what are you?" it asked.

"Don't eat me!" Faye screeched stupidly, rushing backward. She tripped on a rock, sending her toppling backward. She cried out in pain, clutching her knee. "P-please don't eat me," she begged softly, feeling tears burn in her eyes.

The creature stood there, looking just as shocked as she felt. It looked around disbelievingly, as though it couldn't understand how it was at the Gate's borders. The creature's expression was a replica of the emotions churning within her. Fear, confusion, disbelief.

Curiosity.

"Are you the beast?" the creature asked suddenly. It stepped forward, wrapping its hands around the Gate. "Are you what the Legend always speaks of?"

Faye struggled to stand up. The thought this creature was thinking up was ridiculous. Her, the beast? If a girl at Eve High asked such a question, Faye would laugh in her face. Faye was nothing like a beast would look like. She was just a normal girl who went to a normal school. This thing on the other hand, was not. "N-no," she forced out, finally finding the courage to speak. "A-a-are you?"

"You can speak my language?" the creature gasped.

It was then that Faye realized that she could understand what the creature was saying. She'd been so wrapped up in her fear that she didn't stop to pay attention past the creature's appearance.

"Why do you look like me?" she demanded, stepping closer. "Why do you talk like me? You're supposed to be a humongous monster that's going to eat everything in sight!"

The creature chuckled. She could hear the nervousness in the chuckle, but it was a chuckle all the same. "Me?" he exclaimed. "That's what you're supposed to be."

"So what are you?" Faye asked after a moment of confused silence. She reached the Gate, clinging to the metal. The creature stood right before her, its face so close to hers. But, she wasn't as afraid anymore. It hadn't done anything to her so far, and it sounded just as afraid as she did.

"I'm a boy," the creature muttered in disbelief. "What are you?"

"I'm a girl." Faye tilted her head to the side. "Do you have a name?"

"Kole."

Faye bit her lip. "I'm Faye."

Kole stepped back from the Gate. "Well, thank you for not killing me, Faye," it said with a small smile, "but I have to go find my friend, Terence. He ran off."

"He?" Faye murmured, tilting her head to the side. "What's a he?"

"He, his, boy, they're all the same," Kole said with wide eyes. It was as though it couldn't believe she didn't understand. "It's what we refer to a boy as."

Faye didn't understand. "I'm sorry," she whispered. "I don't follow."

Kole searched around in exasperation. "I'm sorry," it whispered. "I have to go."

Faye stepped away from the Gate, watching as the boy rushed away, scurrying off into the night. She stared after it as it went, trying to understand what it meant. He? His? Those words were so foreign to her. She shook her head. She couldn't risk staying at the Gate's borders any longer. She had to get back to the girls.

Faye ran the whole way back to the Campout area. Her legs burned, her lungs felt like they were on fire. But she didn't stop. If she stopped to rest, there would be no way that she could start again. She would collapse out of exhaustion, and everyone would worry about her absence when daybreak came.

The tent came into view. Faye slowed to a walk, rubbing her side where a cramp had emerged. All she wanted to do was collapse in her sleeping bag and sleep the whole day away. But she knew that in a few short hours Errika would awake, and Faye wouldn't be able to resist telling her what had happened.

Faye let out a spur of laughter. She couldn't understand where the laughter came from. All she could think was what an unbelievable night she'd had: she'd reached the Gate's territory and made it back without being arrested; she'd met the beast, learned what it was called, and survived; she'd learned that the beast wasn't really a beast at all. It was human, just like her.

"I'm going to kill you!"

Kole felt his hands curl into fists as he stormed toward Terence. Terence tried to calm his friend down, tried to apologize, but Kole wasn't hearing any of it. All he could remember was the excruciating fear he'd just experienced, the moments of terror within the Gate's territory.

"Man, calm down, I said I was sorry!" Terence called out as Kole reached him, curling his fingers around the collar of his shirt and pulling him toward him threateningly.

Kole glared into his friend's face. "Sorry?" he spat, throwing Terence away from him. "You just made me go through a night of hell, and all you say is sorry?"

"I was drunk, I'm sorry!" Terence screamed. His eyes ignited with anger. "Look, you're out in one piece, obviously you didn't make it into the Gate's territory, otherwise you would have been arrested. Everyone's fine!"

Kole froze, remembering the moments with the creature at the Gate's borders. Faye was its name. A girl. He couldn't understand why it couldn't process what "he" and "his" meant. They were such normal words used by everyone in Cesve.

Weren't they?

Were there more girls like there were boys? Were there thousands? Did they have schools, friends like he did? The girl had seemed as terrified as he felt. Could it have been fed the same Legend as well? The Legend of Friar creating the Gate to save the boys from the evil beast threatening to destroy them all?

"Kole?" Terence demanded, waving his hand in front of Kole's face. "Kole, man, are you okay? You look like you've seen a ghost."

Kole blinked, returning back to the real world. Or, what Kole thought was the real world. What if his world was some illusion and it was really bigger, more terrifying than it seemed? "What?" he muttered, shaking his head. "I'm fine."

"What happened in the forest?"

The question caught Kole off guard. His eyes widened, and he involuntarily took a step back. "What are you talking about?" he forced out, trying his best to sound confused instead of nervous.

Terence's jaw worked angrily. He grabbed Kole's shoulders, shaking him slightly. "Dammit, Kole, something happened in there and you're going to tell me what!"

Kole glanced around fearfully before slamming his hand over Terence's mouth. "Stop talking," he hissed. "Someone will hear you."

Terence slapped Kole's hand away. "Tell me."

Kole sighed in defeat. He felt his shoulders sag, the tension all but leaving his body. What was the point in fighting him? He looked up at Terence and shook his head. "Not here."

Terence glanced around before sighing as well. "We'll go to your house then. My dad's home, and your family isn't home, right?"

Kole nodded, hoping his friend was right. "All right. Let's go."

"Laney, I'm not going to ask you again!" Errika screeched, her jaw working in irritation. "Roll up your damn sleeping bag or I'm going to roll you in it and chuck it in the brook behind my house!"

Faye watched as Laney Trayne grumbled incoherent things under her breath, stomping over to her sleeping bag and rolling it up carelessly. It ended up unfurling and she had to begin the whole process over again. Usually Faye would find that incredibly hilarious, but her mind was elsewhere. Her thoughts kept straying to Kole, the boy on the other side of the Gate. Faye yearned to tell Errika about her discovery, but she couldn't. Not with all these girls around. She would be reported without a doubt.

"Are you all right?"

Faye blinked, turning to face her friend. Errika placed her hands on her hips, her head tilting in confusion. "What? Oh, yeah, I'm fine." Faye smiled distractedly.

Errika's eyes narrowed. "Is there something you want to tell me?"

Faye almost smiled. She didn't have the ability to hide anything from Errika. She always caught on right away. It was impossible to lie to her, and for the most part Faye liked that. "Yes," Faye whispered, fixing the strap of her backpack, "but not here."

Errika stared at Faye for a long moment before nodding. "All right," she murmured. She glanced up, her curiosity transforming into anger. "Laney, seriously? If you think you're invited to the next Campout, you're dreadfully mistaken!" She huffed, glancing at me. "I'll be right back. I'm going to go kick her ass."

Faye shook her head, grinning as Errika stalked away from her, her arms flying as she screamed at Laney. Errika had never been accused of one to hold in her anger. She always let it out, not finding the need to pretend everything was okay when it wasn't. That was one of the things that Faye loved about Errika. Her need for the truth and nothing but the truth. Even when it was painful, it was what Errika wanted.

"Hey, can you help me roll this up?"

Faye turned, her eyes meeting Tannie, a fourteen-year-old. She was small for her age, and the only one who had even close to the same color hair as Faye's. It was just a shade lighter than Faye's, making it more strawberry blond than red. Tannie's face full of freckles constantly reminded Faye of a giraffe, though she couldn't understand why. And Tannie's eyes were the exact same color of Tannie as well. Faye couldn't put her finger on it, but the two of them looked very much alike.

Faye's mind turned to the events of the night before. Even though the Legend didn't seem plausible, it was more likely than what was actually there. What she didn't understand was why girls like her were being protected by creatures exactly like them. How could they possibly be so dangerous as to keep their existence hidden?

"Thank you!" Tannie gushed as Faye finished rolling up the sleeping bag. She took it from Faye's arms, smiling. "You're a life saver."

Faye laughed, shaking her head. If only she were a life saver. So many problems could have been solved. "No problem."

Tannie smiled brightly, her teeth flashing as she clutched the sleeping bag tightly within her arms and trotted off, oddly cheerful while everyone else seemed distracted and grumpy. Faye had to hand it to the girl: she really knew how to keep her spirits high.

"Five minutes until we leave!" Errika called out, irritation seeping into her voice. "Whoever's not ready is going to be left here!"

Faye looked around, noting all the unready girls. Over half of them would probably be left behind. With a deep sigh, Faye took a step toward a girl struggling to fit everything she brought into her pack. Well, she could at least attempt to help them out. Anything to keep her mind off the Gate and the creatures behind it.

"You're joking, right?"

Kole glared at Terence, crossing his arms over his chest. They were sitting in Kole's bedroom, Terence lounging on Kole's bed while Kole himself was plopped on his desk chair. Kole glanced around his room, trying to calm himself down. There wasn't much to see. A bed tucked in the corner with a plaid comforter draped over the top. Besides his bureau with his television on top across the room was his desk, cluttered with objects. A computer sat on top of the desk, the only thing that actually had use to him. Kole had dragged the chair across the room, seating himself in front of his bed in order to face his friend.

"Why would I joke about something like this?" Kole demanded finally, trying to keep his voice calm.

"You're saying that you met the beast on the other side of the Gate, and that it wasn't really a beast at all? Do you know how crazy that sounds?"

"I know how it sounds!" Kole barked, glowering. "But I know what I saw, all right? It called itself a girl. Its name was Faye."

"So this thing had a name?" Terence cocked an eyebrow. "Dude, are you sure you didn't drink anything last night?"

Kole stood up, his hands clenching into fists. He'd gone through a night of hell because of Terence and Terence had the nerve not to believe him? The urge to punch Terence in the face was almost too strong to resist. "I'm not making this up!" Kole hollered. "For some reason the cameras didn't catch me, all right? The girl was just as freaked out as I was—maybe even more."

"What the hell is all this talk about a 'girl'?" Terence demanded, confusion obvious in his voice. "What the hell is a girl, man?"

Kole sighed exasperatedly, throwing his arms in the air. "That's what I've been trying to tell you!" He let his hands fall. "A girl is a creature that looks freakishly like us, but with a few different qualities. And they speak the same language. But, apparently, they're dangerous because we've been kept away from them."

Terence cocked and eyebrow. "You say that like you don't think they're dangerous."

Kole shrugged, dropping back onto the chair. "It didn't seem all that dangerous to me. Like I said, it sounded freaked out. It even asked if I was going to eat it."

Terence scoffed, shaking his head. "Sorry to be so skeptical," he drawled, "but this is really hard to believe."

"Yeah, well, it's true," Kole replied coolly. "It's your fault I'm in this mess, by the way. I told you I didn't want to go to Xia, and what do you do? You make me go anyway. I'm never going to that club ever again."

"It's not the club's fault you ended up in the Gate's territory," Terence defended. Kole scoffed mentally. Sometimes Terence could be really pathetic. "You're the one who ran in there."

"Yeah, chasing after a very drunk you," Kole snapped. "Damn, do you even listen to yourself sometimes?"

Terence sighed. "Look, I'm sorry, all right? I took ten steps in, heard a bunch of noises, got freaked, and ran back out. I didn't know you were in there."

"Whatever, man, okay? What's done is done." Kole scowled. "But for you to sit here and act like I'm a liar is not okay. If you're not going to believe me, you can leave."

Terence stared at him for a long time. Kole began to think that Terence was actually going to believe, that the person most likely to believe him was going to act like what he said was completely false. But Terence didn't leave. Instead he sighed deeply, stretching his arms over his head. "I believe you," he proclaimed finally. "How about you try and get some proof to make it official?"

Kole scoffed in disbelief. "Proof? And how do you expect me to do that?"

Terence shrugged. "Isn't it obvious? Go back to the Gate."

Kole's mouth dropped. "Are you an idiot or something? I could get arrested!"

"Well, obviously the cameras must be malfunctioning or something, because you weren't caught. All you have to do is go up to the Gate, snap a few pictures, and then you're all set."

Kole shook his head. What Terence was suggesting was insane. He couldn't just walk into the woods, up to the Gate, and then snap a few photos. What if Faye wasn't there? And what if the cameras started working again and caught him? It would all be for nothing. Why couldn't his friend just accept what Kole said as true? He would have done the same for Terence if he came to him with such information.

Wouldn't he?

Kole couldn't help but doubt his thoughts. Terence was known to exaggerate and make up stories to make himself look strong and brave. And he was a known partier—a drunk—throughout the whole community. Even the adults knew it, and they accepted it. Terence wasn't the most truthful of people. So, naturally, wouldn't Kole demanded proof too?

Kole sighed, shaking his head again. "You're crazy," he muttered. He paused, his gaze meeting Terence's. "You're giving me your camera."

"So what is it you wanted to tell me?"

Faye shook her head. "Not here."

Faye looked around her kitchen, at her mother pulling a tray of cookies out of the oven. She refused to bring her family into the mess that she'd somehow gotten herself into. She didn't know how bad the situation she was in was, but if she was in actual trouble, she didn't want to chance having Mary or Kat in danger. At least Errika would be protected. It was highly unlikely that they would suspect she knew anything.

"How was the Campout?" her mother inquired, placing the tray on top of the counter. The smell of chocolate chip cookie wafted through the air, making Faye's stomach rumble.

"Good," Faye and Errika said simultaneously.

"Did you scare the girls silly with the Legend?" Faye's mother teased, plopping down at the table across from Faye. She smiled brightly.

"Totally!" Errika exclaimed, her hands flying in the air animatedly. "We did that scratching the tent thing that I was telling you about. Everyone thought they were going to die."

Mary smiled warmly. "Well, aren't you two the sweetest?" She stood up, putting on her oven mitts and grabbing the tray. "Now, why don't my sweet peas have a couple cookies?"

The two girls didn't have to be asked twice. They instantly grabbed at the cookies, chomping on them happily. Faye loved her mother's cooking, the way the food melted in her mouth. She could eat her mother's food all day. But, sadly, her mother rarely baked because she was such a busy woman.

"Where's Kat?" Faye asked, plucking another cookie from the tray.

"She's at Bella's house," Mary replied, taking a cookie for herself and munching on it thoughtfully.

"Oh," Faye murmured. "I thought they were fighting."

"Apparently not."

Faye glanced at Errika. Errika rolled her eyes, picking up another cookie and practically shoving it into her mouth. Kat was always in drama with her friends, always in a fight with someone. And then, as though nothing had happened, they would be like the best of friends again. Well, before one of them found something wrong with the other again.

"You guys didn't have any trouble, did you?" Faye's mother inquired, sitting back down at the table again.

"Trouble with what?" Faye asked, her eyebrows rising.

"Making sure you didn't go into the Gate's territory. Everything went smoothly?"

Faye choked on her cookie in shock. In an instant, Kole flashed in her mind, its eyes wide with fear. She closed her eyes trying to rid herself of the image, but the image wouldn't leave.

"Faye, are you all right?" her mother demanded, worry filling her voice.

Faye opened her eyes, her coking coming to an end. "Sorry," she muttered softy, rubbing her throat. "Choked on my cookie."

"If you die from eating my food, I'd have to kill you," my mom said lightly, the worry leaving her eyes. She turned to Errika. "So everything went smoothly?"

Errika nodded, casting Faye a suspicious glance from the corner of her eye. "Yeah, everything went fine. It was last minute so I had to hurry, but I got the work done."

"That's what I like about you," Mary mused, tucking her fist under her chin. "You don't bow under pressure. That's a great attribute to have."

Errika smiled. "Thanks, Mary."

Faye sighed deeply, stretching her arms out. "Mom, Errika and I are going to go into my bedroom now, all right?"

"All right!" Mary flashed a smile. "I'll see you chicas in a little while."

Faye and Errika nodded, standing up from their chairs and shuffling towards the stairs. They were silent as they headed to Faye's room, and Faye was thankful for that. She didn't want to begin the conversation while her mother was still in ear-shot.

"What was up with that?" Errika asked immediately as Faye closed her bedroom door behind her.

"What was up with what?" Faye replied stupidly.

"You know what." Errika's hands went to her hips. "You choking on the cookie after she asked the question. Is that what you wanted to talk to me about? Did something happen last night?"

Faye gestured for Errika to sit down. Errika grumbled incoherent things under her breath, plopping on Faye's bed. Ignoring her friend's annoyance, Faye collapsed next to her, staring blankly off into space. "I had the dream again."

"I'm sorry to hear that." Errika's arm draped around Faye's shoulder. "Is that all you wanted to tell me?"

Faye shook her head. "I went outside the tent to get some fresh air. I wanted to walk the dream off."

Errika was silent as Faye explained what had happened the night before. She was even silent when Faye told her about touching the Gate, gripping on to the metal bars. Faye appreciated this. If Errika began to talk, Faye wasn't sure she'd have the strength to continue.

"You saw what was on the other side of the Gate."

It wasn't a question. It was a statement. Faye sighed, almost falling back in her bed with relief. Errika believed her. She'd been afraid that she wouldn't. "Yeah," Faye mumbled.

"And it seemed as afraid as you did."

"Yeah."

"And you asked it if it was going to eat you."

At this Faye had to laugh. "Yeah, not my greatest move."

Errika grinned, knocking Faye's shoulder. "What a brave lion you are."

"Shut up!" Faye exclaimed, shoving Errika away playfully. She sighed, becoming serious once more. "What am I supposed to do? Do you think the Government will find out I was there?"

Errika shook her head. "I think something's wrong with the cameras."

Faye cocked an eyebrow. "What?"

Errika shrugged. "The cameras must have stopped monitoring if you weren't caught." She smiled devilishly. "You should totally go back! What if the boy is there again?"

Faye's mouth almost dropped. "Are you crazy? What if the cameras got fixed?"

Errika waved her hand dismissively. "Yeah, right. I very much doubt they've been fixed." She grinned. "You could learn the creature's ways, and how it talks! You said that it said weird words like 'he' didn't you?"

Faye sighed. In truth, she really wanted to know what Kole meant by that. It was just so odd. "I don't know . . ."

"Come on, Faye!" Errika exclaimed, standing up. "You've made a miraculous discovery. Are you telling me that there's nothing you want to do about it?"

Faye sighed again. "I don't know! I don't want to get in trouble or end up in prison."

"Take a risk." Errika smiled, obviously trying to show her that everything would be all right. "You got to the borders once, didn't you? Why couldn't you again?"

Faye rubbed her face with the back of her hand before letting it fall helplessly to her side. "I'll think about it," she said finally. "No promises, though."

Errika grinned, falling back onto the bed. "That's good enough for me."

CHAPTER 5

Something was wrong.

Faye couldn't understand how she knew this, but she could feel it deep within herself. Something was terribly wrong. As she looked around the room, at the police women, at her mommy, she could feel worry unfurl in her stomach. Her mommy was crying. Why was her mommy crying? She never cried.

"Mommy, what's wrong?" Faye whimpered. When her mommy didn't answer, she asked again. "Mommy, what's wrong? Where's Terra?"

Terra's absence frightened Faye. She was always around, especially when something important like this was going on. She wouldn't leave Faye and their mommy to be alone with the police officers. No, she would want to be here to support them, to help them through whatever problems had aroused.

"Mommy, why aren't you answering me?" Faye shrieked, grabbing at her mommy's shirt. Her mommy finally looked at her, and Faye could see the tears streaming down her cheeks.

"Mommy will be right back," her mommy murmured softly, kneeling in front of her and holding onto her arms. "I need to go with these nice people, all right?"

"Why do you need to go with the police ladies?" Faye mumbled, glancing discreetly at the two police women standing awkwardly next to the kitchen table. "Mommy, what's going on?"

"Everything will be all right," her mommy whispered. She kissed Faye softly on the cheek. "Stay here. Errika and her mom will be over any minute now, okay?"

Faye nodded, sniffling. Panicked tears pricked her eyes. She was scared. She needed Terra to comfort her, to tell her that everything would be all right. When her mommy couldn't succeed, Terra always could. A tear fell down her cheek. Where was her sister? Where was Terra?

Faye watched silently as her mommy stood up and followed the police women outside. She glanced around, nervous. She didn't like being home alone. Even if it was for only a little while, she couldn't bear the empty house.

She glanced toward the front door. Any moment now Errika and her mommy would come through the door, swearing that everything was fine. But nothing was fine. Her mommy was crying and Terra was nowhere to be found.

Before Faye could even think about what she was doing, she rushed to the front door, throwing it open. The police women and her mommy had disappeared down the road in the police cruiser. Faye bit her lip. She couldn't follow them if she had no idea where they were.

But she had to try.

Faye hurried down the front porch, hopping onto her bicycle that leaned against the side of the house. She pedaled down the road, following it even though she didn't know if she was going the right way. She glanced at the houses to her right as she passed, noting that people were standing on their porches, speaking in hushed voices and discreetly glancing at her. She knew immediately that her mommy had gone through here.

She kept straight. She didn't want to turn down any roads and get lost in the process. Her mommy would never forgive her if she got lost while leaving the house when she wasn't supposed to.

The sound of sirens almost sent Faye flying into a bush. She gripped the handlebars tightly, searching fervently for the source of the sirens.

And then she saw it.

It was a group of people flowing beside and around two police cars, an ambulance, and a fire truck. She spotted her mommy standing beside the two police women that had been at her house. Faye's stomach clenched when she saw that they were standing over something.

She didn't have a good feeling about this.

Faye discarded her bike on the side of the road, running toward the group of people. She shoved her way through until she made it to her mommy. She stood, gaping at the scene in front of her.

Her mommy was crying freely, screaming, "No, it can't be!" over and over again. The thing she was standing over was a table with a white fabric draped over something. It looked like a body. Faye creeped forward, dread flowing within her. "Mommy!" she cried. "Mommy, what's going on?"

Her mommy looked up. "Faye, what are you doing here?" she demanded, her voice cracking. "I told you to stay home!"

Faye glanced down at the table. Who was it under the blanket? "Mommy?" she whispered. "Where's Terra?"

She felt the weight of everyone's stares around her. Faye looked up tearfully at all the women. "Where's my sister?" she called. "Does anyone know?"

"Honey," her mommy said suddenly. "Terra's not here anymore."

Faye whipped back to face her mommy. "What?" she demanded. "What do you mean?"

Her mommy sniffed loudly. "Terra's gone, baby. She's not coming back."

Faye looked back down at the table and then she knew.

The girl on under the white fabric was Terra. Her throat contracted. No. Not, it couldn't be. "No, Mommy!" she cried. "No, she's not gone!"

Her mommy nodded. "Yes, honey, I'm sorry."

Faye frowned, stepping forward. "No!" she hollered. "Terra wouldn't leave us like that, Mommy! She loves us!"

With that she ripped the white fabric away from the table. She'd hoped that it would be someone else, anyone but her older sister. But, as the white fabric settled on the ground, Faye stared helplessly at Terra.

If she didn't know better, Faye would have guessed she was sleeping. But, Terra wasn't sleeping. Her body was too pale, and when Faye touched it, she realized it was too cold. Terra's eyes were closed, her palms facing upward.

Faye took a step back. "T-Terra?"

"Somebody put the cloth back on the body!" a police lady shrieked.

All of a sudden her mommy's arms were around her. "Terra's gone, baby. Terra's gone."

"Faye, are you even listening to me?"

Faye blinked, shocked when she felt moisture there. She quickly wiped the tears away before Errika could see them. She didn't understand where that came from. One minute she was listening to Errika list off the pros of going back to the Gate, and the next she was ten years old again and staring down at her sister's body.

"Yeah, I'm listening to you," she forced out, remembering that Errika said something and was waiting for an answer. "And you're right. I'll do it, okay?"

She didn't know what made her agree to Errika's ridiculous plan. It was impulsive, slipping off her tongue before she could even register what she was saying. It reminded her of the night when she first reached the Gate's borders. Trying to shake off haunting memories. Trying to run away from the past.

"You will?" Errika's eyes were wide. "What happened to the 'Errika, it's a really bad idea!' thing you had going on there?"

Faye sighed deeply, rubbing her face with the back of her hand. "Look, I said I'll do it, all right? Don't make me change my mind."

Errika looked as though she wanted to say more on the subject, but kept her mouth shut. Faye was thankful for that. She didn't want to talk about her flashback or how it made her feel exactly like she felt the day Terra was found: betrayed, hurt, angered, depressed, and guilty.

She hated feeling that way. She wished it would stop.

Errika tilted her head to the side, and Faye instantly knew that she'd caught the drying tears on her cheeks. "Are you crying?"

"No," Faye muttered, shaking her head.

Errika's eyes narrowed. "But you were."

Faye shrugged, not bothering to hide it. There was no point. Errika wasn't stupid; she'd be able to tell. "I guess."

Errika glanced at the doorway before looking back Faye. "Why were you crying, babe? What memory was it this time?"

Faye tensed. She wasn't surprised that Errika guessed the reason for her tears, but she didn't feel relieved either. Now she would have to explain the memory and why it made her cry. Faye just wanted to get on with her day. "The day she died." Faye shrugged as nonchalantly as she could. "It's whatever. Let's move on now, okay? When are we going to the Gate?"

Errika smiled. "We can go now."

Faye's eyebrows rose. "What if we get caught? Won't it look suspicious if we just go into the woods?"

Errika waved her hand dismissively. "If someone asks, we left something at the Campout site. I've got us covered, all right?"

Faye sighed, standing up and stretching out her arms. "All right. Let's go."

"Remind me why I listened to you again?"

The second they stepped outside Kole began to regret his decision. What was the point of this? It was only going to get him arrested. What would Alex or his father think about that? They would call him a hypocrite. How could he ever call someone else stupid for going to the Gate's borders, if he was doing that himself?

"Because, even though you pretend to hate the prospect of taking a risk for once in your life, you're just as curious as the rest of us." Terence grinned. "You want to meet the girl creature again, and we both know it."

Kole sighed deeply. It was true. He did want to see the creature again, to learn its ways. But he didn't want to risk getting arrested and deserting his family for the rest of his life. He wanted to stay safe. He wanted his family to stay safe.

He didn't want to be in the mess he was dragging himself into. So why? Why do this?

It was simple. He wanted his friend to believe him.

Kole knew it was stupid, but if Terence didn't believe him, he didn't know what he'd do. He needed someone he could trust. Someone who believed his story. And Terence was the number one person that Kole could go to. If Terence didn't believe him, who would?

Who would?

"You know where your camera is, right?" Kole muttered finally.

"Yes, of course." Terence shook his head, rolling his eyes. "My dad would kill me if I lost it."

"He'd kill you if he found out what pictures you put on it," Kole mumbled.

"What was that?"

"Nothing."

Terence looked as though he wanted to press more on the subject, but he didn't. An awkward silence developed as they made their way to Terence's car, hopping inside. Terence slid the key into the ignition before pulling out into the driveway. Kole glanced up at the ceiling. There was no turning back now.

"I could have sworn it was right here," Terence exclaimed, shifting papers around aimlessly on his desk.

Kole sighed deeply. He should have known that his friend didn't actually know where his camera was. It wasn't unlike Terence to misplace his things, no matter how expensive they were. "Guess there's nothing we can do. I'll just go home and—"

"Nuh-uh." Terence shot Kole a glare. "Help me find it."

Kole cast a reluctant glance around the room before giving off a short nod. He decided to ignore Terence's curt tone, or that he didn't even want the camera to be found. If it was found that would mean that he had to go back to the Gate's borders. And, frankly, Kole was terrified of even the prospect of returning.

"Fine," he muttered, sauntering around the room, rifling through random objects. Kole could never accuse Terence of being organized. His room was like a pigsty with clothes scattered across the floor, mixed in with random stuff that was never touched. Kole couldn't help but wonder how life was going to be for Terence when he grew older. His house was going to be a complete disaster.

"Where the hell is it?" Terence seethed, throwing a dirty shirt aside. Kole watched blankly as it fell to the floor, landing on another, equally as dirty, shirt.

"I don't know," Kole mumbled resignedly. "Did you check on the floor underneath the rest of your crap?"

Terence chucked an irritated scowl in Kole's direction. "Why don't you start actually helping?"

Kole's eyebrows rose. "Why don't you stop acting like an asshole? Maybe then I'll start."

Terence sighed, shaking his head. "Look. I'm sorry, all right? It's just ..." He shook his head again. "Never mind. Can you please just help me fine the damn camera?"

Kole nodded, kneeling down and picking between piles of clothes. It amazed him that there could be so many clothes on the floor, yet still so many clothes within the confinements of his dresser. Terence, Kole observed, has a lot of clothes.

"I found it!" Terence called out suddenly. Kole looked up just as Terence pulled the camera out of a box marked for CD's. Kole couldn't fathom why Terence would put a camera in there, but he did.

"Great," he muttered, not sounding pleased at all.

Terence grinned. "Let's go play spies like we did when we were younger."

At this Kole had to smile. When they were younger—no older than ten—he, Terence, Seth, and Zander all used to play spies. Two would be the good spies; two would be the bad spies. They would play the game for hours, talking in hushed voices and crawling around the house to attack the other two by surprise. Kole wished, not for the first time, that he and his friends were ten again. Life was so much simpler back then.

"Let's go," Terence said suddenly, ripping Kole away from his reverie.

Kole blinked, nodding. "All right."

Together, they bounded down the stairs and out the door, telling Terence's father that they were going to go catch a movie at the theaters. That, Terence told Kole, would buy them at least two hours before they had to return. Kole sighed internally. He didn't want to be in the woods for two hours. It would look suspicious.

"So what if the girl isn't there?" Kole demanded as they headed down the street. He leaned back in his seat, glancing at Terence.

He noted dully that Terence looked awfully relaxed as he drove for someone who was about to pull an awfully risky move.

"Then we go home and go back another time. Like tomorrow." He grinned. "I bet it's going to be there."

"What makes you think that?"

"Because there's obviously no law for the creature on the other side not to go. I mean, if they could control it, why keep it behind bars?"

Terence had a point. If the Government was controlling the creatures on the other side of the Gate's borders, what would be the point of keeping them behind the Gate in the first place? Why not just unite them all as one? Kole shook his head. No, the Government couldn't have been controlling the other side. That wouldn't make sense.

"But what if the cameras are working again?" Kole demanded, panic flourishing inside him. He didn't want to be arrested. He didn't want to be seen as some insane rebel. "What if I get caught?"

Terence sighed. "Kole, chill. You're going to be fine. A whole forest of cameras can't be fixed overnight, all right?"

Kole pursed his lips, his jaw working. It was easy for Terence to say. He wasn't going to be putting himself in any danger. He would probably hang out on Kole's hill while Kole did all the dirty work, risking everything just to take a picture or two. "Whatever," he snapped, irritation flashing. None of this was worth it. None of it.

"You don't have to come with me, you know," Faye said for the third time since they entered the forest thirty minutes before. Before they'd gotten out of Errika's car, Errika announced that she was going with Faye to the borders, saying that it wouldn't be right to send her in there alone. She could have gotten lost without her. Errika would feel guilty if she actually did get caught and she wasn't penalized at all. All very uplifting excuses.

"Yes, I do," Errika replied, plucking a leaf from a branch and ripping it apart within her fingers. She glanced up and smiled mischievously. "Just admit it. You need me."

"I do." Faye shrugged. "But that doesn't mean you need to risk anything."

Errika laughed, shaking her head. "Of course I do. It wouldn't be right to preach for you to take a risk if I'm not taking one myself."

Faye would be lying if she said that thought hadn't occurred to her. When Errika prodded Faye's mind, tempting her back to the Gate's borders, Faye couldn't help but feel irritable. Who was Errika to tell her to go back if she'd never taken an overly huge risk before herself? Faye was irritated that she was being told to do something so nonchalantly that no one else had ever been able to do.

"It's probably not going to be there," Faye mumbled, changing the subject slightly. For some odd reason, it felt wrong to call the boy an "it". It didn't seem right. That was what you called an animal or an inanimate object. Kole was neither of these. At least, she didn't think so. Could the boy be considered an animal? Or was it considered a person like her?

"Sure it will." Errika smiled. "I mean, it's probably just as tempted as we are, right?"

Faye doubted it, but nodded. "Whatever you say."

It was silent for a while excluding Errika mumbling to herself about the path to the Campout. They both agreed that it would probably be smart to start from where the journey really began:

the campsite. They were lucky the markings were still on the trees, otherwise they'd be lost.

"You were crying earlier," Errika said suddenly. "And you lied about it. Why?"

Faye sighed deeply. She should have known that Errika wouldn't let that slide. "I was thinking about the day Terra died," she said softly. "Me seeing her body. It just randomly popped into my head, and I don't understand why."

It was Errika's turn to sigh. "It's getting worse," she murmured. "You're starting to torment yourself more than usual. You were getting better. Why is it getting worse?"

Faye shrugged. "Honestly, I have no idea."

And she didn't. Just when she thought that maybe she was getting better, that Terra's death was finally becoming a part of the past, more memories seemed to emerge. The dreams were becoming more intense, and everyday something would remind her of her. Faye knew that she would never forget Terra completely—and she didn't want to. But she thought that maybe she would at least be able to keep the painful memories at bay. Maybe be able to think of her sister without feeling a pang in her chest.

But it wasn't happening any time soon.

"I can't believe she did this to you," Errika snapped suddenly. "I'm pissed that Terra left, and left you broken." She glared at the ground. "It's a good thing that you're as strong as you are, though. Because if you were weak, you'd be lost."

Errika's outburst shocked Faye. Faye's eyes widened. She expected to feel anger for her speaking about Terra in such a way, but she didn't. What Errika said made sense. And, for the first time, it wasn't just to console her. It was what Errika truly felt. "I don't know why she did what she did. But she did, and my stupid brain just has to learn to accept that Terra's dead and she's not coming back."

The words hurt even as she spoke them, stinging like pricks of needles. But they were true. And the faster Faye accepted them, the better off she would be.

Errika shot Faye a smile. "That's what I like about you," she drawled. "You know the truth whether you like it or not. And, unlike some idiots out there, you attempt to accept it. Sure you fail sometimes—like when you refused to believe that the tooth fairy didn't exist—but you try."

Faye laughed, shoving Errika playfully. She was attempting to lighten the mood, and she'd succeeded. "You jerk! I can't believe you actually video-taped my mom putting the tooth under my pillow just to get me to believe you."

"Well, you know me," Errika teased, sticking out her tongue playfully. "I need everyone to know the truth once I know it."

Faye sighed, her laughter coming to an end. "That's very true."

They came to a flat area. Errika stopped walking, peering around. "I think it was here," she murmured. She glanced around, meticulously looking over the details of the woods. Faye closed her eyes for a moment before opening them. She could picture the Campout with its large tent and campfire. She glanced to the right of where she imagined the tent to be, a smile pricking her lips when she saw a destroyed fire pit.

"It was here," she agreed, pointing. "Fire pit's right there."

Errika nodded. "All right. Lead the way then."

Leading the way was more difficult than Faye would have thought. She couldn't remember the directions she took at all, so she did the same thing that she did the day she found Terra's body. She walked in the same direction, never turning. Besides, she tried to reason, the Gate was long enough, so she had to reach it sometime, right?

"You must have had a really bad dream," Errika mumbled, sounding breathless. "Because you walked a long way."

Faye laughed. "Yeah, I did."

"Damn, I need to get in shape!" Errika whined, shaking her head. "Do you think we're in the territory yet?"

Faye nodded. "We must be getting close."

Errika laughed shakily, her exhaustion showing off freely. "Girl, if we're lost, I'm going to blame you."

Faye grinned. "All right."

Kole plucked a branch up from the ground with his free hand and tossed it aimlessly. In his other, he clutched Terence's digital camera tightly, slightly nervous that he was going to drop it. He would never hear the end of it if he broke it, but he couldn't bring himself to care enough to hold it with both hands.

The woods were taunting him as he tried to navigate his way through. He struggled to recall the path he took while he searched for Terence, but he was trying in vain. He'd been so frantic, and it had been so dark. It was next to impossible.

He regretted agreeing to Terence's stupid plan. If the Government didn't catch him on the cameras, they sure would when his father reported him missing. They would find him cowering behind a bush, probably gone mad from looking for the Gate's borders. And then, once they found him, he'd be taken straight to the prison wards.

Kole froze when he heard a branch snap. He twisted, staring hard at the few pairs of trees. They looked awfully familiar ....

Kole gasped, rushing forward and pushing through the branches and underbrush. This was the place—he knew it was. He cursed as the branches scraped his skin, leaving little scratches in their wake. He wanted to stop, to turn, to go back. But he couldn't. He'd made it so far.

All of a sudden the branches were gone, and his arms whacked metal. Kole groaned, rubbing his now-sore hands together irritably. He looked up. In front of him stood the Gate, staring down at him intimidatingly. Kole gulped, stepping back and peering around. He felt his stomach drop when he saw that no one was there.

Kole cursed, stomping his foot. He knew that Terence was crazy. He knew that the girl wouldn't come back. Why had he let Terence get into his head and jerk? Why couldn't he have just stood his ground?

Kole turned to leave.

And then he stopped.

There was movement within the bushes on the other side. Kole twisted back, his fingers curling onto the metal as he gazed around the other side. His eyes sought for the movement in the bushes. He bit his lip, not knowing whether to be excited or frightened. Was it Faye? Or was it some other creature that actually would harm him? No matter what Terence said, he didn't believe that Faye would hurt him. It'd been too scared that night.

Kole's breathing came to a stop as two figures appeared. He pulled away from the Gate, clutching the camera tightly within his hands. There were more of them?

"Hello?" Kole called, trying to keep the timid-ness out of his voice.

The figures moved toward the Gate, and Kole began to see details in the creatures. One of the girls was Faye, its red hair blazing. The other girl reminded him of his brother, Alex. Long, dark brown hair. Tall, with its head held high. And, when it grew closer, he saw that the girl and Alex had the same large, wide, blue eyes.

Faye and the other girl came up to the Gate, grabbing hold of the cool metal. Kole could see that Faye'd gained some courage, that it wasn't as scared as it used to be. But, like Kole, the apprehension was still clear in its eyes.

The other girl didn't seem frightened at all. It seemed excited, though it contained it very well. Kole stared at them silently, wondering if he was supposed to make the first move. But then, finally, the brown-haired girl stuck her hand through the Gate as though it was greeting him. "Hi, I'm Errika," it said cheerfully. "And you are?"

CHAPTER 6

K ole stared at the outstretched hand for a long time before finally taking it in his and shaking. Errika smiled, pulling its hand away and placing it back onto the Gate. Kole glanced at Faye, noting its shocked expression. Apparently, this girl had just done something unexpected, even to Faye.

"I'm Kole," he said finally, shifting his feet in the dirt awkwardly.

The girl nodded, seeming satisfied. "So you're this mysterious boy Faye has been talking about? She didn't want to come back, but I forced her—"

Kole was lost. What did the girl mean by "she" and "her"? Those words were so foreign to him. "What do you mean?" he said suddenly. "She and her? What are those words?"

Errika and Faye cast a glance. "They're pronouns," Errika drawled. She seemed to be struggling with explaining what the two words meant. "Like, when you're talking about someone else, like Faye for example. She is going to the store. She ate a frog for breakfast."

Kole was lost as Errika struggled to explain the concept. He still didn't understand what it meant. He blinked. Wait—what if it wasn't an it? Was that what Errika was trying to say? It was a she? He thought hard. That sounded right. And that made sense, seeing how it sounded like he. Did that mean her replaced him then?

"Oh," he murmured, looking up. "I get it."

Errika blinked, surprised. "You do? Because I suck at teaching—I really do."

Kole smiled. "Yeah, I get it. She replaces he and her replaces him."

Errika and Faye stared at him blankly. "What?" Errika said after a moment. She glanced at Faye as though sending a telepathic message before turning back to him. "What do you mean?"

"It's the same concept," Kole explained awkwardly, feeling Errika's pain. "Instead of saying she, for a boy it's he. And for a boy it's not her, but him."

Faye seemed to be understanding now. "Oh," she murmured. "So it's like he went to the store?"

Kole nodded, grateful that at least one of them understood. "Yeah."

Faye smiled. Kole smiled back, all fear of her diminishing. She was nice, not frightening. Shy, not ravenous. Why would the Government want to hide creatures exactly like them? "So what kind of creature are you?" Kole murmured, his fingers curling around the metal of the Gate. "Human like me?"

Faye nodded. "Yes," she said softly. "Human, person, people."

Kole felt his lips prick up into a smile. Faye reminded him of himself in some ways. She was shy, but didn't let that stop her from asking questions when she needed to understand something. She thought before she did things, made sure that they were good ideas before doing something completely idiotic. But, like Kole, she bended under the pressure of her friends.

"Um," Kole murmured, feeling the weight of Terence's camera within his hands. "I was just wondering if I could take a picture of you guys?"

Faye glanced at the camera in Kole's hands, and back to him. Kole braced himself for a refusal. "A picture?" Her eyebrows crinkled together. "What for?"

"My friend wants proof so he knows I'm not crazy," Kole replied, awkwardly bringing a hand through his hair.

Faye looked down at the camera again, thinking over the request. Kole watched her nervously, praying that she would allow him one picture. If he came out with nothing yet claimed that he talked to Faye and now Errika, Terence would have him committed.

Errika rolled her eyes at what Kole guessed to be Faye's hesitance and sighed deeply. "Of course you can take a picture. If your friend is too cowardly to come in here himself, then we should at least give him a little what he's missing out on."

It was amazing how fluent Errika became with the "he, him, his" business. She was a quick learner, he couldn't help but notice. After she got the hang of something, there was no stopping her. Though, Kole himself had gotten the hang of the "she, her, hers" business pretty fast, too. It came naturally to him. He didn't know why, but it did.

"You sure?" Kole asked softly, glancing at Faye for reassurance. Instead of meeting his gaze, she turned to Errika for a moment before turning back to him, her eyes trained on the camera. She looked up, finally meeting his eyes. There was still hesitation swimming within them. "Please?" he murmured.

Faye sighed after a moment, nodding. "Sure."

Kole smiled, stepping forward and fitting the lens between one of the spaces between the metal bars. He didn't want the Gate to obscure the view of the girls. He leaned down, his eye looking through the eyepiece on the camera. "Can you take a step back?" he asked softly.

The girls obliged. Errika grinned, wrapping an around Faye and pulling her close. Kole couldn't help but wonder what it would be like to hold a girl like that. The thought seemed so weird—holding a girl, hugging a girl, even high-fiving a girl. Contact with them was just so … foreign.

Kole shrugged the feelings off, positioning himself correctly for a good photo. He wasn't very familiar with photography, but Terence had taught him a thing or two. He took a deep breath, concentrating on getting a good focus point. He zoomed in so that their faces would be shown better but you could still see their whole bodies. And then, after a few moments of sitting there making sure he'd made the correct choice, he took the photo.

Faye and Errika moved apart almost immediately after the photo was taken. Kole straightened up, moving the camera away from the Gate. "Thanks," he said with a smile.

Errika suddenly squealed in excitement, pulling Faye back to her again. "Oh, oh, oh!" she called out. "You should take another one except with us making funny faces."

Kole cocked an eyebrow while Faye shot her a disbelieving look. "All right," he said, not able to hide the smile that was beginning to etch on his face. Errika was so energetic; it amused him.

Errika smiled smugly in Faye's direction before pulling her back to her. Errika created little bunny ears with her fingers, placing them about Faye's head before making a crazy stance that almost made Kole break out into laughter. He'd never seen anyone do something like that. Not a boy, anyway.

"Faye," Errika drawled, managing to keep her face and position exactly the same as she reprimanded her friend, "make a funny position and face right now."

Faye sighed and did as she was told. Kole gave her a thumbs-up before leaning forward and quickly snapped the picture. This photo required a sense of spontaneous-ness. He didn't want to put too much concentration in it.

Errika abruptly pulled away from Faye as something began to ring. Kole's eyebrows knitted together as she pulled out what looked like a cell phone. So girl's had the same technology as them as well?

She threw Kole and Faye an apologetic look. "It's my mom," she murmured. "Sorry, I have to take this."

Kole watched as Errika moved a couple feet away flipping open her phone and speaking softly. He couldn't help but wonder what she'd meant by "mom". He'd never heard the word before, but then again, why would he? Girls had different words for different things.

Faye glanced at her friend for a moment before moving closer to Kole. Kole smiled at her. "What's a mom?" he murmured, leaning against the Gate.

Faye brought a hand through her hair, glancing at Errika again before answering. "A mom is a parent. Someone who looks after you."

Kole nodded, crossing his arms over his chest. "Oh, right. We call them dads over here."

Faye sighed deeply, rubbing her eyes with the back of her hand. "This is just all so weird to me," she muttered. "So many new words, and it's just so hard to comprehend." She let her hands fall. "All my life I was taught that the Gate hid a humongous beast that would rip you to shreds if you went near it. That's why the Government keeps us away. But now . . . ."

"I was taught the same thing," Kole replied, closing his eyes for a moment before opening them.

"I just don't understand," Faye murmured, looking past Kole, seeming as though she was in a completely different world. She blinked, and for a moment Kole saw raw fear in her eyes. But it was gone as quickly as it came.

Kole was about to answer, but Errika cut in before he could get a word out. "Hey, I'm so sorry, but we have to go." She appeared beside Faye, leaning against the Gate as Kole was. "My mom is wondering what's taking so long to find some supplies from the Campout."

Kole didn't understand what she meant by that, but decided not to question it. "All right."

Errika nodded, saying a quick goodbye before turning and starting back from where they came. Faye glanced back at Errika before turning back to Kole. "Bye," she whispered. "You might want to delete the pictures after you show them to your friend. It would be dangerous if the Government saw them."

Kole nodded. Faye was right of course. But he didn't have the ability to burn the photographs. Terence's dad used a film camera, the pictures saved on a roll of film inside. He'd have to burn the photographs and the negatives to make the evidence disappear completely. "Bye," he said finally.

Faye turned to leave. Before Kole could even register what he was doing, he was calling out to her, asking for her to wait. Faye turned, waiting patiently for him to say what he wanted to say. Kole didn't understand what was going on—it was like he didn't have any control of what he said. Words were sputtering out before he could understand that he was even speaking. "Will I see you again—I mean will you—won't you—are you—going to come back?"

Kole couldn't fathom how Faye understood what he said, but she smiled, obviously understanding his words. She took a step back to the Gate, the hesitance clear in her eyes. "I don't know . . . it's dangerous, isn't it?"

"Yes," Kole agreed. "It's very dangerous."

Faye looked Kole over for a long moment before exhaling softly and nodding. "Sure, I'll come back. But I have to know that you'll be here on the other side."

Kole smiled. "This spot on Friday at seven?"

Faye nodded. "Sure."

And then she was gone, jogging to catch up with her friend, disappearing behind a group of trees.

The Gate

Faye looked all around her, memorizing the patterns of the trees, the ways the branches folded over each other like vines. She studied the ground, noting the organization of the rocks on the dirt, the way everything was positioned. She took everything in, willing her mind to trap the images. She needed to remember everything in order to make her way back to the spot again.

"So Kole was nice and not dangerous at all," Errika commented, an amused smile on her face. "I can't believe you asked him if he was going to eat you."

Faye shook her head, smiling a small smile. "Shut up."

She couldn't believe how easily it came to refer to Kole as "him" now. It was as though she'd know the words her whole life, when she in fact didn't. This new vocabulary was so strange, yet they seemed familiar. She'd meant what she said to Kole—she couldn't comprehend recent events, and everything was just so weird to her.

But it seemed so ... right.

Maybe that was why she agreed to meet with Kole again. There was something about him that she couldn't place. She couldn't help but want to see him again.

"So, are you going to go back?" Errika asked, wriggling her eyebrows.

Faye nodded. "On Friday."

Errika squealed, clapping her hands in delight. "And I didn't even have to talk you into it this time!" she shrieked. "Oh, this is going to be great. Don't worry I'll be your alibi, all right? Just say that you're coming over to my house."

Faye eyed her friend curiously before nodding. "Okay."

Errika started speaking animatedly about how awesome this discovery was and how they were the only ones who knew about it. They were lucky, they were special. Faye blocked her friend out as she began scoping the place out, noting important factors about the forest as they walked by. She just hoped that in two days, the images of the forest would stay clear to her.

"We should mark some trees or something," Errika muttered, her arms flailing around. "We don't need you getting lost, do we?"

Faye sighed deeply, wishing Errika had spoken up about that sooner. "It's a little late now, don't you think?"

Errika waved her hand dismissively. "Don't be ridiculous. I'll come in tomorrow and mark some of the trees, maybe clear out a path. Don't be surprised if I don't show up to school."

Faye's mouth almost dropped. Errika would do that for her? "Errika, you don't—"

"Don't give me a speech about what I don't have to do. I want to do it, all right? Now, I'm not going to make it obvious because the Government could scout the place out at night or something. But, I'll try and make it so you can notice."

Faye nodded. "All right. Thanks."

Errika grinned. "No problem!"

Miranda Blatt scurried through the deserted hallway, clutching the stolen key within her hand so tightly that the key cut into her skin. She felt as though the walls had eyes, watching her every move as her shoes pounded against the floor. She twisted around, her eyes searching for a guard—or worse, Courtnie. If she was caught, she'd be shot, it was a simple as that.

Miranda sighed shakily when she realized that no one was following her. She was safe. For now.

A trembling hand made its way through her frizzy brown locks of hair. Miranda sighed again, trying to contain herself. This wasn't the first time she'd been sent out on a job like this. The Miss trusted her to do her bidding. She'd done countless jobs before for the Miss, putting her trust in her that this was for the greater good.

But that didn't stop her from being frightened, however.

Courtnie scared her more than anything in the world. She couldn't believe she even had the strength to do the Miss's bidding. She was terrified that Courtnie would catch her, torture her, and murder her before she could even blink. Miranda was smaller than most of the workers in the Government building, younger too. She was only nineteen years of age. Since her mother died, she'd been sentenced to work in the Government building. Miranda didn't understand why she had to work here; there were other, more capable people to do the job.

Miranda shivered, her eyes roaming around the hallway again. What if she hadn't done the job correctly? No—she couldn't have done it wrong. Courtnie had come into the security room, furious that the cameras had stopped monitoring. And she'd done exactly what the Miss told her to do: tell Courtnie exactly what happened. The cameras stopped monitoring. It was true that they did, she just didn't give the full story. She was the one that caused the cameras to stop monitoring. She was the one at fault. She didn't how she did it. The Miss simply handed her a flash drive and told her to stick it into Courtnie's computer. She said to download the file, and then the cameras would stop monitoring. And, the Miss had continued, only she knew how to get them to work again.

The Miss was so cunning, so smart. Miranda looked up to her, though the Miss wasn't much older than she was. She never quite saw her face in the darkness, but she could tell by her height and the sound of her voice, that their ages weren't that far apart. She wished to know the Miss's name, but the Miss refused to tell. She said that it would only put both of them in danger is she knew. So Miranda never asked.

Miranda sighed in relief as she reached the door of the prison wards. She opened her palm, staring at the key for a short moment before blinking and reaching to unlock the door. She let out another sigh as the door unlocked, swinging open at ease.

Miranda moved quickly down the rows of prisoners. They all cried out for her to help them, to let them out. Miranda felt sick to her stomach every time she came in here. She wanted to let the prisoners free, let them run back to their lives. But she couldn't. She had to stick with the plan. The Miss assured her that after the plan was complete, the Government would be no more and everyone would be free to go.

Miranda reached the last cell, moving forward timidly. "Miss?"

The Miss was lying on her bed. She sat up at the sound of Miranda's voice, rushing forward to the entrance of her cell. "Miranda," she breathed, her fingers wrapping around the metal bars. They were slender, elegant. "Did you do it?"

Miranda nodded vigorously, dishing into her pocket and pulling out the flash drive. She outstretched her hand, glancing around fearfully. Guards weren't supposed to be patrolling this section for another ten minutes. That was what the Miss said. But what if someone decided to come early?

The Miss took the flash drive from her hand, curling it within hers and sighing. "Thank you for doing this," she said after a moment, sticking the flash drive into her pocket. "I know the risk your taking. I appreciate it."

Miranda nodded. "Thank you for trusting me."

The Miss smiled, her white teeth flashing in the darkness. "Of course I trust you, Miranda." She paused. "So the cameras have in fact stopped monitoring?"

Miranda nodded, struggling to smile. She was taking too much time here. She had to leave before someone saw. "Yes," she said swiftly.

The Miss bit her lip. "And she doesn't suspect you?"

Miranda heard a note of worry in the Miss's voice. Had something happened that she wasn't aware of? "Not that I'm aware of," she said cautiously. "Did something happen, Miss?"

The Miss was quiet for a moment before shaking her head. "No, Miranda, everything's fine." She looked down the hall, as though searching for a danger. "Come back when you can and give me an update, all right?" The Miss watched as Miranda nodded. "Now go before someone spots you."

Miranda didn't have to be asked twice. She pulled away from the cell, only pausing a moment to watch as the Miss moved back in her cell, collapsing on her bed. The Miss seemed to be hiding some sort of regret, some sort of sorrow. Miranda wondered what she could have been hiding. Did someone important to her slip away? Or was it just because she was trapped there, stuck in the cell defenseless? Not that she was truly defenseless, anyway. She still managed to have her plans of sabotage leak into the Government. How she managed to get her supplies—like her flash drive—Miranda would never know.

Miranda blinked, turning away from the Miss, away from the prisoners within the prison wards, and hurried down the long hall, back the way she had come.

CHAPTER 7

"**A**re they almost done?" Kole demanded, his eyes latching on to the clock for the tenth time in the last five minutes. "I need to go."

He and Terence were standing in the darkness, only the dull yellow-lights coming from the ceiling providing them a small share of light. Kole hated being in the darkroom, hated how dim it was. It set him on edge. He always felt like there were things lurking in the corners, waiting to snatch him while he wasn't paying attention.

"Almost," Terence replied stiffly, plucking the two photographs from the tub marked Stop-Bath and setting them in the tub marked Fixer. He used the wooden tongs in his hands to dunk them into the chemical, making sure the pictures were fully enveloped in the water. "They have to sit for two minutes in the Fixer before I can put them in the water."

"How long do they have to stay in the water?" Kole demanded, leaning back against the wall. He crossed his arms impatiently over his chest, his hands curling into fists.

"Four minutes."

Kole groaned internally, glaring at the clock. It was moving fast, his time swiftly dwindling before he had to meet Faye at the Gate. He'd wanted to head out thirty minutes ago, but Terence insisted that they develop the photographs before he went out. Terence had processed the film the day before, promising that the pictures would be developed today. Kole hadn't thought anything of it at the time. Now he was regretting letting Terence take his sweet time.

"I'm going to be late," Kole snapped before he could stop himself. "Can't you just cheat? Keep them in for less time?"

It seemed perfectly fine to him, but Terence didn't seem to think so. "Of course not," Terence replied through an icy glare. "Just wait a few minutes. You'll be fine."

Kole grumbled to himself under his breath, deciding it was pointless to argue with Terence any further. He still wouldn't make it on time to the Gate. By the time he got there Faye probably would have already left, thinking that he decided not to come. And then Kole would never see her again.

He looked up at the clock again. He just hoped that wouldn't happen.

"Where's my cellphone, Faye?"

Faye groaned, not at all in the mood for an encounter with her sister. She looked up from the bag she was packing, her gaze meeting with Kat's infuriated one. It wasn't unusual for Kat's face to be fitted in a scowl. She was always upset about something, and, sadly, her anger was usually directed at Faye if not her friends.

"I don't know," Faye replied stiffly, zipping up her duffel bag and standing up. She made her way toward her bedroom's door, trying to think of how she was going to fit through the doorway without shoving Kat out of the way. As she got closer she realized that there was no way around it: her sister would have to be shoved. "Did you leave it at Bella's house?"

"No!" she hissed.

Faye paused as she reached her doorway. Kat didn't look like she was willing to move, but Faye had to try anyway. "Can you move?" she demanded impatiently.

"No." Kat glowered. "Not until you tell me where you hid it."

"I didn't hide anything, Kat," Faye snapped, shoving past her sister and heading down the hall. She turned, hurrying down the stairs. She was going to be late.

"Yes you did!" Kat hollered, following her down the stairs. "And you're going to help me find it."

"No, I'm not, because I have to get to Errika's."

Faye skipped the last step and fumbled for her car keys. After getting a confident grasp on them, she held them tightly within her hand, her pace quickening. She had to get to Errika's to sneak out her window so she could get to the Gate without suspicion. She and Errika both agreed that if Faye showed up, they'd be less likely to call if her mother called while she was gone.

But, of course, Kat was going to try and ruin her plans.

"I'm going to tell Mom that you hid my phone again," Kat threatened as Faye rushed toward the front door.

Faye didn't even turn to see her sister's expression. "Go right ahead. Last time you tattled you got grounded for a week, remember?"

Kat growled under her breath, throwing herself in front of Faye, her arms crossed over her chest. "Faye, this isn't funny! I have to call—"

"You're right," Faye agreed, "it's not funny. Cutting people off is quite rude." She put her hands on Kat's shoulders and pushed her out of the way. "Now, why don't you go look around your room? Under your bed, in the disaster zone you call a closet."

"You hid it in my room then?"

Kat was relentless. Faye sighed deeply, deciding that she'd be better off ignoring her sister than answering. Either way Kat would chase after her demanding to know where her phone's location was. Usually Faye found great pleasure in her sister's anger, loving the way her eyebrows arched up so high they almost disappeared behind her hair. But today that didn't amuse her. If anything it made her angry.

"Hey!" Kat called when she realized that Faye wasn't going to answer her. "You can't just ignore me."

"Watch me," Faye called back. She was almost to the door now. Just a couple more feet—

"You know, you're being really dodgy today!" Kat's fingers scraped at her back. "Why are you in such a hurry, anyway? Errika's house will still be there when you get there."

"And your phone will still be missing as long as you keep harping me for answers I don't have," Faye snapped. She reached the door and jerked the door open with an irritable twist of the hand on the handle. She spun around, almost whacking Kat in the chest. She reeled back, disgruntled. When had she gotten so close? "Do yourself a favor and clean your room," Faye snapped, clutching her sleepover bag tightly. "Have a good night."

With that she stepped onto the porch and slammed the front door shut.

Faye let out an exasperated sigh, pulling out her cell phone and checking the time. She was so late.

"Where have you been?" Errika demanded as Faye bounded up the steps of Errika's house.

Faye shot her friend and apologetic look, pushing her way into the house. "I'm sorry!" she exclaimed. "Kat kept me."

Errika slammed the door behind her, leaning against it for a short moment before grabbing Faye's arm and pulling her down the hall. Unlike Faye's house, Errika's only had one floor. Faye liked that she didn't have to travel upstairs to get to Errika's bedroom. It made traveling so much easier. And, in this case, it made sneaking out easier.

"You need to get out of here fast," Errika whispered harshly. She paused for a moment to say loudly, "Oh, Faye! It's nice to see you! Come on, let's go to my room."

"Hello, Faye, dear!" came a call from the other room.

"Hi!" Faye replied lightly, trying to hide her unease. It would be so simple for them to get caught. If her mom went into the room while Faye was leaving, she'd automatically know that something was up. If that happened she'd never get to the Gate on time.

Errika's bedroom door slammed behind them as they entered the room. Faye threw her bag on the bed, taking a quick look around. Errika was what you would call a neat freak. Everything had a place and it was imperative that everything was put in its place. Not a thing was out of order in Errika's room. Books were neatly placed on a bookshelf in the corner of the room; papers were stacked perfectly on her desk. There wasn't a single wrinkle on her bed. Faye couldn't help but wonder how Errika managed to keep everything so tidy. She worked hard just to keep her room half-decent.

"Don't look around," Errika hissed, pushing Faye toward her bedroom window. "Get out of here!"

Faye complied immediately, jogging to the window and pushing it open. She struggled to get into a sitting position, holding onto the walls as though they were a lifeline. She leaned forward slightly, looking down at the ground. Even though the distance wasn't that great, she felt as though she was sitting atop a cliff, waiting to fall off the edge.

Faye flinched as an image of Terra appeared, her body mangled, her eyes wide, and her mouth agape. Her lips ran dry. Was this the feeling Terra felt before she jumped? Terror mixed with the anticipation of the landing? Or did she not care at all? Did she simply run off the edge, not able to wait until her life was over?

"Go!" Errika whispered angrily. Faye turned, catching Errika as she gestured frantically with her hands for Faye to make the decent out the window.

After taking a deep breath, Faye let her hands fall and she slid out of the house. Her feet collided with the ground, and Faye felt herself sag in relief. She'd thought that that would be more painful. She inclined her head, looking up at Errika's window. She glanced at the driveway, spotting her car parked besides Errika's. It would be a lot faster if ... "Can I have my keys?" she asked hurriedly, balancing on her tippy-toes to be taller.

Errika appeared at the window sill, dangling her car keys. "That would be suspicious," she warned. "Do you really want to take that risk?"

"I'm going to be late!" Faye exclaimed as softly as she could. "I don't really have a choice."

After a moment of thinking the Faye's words through, Errika smiled, dropping the keys form her hand. "Be careful," she ordered, gesturing to Faye's car in the driveway. "And what happens if my mom comes in, demanding to know why your car is suddenly leaving the driveway?"

"Say I'm going to the store," Faye replied briskly, already moving toward the driveway. "Text if you end up needing me to come home with proof."

"Do you have any money?"

Faye patted her pockets, sighing heavily when she realized she didn't have anything. She would check the car, but she didn't want to waste any more time. This conversation was already making her later by the second. "Can I borrow twenty bucks?" she asked swiftly, shooting her friend a pleading gaze.

Errika nodded and disappeared from the window sill. Faye hopped on her feet, nervous that Errika's mother was going to come outside and see her standing outside Errika's window. That, Faye knew, would be nothing but trouble. She'd never make it in time if that happened.

A moment later Errika reappeared, dropping a twenty dollar bill into Faye's outstretched hand. She smiled at Faye for a short second before flicking her hand in the direction of the driveway. "Now go!"

Faye didn't have to be told twice. She spun, pelting toward the driveway and hopping into her car. After a short moment of struggling with the keys in the ignition, she started the car and backed out, heading toward the park.

The only thing there was to do now was hope he'd be there when she got there.

Underbrush crinkled and snapped under Kole's feet as he made his way through the forest, his eyes trained on two photographs. He couldn't explain why, but he loved them. He love the way Faye's shy smile was shaped, the way she and Errika were so familiar and comfortable with each other. He loved everything about them. It was so foreign, so . . .

Beautiful.

Kole looked up, glancing around him to make sure he was going in the correct direction. He smiled around at the trees. The cynical part of him—the part that deemed this whole thing a bad idea—was beginning to fade. He was beginning to realize what Terence meant by the excitement and the wonder of this. How many people were able to come to the Gate without being arrested and speak to the girls from the other side? None.

Kole pushed through a batch of trees, careful not to scratch the images. He wanted to ask Faye if she wanted them before he burned them. It wouldn't be suspicious if girls had pictures of themselves, would it?

The Gate was in view now. Faye was nowhere to be found, however. Kole sighed deeply, hoping he wasn't too late. What if she'd already been there? What if she'd thought he wasn't coming and she didn't show up?

The pictures tight in hand, Kole allowed himself to fall into the ground, leaning against one of the trees. If someone—like a Government official—came around, they'd only see the tree and wouldn't think anything of it. Kole, for now, was safe.

Kole jumped and cursed as his phone went off within his pocket. He set the photographs gingerly onto the ground before dishing his phone out and bringing it irritably to his ear. "Yes?"

"Is that any way to greet your brother?"

Kole relaxed instantly, allowing himself to grin. "Hey, Alex."

"Hey!" Alex chuckled. "That's more like it."

Kole rolled his eyes, looking at the trees around him. His voice seemed so much louder out here in the wilderness than it ever did back in town. It echoed off the branches, the leaves. His voice projected so loudly it scared him—what if someone heard him? "Is there a reason why you decided to call?"

"Yeah, actually there is." His voice lowered, growing more serious. "Dad wants you home."

Kole's eyes narrowed. "Why?"

He could just visualize his brother shrugging. "He just said that he wanted you home. I think he's going through one of those withdrawals again—you know, where all of a sudden family is the most important thing there is."

Kole couldn't help but laugh. "Damn. I don't think I want to come home, then."

Alex sighed. "You're not leaving me alone in this. Come home, now."

"Not now," Kole muttered before he could stop himself. "Soon, I will. I just need to do something first."

"Like what?"

"Like take a long walk thinking about how stupid I am to go home to a sentimental man in his fifties."

With that Kole hung up the phone and pocketed it. He leaned back, closing his eyes. If he waited too much longer his father was going to go looking for him. And when he found out that he wasn't at Terence's like he said he would be, he'd be forced to explain things that he couldn't explain.

"Kole?"

Kole's head snapped up in the direction of the Gate. And out of nowhere, Faye was there, smiling shyly and waving her hand. Kole smiled slightly, pushing himself off the ground and shuffling toward her. "Hey," he said, his smile growing as he reached her. "I can't stay long, my dad wants me home."

Faye nodded understandingly. "I snuck out of my friend's house so I don't have much time either."

Kole glanced behind her for a moment before looking down at the photographs still within his hands. "Um," he mumbled, his eyes meeting hers once more, "my friend developed these, and I wanted to know if you wanted them before I had to burn them."

Faye's eyebrows rose slightly as she spotted the pictures in his hands. Kole rolled them up and stuck them through one of the holes in the wire, careful not to scratch his hand. Faye reached up, grabbing the pictures. She smiled and looked them over. "They're beautiful," she murmured in amazement. She looked up. "You take great pictures."

"Thanks." Kole shoved his hands into his jean pockets, suddenly self-conscious.

Faye's smile grew. "I can have them?"

Kole nodded. "Yes."

She grinned. "Thanks. What do I tell my family when they find the pictures, though?"

Kole shrugged, a smile pricking on the tips of his lips. "You'll figure something out."

Faye smiled brightly, her eyes still on the photographs. Kole noted how much more comfortable she seemed, how relaxed her posture was. When they first met she was stiff and nervous. Now she leaned against the Gate, her eyes alight and her lips pricked up in a smile.

Faye looked up suddenly, the spark of excitement still in her eyes. "Thanks," she said again.

Kole nodded, gazing past her, through the trees. He wondered, not for the first time, what lay beyond the never-ending trees. What did things look like where Faye lived? Did they live in houses like he did? Or did they live in caves like cavemen from story books?

"What are you thinking about?"

Kole blinked, his gaze turning back to Faye. She stared back at him, her green eyes like jade orbs. Kole bit his lip. Something about her eyes—though he couldn't place what—made him get lost in them every time they caught his. He'd never felt anything like it before. Was this a girl thing? Did they have supernatural powers that held boys captive against their will? Kole blinked again. Should he ask her? No, she'd think he was crazy and she'd stalk away, never to return.

"Kole?" Faye tilted her head to the side.

"I'm sorry—what?" Kole snapped out of his reverie, avoiding her eyes as to not get lost in them again.

"What are you thinking about?" she repeated, her eyes alight with amusement.

"I was just wondering what it looked like on your side," he answered sheepishly, rubbing his arm awkwardly.

Faye smiled, twisting around and peering through the trees. She spun around and for a moment Kole thought that she was going to tell him all about it, divulge the secrets of her home. But she just shook her head. "I'm sorry," she murmured. "I wouldn't exactly know how to explain it." She wrapped her fingers through the Gate's bars. "I wonder the same thing about your side."

A thought blossomed in Kole's mind. It was a crazy thought, one that he knew she would never agree to. It was one that could get them thrown in the prison wards, or even worse—sentenced to death. Death sentences rarely happened, so rarely that there hadn't been one since before Kole's father had been born. But it was still a possibility. Though, wasn't standing there at the Gate risk enough? They could get thrown in the prison wards just standing there talking.

"What if you came over here?" he said breezily before he could stop himself.

Faye just stared at him. He stared back, willing himself to look braver than he felt. What he'd uttered was the most reckless thing he'd ever said in his life. And for him to put her at risk as well .. . well, that was hardly fair. He should have offered to come over there instead. At least that way if they were caught, he'd be the offender, not her. He should have—

"I don't know..." Faye murmured, looking uncertain.

Kole brought a hand through his hair. "I'm sorry, I shouldn't have put you on the spot like that—"

Faye shook her head, cutting him off. "No, it's okay. I just need some time to think it over." She glanced behind her as though nervous. "Can we meet again?"

Kole nodded immediately. "Of course."

Faye took a step back. Kole knew instantly that their meeting was over, that they now had to go different ways until they met again. But when would that be? In a week? Two? Kole didn't know if he could wait that long. He thought of the next two weeks without seeing Faye, wondering how she was doing—what she was doing. He felt his stomach turn. He didn't want to wait that long.

Obviously, neither did Faye. "Same time next week?" she murmured.

Kole nodded even though he couldn't help but feel a little disappointed. A week. That seemed like a long time. But Faye needed time to think over what he'd just proposed. So he understood. He'd need at least a week if she'd suggested going on the other side, too.

After an awkward goodbye, Kole turned, heading away from Faye and the Gate, back toward civilization where his father was probably waiting, his eyes trained on the door, for his son to come home.

"No."

Courtnie growled under her breath, her slamming down on Fortis Caine's desk. Papers flew, fluttering to the floor like snowflakes upon the ground. Courtnie glared at Fortis, her eyes narrowed in anger. Fortis didn't seem at all fazed by her outrage, however. He sat back nonchalantly in his seat, rubbing his hand on his five o'clock shadow. He had his slender brow raised, looking fairly amused. This only made Courtnie angrier. What right did he have to be amused during such a serious matter?

Fortis reminded Courtnie of her father when he was younger. Well-built, always keeping his facial hair contained but present, and keeping his brunette locks of hair gelled and perfect at the top of his head. He had beady eyes like her father, the same dark brown that seemed to stare right through you instead of at you. They were even similar in the way they dressed: jeans, a shirt fit for a suit, a suit jacket, and four rings on his left hand (one for each finger excluding his thumb).

These similarities were to be expected of course. Courtnie's father was Fortis's father as well.

"Fortis, this can't go on any longer," Courtnie hissed, pushing her hair back from her face. "She's put our entire life's work in danger—"

"She couldn't have possibly done anything," Fortis said, waving his hand. The rings glinted in the light from his office's window. "She's been in a cell for years."

Courtnie tried to contain the fury that was bubbling up inside her, her eyes searching for something to stare at. Fortis kept his office neat—neater than her office, anyway. He had bookcases lined on the back wall, filled with information about all the citizens of Cesve, both male and female. There were books of lists of all the citizens, of their jobs, of their personalities. There were books filled with the history of Cesve, how it came to be and why it came to be.

His desk sat in the middle of the room. Fortis liked to be in the middle of things, Courtnie had learned over the years. It made him feel important, like he mattered. Papers stacked up on the surface of his desk, surrounding his laptop in the middle. His neat piles had been destroyed when Courtnie's hand landed, sending them flying.

"She must have found a way," she snapped through gritted teeth. "You and I both know she has her ways."

"That was when she was outside and free," Fortis said with a shake of the head. "She's contained now. She can't pose any threat anymore."

Courtnie's nostrils flare. She was so tired of Fortis sticking up for her. No matter how many times Courtnie pleaded for him to listen, to see her way, he always took her side. "You need to stop protecting her, Fortis." Her hands balled into livid fists. "You need to wake up and see her for who she is."

"I know who she is." Fortis scowled. "She's a girl who rebelled against the Government. I know."

"She almost exposed everything we've tried so hard to keep hidden!" Courtnie exclaimed, her hands flying in exasperation.

"I'm aware." Fortis stood up, patting his shirt. "But she is contained now."

Courtnie glared at him, letting as much venom as she possibly could into the next sentence. "We need to get rid of her, Fortis. This has gone for far too long."

"She hasn't done anything since we caught her." Fortis refused to relent.

Courtnie braced herself, knowing that she had to say what she was about to say next. It would hurt him, she knew it would. But in order for him to see that she had to be rid of from the world forever, he'd have to hear it. "She's not Daneigh, Fortis. Daneigh is dead. No matter what stupid things you do to protect her memory, she will always be dead. The sooner you get that through your head the better."

She stalked to the door, grabbing the handle within her hand and twisting it open. Before leaving she spun around, trying to ignore the pained look on Fortis's face. "You know it's the right thing to do," she said, making sure she sounded stiff and emotionless.

And then she slammed the door, leaving Fortis alone with his guilt and misery.

CHAPTER 8

"Now, for centuries, we men have been protected from the terrible unknown creature on the other side of the Gate."

Kole internally scoffed at his history teacher, Mr. Banally. Mr. Banally constantly reminded Kole of a river otter with his bucked teeth protruding from underneath his bushy mustache. He was lanky, taller than most of the men in the school. He had large circular glasses perched at the bridge of his nose; he was constantly pushing them upward, trying to keep them in place—in vain of course.

But, more importantly than his appearance, Kole hated the way he taught. Mr. Banally was so stubborn that your opinion didn't matter in the four walls of his classroom. All that mattered was that he was the teacher and he was always right. A boy by the name of Farland contradicted him once the year before and found himself with a week's worth of detentions.

No one had contradicted him since.

"Does anyone know what's behind the Gate?" Mr. Banally challenged, leaning casually against the chalkboard in the front of the room.

Five hands rose in the air. Kole stared at them all, internally feeling sorry for them. They had no idea what—who—was really behind the Gate. They had no idea that the people on the other side weren't really dangerous at all. They were friendly. Sweet. Shy.

An image of Faye flashed before Kole's eyes. He could visualize the way her lips pricked up in a nervous smile, the curves of her lips steadily relaxing as the conversation went on. He could see her play with her hair, a gesture that she seemed to take on when she was thinking an offer through. He could see her in all her girlish glory.

"Kole, how about you?" Mr. Banally called suddenly, despite the fact that Kole, unlike his fellow classmates, had kept his hand tucked under his chin.

"Gir—a beast," Kole replied, mentally cursing himself. How could he have let it slip like that? What if the Government had chosen that moment to play their security cameras on the classrooms? They did that once and a while—watched classrooms as they were being taught, making sure that the teachers were following the rules. Kole suddenly wondered if the Government was making sure that the teachers didn't tell their students the truth about the Gate and what was behind it. Was that at all possible?

"That's right," Mr. Banally said with a nod, either not hearing Kole's initial response or ignoring it entirely. "A beast." He stared around at everyone, his eyes bright. Kole didn't understand why. Everyone had had this conversation thousands of times already.

Not a day went by when a teacher would ask, "What is the creature that lies behind the Gate's borders?"

"And what, Carter Hengan, will the beast do if it escapes from behind the borders?" Mr. Banally continued, grabbing a ruler from his desk and pointing it in Carter's direction.

"It will kill us all," Carter replied automatically as though the answer came naturally to him. And why wouldn't it? It was what they were taught to do their entire life. What was behind the Gate? A beast of course! And what would happen if it escaped? Total annihilation. What exactly is the beast on the other side? No one knows.

Kole's eyes darted to the clock settled on the far side of the room, tick-tocking its way to the end of the class period. Kole willed it to move faster, for time to speed up. He needed class to end. He needed the school day to end. The sooner school let out, the sooner he could get to the Gate and to Faye. He knew that he could be waiting there for hours for her to come—they'd agreed on the same time, after all—but he wanted to get there sooner than later.

Mr. Banally rambled on and on, insipidly informing everyone about the Gate's dangers and how everyone needed to be more careful about where they hung out in the woods. Kole blocked him out, his eyes trained on the clock. At that moment he didn't care that the Government would haul him off to the prison wards if they caught him. He didn't care that the Government was only trying to protect them from the beast on the other side. He didn't care that the beast would rip him to shreds. All he cared about was meeting Faye again.

"Mr. Frost," Mr. Banally said suddenly, pulling Kole from his reverie. "Is there a reason why you're looking at the clock instead of at me?"

Kole immediately turned away from the clock and back to Mr. Banally. "Sorry," he said, not feeling sorry at all.

Mr. Banally opened his mouth as though to say something else but at that moment the bell rang, signaling that class was finally over. Kole was up immediately, grabbing his bag and tossing his things aimlessly into the opened pocket. His classmates followed pursuit—with significantly less enthusiasm—standing up, their chairs sliding behind them. Kole zipped up his bag and threw it over his shoulder, giving a deep sigh before heading down the rows toward the front door.

He dodged Michael Berns, a lanky boy with dandruff-filled brunette hair, who was scratching his forehead as he stared blankly into space. Usually Kole didn't mind Michael—he was nice enough. But today all he was was an unneeded obstacle that Kole would rather do without.

"Mr. Frost!" Mr. Banally called before Kole could reach the doorway. Kole stopped mid-step, silently cursing. Of course Mr. Banally would feel the need to reprimand him for not paying attention in class. He always did. Mr. Banally believed in order, and if you failed to keep in line, he'd keep you after class as long as he wished. And, to Kole's horror, that could be for a very long time.

"Yes, Mr. Banally?" Kole mumbled, moving back toward the desk. He watched grudgingly as his classmates flooded out the doors, happy to be done with class. A few classmates shot him sympathetic glances, but other than that, they completely ignored the torture Kole was probably about to endure.

"You seem to have trouble paying attention in my class," Mr. Banally drawled, leaning back on his desk.

Kole teetered on the heels of his feet, resisting the urge to take another glance at the clock. "I'm sorry," he said softly, bringing a hand through his hair. At that moment he wished that he were somewhere else—anywhere else. He didn't care if he was stuck at Xia. He just wanted to be out of Mr. Banally's clutches.

"Any explanations?" Mr. Banally cocked a furry eyebrow. He waited a moment for Kole to answer. After a moment he added, "Any at all?"

Kole chomped down on his cheek, willing himself to think of an excuse. But what excuse could explain the fact that he was daydreaming about meeting a girl—a creature that no one on this side had ever heard of—again after trespassing into the Gate's territory? And what plausible excuse could he have for looking at the clock? Everyone knew he wasn't very outgoing. He didn't play sports, didn't socialize more than he really had to. He just went to school and went home. That was it.

"No explanation then?" Mr. Banally persisted after a few moments of awkward silence. He sighed deeply, moving slowly behind his desk and toward his chair. Kole kept his eyes locked on his teacher, dreading what was coming next. He was trying to intimidate him, Kole realized as Mr. Banally paced his walks to keep Kole waiting. He was trying to show him that he had something to fear.

Well, it was most definitely working.

"I'm just . . ." Kole fumbled for words, but it seemed that words had completely deserted him, "distracted," he settled on, knowing that he hadn't given his teacher a good enough excuse.

"Distracted?" Mr. Banally regarded Kole coolly. "Well, I'd say so. But what is there possibly to be distracted about when you're learning in my class?"

Kole shrugged, not knowing what to say.

Mr. Banally smiled an icy smile, his teeth all but digging into his lower lip. "Well, I have the perfect solution to your distraction problem." Kole cringed as Mr. Banally's smile grew. He watched nervously as his teacher grabbed a sheet of paper and a pencil from his desk. Mr. Banally slid the contents in front of him, his eyes alight with anticipation. "Write 'I will not be distracted in Mr. Banally's class,' one-hundred times before you leave."

Kole inwardly groaned, taking the piece of paper silently and dragging his feet toward the front desk. He flopped into the seat, dropping his backpack haphazardly onto the floor. He glanced at the clock again. He had approximately two hours before he had to meet Faye.

I will not be distracted in Mr. Banally's class, Kole wrote, one hand tucked under his chin.

One line down. Ninety-nine to go.

Faye brought a hand through her hair, growling under her breath as she struggled to complete her English homework. English had never been her best subject, nor had it ever been her favorite. She had never been one for writing—nor would she ever be. That was Terra's thing. She could remember when Terra used to sit on her bed, jotting ideas into her notebook, completely lost in her fantasy worlds. Faye had tried to read her sister's writing once, but Terra had snapped the book shut, making Faye promise that she'd never read what Terra wrote. Even though Faye had been hurt and didn't understand why Terra wanted to keep her writing a secret, Faye had agreed.

Faye bit her lip, willing herself not to think of Terra at a time like this. She had to finish her homework so she could meet Kole. She didn't have time to willow in misery. But no matter how hard Faye tried, Terra kept interrupting her thoughts with her pen in her hand, scrawling adventures onto paper.

"I give up!" Faye hissed, throwing her paper to the side. She leaned forward, letting her head fall into her hands. If Terra were here, she would be able to help Faye on her homework. She'd know all the answers. She used to have all the answers.

Used to.

Faye blinked, cursing herself as she felt tears burn in her eyes. She had to stop this. There was no point in thinking about what could have been. Terra was gone. She'd seen her body. It was seven years ago. Mary managed to move on, so why couldn't she? Why couldn't she let Terra go?

"Faye, are you all right?"

Faye looked up to see her mother staring down at her. She quickly blinked the upcoming tears back, not wanting to cry in front of her. She hated crying in front of others, especially when it came to Terra. If her mother realized that Faye was still hurting, still missing Terra so much that she could scream, she would probably break down. Faye wouldn't be able to bear it if her mother cried over Terra again. It had been heartbreaking enough the first time.

"I'm fine!" she assured her mother, standing up and wiping her hands on her pants. "I was just going to take a walk," she continued, trotting toward the front door and slipping on her shoes. "Is that okay?"

"A walk?" Mary shot a shocked expression in her daughter's direction. "Since when do you like to take walks?"

Faye gulped. "Since now," she said, putting on a bright smile. "I just have a lot on my mind. Walking will help me think it over."

Her mother stared at her for a long time before nodding. "All right."

Faye sighed in relief, grabbing her sweatshirt from the couch and throwing it on. She threw a smile in her mother's direction. "I might stop by Errika's," Faye told her, scrambling to think of an excuse for why she'd be gone way longer than the usual duration of a walk around the neighborhood.

"All right!" Her mother's posture instantly relaxed. "Have fun."

Faye hurried outside, her feet pounding down the porch. She glanced at her car and sighed. She should have told her mother that she was going to Errika's instead of telling her that she was going for a walk. At least that way she could use her car.

Oh well. There was no taking it back now.

Faye made her way down the street, looking up at the sky. It was scattered with clouds today, as it had been all week. She smiled faintly as she looked closely at a single cloud. She tilted her head to the side, her smile growing as she saw what resembled a fire-breathing dragon. For years she thought that dragons were behind the Gate and that they were going to fly over the border and come for her. But Terra had assured her that if the beast were a dragon there would be no point in creating the Gate in the first place.

Faye frowned. Was it possible that dragons did exist? She'd immediately deemed them fictional as soon as Terra told her that it wasn't possible for dragons to be the beasts. But if there were creatures like boys, why not creatures like dragons? What if there were zombies? Mummies? Who was to say that these creatures didn't actually exist and the Government wasn't hiding them from them too?

Why did the Government hide the boys' existence? And why did they hide the girls' existence? It seemed so right for them to be together, to speak to each other. So why take that away? Why put people in jail if boys weren't dangerous at all?

It just didn't make sense.

Faye paused, waiting for a car to pass before crossing the street. She jogged across, ignoring the awkward feeling that was bubbling up within her. She hated jogging—especially across the street. Jogging, running, any fast movement. It made her think that she was going to fall. And she hated falling.

Feared it.

Ever since the day Terra threw herself off the cliff, Faye had been terrified of falling. When she tripped on the ground, she would screech at the top of her lungs, feeling like she'd fallen a hundred feet. The day Errika made her jump out the window had been terrifying all in itself. She wasn't quite sure how she did it.

Faye closed her eyes for a moment. What was she going to do when she climbed over the Gate, onto the other side? She opened her eyes again. Was she even going to go onto the other side? The idea was tempting—more than tempting, actually. But was she willing to take the risk?

What terrified her more than falling was that yes, yes she was.

Kole leaned against the Gate, closing his eyes. His right hand ached from all the writing he'd been forced to do. Mr. Banally forced him to start over when he saw that Kole misspelled a word. "Start over," he'd said, giving the paper back to him with a triumphant, evil smirk on his face. "You made a mistake."

And he'd been forced to start over. Just like that.

He opened his eyes, letting out a long sigh. Why did Mr. Banally have to harass him today of all days? Why on a day when he was supposed to meet with Faye? He had any other day to torture him, but he chose today? Kole just didn't understand. Did the world hate him? Probably.

Kole rubbed his hand irritably, attempting in vain to make the soreness go away. There was no point, really. His hand ached so terribly that Kole feared it was going to fall off. Mr. Banally would probably smirk if that happened. He loved to see his students in pain.

"Kole?"

Kole twisted around, shocked by the sudden noise. He sagged, letting out a relieved breath of air when he saw it was only Faye, her eyes and smile bright. Her hair was as long as ever, draping down her shoulder blades. Kole found himself smiling at her as he curled his fingers around the Gate's metal. "Hey," he murmured.

She held up a slender finger before pulling what looked like an elastic band off her wrist. Kole watching in amazement as she wrapped her hair, pulling it into what looked like a knot. He'd never seen anything like it. No one on his side of the Gate had hair long enough to tie into strange designs. What Faye was doing . . . it was mesmerizing.

Faye caught his stare and said, "My hair has been all over the place all day."

"I've never seen anything like that," Kole murmured, his eyes locked on Faye's hair.

Faye shrugged, rubbing her arms awkwardly. "Our hair is long enough over here," she mumbled. She smiled shyly. "We're able to put our hair in buns, ponytails, knots ..."

"You put your hair in buns?" Kole's eyebrows rose as he involuntarily imagined girls stuffing their long hair into the buns that they kept on the kitchen table. Wouldn't it be awkward having bread crumbs all over you?

Faye seemed to realize what Kole was thinking because she quickly explained herself. "Not that kind of bun! This kind of bun." She pointed at her entangled hair. "We call that a bun."

Odd, that they would name a hairstyle after a food. Kole shrugged, not really understanding but not wanting to waste their entire time together talking about hair. "So," he murmured, deciding to change the subject. "Did you think about it?"

Even though Kole didn't directly say, "Did you think about coming on my side?" he knew that she understood. She stiffened, eyeing the Gate up and down nervously. She bit her lip, grabbing a stray strand of hair and twisting it as she dug her sneaker into the ground. Kole braced himself for the deny he was probably about to receive.

"I did," was all she said.

Kole stared at her for a moment before persisting with a soft, "And?"

Faye smiled slightly. "I've decided ... yes."

"Yes?"

Faye nodded. "Yes."

Kole couldn't believe his ears. He'd been so sure that Faye was going to refuse, especially from her reaction when he'd initially asked. She didn't seem like the type of person to do anything rash. But, then again, how well did Kole really know her? The thought hit him so hard that it almost threw him off balance. He'd felt like he'd known Faye forever. It was so hard to believe that they'd only met a couple times.

He smiled, gesturing with a wave of the hand. "Come on, then."

Faye took a deep breath, looking the Gate up and down again. Kole watched her, his eyes expectant. Faye pursed her lips. She tried to bring herself to walk up to the Gate, to begin her climb, but she couldn't. Something held her in her place.

"You don't have to if you don't want to," Kole reassured.

Faye shook her head, shuffling to the Gate and wrapping her hands around the metal. She took a deep breath, mentally preparing herself for what she was about to do. She closed her eyes for a moment. What if she—what if she fell? How many bones would she break? An image of Terra flashed and she cringed. Would she look like her sister? Completely mangled, almost unrecognizable?

Faye opened her eyes. No. She was going to do this. "I'm fine," she whispered. "I'll do it."

As Kole nodded, a small smile curling up his lips, Faye looked the Gate up and down. How was she supposed to climb up the Gate without scraping or hurting herself? Or worse—falling? The holes were so small ...

Faye took a deep breath before beginning her climb. She made sure not to look down, not to direct her gaze anywhere but right in front of her. She had no idea how close she was to the top, how far away. All she knew was that she was climbing. And she wasn't falling.

"You're doing great!" Kole complimented as Faye continued her ascent. "You're almost there."

And she was. A few more feet higher and then she was there, gripping the top of the Gate. She let out a small cry of fear mixed with relief. She didn't exactly know how she managed to make such a cry, but that's what it was. "What do I do?" she forced out, afraid to look at Kole. He was below her, and if she chanced looking down, she might fall.

"Just put one leg over the side and then the other," Kole said calmly. "Move slowly, carefully."

Faye took a deep breath, willing the image of Terra's mangled body to disappear. She followed Kole's advice, putting one leg over and then the other. She held her breath, afraid that if she breathed she would topple over. It was an irrational fear, she knew. But she was so scared of falling that she didn't want to chance anything.

It was harder descending than it was ascending. Everything was backwards, upside down. She didn't know where to put her feet, her hands. Every movement felt like a sudden jolt. Faye found herself pausing several times, so frightened that she was about to refuse to move. But she kept on going, knowing that she was almost to the ground.

She flinched, almost losing her grip when she felt a pair of hands on her back. "I've got you," Kole whispered, his voice close. "You won't fall."

Concentrating on Kole's hands supporting her back, Faye finished the rest of the way down. She turned, facing Kole. He seemed so different without the Gate obscuring her vision of him. More real. More human.

"I did it," she whispered.

Kole let his hands fall away from her and back to his sides. He smiled as though by reflex. "You did."

Fortis Cain made his way through the prison wards, his gaze cast to the ground. He, unlike his sister, did not enjoy the prisoners' angered cries from their prison cells, their pleas to be let go so they could go back to their families. He hated their scornful glares they shot at him every time he came in. He hated their infuriated screams they shot his way when he refused to let them out. It was his fault they were trapped there. It was his fault they were without their children. It was all his fault.

Over the years Fortis tried to convince himself that it wasn't his fault. It was theirs. They were the ones that decided to let the curiosity get the best of them. They were the ones that broke the law. If they had just let it be, they would be with their families right now, eating delicious food at the dinner table. But, instead, they'd decided to throw it away just to see what was on the other side of the Gate.

But, the thing was, it wasn't their fault. If Courtnie gave up on the shriveling hope of separating girls and boys, then none of this would be happening. Daneigh wouldn't be dead. And she wouldn't be trapped in a cell. He couldn't even bring himself to think of her name. It was too painful. Courtnie spoke it with such vile contempt that it contaminated her name. It was all Fortis could do not to change her name altogether.

He reached the cell of his choosing, standing awkwardly in front of the very last cell. He remembered the day he brought her here.

She'd come kicking and screaming—she even bit him. The officers had suggested just doing away with her—getting rid of the vile animal that she was turning in to. Courtnie immediately agreed with them. She told Fortis not to delay the inevitable. They had to get rid of her before it was too late.

But Fortis couldn't bring himself to.

He blinked, torn away from his reverie as she moved in her cell. She didn't move very far, not that he expected her to. She didn't like to keep a close proximity to him. He would never say so, but it killed him inside that she abhorred him so much.

"What are you doing here?" she spat.

"I came to check up on you," Fortis said softly, dragging his feet toward the cell's door. It pained him to see her like this—trapped and confined like some wild animal. But that was the only way to keep her alive.

"I don't need any checking up on." Even though Fortis couldn't see her in the darkness, he could feel her glare. "I don't need you."

"Honey—"

"Don't call me that!" She stood up then, rushing toward the cell's door. She slammed into it, her eyes blazing like fire. "Don't you ever call me that. You may be my father, but I do not love you. Understand that? I hate you. Hate. If I were to never see you again it would be too soon."

Fortis gulped down the pain her commented inflicted upon him. "I understand you're angry," he said softly. "And you have the right to be—"

"I have the right to be?" She laughed. "You're damn straight I have the right. It's your fault Daneigh is dead. If you and your officers hadn't come and destroyed everything, Daneigh would still be alive!"

Fortis took a step back. Her words stabbed him like a thousand knives piercing his skin. He stared at her, unable to say anything. She'd said exactly what he'd been thinking all along: it was his fault that Daneigh was dead.

His fault.

She let her hands fall from the bars, her rage simmering down to a dull annoyance (or though it seemed). She settled an icy glower in his direction, her contempt freely showing. He wondered, not for the first time, what look she treated Courtnie to whenever she came to her cell. Did she give her the same hate-filled look? Was it even more hate-filled—if that was even possible? Or was it possible that she hate him more than Courtnie?

"Just go," she whispered, her voice almost devoured by the cries of her fellow prisoners around her. "Go."

Fortis stood there for a moment, unable to move. For years he'd tried to get through to her, to at least weaken the contempt she held for him. But no matter how hard he tried, nothing seemed to work. He'd lost her forever when he arrested her. She blamed him for everything.

As Fortis finally found the strength to turn and leave, he couldn't help but think that it was all right. He blamed himself too.

CHAPTER 9

Faye's eyes were wide.

As Kole led her through the forest, gesturing with his hands as he explained how where he lived was set up, Faye's head kept twisting around in all directions. She didn't know why, but she expected his forest to look different than hers. Maybe she expected it to be more terrifying, more dangerous-looking. But it wasn't. It was light, friendly seeming. Just like Kole.

Her mind drifted away, back to the Gate, to Kole's hands on her back. At the time she hadn't thought anything of it—a boy's hands touching her. But now? She was amazed. Amazed that his hands were so gentle, so warm. She'd expected his hands to be rougher. But they weren't. She glanced up at Kole's hands as they flew around him (probably to describe some large building). She wondered if they were soft like silk. She wondered if they were smooth. The sudden urge to take his hand in hers surprised her.

"We'll have to be careful so you don't get spotted by anyone," Kole muttered, glancing at her. "It will be safer once we get to my house. If Alex is home he won't say anything. He likes secrets."

Faye pushed down her thoughts of Kole's hands and raised her eyebrows. "How many of you are there?" she asked.

"A lot." Kole shrugged. "How many of you are there?"

Faye let a small smile prick the ends of her lips. "A lot," she said, copying Kole's answer.

Kole looked at her and laughed. She couldn't help but laugh back.

Faye looked around her. What would her mom say if she found out that Faye had seen the creature on the other side of the Gate, had even travelled with him to the other side? Would she just stare, wide-eyed? Would she get angry? Or worse, would she not believe her at all? Faye bit her lip. It was impossible to tell. She knew that her mother wouldn't report her if she found out, but Faye doubted that she would be supportive. She'd probably force her to cut off all connection with Kole, would probably force her to stay shut in the house all day for the rest of her life.

One glance at Kole, and Faye instantly knew how much she did not want that to happen. She loved meeting Kole, talking with him. She couldn't imagine not coming to the Gate and just . . . speaking to him. Sure, their conversations weren't long, and they were even sometimes a little awkward. But she loved it. Every single second of it.

What would have happened if she hadn't had that nightmare? What would have happened if she hadn't dreamed of Terra's death—if she had had a nightmare-free night? Would she have still taken that walk? Definitely not. Would she have frantically looked for a release? No. Would she have even gone to the Gate at all? Not a chance.

Odd, Faye couldn't help but think, that her nightmares had actually brought something good.

She twisted around in her cot, peering around in the darkness.

The cries of those imprisoned surrounded her. When she first arrived, those cries had almost driven her mad. There was a time where she wanted to cry with them, to beg to be let out. But she never did. She had too much pride, too much anger and hostility toward her captors. If she were to beg to them—to get down on her knees and beg—then she'd lose.

And they would win.

She let a small smirk curl up on her lips as she twisted back to face the door of her cell. Her captors would never win. They thought they were so smart with their cameras tracking Cesve's every move, but they weren't. They were naïve, stupid. Courtnie especially. She thought that because she sat in the big seat, had the biggest, comfiest chair in the joint, that she had all the brain power. But what she didn't know was that there was someone much, much smarter than her.

And she was going to take the Government down.

She'd already taken away their precious cameras, the one thing that they had that they could use to arrest anyone they felt like it. She'd watched woman after woman—hell, man after man—be arrested for so much as stepping into the forest. They hadn't even been near the borderline to the Gate's territory.

But they didn't care. They didn't care that they were taking mothers away from daughters, fathers away from sons. All they cared about was power. Power was what drove them to keep everyone separated. Fortis would deny it, of course—he wasn't power hungry, oh no—but she knew better. All they cared about was the influence they had over every single person in Cesve.

They disgusted her. All of them.

"Miss?"

She looked up, her eyes wide. "Miranda!" she called softly, jumping up from her bed and hurrying to the door of her cell. Miranda stood there, looking vulnerable as she glanced everywhere around her, frantic as she searched for security guards. But there was no danger. She knew that. The security guards were stupid, just like their bosses. They didn't play close enough attention to what was really going on.

"Do you have it?" she whispered, her eyes locked on Miranda's nervous figure. She hated asking for Miranda to do all these things for her. She hated making her an accessory to her crimes. But Miranda insisted. She wanted to see the Government taken down just as much as she did. And she loved that about Miranda.

Miranda nodded, pulling a slender-looking electronic device out from under her shirt. She slid it through the bars, handing it to her with a small smile on her face. "I do," Miranda murmured. She took it from Miranda's hands, sighing in relief. She hadn't been sure if Miranda would be able to get it without Courtnie finding out.

"Thank you," she breathed as she set the device gingerly onto her bed, not wanting to damage it in any way.

Miranda nodded again. "If I may ask, why do you need a laptop?" she asked, her eyes darting from side to side. She looked down and noticed that Miranda's hands were trembling. "Is this the next part of the plan?"

She nodded, smiling comfortingly at Miranda. "We're almost there," she assured her. "Now go. I don't want you getting caught."

As Miranda instantly turned away, hurrying back the way she'd come, she opened the laptop, her eyes bright with anticipation. As the laptop powered up, she patted her hands on her pockets, searching for her flash-drive. She smiled as she pulled it out of her left pocket, holding it out in front of her. This single flash-drive would end Courtnie and her reign over Cesve. This would end the Government, their need to keep the genders hidden from one another.

Everything would be set right.

Just like she and Daneigh wanted.

She sighed, quickly typing in the password. She'd asked Miranda to write down the password beforehand, which was easy enough seeing how Miranda worked in security. After she memorized the password she'd given the slip of paper with the password written on it back to Miranda and ordered her to burn it. No trace of her plan could be left in the open. None of it.

Otherwise they were doomed to fail.

She took the flash-drive and plugged it into the laptop, sitting back and cracking her knuckles. She glanced around, making sure that no one was looking. This was ridiculous of course—to think that someone was coming. They barely ever patrolled on her side of the wards. Courtnie and Fortis came too often for them to care all that much. Of course, what they didn't know, was that they only came to yell at her. They didn't really care about the other prisoners. Not at all.

She felt a smile creep onto her lips as the file on the flash-drive began to load. What Courtnie didn't know was that she didn't just put a virus on her precious computers. Oh, no. She did something much more than that.

She'd taken complete control of the cameras.

The only way that you could get the computers to monitor again was if you had the flash-drive that was in her possession. Other than that, you were blind. Blind and frantic because you couldn't be the control-freak that you really were.

She paused as the camera-monitoring system popped up on her computer. She leaned forward, resting her chin on her hand as she sifted through the images that had been caught on the cameras while the Government was left blind. Nothing much really happened. A group of girls camped out in the woods. A drunk-looking boy threw himself into the woods while a sober-looking boy ran after him.

Her eyes narrowed as she continued to watch the two boys. The drunk-looking boy staggered out of the woods a few minutes later, all but collapsing onto the ground. He laughed hysterically, throwing his arms into the air and shouting something that she couldn't hear. But she didn't care about the drunk boy. The sober boy hadn't come out of the forest yet.

She searched through the images until she saw him again. He was running frantically through the forest, probably searching for his friend that had already left. She watched as he ran, something growing in the pit of her stomach. He seemed deep in the forest—deep enough to be in the Gate's territory.

And she was right. Seconds later he'd reached the Gate, staring at it with wide, frightened eyes. She stared at him, interested in what he was going to do. Was he going to attempt hopping over the other side? Was he going to run away?

Apparently neither. He crept toward the Gate, his eyebrows crinkled together. Her eyebrows knitted together as well when she noticed that he was speaking. What was there to talk to? The trees on the other side? The squirrels? She wondered if she'd been mistaken—that this boy wasn't as sober as he seemed.

But one look at the cameras on the girls' side of the Gate proved otherwise.

Her eyes widened and her mouth dropped as she saw a girl standing on the other side of the Gate, looking terrified as she spoke to the boy on the other side. She shook her head, covering her mouth with her hand. No. This couldn't be. She could understand a boy or a girl ending up at the Gate—but to meet? The odds were so small.

But there it was. A boy and a girl, speaking to each other in the darkness.

She couldn't help but smile as the scene played out before her. Two people besides those trapped in the prison wards knew about the Government's secret. Two people, one on each side.

She closed the laptop with a content smile on her face. If she wasn't able to get the word out to the people of Cesve, maybe there were two people that could.

And that was such a comforting thought indeed.

"What happens if someone sees me?"

Faye asked the question frantically, worried to death that someone would find her and report her to the Government. The thought of being trapped in the prison wards for the rest of her life wasn't exactly a comforting thought. She bit her lip, closing her eyes as she tried to calm herself. There was no point in being scared like this. She'd already committed the infraction on the law, hadn't she? Why spend the entire time on the boys' side in misery? Why would she rather worry about the Government catching her than be amazed by how the boys' lives worked?

Because she was Faye. And Faye couldn't help but worry.

"If someone sees you, they're going to think that you're a lunatic boy who looks freakishly different than everyone else," Kole replied, shooting a smile in her direction. "Don't worry."

Easy for him to say. Her hair all itself called attention to everyone around her. If someone noticed her just by the brightness of her hair, they were definitely going to notice the "abnormal" length to it. And once they noticed the length, they were going to notice that she had breasts—unlike everyone else on this side (she thought at least). And then when they noticed that they would notice that she had slender-er hips and an all-around smaller body.

They would notice she was different. And then they would assume that she was evil.

And then she was going to be captured and die.

The thoughts of her death were shattered when a piece of clothing was thrown in her face. She let out a shriek as the clothing made contact with her head, blocking everything from view. She pulled it away from her and held it out. It was a pale blue hoodie—Kole's. She glanced up at him, confused. Why...?

"It'll be baggy on you," Kole murmured, now in plain V-neck gray T-shirt, "but it'll hide your figure. That's what you're worried about, aren't you?"

Biting down the shock that Kole knew exactly what she was thinking, Faye nodded. She slipped her arms through the arm-holes, pulling the hoodie around her. She bit her lip. The hoodie was so soft, so warm. It was so comfortable. She zipped it up, hugging herself in it. Kole was right—it was baggy. Baggy enough to keep her figure hidden anyway.

Faye pulled the hood over her head, smiling as her long hair was now concealed from view. She felt so much safer hiding in his hoodie. More invincible. "Are you a mind reader?" she demanded, cocking an eyebrow. "Is that what boys do? Read minds?"

Kole laughed, shaking his head. "No, I'm not a mind-reader. Your face just made it really obvious."

Faye pursed her lips. Her face made it obvious? She supposed that made sense. Errika had always accused her being like an open book—easy to read and to figure out. She'd always figured that Errika was just a genius. Maybe she was just terrible at hiding how she was feeling.

"We're almost there," Kole assured her.

"You said that ten minutes ago," Faye mumbled, not at all believing him. The whole walk he'd told her that they were almost there, that they were so close. She believed him at first. Now she didn't even bother hoping they were almost there. It didn't really matter, anyway. She was with Kole on the boys' side of the Gate. That was all that mattered.

"Well, this time I mean it."

Faye snorted. "Okay."

Kole was about to reply, but suddenly Faye's cell phone went off. She cursed under her breath. She'd forgotten to tell Errika that she'd used her as an excuse to leave the house. What if her mom checked in to see if she was there? What if she stopped believing that Faye was taking a walk and started to get suspicious?

She took a breath, willing herself to calm down. She'd been too quick to jump to such horrendous conclusions lately. She needed to stop before she literally worried herself to death. With a short glance in Kole's direction, Faye grabbed her cell phone from her jeans pocket and flipped it open. "Hello?" she said softly, praying that it wasn't her mother.

"Faye!" Errika called out.

Faye sighed in relief. "Hi, Errika," she mumbled, letting a smile find its way to her lips. "What's up?"

"Do you want to hang out today?" she asked. "I mean, I'm pretty sure it was planned yes?"

Faye instantly groaned. So her mom had called. "Did you tell my mom I was there?" she demanded softly. "Please, please, please tell me you told her I was there."

"I told her you were here," Errika assured her. "You're lucky I'm here alone. My mom would have been a little suspicious if she were here. Next time, babe, inform me when you're going to use me as a cover-up, okay?"

Faye nodded even though she knew that Errika couldn't see her. "Sorry. I was going to call you but then I was too busy concentrating on not getting lost."

Errika laughed. "Yeah, I thought it was something like that. You would get lost." She paused. "Are you on the other side?"

She said the last part in a whisper. Faye didn't really understand why, seeing how Errika was home alone. But, then again, Errika probably thought that the Government may have their eyes on the house. Those were just rumors—the Government keeping bugs in houses so they could hear what was going on. But she didn't blame Errika for being cautious.

"Yes," she said, her voice a notch higher than Errika's had been. "What's it like?"

"It's full of trees," Faye said lightly. "We haven't made it out of the forest yet. I'll call you when I get back, okay? I'll stop at your house."

"Good. That way you're not lying." Errika snickered. "Talk to you later, babe!"

And then she was gone, their connection lost.

Faye hung up her phone, turning to Kole. He was staring at her, his eyes wide. She looked down at her phone and back to him. Why did he seem awed at the fact that she had a cell phone? Did he not have one? Did boys not have cell phones? If they didn't have cell phones, what else didn't they have? Laptops, televisions, cars? "What?" she asked.

"You have cell phones on your side, too?" Kole exclaimed, shocked.

Faye nodded slowly. "Yes. Do you?"

It was a stupid question, really. If he knew what the device in her hand was then he obviously had seen one before. And where else would he have seen one except for on his side of the Gate?

Kole didn't seem to find the question stupid at all. Instead he nodded and said, "Yeah, we do. Do you have computers?"

Back and forth the questions went. Faye found herself forgetting about the fact that she was breaking the law, the fact that people might notice the difference between her and them. Her entire attention was on Kole and his questions. Did she have a television? What about a flat-screen? Did they have ovens, stoves, microwaves? Had she ever had pancakes? Chocolate chip pancakes?

"Have you ever been to the movies?" Kole asked, his eyebrows knitted in concentration as he tried to think of more questions.

Faye snorted. "Of course I have. Who hasn't been to the movies?"

Kole shook his head, sighing. "I don't get it. If we live the exact same type of life, then why do we have to be separated?"

Faye shrugged. "I don't know," she murmured.

And she didn't. Now more than ever, she wondered why. Why did the Government keep them separated? It seemed so right being with Kole. Like something missing in her life had been pieced together. She didn't know what it was about him—if it was really anything—but the feeling was strong, and it was there.

She just didn't know what it was.

She came to a stop as she caught sight of an opening in the trees. Kole, not noticing that she stopped, continued walking, his arms moving back and forth carelessly at his sides. He turned. "Faye?" he said, his eyebrows rising. "You okay?"

Faye took a deep breath. "Fine," she muttered. She paused, letting out a long breath of air before nodding. "Yeah, I'm fine. Let's go."

With that, Faye shook off the apprehension fluttering around in her stomach and followed Kole out of the forest and into the unknown.

Kole led Faye out of the woods, up toward his hill. Anticipation and fear dripped in the pit of his stomach, slowly but surely taking over any rational part of his mind. Faye was here. On his side. He'd never say so, but he was a little frightened for Faye. What if someone did find out that she was different—too different? What if someone did report her?

Kole bit his lip. Would showing her his house be safe? He knew that Alex wouldn't say anything, but what about his father? He'd be lying if he said that he had total faith that his father wouldn't report Faye to the Government. He'd probably think it was the right thing to do. Get rid of Faye and clear Kole of all charges. But it wouldn't the right thing to do. Not at all.

He pushed back any more pessimistic thoughts that were trying to sprout into his head and turned to Faye. Her eyes were wide as she looked around her, amazement clear on her face. Her head twisted in all directions, trying to get a good look at everything around her before they passed. Kole couldn't help but smile at her. They hadn't even reached town yet.

"It's beautiful," Faye breathed as they mounted his hill, her eyes so wide that Kole feared they were going to pop out of her skull.

Kole smiled faintly. His eyes flicked around at the scenery. He didn't understand how this was considered beautiful to her. Sure, he loved the surroundings of his hill, loved the way the forest greeted him with what seemed like open arms. But he'd seen much more beautiful sights, scenes that truly took his breath away.

Did they have scenery like that on her side? Did they have breathtaking beauty? Or was everything bland—lifeless? Did they even have hills on her side? Or was everything flat? He couldn't know for sure. She didn't look surprised at the slant in the ground, but, then again, she was so concentrated on the world around her that she wasn't looking down.

"Where are we going first?" Faye asked softly, turning her atten-tion back to Kole. Kole watched as her hand slipped under the hood to itch the back of her head. She looked around again, her eye wide with admiration.

Kole shoved his hands into his jean pockets, glancing around. Where should he take her first? Should he take her around toward Xia, or should he start toward the library and the other work buildings? Should he start toward the school, or toward the park near his house? His eyebrows knitted together as he tried to think of a starting point. The park would have to be last—that way they'd end at his house before he brought her back. But where to start?

"Kole?" Faye murmured, her eyebrows raised.

Kole sighed, rubbing his face with the back of his hand. "I'm not really sure," he confessed.

Faye smiled understandingly and nodded. "Well," she said, her hands going into Kole's sweatshirt pockets. "Let's get started then."

Despite the utter normality of the boys' side, Faye couldn't help but be amazed.

She never thought that this was what was on the other side of the Gate. And why would she? Everything was so normal, so every day. There were buildings, people that were out on the streets. Hidden behind Kole's sweatshirt, Faye felt like she was one of them. Even if they were completely different, she felt completely the same.

Kole showed her everything. He showed her stores, houses, streets, libraries. He showed her where he and his friends usually hung out, and this club called Xia that allowed boys of all ages to attend. Apparently it was Xia that was the initial cause of Kole reaching the Gate in the first place. Faye silently thanked Terence—whoever he was—for getting drunk and jumping out of Kole's car. If he hadn't . . . well, Faye wouldn't be where she was now.

"Everything is so different," Faye breathed, her eyes latching onto everything she could. There were boys in groups, sauntering down the streets in baggy pants and shirts. There were also boys who were dressed in not-so-baggy clothes, rather clothes that were almost like her own. They reminded her of the group of girls prowling around, the cliques circled around to gossip about nothing important. "Yet, it's completely the same."

Kole, a soft smile on his face, replied, "Come on. I have one last thing to show you."

Faye nodded, excitement bubbling within her. What else could he possibly have to show her? She'd seen so much already—so much. Did boys have something special, something that girls did not have? Faye couldn't help but doubt it. Everything else had been the same (for the most part anyway). So why would that change now?

Kole lead her through a copious amount of streets, never once divulging where they were headed. Faye begged him to tell her, groaning every single time when he refused to relent. She sighed, bringing a hand through her hair. She hated not knowing. Not knowing what was going to happen. That was why she rarely ever took chances. It was a wonder that she'd chanced coming back to the Gate at all.

"We're almost there," Kole reassured.

Faye blinked. She'd been so lost in thought that she almost didn't hear him. She looked up, glanced around her, and then turned back to Kole. She smiled. "Should I believe you when you say that?" she teased. "Or is this like our way out of the forest?"

Kole snorted. "No, you should believe me."

Kole was right. Within five minutes they'd arrived at their destination. Faye stared at the building, utterly confused.

It was a house.

Just a house.

There was nothing special about it, were Faye's first thoughts. Why had Kole saved this specific house for last? It was a simple white two-floored home with black shutters. It reminded her of a girl named Donnie's house. In fact...it looked exactly like Donnie's house. The front porch, the red front door. The upstairs windows. Everything.

The exactness of the two houses startled Faye, to be honest.

"This is your house, isn't it?" Faye asked, the words slipping off her tongue before she thought them through. And that's when she realized—it was his house. No wonder he'd left it for last.

"Yeah." Kole brought a hand nervously through his hair. "Full warning, my brother might be home. He won't say anything about you if he figures out, though, okay?"

Faye felt something deep in the pit of her stomach. She wasn't sure what it was. Fear that Kole's brother would find out? Maybe. Or maybe it was excitement that she was going to see the inside of a boy's house. Or maybe it was anxiety, nervousness from doing something new. Or maybe it was a mixture of the three. She wasn't sure at all. "Okay," she mumbled finally, shoving her hands into Kole's sweatshirt pockets.

She suddenly felt self-conscious. Like if she could curl up into a ball and disappear that wouldn't be invisible enough. She didn't know why these feelings suddenly surged within her, but they were there. And they were strong. Almost so strong that she almost spun around, ready to run back into the forest—back to her side of the Gate's territory. She gulped, willing herself to calm down. She used to get like this when she was little—when Terra was still alive. Terra would comfort her, telling her to breathe slowly. In. Out. In. Out.

But Terra wasn't there to comfort her now.

"Faye, are you okay?" Kole asked, concerned. "You look pale."

Faye nodded, taking a deep breath before answering. "I'm fine. Let's go in, shall we?"

Kole stared at her for a moment before nodding. He gestured for her to follow as he made his way up the short path toward his house and up the steps to his porch. Faye pulled her hands out of Kole's sweatshirt and wrapped them around herself, hugging herself so tightly that it began to hurt. She didn't untighten her grip, though. The thoughts of Terra still fogged her mind, threatening to consume her.

She refused to let herself become consumed, though.

"Alex, are you there?" Kole called as he opened the door. Faye stood close beside him. Who was Alex? His brother? Probably.

"Yeah!" came a distant voice.

A few moments later, a boy stood in front of them, a bright smile on his face. Faye stared at him, wide-eyed. Except for his boyish features—the short hair, the harder jaw line—he looked exactly like Errika. The same dark hair, the same eyes. Even their eyebrows were the same. Of course, Errika's were barely ever arched with confusion, but still. They were the same. The boy, Alex, Faye presumed, was probably only a year or two older than she and Kole. He crossed his arms over his chest, his white long-sleeved shirt creasing. It was an Abercrombie and Fitch shirt, Faye observed. And so were his jeans. "Who's this?" he asked lightly, though it was obvious in his eyes that he was on edge. Kole must not have had new people over often.

"Yeah, Kole," came a voice from the right. "Who—I mean, what rather—is this?"

CHAPTER 10

K at Caldwell was snooping.

She didn't know why she was snooping, or even who she was snooping on. All she knew while she rummaged through random things in her family's attic, that she was doing just that. She glanced over her shoulder, toward the hole in the floor where she'd dropped the ladder to make her ascent in the first place. She pursed her lips, wondering if she should shut it. Her mother wasn't home—she'd gone to the store to buy some things for the house. But still. What if Faye got home early from Errika's and caught her up here? She'd demand to know what she was doing, would scream at her for snooping around where she shouldn't have been.

Kat wasn't allowed in the attic. She didn't know why, but it made her crazy. What was up here that was so special that she couldn't even take one step into the room? What special things did Faye (it was so obvious that her sister knew) and her mother hide up here? And why couldn't Kat know about them?

Shaking her head, Kat sauntered to the fallen stairs and knelt down. She glanced down at her All-Star Converse, a frown curling on her lips. As much as she loved the shoes, she hated the fact that they were Faye's hand-me-downs. Her mother didn't see the point in buying anything that they didn't need. Apparently Kat's own set of clothing—really, her own set of clothing—did not apply to that category. Kat felt herself constantly wondering if Faye ever had to endure hand-me-downs. Probably not. Everything that came before Faye belonged to Terra. And Terra was a burden on their memories.

Kat felt something deep in the pit of her stomach. Maybe anger, maybe guilt. Maybe both. She couldn't help but feel guilty that the only reason she belonged to this family was because Terra was dead. If Terra were alive, Kat would be with another family or still in the orphanage. All the time disturbing thoughts flashed through her mind: would they rather Terra be there instead of her? Would they like it better if they never got her, but still had Terra in their lives?

Would they choose Terra over her?

Kat blew a few stray blond strands of hair out of her face, her frown growing deeper. She reached forward, grabbing the thick rope in front of her and pulling the attic stairs up toward her. She closed the hole in the floor, standing up. Everything was significantly darker now—a point that she'd definitely not thought through—but she could still see. After a deep sigh, pushing the thoughts of Faye's late sister away, Kat stepped toward the stack of boxes a few feet away.

Grabbing the first box at the top, Kat sat down with the box set out in front of her. She pulled the tabs open, peering inside. She took a deep breath as she stared at the contents. She brought a hand into the box and pulled an object at random out.

It was a shirt.

Her eyebrows creasing, she dumped the all the contents of the box onto the floor. They were all clothes. Shirts, jeans, shorts. A variety of clothing mixed into one. Kat didn't understand. She was banned from the attic because of clothes? It just didn't make sense.

She looked up. Boxes surrounded her, filling the entire room. She stood up again. There had to be something there. Something that was useful. Something that meant something.

She searched through a copious amount of boxes, trying to get a glimpse at something important. But there didn't seem to be anything. Almost every box she opened was filled with clothes. Kat could have groaned in frustration. It seemed absolutely ridiculous that she was forbidden to go somewhere over clothes — and stylish clothes at that.

Kat held a shirt in front of her, tilting her head to the side. It was a tank top, a pretty maroon color with a floral pattern. The top was bejeweled — just how Kat liked it. She could see herself wearing it, flaunting in it as she sauntered through the middle school's halls with Bella and her other friends. They would ask her where she got it; they would tell her she looked absolutely amazing. And Kat, taking in the attention, would simple smile mischievously and say, "It's a secret, girlies. Can't have everyone copying my style."

Kat let the shirt fall from her fingertips. It glided to the floor, the silk fabric looking elegant even in the darkness. There was no point in wondering what it would be like to actually own an outfit that she truly enjoyed, basked in. She would never get it. She never really got what she wanted. Not here.

Because the only thing she wanted was to be noticed. And to be noticed, she needed a whole bunch of things: clothes, hair projects—just anything that gave her glam. But her mother didn't believe that Kat needed that to be noticed.

If only she knew.

Kat let out an irritated huff, reaching for the next box. She knew it would be the same: clothes. What else could it be?

But, when she opened the box, she realized that they weren't clothes at all. They were books. Not novels, but notebooks. Kat pulled one out, biting her lip. In a neat scrawl at the top, the Composition book was labeled Geometry. Kat shook her head disbelievingly. The most exciting thing she'd found was some-one's—probably Faye's—Geometry work?

With a roll of the eyes, Kat flipped the first page open. She didn't know why she did. Geometry wasn't what she labeled as interesting. But, there she was, opening the cover and averting her gaze to the first page.

When she saw what was written there, her mouth dropped, the book almost falling out of her now-trembling hands. Without a word, she tossed the book back into the box. She took a step back. And then another. Her legs began trembling so hard the she almost fell to the ground. She didn't know why the words on the paper affected her the way they did. They were so mundane, so normal.

But, still, the words seared her mind burning an imprint on her memory.

What were the words?

This is the property of Terra Caldwell.

"So, Kole," the bitter voice continued after a long moment of silence. "Are you going to answer me or what?"

Kole felt his jaw tighten. Seth stood in front of him, his arms crossed irritably over his chest. His friend's jaw was working, only showing how angry he was. Kole couldn't understand why Seth was angry—or why he had the expression of betrayal on his face. Kole snuck a glance in Faye's direction, suddenly terrified for her. He'd never seen Seth this way before—at least, not at this level. What if Seth was so angry that he'd turn Faye in? He didn't care much if he got caught—but if Faye got taken to the prison wards he'd never be able to forgive himself.

"What are you doing here?" he demanded softly.

Seth glared at him. "Does that really matter?" He waved a hand, cutting off Kole's response. "No, it doesn't. What matters is that you got to the other side, met the creature there, and then had the audacity not to say anything about it!"

Kole's eyes shot to Faye again. He had the sudden urge to stand in front of her, to protect her from what Seth might do. There was no knowing what he would do at that moment. He could attack, could lash out; or worse, he could report. "How did you—?"

"Find out?" Seth sneered. "Terence, unlike you, doesn't keep secrets from his friends."

"Seth—"

"How many other secrets are you keeping from us, Kole? Are there any bigger secrets that you have hidden? Do you tell them all to Terence and make him swear not to tell? Or is Terence not even important enough to—"

"For the love of god, Seth, shut up!" Kole hissed, cutting off the rest of Seth's furious sentence. He took a step in front of Faye, covering her from view. "I didn't tell you because the more people who know, the more dangerous it is for Faye. I wasn't even going to tell Terence, all right? If I thought it was safe, I would have told you. Now will you stop spewing random shit about trust? Because, obviously, you didn't trust me enough to know there was a good reason for me not telling you."

Kole crossed his arms over his chest, his jaw working along with Seth's now. He could see his brother in the corner, watching the fight between Kole and his friend go on. He almost gulped at the look on his brother's face. Alex had an expression that could only be described as confusion—and confusion wasn't something that Alex took very well. Alex Frost was the type of person who needed all questions answered for him. Which was why the creature on the other side of the Gate always bugged him.

"Kole," Alex drew out slowly, coming to stand beside Seth. "Could you please explain to me what's going on?"

"Yeah, Kole," Seth seethed, apparently not understanding Kole's rant. "Why don't you tell us what's going on?"

Kole ground his teeth together. He'd expected maybe a few questions from Alex—nothing too bad. But Seth was making this situation almost unbearable. He couldn't imagine how Faye was feeling right now. Probably frightened—more than frightened, actually. Terrified. How would Kole feel if he was brought to a place he wasn't used to and suddenly two other people came in creating conflict? Kole would flee.

Instead of answering his friend's question, he asked one of his own. "Where are Zander and Terence?"

Seth seemed taken aback. "What?"

"Zander and Terence," Kole repeated coolly, taking a step forward. "They have to be here. You probably just found out since you haven't cooled down at all, so Terence has to be with you. Zander was probably there as well." He shrugged, feigning nonchalance even though, on the inside, he was broiling with anger. "A little get together behind my back, eh?"

Seth began sputtering out random excuses, only proving Kole's original point. Zander and Terence were there in Kole's house, not brave enough to come face Kole. Instead they hid, probably in Kole's or Alex's room. And, to make it worse, Alex probably didn't even know that the other two were there. Seth snuck them in, promising not to get them involved. Kole didn't know how he knew this, but he did.

"Where are they, Seth?"

It wasn't Kole who demanded this time, but Alex. He stepped between Kole and Seth, his arms crossing over his chest along with his brother. Kole bit his lip to keep from smiling. He could always count on his brother to come to his rescue. Always. Kole trusted Alex with his life. Always had, always would.

"I—what? You're—Kole doesn't know what he's—"

Alex grabbed Seth by the shoulders, giving him a rough shake. "You sneak into our house with only the intention of screaming at my brother for no other reason but feeling angry. And you go and hide Zander and Terence so they can't stop you?" Kole could just feel the glower on Alex's face. "That's low, Seth, and you know it. Now where are they?"

Kole turned as he felt a hand on his back. Faye stood there, a nervous expression on her face. His stomach dropped when he saw fear mixed with the nervousness. She was afraid, just like he'd predicted. "Maybe this was a bad idea," she whispered to him, her voice cracking. "Maybe I should just go."

Not even thinking about what he was doing, he placed his hands on her shoulders. "It's okay," he assured her. "Seth just has anger issues. He wasn't supposed to be here. He'll be cooled down in a minute."

She searched his face. Kole forced a smile, hoping that that would comfort her enough into staying. He silently cursed Terence. If he learned to keep his mouth shut then he wouldn't have this problem. He should have lied to Terence about what he'd seen in the forest. If Kole had just made up a story, then everything would be fine.

But would everything be fine? Kole wasn't so sure. He'd have broken eventually, spewing his words to probably the worst person possible—like his father. Terence might have told his friends, but he'd kept his mouth shut for the most part. And that Kole was thankful for.

"They're upstairs," Seth muttered finally. "In Kole's bedroom."

"No we're not," came a voice.

Kole spun as Terence entered the room, his hands shoved into his jean pockets. Zander followed pursuit, his hands tucked under his armpits anxiously. Neither of them would meet Kole's gaze. Instead they stared at the ground, where they probably felt safer. Kole didn't really understand why. It wasn't like Kole was going to attack them. Though, he had to admit, he could understand why his friends would think so. He didn't exactly control his anger very well.

Alex shook his head, turning to Kole now. "Can you please explain what's going on now?" He gestured to Faye. "Is Seth telling the truth—that's the creature from the other side?"

Kole let his arms fall from Faye's shoulders as he nodded. He cleared his throat before saying, "I'll explain everything. Can we just move out of the doorway? You guys are making Faye nervous.

Faye wrapped her arms around herself, holding herself tightly as she followed Kole out of the doorway and further into the house. The house, she realized, was set up as one huge hall connected by rooms on the sides. She tilted her head to the side, intrigued. She'd never seen a house designed this way—usually homes were connected room by room instead of separated completely by a hallway. It made her wonder if Donnie's house was set up the same way.

Finally the hall ended, opening up into a large sun room. The walls were covered with windows, letting light shine freely onto the carpet and furniture. Sitting against the back wall was a sea green, three-pieced couch. It spread out across the wall, cutting off with a shay lounge at the very end. Faye was amazed. She'd always wanted a couch like that.

Her eyes flicking around the room, Faye realized that there was barely any other furniture. There was a lamp next to the couch, probably for when someone wanted to read in the dark. Besides that there was only a small table with a glass table top sitting a few feet away from the couch. There was no television set, no television cabinet. The room seemed…freeing. Technology didn't seem to hold the room down like everywhere else.

"All right," Sean muttered coolly as he settled onto one of the couch cushions. "Now tell us everything."

Faye turned, staring as Kole simply ushered everyone to take a seat, his face pinched with irritation. Faye bit her lip before moving toward the shay lounge, silently praying that no one planned on sitting there.

No one had. Faye couldn't help but smile as she sank into the seat. It was just like she'd always imagined: so comfortable she could lie there forever.

Kole, unlike everyone else, stayed standing. Faye kept her eyes on him, studying his features. His eyes were like dark chocolate, swirling with anger as he glared his friends down. His jaw was set, his arms crossed irritably over his chest. Faye's eyes flicked to his lips, now pursed. Kole, Faye realized, was not one to hold his temper.

"Kole," his brother drew out, hesitant, "will you please explain what's going on?"

"I will in a moment, Alex," Kole replied dryly, clearly attempting not to snap. Faye bit her lip to keep from smiling. His attempt hadn't worked so well.

Faye allowed herself to look away from Kole and to the boys sitting with her on the couch. Seth, seated on the cushion farthest away from her, reminded her of a hawk with his shark facial features. His light brown hair, though Faye couldn't really understand why, seemed sharp as well. The other boys had softer features. One had brunette hair, pale skin, and blazing blue eyes, while the other had black hair, olive skin, and dark eyes. The boy with the olive skin seemed like he had something weighing him down, Faye observed. Like there was an inner torment that he kept solely to himself.

Alex, plopped between Seth and the olive skinned boy, sighed deeply. This, Faye noticed, was something that Errika would do. Alex, like Errika, seemed to need all the answers—he hated being confused. They were more alike than just by their looks. Their attitudes seemed to match as well.

Kole cleared his throat. Faye, along with the boys, turned to face him, ready to listen attentively. "I'm going to explain this once," Kole said slowly, enunciating each word carefully, "and once only. Do you understand?"

As the boys nodded, Faye couldn't help but wonder who Kole directed that sentence to. It didn't seem like it was directed at everyone; the edge in the tone, the ice hidden inside, couldn't have been aimed at more than two people. It was probably Seth and Alex, Faye thought. They were the only ones demanding answers after all.

"After you and Terence got trashed," Kole began, settling an irritated glower in Seth's direction, "and after Zander and I dumped you on your porch, I began driving Terence home."

He gestured to the blue-eyed boy. So he was Terence. Faye nodded mentally to herself, trying to force herself to memorize the name with the face. Which meant, she thought, her eyes flicking to the olive skinned boy, that that must have been Zander.

"Terence," Kole continued, being the idiot—no offense Terence—that his is, decided to jump out of the car and run toward the forest. He wanted to find out what creature was on the other side of the Gate. I chase after him, not wanting him to get arrested just because he pulled a stupid move while he was drunk."

Faye leaned forward, listening attentively even though she already knew the end of the story. She listened, watching as Kole unhooked his arms and flailed them about. He spoke with his hands as he continued on with his story. He explained about meeting Faye that night at the Gate, how he told Terence about it after. Faye couldn't help but let out a short snicker when Kole said he grabbed Terence by the shirt while he screamed. He really didn't know how to control his anger, did he?

After Kole finished explaining, it was silent. Even Seth, who didn't seem to know how to keep his mouth shut, had his lips pressed into a straight line. Faye glanced between Kole and the other boys. Was silence a good thing? Or was it a bad thing? Faye glanced at Kole again. He met her gaze and struggled out a smile. She smiled back, unease fluttering around in her stomach.

"So." Alex stood up then, shoving his hands nonchalantly into his pockets. "So this is a girl?"

He pointed to Faye. Faye stared at his finger. She suddenly felt like an insect under a microscope, like she was being examined closely. She felt naked under the boys' eyes despite the number of layers she wore. Faye crossed her arms tightly over her chest, hoping that it would make her feel more secure, but it didn't seem to matter. Their eyes burned through her skin all the same.

"Yes," Kole replied.

"She—that's what girls are called right?—doesn't look much different than us." Alex tilted his head to the side. "In fact, I don't see any differences at all."

Kole shot Faye a look that she couldn't decipher. She averted her gaze, plucking at his sweatshirt absently. Kole's eyes continued to bore through her, however. There was no escaping it. "Faye," he said softly.

Faye looked up then, eyes locking with Kole's. "Yeah?"

Bringing a hand through his hair, Kole sighed. "Can you take off my sweatshirt, please? And comes stand over here?"

Faye hesitated before nodding. She pushed herself off the shay lounge, swallowing hard. The thought of stripping—even if it was just a sweatshirt—in front of people, boys no less, she didn't know made her extremely uncomfortable. She bit the inside of her cheek and stepped beside Kole. She took a deep breath. And then, after closing her eyes, Faye pulled the sweatshirt over her head.

The boys gaped as Faye's hair fell over her shoulders. Faye rubbed her arms self-consciously, their stares weighing her down. She wished they would stop, that they'd look away. But they didn't. They stared endlessly like they were never going to stop.

Kole cleared his throat again. The boys snapped to attention, turning to face him. "Stop staring like that," Kole said, rolling his eyes. "You're making her uncomfortable."

Mumbling apologies, they averted their gazes to the floor—well, all but Alex who stood up, his arms crossed over his chest. His expression shouldn't have made Faye nervous; he was just watching her with a pleasant smile on his face. But it did. She felt like he was raking her skin, seeing right through her. She felt like all the feelings she felt like she wanted to keep hidden were spewing all over the floor. No one seemed to notice her fears and sorrows settling in the air, but Faye felt it. Like she couldn't keep anything a secret. Like he saw right through all the walls she tried so hard to keep up.

"It's amazing," Alex breathed finally, coming to stand in front of her. Faye shot a quick, nervous glance Kole's way, but turned away so that Alex wouldn't notice. "I can't believe you're what's been behind the Gate this entire time." He brought his thumb across his lip thoughtfully. "But it doesn't make sense."

It was Kole's turn to glance at Faye now. Faye caught his gaze and held it, not able to turn away. Kole's shot glance turned into a stare, like he too was trying to figure out how exactly she worked inside her head. Faye turned away, not wanting him to find out. There were some things in her mind—like Terra's death—that she wanted to keep hidden.

"It doesn't make sense," Alex whispered again, tilting his head to the side. "Not at all. If you're just like us, there'd be no point in keeping us separated. So—why? Why all the trouble to keep us from meeting each other? Why arrest us for getting close?"

He stared at her like she held the answer. Faye shrugged, showing that no, she did not have the answers he was looking for. "I don't know," she said softly, rubbing her arms again. "I was wondering the same thing myself."

"How many more of you are there?" he asked, his eyebrows lifting. "Or are you the only one?"

"We have about as many girls as you do boys," Faye replied, twitching a hand through her hair awkwardly. She felt so uncomfortable that she wished she would just melt into the floor, away from all these people around her. "Our side doesn't look much different than yours, actually. Some of the houses look the same." Including this one, she wanted to say, but kept her mouth shut.

"So the Government made us all believe that this man-eating creature was on the other side," Alex said, his voice lowering as he concentrated, "but there isn't. It's just other humans."

Faye nodded. "Yeah. We have forest animals and stuff, but you guys do too."

"So it's exactly the same."

"Exactly."

Alex growled in agitation. His hands went into his hair and his fingers curled into fists. Faye watched him, wide-eyed. She'd never seen someone get so irritated for not understanding something—well, except for Errika, of course. Errika brought her hands into fists through her hair when she was angry, too. Faye frowned. The alikeness between the two was really peculiar.

Kole stepped forward, putting a hand on his brother's shoulder. He murmured something into Alex's ear, something that no one else in the room could hear. Faye glanced at the other boys, at Terence, Zander, and Seth, watching for their expressions. Terence was expressionless, which didn't surprise Faye in the slightest; he already knew all this information, after all. Zander was thoughtful, staring off into the distance, his jaw working like he was upset about something. Seth had a scowl on his face, seeming just as infuriated as he had been when he entered the household. Faye wondered what his problem was. Kole had only hidden it from him because he thought it was the right thing to do. That was why she didn't tell her mom, why she didn't tell Kat or anyone else. Because it could put them in danger. Why did Seth see that?

Kole pulled away from Alex, cutting off Faye from her thoughts. He smiled at her, and she smiled back. Then he looked at Seth, his smile instantly falling from his face. "You're still mad?" he demanded, sounding angry himself. "Seriously, Seth?"

Seth snorted, standing up and stretching his arms out. "You explaining what she is doesn't change the fact that you hid it from us."

Kole glowered icily. "It was for your protection. What do you think will happen if the Government finds out that I've been hanging out around the Gate's borders with the 'creature' from the other side? Do you think that they won't question everyone I associate with to see what you guys know?"

"They haven't before—"

"That's because they didn't make it to the Gate, Seth," Kole said, his voice scary-calm. It was like he'd lost all motivation to try and convince his friend that he was doing the right thing. "If they found me, they'd probably think that you guys all knew about it. And they'd probably question you. That's why I didn't tell you. I didn't need you all becoming liable."

"Well, we are now," Alex said lightly, a smile on his face. He clapped Seth on the shoulder, holding his hand there. "Seth," he continued, his voice still light. Despite the lightness, Faye could see the threatening and menacing posture through it all. She shivered, "you need to get over this little tantrum of yours. We could always not tell you whenever we meet Faye here again." He smiled coolly. "You wouldn't want that now would you?"

If Errika were here, she'd probably be high-fiving him, congratulating him on pulling off such a threat without seeming mean or angry at all. Even though the threat wasn't all that huge—just forcing Seth to stay away from all of this—Faye could see that it affected Seth hugely. He'd gone rigid all over, his face almost turning a gray sort of color. He looked mortified, like the prospect of not being in on this secret terrified him more than anything else. Faye's eyebrows rose. Why? Why would he feel that way? She just didn't understand him. Not at all.

Seth forced a smile. "Sorry, Kole. I understand completely why you did what you did."

Alex's smile grew, this time triumphant. "That's what I thought." He pushed Seth away slightly, almost causing Seth to trip on the small glass table in front of them. "Now, I say we get something to eat, I'm starv—"

His sentence cut off suddenly as the front door open and a voice sent everyone into silence. "Alex, Kole!" someone shouted. "I'm home!"

"Shit," Kole cursed under his breath. He shot a fearful glance in Faye's direction. He averted his gaze quickly, but Faye still saw it. And her stomach instantly plummeted.

Something bad was about to happen.

"You need to get her out of here now," Alex hissed, pushing Kole roughly toward the living room door. "Hurry up, before he sees you!"

Kole grabbed Faye's hand, rushing her out of the living room. Faye didn't bother asking any questions, just stuck close to him. Her mind whirled, and she suddenly felt like she wanted to vomit. What if this man—whoever he was—saw them coming down the hall. Everything was connected by this hallway, after all. That, Faye couldn't help but think, was very inconvenient.

Kole pulled Faye into one of the rooms, shutting the door behind them. Faye cast a glance around, not able to help herself. They were in what looked like an office. A computer desk with an old Windows desktop sitting on top of it. Books sitting on bookshelves surrounded the walls, books that she'd never seen before. There was a crate on the floor next to the desk, filled with assorted binders of various colors. Despite the ordinariness of it, Faye's eyes widened. Whose room could this be—?

"Come on," Kole whispered, tugging her through the room to the window on the far side of the room. She followed him, her eyes tugging at her surroundings. Who sat here during the day, sifting through the papers, reading the books, and looking through the binders? Who worked in here? She doubted it was Alex, and knew it wasn't Kole. Her eyebrows furrowed. That could only leave.. ..

"Is that your dad?" she whispered anxiously as Kole reached the window. He tugged it upward, letting in the cool breeze. "Is that why we're running?"

"Precisely," Kole muttered, pulling the window open the rest of the way. He snuck a glance her way. "While Alex is understanding about knowing what's on the other side, my dad has a certain . . . feeling of obligation to listen to the law. I don't want to chance him turning you—or me—in."

"He'd turn you in?" Faye was horrified. She couldn't imagine a parent turning in their own child for breaking the law. She worried about her mom finding out, but she didn't think Mary would turn her in to the Government. She loved Faye too much to be able to do that. Was it different for boys? Did fathers not love their sons the way mothers loved their daughters?

"I don't know," Kole said, his voice tight. He gestured for her to join him at the edge of the window. "But I'm not willing to find out."

Faye gulped, looking over the edge of the window. It was just like the drop of Errika's window sill. Small, but terrifying. She could just imagine it now: she'd slip, fall, and break her neck. She'd turned mangled, just like Terra. . . .

"Come on," Kole whispered hurriedly. "We don't have much time."

Adrenaline she didn't even know she possessed coursing through her veins, Faye nodded and straddled over the window. She took a deep breath before jumping, biting her tongue to keep from screaming as she plunged to the ground. She landed on her feet, her hands digging into the dirt. She stood up, eyeing her palms. Little rocks indented in her skin. She winced, thankful that she was otherwise unharmed.

A moment later Kole was beside her, taking her hand in his again. "Let's go," he said softly. "We have to get out of here before my dad notices I'm gone."

Faye nodded, allowing herself to be pulled into a run as their feet slapped against the pavement. They rushed down the driveway, down the street. In the back of her mind, Faye knew that she no longer had Kole's sweatshirt for protection, that anyone who saw her would be able to tell that she was different. But she couldn't bring herself to care. She couldn't do anything but concentrate on running, on getting to the forest before time ran out. Whatever Alex thought up for an excuse—and Faye knew that he would think of something—wouldn't last forever. Kole needed to get home sooner rather than later.

"What happens if he does notice you're gone?" Faye gasped out, not able to stop herself from asking the question. She regretted asking instantly. Her lungs burned painfully, her breathing labored with every step. She wanted to stop running, to slow to a walk, but she knew she couldn't. She wouldn't risk getting Kole in trouble, either.

"Then I get grounded and questioned," Kole replied, his voice seemingly rusty and tired. He was just as worn down from running as she was, Faye observed. For some reason she'd imagined them being able to run for hours, never tiring. Though, Faye thought, that was probably just her imaging them as supernatural in some form or fashion. Faye knew that she needed to stop linking boys to supernatural activities, but she couldn't help it. There had to be some reason to why they were separated.

Didn't there?

"Oh." Faye didn't even know if he'd be able to recognize that as a reply. It was more like a little gasp of air than anything else.

Whether he recognized it as a response or not, she didn't know. He didn't say anything else, just ran. Faye kept her mouth shut for the rest of the run to the forest, not wanting to waste any more oxygen that she desperately needed.

Alex Frost crossed his arms over his chest, trying to seem non-chalant.

Kole and Faye were long gone by now, he hoped. When Kole raced into their father's office, he knew that they were going to get out unseen. For a short moment he'd feared that Kole would try to hide them upstairs, would try to chance running to the kitchen where the stairs were. The stairs, Alex observed for the thousandth time, were oddly placed. Instead of separating two rooms like any other house, the stairs sat in the corner of the room, seeming so out of place in the rest of the house. Alex always knew that their house was set up strangely—every room seeming to connect by a single hallways instead of to each other. But that was only because the house used to be a small hotel, made by a family hoping to get some cash. It didn't work, obviously.

"Alex?"

Alex's thoughts about his home were cut off by the sound of his father's voice. He looked up, breaking into a bright smile. "Hey, Dad!" he said, keeping his tone light.

Nathaniel Frost always reminded Alex of a puppy. Not at all because of his body, which was more intimidating than friendly like the small canine; he was incredibly muscular, a result to the amount of time he spent at the gym every week. He was tall too, a head over Alex's height, and Alex wasn't short. No, what reminded him of a puppy were his big, green eyes that were like emerald, so green that some people questioned if he wore contacts. He had laugh lines engraved into his cheeks from all the smiles and laughter he'd shared with his family and friends over the year. Even his hair, curly and a light brown, flopped playfully over his head like he just rolled out of bed.

"Where's Kole?" he asked, cocking an eyebrow. His eyes latched onto Kole's friends, and his other eyebrow rose as well. "Why are his friends here but not him?"

"Kole and Seth got into a fight, and Kole stormed off," Alex lied smoothly. At least part of it was true. Kole and Seth had gotten into a fight after all. He slid his gaze Seth's way, praying that the boy had his expression in check. If too much shock lit up, Nathaniel was going to know that his son was lying. "You know how he is," Alex continued, smiling slightly. "He storms about before he punches something. You're lucky there's not a hole in the wall, actually."

"Seth and Kole got into a fight?" Alex watched as Nathaniel's eyes flicked over to Seth. "Care to explain what over?"

Alex feared that Seth would draw a blank, wouldn't be able to explain—or make up, rather—what was going on. But he was wrong. "I thought he took my video game," Seth said, sounding oddly convincing. "I couldn't find it anywhere and the last time I saw it Kole was ogling at it. So I thought he took it while I wasn't looking." Seth smiled apologetically. "Terence just got done admitting that he was the one who took it, though. He's going to give it back."

"Well, next time look into things before coming over and screaming at people," Alex's father said sternly, shaking his head. "Now we don't know when Kole will be back."

Alex hid a smile. Perfect, he thought. Now all he had to do was get the message to Kole. That he was supposed to have been infuriated with Seth for accusing him of theft and running out of the house right before their father got home. If he didn't, there wasn't much to worry about. Kole knew how to play along when he knew that Alex was making up excuses for him. And Alex did, too.

Alex and Kole were closer Alex was with any of his other friends or family members. Alex could tell Kole anything, and Kole could tell him anything. That, Alex couldn't help but think, was why Kole brought Faye here in the first place. Because he trusted Alex with this secret, with his life. Alex's arms tightened around himself. If anything ever happened to Kole because of this secret....

Alex's eyes narrowed. Faye's image flashed, her bright green eyes blazing with her hair. Something inside Alex tightened. Her eyes, along with the way she held herself together reminded him of.... of his father.

Nah, Alex told himself, shaking his head. It couldn't have meant anything. Not at all.

"Faye," Kole murmured.

Faye twisted around, shooting him an anxious look. They'd reached the Gate, and she was getting ready to begin her climb, all but frozen to her spot already. Her triumph over beating the Gate that morning had vanished, replaced by the icy fear crawling its way down her spine. All she could see was Terra, her mangled body after falling—jumping, rather—off the cliff's edge. She was so afraid, so, so afraid, that she was going to end up just like her.

Except Faye wouldn't do it on purpose.

"Yeah?" she squeaked out, her voice sounding thin to her own ears.

"Are you afraid of falling?"

It was a normal question, one that someone usually asked when someone was about to climb something of massive height. But Faye could feel the weight of the question, and she knew that Kole meant something more than the simple question. He'd noticed her fear at the window sill, Faye realized. He knew that she'd been terrified of falling despite the small distance.

"W-what makes you ask that?" she asked anyway, her voice cracking. She looked up at the Gate again, her eyes widening with new fear fluttering around inside her. She gulped, looking away.

"You seem petrified," Kole said softly, coming to stand beside her. He reached up, touching her hand slightly. The feeling of his hand on her sent warm shivers down her spine. Why, Faye didn't know. All she knew was that it felt good. "Not in the usual way that people are when climbing up or down something. You looked like you were going to faint when we hopped out of my dad's office's window."

Faye sighed deeply, unlatching herself from the Gate and setting her feet on the ground. She felt so much safer on the ground, so much safer with no distance between she and the dirt under her feet. "Okay," she said, giving in. "I'm terrified of falling. Every time I have to jump I feel like I'm going to die—and that's exactly what I picture. Me with a broken neck. And it scares me."

Faye's stomach hurt. She'd never told anyone, not even Errika, about her fear of falling. Everyone would pity her, look down on her. They would all know the reason why she was terrified of falling, the reason why she couldn't go on anything that lifted her off the ground. They'd know it was because she was still haunted by Terra's memory, unable to let go.

But, looking at Kole, Faye wasn't afraid of that with him. She felt like he wouldn't pity her, wouldn't look down on her. He'd accept her fear and that was it. Even if he did know about Terra, about how she couldn't let her sister go. Kole didn't seem like the pitying type. And that, Faye thought, she was incredibly thankful for.

Kole's eyebrows drew together. "You visualize yourself with a broken neck?"

Faye nodded, biting her lip and praying she hadn't made a mistake.

Kole took a step forward, his hand touching her arm. Faye tensed, but then relaxed. His hand was so gentle, so warm. It was nothing like she'd ever experienced before. Was this because it was a boy, and not a girl touching her? Did their hands cause different reactions? "What happened to make you imagine that?" he whispered. "Fears like that—they're caused by something."

"How do you know they're caused by something?" Faye asked softly, her gaze averted to the ground.

"My dad's a therapist," Kole explained. "He talks to people, tries to get them over their fears. Not one person has had the fear for no reason—at least, not the ones where you almost faint and paralyze at the thought of being forced to deal with it." He paused. "You don't have to tell me if you don't want to. I understand."

Faye was silent for a moment. She stared down at the ground, her feet kicking into the dirt. Her stomach ached with longing. Facing this, telling Kole about her fear, brought so many memories back to her. Terra lounging on the couch writing in her journals. Terra playing hide-and-go-seek with Faye over and over again. Terra cooking in the kitchen while their mother was out.

Terra, Terra, Terra.

"Terra," Faye whispered before she could stop herself. She looked up at Kole, her eyes glistening with tears. "Terra."

Kole stared at her, uncomprehending. "What?"

"Terra," Faye said again, her voice thick. "She is—was—my sister." She sniffed, wiping a tear from her cheek before it could slide off her chin and onto her shirt. "She was my best friend. She was always there for me." She paused, sighing shakily. "And then she was gone."

Kole's eyes widened. "What happened to her?"

"She killed herself," Faye said, her voice dead to her own ears. She blinked back more tears, not believing herself. Any other time she talked about Faye—when she was with Errika—she didn't cry. She usually cried when she was thinking about her, lost in thought. When she was by herself. But talking about it with Kole—Faye couldn't stop herself from crying even if she wanted to. "She threw herself off a cliff."

Faye gasped as Kole reached out, wrapping his arms around her. Faye hugged him back, crying softly into his shoulder. He cooed comforting things into her ear, whispering that everything would be okay, that she would be okay. Faye had grown so used to people telling her that, so used to people telling her that she'd be able to move on someday, that she'd learned to block the comforting words out. But with Kole, she felt something. Something tugging her in the pit of her stomach. Like everything would be okay. She would be okay.

"So, that's why I'm afraid of falling," Faye mumbled as they pulled apart, wiping her eyes. "Every time I go to jump, I see her. She's mangled just like she was the day she fell—jumped—off the cliff."

Kole's eyebrows drew together again in confusion. "You—you know what she looked like?"

Faye nodded, sniffling again. "My mom told me to stay home, that Errika and her mom would be over soon. But I knew something was wrong. My mom was crying, Terra was missing, and there was a police woman there. So after they left I got on my bike and followed them." She swallowed. "There were a bunch of women surrounding a table with a white blanket on top of it. I begged people to tell me where my sister was, where I could find Terra, but no one would tell me. My mom told me that Terra was gone—that she wasn't coming back. But I wouldn't listen. I ripped the blanket off the table...."

Kole's eyes were sad as he said, "I'm so sorry. I can't imagine what it must have been like to go through that."

Faye shrugged, wiping her eyes again. "It was seven years ago. Everyone's seemed to have moved on."

"But you haven't."

Faye met Kole's gaze. "No, I haven't."

Kole looked like he wanted to say something about Terra, about what happened, about Faye's fear, but he didn't. He seemed to know that Faye didn't want to talk about it. He knew that she didn't want pity or sympathy. She just wanted him to leave the topic alone. Instead, he cracked a smile and said, "So, when do we meet again?"

She smiled back, happy for the excuse not to talk about her sister anymore. "Same day next week?"

Kole shook his head. "Not soon enough."

Faye rolled her eyes, grinning. "Well, if you plan on coming onto my side, it has to be when my mom is working late and my sister is over at a friend's house. They can't know that I've been hanging out at the Gate's borders." She smiled. "So we can either do this on Wednesday, or wait until same day next week."

"Wednesday," Kole said instantly. "Definitely Wednesday."

Faye smiled, unable to help herself. There was something about Kole that made Faye smile. She couldn't explain it, but it was there. "Are you going to be able to survive until then?"

"No."

Faye and Kole laughed together, the sound chasing birds out of nearby trees. Faye shook her head, bringing a hand through her hair as their laughter subsided. "Well, then how do you suppose we solve that problem?"

"You," Kole drawled, grinning, "should give me your phone number."

Faye blinked. She'd expected a joking answer, not an actual solution. "Kole," she said softly, suddenly turning serious. "What if the Government can tell if boys and girls are sharing phone numbers? And what if—?"

"If they were going to figure out anything it would have been that we were coming here in the first place," Kole pointed out. "I think it will be safe."

Faye searched Kole's face, trying to read his expression, and then sighed. "Fine."

They exchanged phone numbers, quickly reading the numbers off to each other. Faye glanced around her, suddenly anxious that someone was listening in. She glanced up and saw why. There was a camera sitting right in front of them, looming over them like it could take them out with a single flick of the finger. Faye gasped. "Look up there," she whispered.

Kole obliged, his eyes shooting up to were Faye was looking. "I never noticed that," he said softly. He glanced at her and smiled. "More proof that everything is fine. The Government must have something going on with the cameras, otherwise they would have picked us up a long time ago."

Faye shook her head, smiling despite herself. She pocketed her phone, bid goodbye to Kole, and then made her way over the Gate, heading back the way she had come.

Faye closed her bedroom door behind her, blowing air through her teeth. She suddenly felt tired, like she could collapse onto her bed and sleep for hours on end. She closed her eyes, smiling softly. Today, despite the conflict and the tears shed, had been a great day. She'd gone on the other side, gone to where Kole lived. She'd met other boys from the other side. It was all so unreal, all so unlike anything Faye had ever done before.

Before she'd stumbled upon the Gate, she never would have been caught dead doing something so reckless. She hated the thought of getting in trouble, let alone captured and thrown in jail by the Government. But now? Now Faye couldn't wait until Wednesday when it would be Kole's turn to come on her side. She was suspicious of the Government's intentions, and didn't feel at all loyal to them. She'd never really understood the Government, and always felt like she and the other women of Cesve were being oppressed, but now she felt like the Government was doing it for no reason. Like they were doing it just because they could.

Faye's eyes flicked to her bed longingly. Her eyes trailed from the pillow, to her comforter, to ...

She froze. There was a cardboard box sitting on top of the bed, glaring back at her in the darkness. Faye fumbled for her bedroom light switch, her stomach feeling like it was going to explode. Her fingers trembled as it flicked the light switch up, letting light into the room. The box, as normal as it seemed, continued to glare at her, like it could tear her apart with its eyes.

Faye crept forward, her legs like water. She could barely stand, barely keep from collapsing on the floor. The cardboard of the box was worn out, she noticed with a sickening realization as she reached the foot of her bed. Like it had been around for many, many years.

Seven years, in fact.

Her hands shaking harder now, Faye lifted the tab open of the box. Inside sat Terra's old notebooks, her old school things. Tears burning in her eyes, Faye brought her hand down on her Geometry notebook. She could remember when Terra would have her Geometry book out in front of her, scrawling into the notebook as she completed her homework. Faye would watch her, amazed by how quickly Terra could write. She never tried to look over her sister's shoulder, however. Terra hated it whenever Faye did that, and had asked her to stop. Privacy, Terra had told her, was something that everyone deserved. Even if it was just math homework.

Faye slammed the box shut and threw it on the ground, a small cry escaping her lips. She and Mary had put everything of Terra's in the attic so that they'd never have to face them again. They couldn't bear to get rid of it—they were Terra's. But they couldn't bear to look at it, either.

Faye threw herself on her bed and closed her eyes. She didn't know how the cardboard box got there, and she didn't know why it was there. All she knew was that the memories flooding back to the surface were too strong, and even though it was what Faye feared most, she could feel herself falling, falling back into the memories of Terra Caldwell.

CHAPTER 11

She was running.

Running as fast as she could. Her feet pounded against the pavement, her hair whipping in front of her face. She didn't take the time to brush it away. Instead, she concentrated on running. On getting away. If she didn't concentrate on that, then all would be lost. All of it. Everything they'd worked for. Everything they'd uncovered. It would all be gone.

"Daneigh!" she shrieked, her feet pounding harder as she dashed onto the other girl's street. She breathed hard, her lungs aching. She wanted to stop. To stop running. To stop and lie down. She wanted to collapse, to close her eyes and sleep.

But she couldn't.

Her enemies were hard on her heels, shouting at her to surrender. To give up. The Government had found her. She could either come quietly, or she could deal with the consequences of resisting. Death. That's what they meant. If she resisted, the Government was going to kill her. She wasn't a fool. She knew what the

Government did to traitors like her. They made sure the threats were taken care of.

"Daneigh!" she cried, her voice rising with hysteria. She had to get to her. To warn her. The Government new the other girl had had a part in this treacherous act. They knew that the two girls had collaborated, and they had worked out a plan to take down the Government once and for all. Even if she let the guards take her now, leaving Daneigh behind, they would get to her eventually. And they would take both of the girls down.

"Daneigh—"

Suddenly a Government official had a hold of her arm, their fingers digging painfully into her skin. She refused to wince, though. That would only give her captors satisfaction. And satisfaction was something she refused to give the Government ever again. "It's too late for you," the man hissed into her ear. "It's going to be death row for you."

She didn't answer the Government official. Instead, her eyes shot to the house in front of her. A girl stood on the front porch, her brunette hair blowing in the wind. Her eyes, like burning chocolate orbs, stared down at her in terrified shock. She stood stock still.

"Daneigh," she whispered.

Daneigh opened her mouth, ready to say something, and then—

"Miss!"

She ripped her eyes open, gasping in shock as her nightmare fell away from her. She felt like she was suffocating, her lungs not taking in the air she so desperately needed. It was just like her nightmare. Running, running, running. Nothing else but running—and the fear. The fear that had threatened to consume her whole that day. The fear that had cost Daneigh her life.

She told Fortis that she blamed him for Daneigh's death. And she did. If it weren't for Fortis and his damned Government, then Daneigh would still be alive. But it was her fault, too. If she hadn't run to Daneigh, if she hadn't taken the chance in getting to her on time, then Daneigh would have realized what was going on and run.

And now Daneigh was gone.

"Miss," Miranda whispered urgently, her hands curled around the bars of her cell. She looked up, her eyes wide. What was Miranda doing here? They weren't due for another meet up for a couple of weeks. Something must have happened.

"What's wrong?" she demanded, hopping up from her cot and hurrying toward Miranda. She struggled to keep her voice in a whisper, not wanting anyone to overhear them. Not that it mattered. All of the inmates knew of her plan to get everyone out. That was the only way that the other women survived. That was the only way that the other women made it through the day. Hope.

"Courtnie," Miranda whispered hurriedly, shooting a quick glance behind her. "Courtnie's coming. Surprise cell check."

She gasped. A surprise cell check? They hadn't had cell checks in years. Years. "Courtnie is using an excuse to see if I'm pulling anything," she whispered. She looked up at Miranda, keeping her voice steady despite the fact that her mind was reeling with anxiety. "Thank you, Miranda. Hurry and get back before Courtnie catches you."

In an instant Miranda was gone. She sighed deeply, darting back to her cot and pulling the laptop out from under her sheets. She should have asked Miranda to take the laptop with her. No, she immediately argued. If Miranda took the laptop, there was no certain time when she would get the laptop back. And she needed the laptop. She needed to keep her eyes on the boy and the girl who crossed paths at the Gate. She needed to make sure that they hadn't gotten caught.

Frantically, she began pulling at the bricks of her cell. When she'd first been brought to the prison wards, she'd tried to dig her way out through the walls. And she'd almost succeeded. If it hadn't been for Courtnie catching her, then she would have been long gone by now. But that didn't matter now. What mattered was that there were still a few loose bricks on the wall.

It was just a matter of finding them.

She clawed at the bricks, silently cursing as time ticked on. Courtnie could be anywhere. She could be right outside, unlocking the door to the prison wards. She could be inside the prison wards. She could be—

"Ladies, ladies!" came an icy, withered, amused voice. "It's time for a cell check!"

She felt her heart stop. Courtnie had arrived.

"Faye, come on!" Kat whined, throwing her hands in the air. "Please say something."

Faye studiously ignored her sister, pulling her knees closer to her chest as she propped her novel out in front of her. She pushed herself as far as she could into the couch cushion, wanting nothing more than to disappear completely. Kat hovered over her, staring down with begging eyes. Faye had come to the living room to escape her sister to no avail. Faye wasn't at all surprised that her attempt to block out Kat hadn't worked. Kat was never one to stop prodding where she wasn't welcomed.

"I said I was sorry!" Kat hissed, her eyes burning with irritation. "Like, fifteen-thousand times. Doesn't that count for anything?"

Of course, Faye thought in disbelief, it didn't count for anything. Kat's apologies only made things worse. Like she hadn't realized the deep pain that she'd inflicted upon Faye. The hurt that Faye felt all night, trapped in Terra's memory. The fear that she felt that night when the worst of all her nightmares had emerged from her self-consciousness. Not one, not two—not fifteen-thousand—apologies could fix that. And to make it worse, Kat had walked right up to her the next morning with a triumphant smile and said, "I found that just lying around. Hope it wasn't anything important."

Kat had deliberately dragged Terra's things downstairs and into Faye's room. And for what? Did Kat find Faye's misery amusing? Did she enjoy watching Faye fall apart? Faye would have asked her, screamed at her for an answer, but she didn't want to. Watching Kat squirm in discomfort for the last three days was good enough for now.

Faye let out a sudden cry of shock as her book was ripped from her hands and tossed across the room, skidding on the floor. She gaped at the curled pages, silently cursing the world for bending them. Great. Now her novel was ruined. Just great.

So consumed by anger, Faye almost forgot that she was giving her sister the silent treatment. Her head shot up, her eyes locking on Kat's with disdain. In that moment, Faye could have hit her. She could have done more than hit her. This emotion was so close to hate that it was almost bubbling over the edge.

"Will you talk now?" Kat continued to hiss, showing absolutely no regret for ruining Faye's favorite book. "What will it take for you to just open your mouth?"

Faye stood up, sauntering over to her fallen novel and scooping it into her arms. She bit the inside of her cheek to keep from lashing out at Kat as she attempted to mend what had been broken. Kat had no right to do this. To bring Faye so much pain and grief. It was bad enough that she'd brought Terra's things into her room to haunt her, but this?

"Kat," Faye whispered, her flat, emotionless, "if I were you, I'd stop trying to talk to me—until further notice."

Kat flinched as though Faye had punched her. Her eyes widened, her hands curling into tight fists at her sides. Faye watched her without interest, wishing she could go back to pulling the silent treatment as though she hadn't spoken. In fact, she wished she'd never opened her mouth at all. Kat would never give up now. "Faye—"

"Kat," Faye repeated again, her voice like sharp shards of ice. "What do you want from me, exactly? Do you want amusement? Is that what you want? Do you like causing everyone pain? Because that's all you do." She glared, her eyes as freezing as the words she spoke. "That's all you do."

Without another word, Faye tossed her un-mendable novel back onto the couch and stormed out of the room, leaving a torn-looking Kat behind.

Faye stormed down the street, her hands shoved deep into her pockets. A rage so unlike her threatened to consume her, and she had to fight the urge to grab the baseball bat from the house and beat something with it. She'd never felt so angry before—never.

Not even when Kat had destroyed something very precious to Faye a few years ago. It had been a picture she'd drawn for Terra before Terra died. She'd never had the chance to give it to her.

But what Kat did this time....

It was unforgivable. She went into the attic and rifled through Terra's things. And then, just to spite Faye and her mom even more, she brought one of the boxes downstairs. And then, like the cherry on top of a sundae, she'd thrown the box onto Faye's bed knowing the pain it would cause her. Kat knew that Terra was a subject that pained both she and her mother immensely. So why? Why do it? For attention? Faye always knew that Kat was starving for attention, but was this really the way she wanted to get it?

All she knew was that she wouldn't be talking to her sister any time soon. She'd made the mistake of opening her mouth today, but she wouldn't be again. Not for a long time. For the first time, Faye really wanted her sister to suffer. And giving her no attention at all was just the way to do it.

A sharp ringing cut Faye away from her thoughts, making her jump. After collecting herself, Faye reached into her jeans pocket and pulled out her cell phone. Her eyes widened when she saw who was calling. Kole. "Hello?" she said softly into the receiver, glancing around. She felt like everything had eyes, like everything had ears. Like everything knew exactly what she was up to.

"Hey!"

His voice was so cheerful, so free. Faye couldn't understand how Kole did it. How did he manage to be so light about this situation? Did he not understand the danger they could be in? The risks they were taking? Sometimes she couldn't help but wonder if he actually did.

Great, Faye thought bitterly. Her anger toward Kat was seeping into her thoughts about Kole. That was just great. "Hi," Faye replied, keeping her voice a notch over a whisper. "What's up?"

"It's Wednesday, remember?"

Faye silently cursed herself for forgetting. Of course! It was Wednesday, the day they were supposed to meet at the Gate. In fact, she was—"Shit!" Faye hissed, glaring up at the sky. "I'm late. I'm so sorry—"

"It's all right." Kole chuckled. "Are you coming, though?"

"Yes," Faye replied instantly without a second thought. Even if she didn't want to go, something about Kole attracted her, pulled her toward him. Sometimes on the way home from school she'd have to fight the urge to venture in the woods and climb to the other side.

Maybe that was why they were separated. Because boys were addicting.

"All right." Kole's voice was so cheerful. She wished that she could feel the same way. "I'll see you soon?"

"Yeah," Faye said softly. "We're going to have to change plans, though." She bit her lip, afraid that Kole was going to be so disappointed that he'd cancel altogether. "Everyone's at home."

There was a moment's pause. Faye moved to biting the inside of her cheek instead, showing how nervous she was. She hated the thought of disappointing Kole, especially when he'd been so excited to come onto her side of the Gate. And then all of her nervousness disappeared when Kole said, "Yeah, okay! That's fine."

Faye nodded, forgetting for a moment that Kole wasn't standing there with her. "All right," she said, the tension beginning to sprout in her stomach disappearing. "I'll see you soon then."

"Okay!"

Faye bid Kole goodbye before lurching to the side, switching directions. She could not believe that she'd completely forgotten about her and Kole's plans. She'd been so consumed by her anger with Kat that she hadn't taken into account that she had other things to do besides pull the silent treatment. Faye suddenly felt guilty, so guilty that she almost started running toward the forest. She'd been selfish these past few days—not with Kat, but with everyone else. She'd ignored calls from Errika, skipped out on school, and she barely spoke a word to her mother. She was probably being melodramatic, letting a single box get to her like she was, but she couldn't help it. Memories of Terra were already tearing her apart. That box toppled her off the edge.

Faye quickened her pace, her eyes shooting around her fervently. Even off the phone with Kole, Faye felt on edge. Like the Government was watching her every move. Like they would come at any moment and take her away. And then she would be trapped in the prison wards for the rest of her life, rotting in a cell.

And that scared her almost as much as falling.

But it didn't scare her enough, so it seemed. Otherwise she wouldn't be entering the forest; she wouldn't be making her way through the trees, following the path that Errika made for her; she wouldn't feel the anticipation swirling within her as she drew closer to the Gate's borders. If she were scared enough, she would have stayed home; she would have never crossed over the Gate; she would have never gone back.

But there she was, walking through the underbrush. There she was moving branches to the side. There was she defying the most important rule that hung over the land of Cesve.

And she didn't feel sorry at all.

Courtnie stepped up to the final cell, her hands folded out in front of her.

She'd gone through all the women's cells—every single one. And for what? She knew that no one held anything in here. They were too worn out, too afraid of what the Government would do to them if they were caught stashing weapons. It was for that reason that Courtnie never did cell checks—at least, she hadn't in years. When she first arrived, Courtnie checked the cells at least twice a week. And a good thing, too. If she hadn't, she would have escaped through the walls.

The wall was sealed back up, of course. Courtnie wouldn't tolerate her escaping under her own watch. No. She would not bring doom upon everything she worked for—everything she lived for—just to see that little asshole roam free. Courtnie would not let her win.

She couldn't let her win.

And that was the sole reason why Courtnie decided to do a cell check. She seemed more superior lately, more full of herself than usual. It would be hard for anyone else to notice, but Courtnie could. She'd learned over the years to study how she acted. That was the only way to know when she was plotting a scheme.

And she was definitely plotting something.

The second the cameras went down, Courtnie knew it was she who was to blame. She was the only one who could think of something so vile, so irritatingly brilliant. She was the only one who would be able to ruin everything while sitting inside a cell. Fortis continued to believe that she was innocent, no matter how many times Courtnie plead with him. She'd thought that the reference with Daneigh would do the trick, but no such luck. All it had done was make him angry at her.

And now she was on her own to figure out what she was doing. Well, not like she wasn't on her own anyway. Fortis had never helped her in connecting the dots—and he never would. He believed his precious daughter was innocent despite the wreck she'd caused. Courtnie could not believe how blind her brother was.

Courtnie came to stand in front of her cell, a smile filled with malice on her face. Today would be the day that Courtnie caught her once and for all. Today would be the day that Courtnie would finally make Fortis see. All she needed was a small shred of proof—that was it. And then she would finally have her brother on her side.

"Hello there," she murmured brightly, unable to hide her anticipation. "Are you ready for your cell check?"

She was lying in her cot, staring up at the ceiling. She didn't seem at all fazed by Courtnie's presence, though Courtnie hadn't expected her to. She knew that Courtnie loved it when her prisoners were afraid, and she didn't want to give Courtnie any satisfaction. She'd made that quite clear when she was first brought in. "Just get it over with," she drawled in a bored voice. "We both know why you're here."

Courtnie didn't have to be told twice. She unlocked the bars of her cell and stepped inside, a superior smile on her face. She strutted forward, gesturing impatiently for her to get up. "You know the drill," she snapped irritably. "Get up and stand to the side."

She rolled her eyes and stood up, crossing her arms irritably over her chest as she stood in the far corner of the cell. Courtnie half-expected her to run, to take the first chance she could get out, but she didn't. She didn't even glance at the cell's open door.

Courtnie turned to her work, digging through her things. She shook out the blanket, lifted the mattress off the cot, and even unzipped the mattress and rifled through it. There was nothing to be found. Courtnie growled angrily, disbelieving. There had to be something to prove her guilt. Something!

But there was nothing. Nothing. Even as she felt at the bricks, there was nothing. Courtnie wanted to scream out. She thought she'd had her. She thought she'd finally succeeded.

But she had nothing. Nothing.

"Satisfied?" she sneered, smiling triumphantly. "There's nothing here. Stop chasing on a wild goose chase you've made up for yourself. Go report to your brother, Featherstrom, and he'll tell you the exact same thing: Quit searching. There's nothing."

Courtnie threw her mattress roughly to the ground, almost bursting with rage. "You did something!" she shrieked. "I know you did! You destroyed the—"

"Destroyed the what, Courtnie?" She cocked an eyebrow. "Is something happening?"

Courtnie could tell by the smile on her face that she knew exactly what Courtnie was referencing to, that she was the one who was doing everything that was tearing the Government apart. Already the cameras were gone. There was no way to scare the citizens into behaving if the cameras were no there to fulfill their threats.

And she knew that.

"There's still the broadcasts," Courtnie hissed, tempted to slap the smile off her face. "You haven't won."

Her smile was filled with as much malice and as much hate as the smile Courtnie had worn when she'd first entered the room. "Not yet," was all she said.

"So what are we going to do?" Kole asked.

Faye scratched at her head, looking up at the sky. She and Kole stood before each other, the Gate the only thing keeping them apart. She bit her lip, tempted to climb over the other side just so she could see him without the bars of the Gate obscuring her view. But then a vision of Terra's mangled body appeared before her, and the urge vanished completely. "I don't know," she murmured.

Kole grinned, and something inside Faye's stomach fluttered. She almost gasped in shock. She'd never felt anything like that before. "Well, you could come back on my side," he mused. "But we don't really want to chance getting in that situation again." He drew his eyebrows together thoughtfully. "I could still come onto your side and we could just stay in the forest."

Faye thought the suggestion over. It was probably the safest suggestion, and probably the only one that would only lead to any success. If they were to go back onto the boys' side, then she would chance being caught by other people—including Kole's father. And, from the looks of it, that was something she did not want to happen. "All right," Faye murmured softly. "We'll have to make sure we stay in the forest, though."

Kole nodded in understanding. "I know."

Faye watched with wide eyes as Kole readied himself to make the climb over the Gate. He grabbed onto the metal with such ease, like it didn't even cross his mind that he could fall. Faye was struck with a sudden jealousy that sent her jaw working. Why couldn't she do things like this without being terrified, without feeling like she was dying right there were she stood? Why couldn't she climb without being afraid?

Why not?

Kole made his way to the top of the Gate and flipped over to the other side. He descended his way toward her, not at all tense as he shifted his position. Faye watched, wide-eyed with awe as she studied his movements. He made it seem so easy.

But it wasn't easy. At least, not for her.

Kole hopped onto the ground, twisting around to face her. He adjusted his shirt, pulling down his sleeves before tossing a small smile in Faye's direction. Faye watched with faint interest as Kole's eyes shot around, his eyes wide. It was like he was in a magical land facing a new mythical power. Part of Faye wanted to roll her eyes—they were only in the forest, after all. But, then again, she'd been the exact same when she'd gone onto Kole's side.

"This is the part where you give me a tour of the woods whilst praying we don't get lost, right?" Kole teased, his eyes finally meeting hers.

Faye laughed despite herself, shaking her head. "Yeah, we better pray we don't get lost," she mused, taking a step toward him. "I don't know the way around these woods except for the path that Errika made out for me. Other than that...."

Kole didn't answer at first. He looked around, his eyebrows knitted together in concentration. Faye watched as he pursed his lips, bringing a thumb to his chin. Wow, Faye thought, he must be thinking really hard. "Why don't we stay with the Gate's border and just pick a direction?" Kole offered suddenly, his hand dropping. He shrugged. "That way we don't lose sight of the Gate at least."

Faye thought the suggestion over. It was a pretty smart idea. If they lost track of the Gate, they'd be more likely to be caught. But it was more dangerous this way.... "What if there are officials further down?" she asked softly, her worried gaze connecting with Kole's nonchalant one. "What if we get caught?"

Kole thought Faye's words overt before answering. "If we get caught, we get caught," he said softly. "Haven't we been taking that risk this entire time?"

He was right, of course. They had been risking getting caught this entire time. Any moment now the cameras could go back on and a helicopter could drop down and take them away to the prison wards without letting them have their final goodbyes to their families. Any moment now, Faye's life, Kole's life, could be destroyed.

That should have frightened her—and it did. But it didn't frighten her enough. She was honestly more scared of falling than being caught by a Government official. "All right," she said softly. "Let's go."

The underbrush crackled and crunched under their feet as Faye and Kole made their way through the forest. Kole's eyes shot all around, his eyes wide. They may have only been in the forest, but he felt like he'd entered a new realm, a realm where anything could happen. He'd been excited to go onto the girl's side, and had been a little down when Faye told him plans had to change, but he didn't mind so much now. They could always do it another time. And, besides, there could be something amazing to be found here in the forest.

Kole felt like he was being tugged forward by an invisible force, like something—or someone—was telling him to come closer, to come and see what they had hidden. He didn't understand why he was feeling this way. He hadn't felt this way on his side of the Gate, though he hadn't stood there long enough to concentrate on it. But as he and Faye walked, the words repeated over and over again like a broken record. "Come on, Kole," it whispered. "Just a little further."

Just a little further to what? Kole didn't understand. They were simply walking through the forest, chatting about nothing in particular. What could be so important that his subconscious tugged him forward—so much that he had to resist the urge to break into a run? What was going on? Was this a girl's power? No, it couldn't have been. He and Faye discussed this already, and neither of the two had any supernatural power to bring to the table. And neither did anyone else, for that matter. At least, no one that Faye or Kole knew of.

"Hey," Faye said urgently, her feet suddenly stopping. Her point- ed ahead of her, her eyebrows coming together in confusion. "Do you see that?"

Kole's eyes followed Faye's finger, and they widened. In the distance, he saw what looked like a big black blob—definitely not something you usually came across in the woods. He tilted his head to the side. What could it possibly be? "Yeah," he murmured. "I do."

Faye bit her lip, a flash of anxiety crossing her face. Kole resisted the sudden urge to wrap his arms comfortingly around her, pulling her as close to him as possible. She reminded him so much of himself. At least, what he used to consider himself.

Lately, all pretenses, all need to be careful suddenly vanished. He just—didn't care anymore. All that mattered to him was meeting Faye.

Something about her—something that he couldn't place—set his heart on fire. He couldn't explain it, but that was how he felt.

"Should we turn back?" Faye whispered, glancing up at him before turning her attention back to the distant blob. "There could be people there...."

The tug Kole felt earlier grew so strong that it was all Kole could do not to rush away, running to the black blob in the distance. He knew instantly that this was what his subconscious had wanted him to find. This was what was tugging at him all along.

"No," Kole said softly. "Let's go see what it is."

"Kole—"

"You can stay behind if you don't think it's safe," Kole offered, smiling kindly at her. "I just want to see what it is."

Faye stared at him for a long moment before sighing. "Fine," she mumbled, shaking her hand and bringing a hand through her hair. It was so bright a color, Kole thought distantly. Her hair was like fire, with its red, oranges, and yellows all collaged into one. He'd never seen anything like it. It was—beautiful. "We can go. But if there's any sign of danger, promise me you'll agree to leave right away."

"Fair enough," was Kole's reply, and he took a step forward. "Come on."

They closed the distance between themselves and the black blob swifter than Kole would have thought. That last one-hundred feet Kole ran, his feet pounding hard on the forest ground. He could hear Faye running behind him, could practically feel her begging him to stop, to be more careful. But he couldn't help it. The anticipation of seeing what they'd discovered, to finally know what it was they'd found, was almost too much to bear. It was all he could do not to throw himself at the building.

This anticipation startled Kole. It was an insane, terrifying feeling stirring within him—something he'd never felt before. He was always the calm one, the one who kept their head in a new situation. But this time it seemed Faye was the one who kept her head.

Kole pushed at the branches blocking his view. Faye stood behind him, waiting for him to move forward. Kole, gesturing for Faye to follow him, took a step forward, out of the underbrush.

And suddenly the forest was gone, replaced by what seemed like a yard. Kole's eyes were wide as he gaped at the scene before him. The black blob was a building. A building unlike anything he'd ever seen before. A building so vast that it stretched outside his line of sight, mixing in with the trees in the far distance. In an abrupt sense of shock, Kole realize that the Gate itself seemed to have disappeared.

Beside him, Faye gasped. "Is this—?"

Kole nodded, a grimace forming on his lips. There was no other explanation except for this one:

They were standing in front of the Official Government building.

CHAPTER 12

F aye's insides felt cold.

It was liked ice shards had dug their way through her skin, piercing her veins and entering her blood stream. If someone were to touch her, Faye feared that she would break, crumbling to ash on the ground. She didn't understand why the sudden feeling swept through her, but it did. It was like something was completely wrong.

Kole took a step forward, his eyes wide. Faye bit down the urge to call him back to her, to beg him not to move. Every important official was in that building. Everyone who was against her and Kole's being together. If they were to be seen—and so close—they would automatically be brought to the prison wards. If they were lucky.

"This is where the Gate leads, huh?" Kole said blankly, as though he felt the need to say something but really had no idea what words to use. "To the building that started it all?"

Faye gulped, willing the ice to melt. "Y-yeah," she stuttered out, crossing her arms over her chest. It did nothing for her, however. She was still freezing. "We should—we should go."

Kole twisted around, his eyes meeting hers. Faye wondered if Kole could feel the ice in Faye's veins, could feel the same prickling sensation. She wondered if it affected him at all, if it scared him as much as it terrified her. She wondered if inside him there was a sense of urgency, a sense that told him to get the hell away from there as fast as he could. From the expression in his eyes, Faye couldn't help but feel that no, he didn't feel that way. He only felt fascination. Fascination that they'd found the source of everything, fascination that they were standing in front of the building that had complete control of their lives.

Whether he noticed the fear in Faye's eyes, Faye wasn't sure. But, when he opened his mouth, his words were full of understanding. "Yeah," he murmured, sneaking a quick glance at the vast building in front of them before nodding. "You're right."

Faye let out a long breath of relief. "Okay then," she said softly, resisting the sudden urge to grab onto Kole's hand. "Let's get back then."

Kole nodded, taking a few steps back before gesturing for her to follow. "Yeah, let's go back. That's enough excitement for today."

With a small smile, Faye followed Kole back into the woods, back the way they had come.

Kole let the front door fall shut behind him, leaning back against the wood. He let out a long sigh, closing his eyes. It had taken a lot of willpower not to say no to Faye, to keep going even though she was so obviously terrified. Kole wasn't sure what had taken over him, what was still taking over him, but he didn't really want to find out.

With another sigh, Kole opened his eyes and moved away from the door. He crept down the hall, listening out for his family members. Whether they were even home or not, he wasn't sure. But if they were, he didn't want to announce that he'd arrived. Not yet. Something about the way his stomach was in knots kept him from wanting to socialize. In fact, if Kole had any choice in the matter, he'd run upstairs to the bathroom and puke.

"Kole?"

Kole's eyes snapped up, locking onto his brother as he stood a few feet away, his arms crossed over his chest. Kole could see from the expression on Alex's face that he knew something was up and he wasn't exactly happy about it. Kole held his brother's gaze, resisting the urge to wrap his arms around himself and to disappear. He didn't know why he was suddenly feeling such anxiety toward the only person he ever really trusted in the world. To be honest, he had no idea about really anything anymore.

"Alex," he said softly, moving forward again. His chewed on the inside of his cheek, willing himself to snap out of this haze. Why was he feeling this way? Why did he have the nagging feeling that he had to go back to the Government building? Why did he feel like if he didn't then something dreadful was going to happen—not just to him, but to everybody? Why did he feel like the Government wasn't only hiding the genders from each other, but something else, something huge?

Why?

"Is everything okay?" Alex demanded. A moment later he was right in front of Kole, grabbing onto his shoulders. "Did something happen with Faye?" His eyes searched Kole's face, trying to find the answers within his eyes. Kole wondered what his brother would find there. Unease? Turmoil? No one could be sure. "What's wrong?"

"Is Dad here?" Kole asked softly instead of answering his brother's questions.

Alex shook his head. "No," he said, his eyes bright with growing anxiety. This was what confusion did to him, Kole knew. The longer you kept him in the dark, the worse off he was going to be. In a few minutes he was probably going to begin pacing. "Why?"

"Because I can't tell you anything with him here," Kole replied shortly. With a sweeping glance at their surroundings, Kole gestured for Alex to follow him upstairs, to his bedroom. Alex, Kole could tell, resisted the urge to mutter out a countless amount of questions as they made their way up the stairs, down the hallway that led to Kole's bedroom. And Kole was thankful for that. If Alex started demanding to know information, Kole didn't know how much of it he'd be able to take.

Kole closed his bedroom door behind him and watched as his brother collapsed onto his bed. Alex's eyes remained on him, waiting patiently—at least as patient as Alex had ever been before—for Kole to continue. Kole chewed on the inside of his cheek again, hating the feelings inside him. He'd never felt anything like it. Not ever. "Faye and I went walking through the woods today," he began.

Alex listened attentively as Kole explained everything. How they talked through the woods, how they reached the Government building. He even listened as Kole told him about the tug he'd had toward the building—the tug that he couldn't explain. Alex didn't say a word as Kole spoke, his eyes simply widening when Kole said something that shocked him. Kole pushed on through his story, not really knowing where to stop. The churning in his stomach continued and so did his words. Kole wondered if it would ever end.

"Wow," Alex murmured as Kole finally managed to press his lips together. "Just ... wow."

Kole nodded. "I don't know what to do." He threw his arms in the air exasperatedly. "Something is telling me that I need to check out what the hell is going on in there. I know it's wrong, and that it could get me arrested, but I feel it. I've never felt this strong of a tug before, you know?" He sighed, dragging one of his hands down his face. "But then when I see the fear on Faye's face, I wonder if I'm going crazy. Maybe I am going crazy. The old me would never do stuff like this."

The old him. Was that how he was now referring to himself? Kole hadn't really taken into consideration that he'd changed all that much. He knew that he was becoming more able to take risks, more apt to go against the Government's wishes, but he didn't know that he'd changed—at least, not enough to label an old and a new part of himself. But, maybe it was true. Maybe he had changed.

"You're not crazy," Alex assured him, standing up. Alex, Kole observed for the millionth time, always held himself with a confident grace, one that Kole could never hope to hold himself with. Kole hated the fact that he wasn't as brave or confident as his brother, that he hid in his own shadow rather than facing the world with a curled fist. He hated that he couldn't make threats sound like small-talk yet still get the message through, that he couldn't intimidate someone with a simple stare—without even glaring. Alex was someone that Kole had always looked up to. And he always would.

"I'm not?" Kole blinked. "How could you possibly—"

"Know that?" Alex snorted. "Kole, just because you've actually sparked some curiosity, doesn't mean you're crazy. It means that you actually care about something for once. And I'm happy for you. I say you go back to that building and figure out what the hell is going on. It's about time someone finally did."

"But—" Kole swallowed. "But what if I get caught? I can't do it alone, and I doubt Faye will be all that willing. You didn't see the look on her face when she saw the building today. She looked like she'd been shot. And, even then, how would I do it?"

Alex grinned, his hands reaching out to grab Kole's shoulders. He gave his brother a slight shake before smiling. "My dear brother, you have me to help you along the way. Even without Faye, you're not alone." He paused, his smile growing. "And, as to how we're going to do it, let's just say . . . I have no freaking idea."

Well, Kole thought to himself, that was a start.

Faye paced through Errika's bedroom, chewing on her fingernails.

Chewing her fingernails was something that Faye hadn't done in years. When she was younger she used to bite her nails all the time, using it as a way to cut some stress from her system. Terra and her mother told her off for the longest time, warning her that her nails were going to look disastrous. But what did Faye care what her nails looked like? They weren't really all that important, right?

And then, after Terra died, she stopped. Just like that. Faye didn't really know why she stopped, but she did. Maybe it was a subconscious need to please Terra after death. Maybe it was something else entirely. Faye had no idea.

"Faye, what's going on?" Errika demanded, her eyebrows coming together. Faye was struck by how much she resembled Alex. Faye had never seen anything like it. The arch of their eyebrows, the way they hooked their arms when they were irritated because they had no idea what was going on. "Seriously. You've been pacing for ten minutes."

Faye's feet stopped moving. She spun around, her eyes wide. "Errika, it's so big," she whispered hauntingly.

"What's so big?" Errika continued to demand. Faye could see the irritation in her friends eyes, and she wished that she could bring herself to explain what she'd seen. But the ice was still in her veins, unyielding. Faye feared it would never melt away. "Come on, babe. You know I need answers!"

"The—" Faye swallowed, shaking her head. She twisted her hands together, forcing her mouth closed as she resisted the urge to bite her nails again. No. She would not destroy her nails because she was nervous. She grew out of that habit. She grew out of it. "The building."

"What building?"

Errika huffed, hopping from her bed and grabbing onto Faye's shoulders. Giving her a rough shake, Errika said, "Come on. Answers. Now."

"The Government building," Faye choked out, her words coming out like spasms. She silently cursed herself. Why couldn't she just say it? It wasn't like anything had really happened. She and

Kole had seen the building and then they'd left. It was as simple as that. But Faye still couldn't shake the feeling that something was wrong. That something terrible had happened—and was still happening—there.

"Okay, why don't you take a sec to collect your thoughts?" Errika muttered, her nails digging into Faye's shoulders. Faye winced. Errika, unlike Faye, had long fingernails—fingernails that never managed to hurt you when they got too close. "Because I do not understand what the hell you're saying with all these fragmented sentences."

Faye nodded, gulping down her anxiety. She had to push it down, to keep it contained. If she couldn't get these words out, then she would never be able to get the problem fixed. "Kole and I found the Government building," she said finally, relieved that the words finally came out.

Errika blinked. "What?"

"We were walking in the woods and then we found the Government building," Faye whispered, her eyes scrambling for the floor. The ice shards were poking at her skin, threatening to stab at her. "There's something completely wrong with the place, Er. So wrong."

Errika brought a hand through her hair, a sheer sign that she was still confused and didn't know how to handle it. No one messed with Errika's hair—not even Errika. "You—you saw the Government building? Like, legit?" Her eyes searched mine. "What do you mean there was something wrong? What happened?"

"Nothing happened." Faye collapsed onto Errika's bed, closing her eyes. In the back of her eyelids she could see the Government building, so vast that it stretched out further than she could see. And then suddenly she was seeing inside—seeing Courtnie Featherstrom as she grabbed onto girls, an evil grin on her face as she ripped their heads from their bodies. Faye's eyes snapped open, suddenly disturbed. She did not like that mental picture. "We just saw the building. But there's something about it. I feel like something is completely wrong with the place. Like terrible things are happening there."

Errika's eyes widened. "Was it a strong feeling?"

Strong? The word seemed insignificant to how she was feeling right now. "Very." Faye nodded. "Something's going on there."

Errika's face scrunched together suddenly, and Faye's eyes widened. She'd never seen Errika make such an expression before—ever. This could not be good. "I've been thinking," she said softly, falling onto the bed beside Faye. "I've been getting the same feeling you have about the Government—it just didn't take me seeing the building to feel it. It just doesn't make sense for us to be separated. There has to be some hidden agenda. Doesn't there?"

Faye shrugged. "I have no idea."

"And that," muttered Errika, "is precisely the problem."

The papers went flying of Courtnie's desk, fluttering to the ground like dying butterflies.

Anger consumed her. No—anger was the wrong word. Fury. Fury consumed her. She'd never felt so aggravated, so infuriated, so malevolent in her entire life. She wanted to take someone's neck and snap it. She wanted to punch a wall. She wanted to set things on fire.

She wanted to tear the world apart.

"Dammit, dammit, dammit!" she shrieked over and over again. Her hands went flying, attacking everything that she could. Books crashed to the floor, as did her writing utensils. Everything went to the floor. Everything flew. Crashed. Fell. Failed. Failed her. Failed to keep standing. Failed. Failed. Failed.

She couldn't rid the awful picture of her gloating face when she realized that there was nothing in her cell. When Courtnie came up dry, the triumphant expression on her face—it was unbearable. To see that little smirk—it made Courtnie want to rip her head off and throw it into a fiery pit. She knew exactly what Courtnie was feeling and she'd taken advantage of it. She'd made it worse.

And she loved every second of it.

She was up to something, Courtnie knew. Courtnie knew that she had been planning something—could sense it from the start. But there was no way to prove it, no way to show her brother that his daughter was no better than she had been since they brought her in so many years ago. There was no way to unmask her. To show Fortis that his little girl was nothing more than a hindrance that needed to be disposed of. That his little girl was going to rip apart Cesve by the seams.

She would not let the world that her family built fall apart. She refused to let a simpleton bring down everything she'd worked so hard to achieve.

Especially not her.

But nothing was going as Courtnie planned. First the cameras were taken away. What next? What did she have up her sleeves? Courtnie knew that there was something coming—and what was coming next was going to be big. So big, Courtnie had to wonder if she would be able to recover from it. Would Cesve be able to recover? Or would this be the time when she finally got her wish—the secrets of the Government would be unleashed?

Courtnie's fist landed on her desk. No. She could not let that happen. She could not let that happen. She. Could. Not. Let. That. Happen.

She lifted her fist, ready the punch her desk again, but suddenly the door to her office flew open. She spun around, agape as her eyes latched onto the figure standing in the doorway. Fortis stared back at her, his eyes wide. His fingers curled onto the doorknob tightly, so tightly that his hands turned red, making his knuckles look ghostly white. He looked horrified, Courtnie observed. Horrified and suspicious.

That was not a very good combination.

"What are you doing?" he demanded, his grip on the doorknob tightening. "Courtnie—what is wrong with you?"

"I—" Her mouth snapped shut and she swallowed. Something in her brother's expression told her that he was no longer going to listen to a single thing that she said. She'd lost him. But, she had to try. "I went to the prison wards," she said, regaining her composure. She stood tall, crossing her arms irritably over her chest. "Do you know who I went to see?"

"You need to stop this," Fortis muttered, pushing away from the door. He stepped into the room, a guarded expression etched onto his features. "You need to leave her alone. You've gained absolutely nothing—in fact, you're losing more than you're winning."

"She's ruining everything!" Courtnie hissed. "Why can't you see that, Fortis? She's tearing down Cesve by the seams. She's already taken away the cameras—"

"Do you hear how you sound right now?" Fortis demanded, his voice cooling. Courtnie blanched, unused to this. No matter how mad she made him, Fortis never talked to her this way. Like they were strangers. Like they were two worlds apart. Like they were enemies. "How do you think she managed to get the computers down, little sister? She's been locked up in a cell. A cell that I've had to keep her in because you don't have the decency to let her go."

"She's paying the price for her crimes," Courtnie seethed, her hands curling into fists. "It is no different than any other perpetrator."

"It's completely different!" The acid in his voice dripped onto the floor, slithering its way toward her and through her skin. She could feel the poison threatening to take over her body, her mind. She'd never seen Fortis so angry, so hateful. This was not the brother she knew. "You would have her killed if you could. You would kill your own blood—just to keep the name of Cesve alive. How does that not disgust you?"

"I am ashamed that she is my blood," Courtnie spat. "She is nothing to me. Nothing. All she is is a little pest that needs to be taken care of. If you weren't blind with this apparent love you have for the girl, then maybe you'd be able to see that she's nothing but a hindrance. A danger to everything that we stand for?"

"We?" Fortis's voice grew soft. "We, Courtnie? There is no we. There hasn't been for a long time. This is all about you. You and your conceit."

Without another word, Fortis turned and stalked out of the room, slamming the door behind him.

Faye lay back on her bed, her eyes blankly staring at the ceiling. She wasn't really seeing anything; at least she wasn't really seeing the speckled wall. All she could really see was the expression on Kole's face when he saw the Government building. The absolute wonder, the curiosity. The need to know what was inside. She felt it too, she did. But it was shoved down deep inside her, locked back in a box with a key that she'd lost in her system. It was devoured by the utter conclusion that something was wrong. That something was completely and terribly wrong.

But if that were the case, wouldn't that be more of a reason to figure out what was going on?

But she couldn't figure out what was going on. That would mean going back to the building, back to the source of all this turmoil. That would mean feeling the ice again, which took so long to get rid of in the first place. And as it was, she could still feel the dull pressure of the ice threatening to poke back out if she thought about this for too long.

Faye sat up, rubbing her eyes. The thoughts within her were battling out, threatening to tear her apart from the inside. They were such conflicting thoughts. Desert the idea of the Government building, or go back and find out what was wrong? Go back and feel the ice, or fall back only to hate herself for not figuring out the problem before it was too late?

"Faye, hon?"

Her eyes barely had time to glide over to her bedroom door before Mary was pulling it open, standing in the doorway. She smiled at her daughter. "Dinner's ready," she said politely, her smile growing. "Will you be joining us tonight?"

Lately Faye had declined eating with her two family members because she hated the sight of Kat. Just seeing Kat's face would make her so angry that she feared she would burst. The day after she found the box in her room, Faye had almost broken her plate from gripping it too tightly. It was shocking to even her mother that she was capable of such emotions. Faye was usually a mellow girl—no explosions, whatsoever.

That was, until Kat brought out the worst within her.

At least, Faye hoped it was the worst.

"I'll be there in a minute," said Faye, her lips pricking into a small smile. "I promise I won't scream this time."

Her mother smiled largely, happy (at least Faye thought) that Faye was finally seeing reason. "Thank you, hon." She moved to leave and then paused. "I'm really sorry about what Kat did. Did you want me to take the box up to the attic?"

Faye's eyes flicked to the box, hidden under a stack of clean clothes. She'd tried to hide the box away, unable to look at it, but unable to bring it back to the attic where all of Terra's other things were kept. The thought of setting the box with all of Terra's other things—she couldn't bear it. Just looking at all of her things . . . Faye didn't want to risk it.

So there the box sat.

"No," she whispered, surprising herself. She wanted the box out of her room. Why didn't she just take the offer? "That's okay." She smiled fleetingly. "I'll be right there, okay?"

Mary nodded before leaving the room. Faye hopped off her bed, stretching her arms out. Her eyes tiptoed toward the box, locking on it. Faye wanted to look away, to go downstairs to where the food was probably already on the table, but she couldn't bring herself to. Something about the box called to her. Screamed at her, even. It was like Terra was ushering her to open it, to look inside.

Something inside Faye cracked. The next thing she knew, her feet were moving across the floor, toward the box. She had no control of her movements, no control of her body. She felt tears burn in her eyes—but not because she was sad. She was terrified. Terrified that something inside her had taken over. Something that she couldn't control.

Faye knelt down in front of the box, pushing the clothes away. She pulled the box toward her, her stomach lurching. She didn't want to open it. She really didn't want to open it.

But she did.

Inside it where Terra's writing things. Her schoolwork, her notebooks. Anything that needed pen and paper. Faye reached into the box, pulling out Terra's Geometry book. She remembered how Terra used to sit on the couch, scrawling into the notebook effortlessly, her math book by her side. Though, she never seemed to really look at the math book. It was like she didn't need it to answer her problems.

Faye flipped the book open. Inside was a message, stating that it was Terra's property. Seeing Terra's handwriting—her beautiful handwriting—made Faye want to throw up. The memories were threatening to overwhelm her.

She flipped another page.

And stared.

There were no Geometry problems, no sign that this was a math-work book at all. Faye, turned to the cover, thinking that she might have read the title wrong. Maybe it actually said English homework, and in a rush Faye had misread.

But she didn't. It said Geometry.

Faye flipped back to the writing, her stomach hurting now. She began reading the words, her stomach dropping with each syllable, with each letter.

Lies. Everything that we've been taught are lies. The false promises, the false statements fed to us by non-other than the people who are supposed to be sworn to looking over us: the Government.

They don't want to protect us. There is no beast on the other side. There's no such thing as this monster that will devour you if you so much as take a step into its territory. They're just lies. Figments of our imagination. Lies. Lies. Lies.

I never believed that there was a beast on other side. Not even when I was a little girl. The thought seemed preposterous—completely stupid. If there were really a beast, it would have overcome the Gate's borders. And if it couldn't even do that, why did everyone have to be afraid?

But now I know. I know.

I know everything.

What's on the other side? That's the question that all girls have been asking since the beginning of time. The Gate has always been here. To "protect" us. But little does everyone know that this Gate hasn't been here forever. Someone built it. And it wasn't that legendary figure that people conjured up to answer their questions. No. Regular people built it. Both girls and the creatures on the other side.

What are those creatures?

Boys.

Faye dropped the book, her hands shaking. The Geometry book snapped shut, collapsing on the floor with a small thud. It looked so innocent from the way it was lying—like it only held simple problems from school.

But it held so much more than that. Faye knew that now.

Terra knew. Terra knew everything. She knew about the boys, she knew what the Government was doing. She knew. She knew.

With a trembling hand, Faye pulled her cell phone out of her butt pocket. Without thinking of what she was doing, she dialed Kole's number. She brought the phone to her ear, closing her eyes. She could feel the tears burn there, just like she could feel the ice falling into her stomach.

When Kole picked up the phone with a casual greeting, Faye sucked in a breath. "I'm coming over," she said simply. "I'm bringing Errika with me. We need to talk. And we need to get into the Government building."

With that, she snapped the phone shut and stood up, moving toward the door and opening it. With one last glance at the fallen Geometry book, Faye pulled the door shut, heading downstairs toward where her family members were waiting.

CHAPTER 13

"**I**s this it?"

Faye barely glanced in Errika's direction as she nodded her head. Kole's house stood before them, daring them to enter with its eyes. It had taken forever to find the place, Faye thought bitterly. A lot longer than she would have hoped. She thought that she might be able to recall the way from the last time, despite the hurriedness of the visit. But, Faye's memory wasn't as intact as she'd thought. "Yes," she said simply.

Her nails dug into the Geometry notebook so deeply that it left indents in the material. The ice had turned to steaming acid, burning her insides, threatening to turn her to ashes. Her stomach clenched as she thought yet again of her sister's handwriting, the complete familiarity of the writing on the pages. And the words. The words on the paper.

Those threatened to consume her whole.

Faye gulped down her anxiety and hopped onto the porch, knocking on the door. Kole had assured her that everything would be fine, that his father wouldn't be home until late. He told her that the whole group of boys she met earlier would be there, but they would be on their best behavior. He told her that Seth would not be outraged again.

But how could he be so sure?

"This looks like that chick's house," Errika muttered breathlessly, coming to stand beside Faye on the steps. "You know, that really annoying one at the Campout."

"I know," Faye said softly.

"Are you okay?" Errika asked, her eyebrows creasing. "You seem like you're going to faint."

Faye shrugged, gulping down her unease. So many questions were circulating through her mind. How had Terra known? What happened for her to realize just how corrupt their government was? How had she found out about the boys at all? What did she do about it?

Did she really kill herself?

That was the question that tortured her most of all. If Terra knew the darkest secrets of the Government—if she threatened to expose them—what would the Government do about it? Faye didn't doubt for a moment that they would kill her. They would kill her mercilessly in order to protect their terrible secrets they preferred to keep hidden.

So did Terra really kill herself? Or had they murdered her and made it look like an accident?

Suddenly the front door opened, cutting off Faye's thoughts. Kole stood before her, his hair ruffled like he'd just woken up. And maybe he had. She had no idea what time boys went to bed, or what time they woke up. For all she knew they were nocturnal.

"Faye," he said briskly, concern clear in his tone and in his eyes. "You're here."

Faye nodded, gesturing to Errika. "Can we come in?"

Kole nodded, stepping aside and gesturing her inside with a brisk wave of the hand. "Yes," he said immediately, his tone and gaze firm. "Definitely."

Faye stepped inside, followed by a much more enthusiastic Errika. Faye swallowed down her impatience as her friend squealed about being in a boy's house for the first time, and how weird everything looked. She could barely hear Kole explaining that the house was weird even for boys—something about the place used to being a hotel? She couldn't be sure.

"Are they here?" a voice called from the end of the hall. Faye's eyes flicked up, her mind finally coming into focus. They were in front of the sun room, and she could see the boys lounging on the furniture. Alex, the source of the voice, was standing a few feet away, a curious expression on his face. "Did they say what they were coming for?"

"They're here," Kole said softly, sliding past Faye and into the sun room. Faye and Errika followed immediately. Faye couldn't help but notice the ease in which Errika was acting; the way she walked without any tension in her shoulders, and how there wasn't a nervous expression on her face. When Faye came here she'd been scared out of her mind. Errika looked like she'd walked into an old friend's house that she hadn't seen in years but was comfortable all the same.

Faye wished, not for the first time, that she was more like her.

Faye caught Kole's gaze and struggled to smile. It didn't work, though. Not that Faye would have expected it to. Her insides were torn and frayed, withered by the beating they'd just endured. She didn't know how much more she would be able to take. She really didn't.

"Faye," Kole said softly as Errika got comfortable on the couch—smack in the middle of the group of boys. "What's going on?"

In answer, Faye held out Terra's geometry book. The boys stared at it blankly for a moment, uncomprehending. But why would they comprehend? To them it was just a book with paper—nothing that mattered. But it did matter. It mattered so much. "This," she drew out, her voice on the border of shaking, "is what's going on."

Errika's eyes widened as her eyes landed on the notebook. She, Faye thought distantly, knew exactly who this belonged to. And now she knew why Faye was acting strangely. That was one of the many things Faye loved about Errika: She caught on so fast.

"My sister died seven years ago," Faye began, her eyes locking on the floor. "My mom and I couldn't bear to see her stuff in her room, but we couldn't bear the thought of throwing her stuff out either. So we stashed it away in the attic. My younger sister was told to stay away from there, but she's not one to listen. So she went in there, found my sister's stuff, and then dragged one of the boxes down to my room just to mock my pain.

"At first I just kept the box hidden away. I couldn't bring myself to really do anything with it. But then today I opened the box and pulled out this." She gestured with the geometry notebook. "It's supposed to be my sister's geometry homework. But it's not. It's filled with my sister's rants about how contaminated the government is and how she knows how corrupt it is. And she's constantly talking about boys. That means that she knew about you guys before any of us did—and she knows Cesve's secrets."

At first all anyone did was stare, their mouths slack. They didn't understand, Faye thought dully, unable to even feel disappointment. All she could feel was the acid in her veins, the acid that had a name: Terra.

And then all of a sudden Errika was on her feet, gasping. "Holy shit!" she exclaimed. Her eyes scanned around at the boys. "Do you not get it? Terra knew. She knew."

"And?"

It was Seth. As promised, he did not look furious as he had last time; in fact, he was as composed as Kole and the others. It shouldn't have surprised her so much to see the boy calm. It was possible for someone to be other than angry. Everyone got angry sometimes.

Faye watched as Seth stood up, his thumbs hooked in the pockets of his jeans. "What difference does it make if this Terra person knew? You guys know—and the Government isn't anywhere near losing its power is it?"

"It makes a difference because my sister killed herself," Faye whispered. Her eyes scanned over the boys, watching their expressions change. Shock flitted through their eyes.

Errika's mouth dropped slightly before she regained composure. "Faye," she said softly, her eyes full of sympathy. "Do you think—?"

"If Terra knew about what the Government was doing, she wasn't going to just sit there and let them continue what they were doing," Faye said, her voice gaining strength. A pride deep within her was sprouting to the surface, and she suddenly felt like she did the day Terra and her team won the soccer tournament. Proud that her sister had been the leader in something so great. "She isn't—wasn't—the type of person to sit back and let everything crumble to the ground. She would have done something about it."

"I still don't get what difference this makes," Seth grumbled, bringing a hand through his hair. Faye could see the deep concern within him, the struggle to understand.

From the corner of her eye she could see Alex moving toward Kole, putting a hand on his shoulder. It was like a protective maneuver, like he thought that an invisible force was going to come take them out and he had to keep Kole from falling to the ground. This information unnerved him, Faye observed. And why wouldn't it? It unnerved her, too.

"Seth," said Alex suddenly, his voice rusty as though he hadn't drunken any water in days. "If the Government knew what her sister was doing...."

Faye's eyes should have been on Seth or Alex, but they weren't. They were on Kole. He was squinting at the floor, trying to figure out what was going on. He was as confused as the rest of them, Faye knew that. And she also knew that he'd be the first one to figure it out (besides his brother, of course). She didn't know how she knew that, but she did. It was like she'd known Kole forever—had studied his habits and grown used to them.

A moment later Kole's eyes widened and his head shot up. His eyes met hers, and she could see the utter discomfort in them. Like the place he'd once called home was no longer a safe place to be. "They would have had her removed," he whispered. He cleared his throat, closed his eyes, and then re-opened them again. "Faye, are you saying that you don't think Terra killed herself at all?"

"That's exactly what I'm saying."

Faye could feel it. Could feel the utter sense that something was off, wrong. The pieces were finally beginning to come together. No wonder no one ever understood why Terra killed herself—she hadn't. She was murdered by the Government. The Government had killed her because she'd gotten close to unleashing all of their secrets on the world. They'd rather push a girl off a cliff and fake a suicide than admit their wrong-doings and fix the mistakes they'd made.

They'd killed her sister. They'd taken her away.

They'd made her think that her sister deserted her.

That was what finally pushed Faye over the edge. The fact that they made Faye borderline loath Terra, made her believe that she'd deserted her for this thing called Death. They'd made her believe that Terra had decided they weren't worthy of staying with anymore. They'd made her believe so many things.

So many lies.

Suddenly Errika was in front of her, holding onto her shoulders. Her eyes bore into Faye's with such determination that Faye almost pulled away. Something about the gaze terrified her. "Faye," Errika muttered hurriedly. "Are you sure the Government—?"

"Yes." Faye nodded. "It makes sense, doesn't it?"

Errika stepped back. Faye's eyes flicked between her and Alex, unable to help but observe the utter identicalness between the two. Despite the feelings swirling within her, she couldn't help but be amazed. How was it that these two could look so alike when they lived in separate worlds?

"If the Government is willing to kill people to keep their secrets safe," came a voice from the couch, "then who knows how terrible those secrets are?"

All eyes shot down. Terence eased off the couch's cushion, standing next to Seth. Zander was the only one sitting now, so out of place in this scenery. He was blank-faced, as though he was miles away from here. Like he had more important things to do than sit here and talk about the Government's secrets.

"That's the question I'd like to know the answer to." Alex glowered. "The fact that they'd kill—"

"It's not a fact yet," Seth pointed out. He shot an apologetic glance in Faye's direction before continuing. "We have no idea if Terra really killed herself or not. We're just assuming the Government did it because of Terra's writings. But—what if she actually did kill herself? What then?"

"Then she did the exact opposite of what she'd always promised she wouldn't do," Faye replied instantly, her voice surprisingly strong when she felt so weak. "She promised she'd always be there for me. Throwing herself off a cliff would damper that, wouldn't it? And she always kept her promises."

"That's true," Errika murmured from beside her. "The girl never told a lie."

No, she didn't lie. That was true. But she had secrets.

And apparently dark ones.

What world had Terra been living in, really? What had she been doing when Faye sat there coloring in school? Was she breaking into places that she shouldn't have been entering? Was she researching the Government and its history? Was she risking her life every single day just to show the Government up?

Had she lived her last moments in fear?

Seth fell silent, his eyes grabbing the floor. Kole stepped away from his brother and moved toward her, reaching out and putting a hand on her arm. Her skin tingled where he touched, through the fabric of her shirt. "Faye," he said softly. "What are we going to do about this?"

Faye's eyes reached his. "We need to get into the Government building," she replied, her tone kept neutral despite the turmoil within. "They're hiding something else—I can feel it."

Kole nodded. "I felt it, too, when we were at the building. Like they were hiding something else. Something big."

"What can be bigger than hiding the other part of humanity?" Errika thought aloud. Faye knew that she wasn't really directing the question to anyone. Errika thought better when she was talking. That was just how she worked.

"That's what I would like to know," Alex grumbled. "Dammit. Why does this have to be so confusing?"

"Confusing or not," Kole drawled, giving his brother a short grin as he patted him on the shoulder, "we need a plan. And a good one if we don't want to get caught."

"But," Errika began, her voice growing so serious that Faye turned to her with concern, "how are we supposed to create a plan when we don't even know what we're fighting against?"

The wind blew through the trees, swaying the branches back and forth eerily as Faye made her way down the street. Her feet slapped against the pavement, the only noise besides the leaves ruffles in the night. Everything had a shadow. A deep, dark shadow that threatened to devour Faye whole.

Faye was never one to be afraid the dark. While all the other girls cowered under their blankets, needing nightlights to keep the scary monsters away, she'd been fine. Whether it was because she felt secure with her mother and Terra around, she wasn't quite sure. But that didn't matter now. What mattered now was that her once steady shield against the terrifying-ness of the darkness was gone.

She was frightened.

Every shadow was a Government official coming after her. Every squirrel was someone getting ready to wrap their hands around her throat, to throw her in the prison wards—or worse. Maybe when they found her they wouldn't bring her to the prison wards at all. Maybe they would do what they did with Terra. Maybe they'd throw her off a cliff and make it look like suicide.

Falling. Falling. Falling.

Faye's feet stopped moving and suddenly she couldn't breathe. Just the thought of falling—gravity pulling her faster and faster toward her upcoming death—rendered her catatonic. She couldn't move. Couldn't do anything. Fear gripped her with its iron grasp, threatening to suffocate her. There was no escape from this madness. No escape at all.

But maybe there was.

"You all know the plan," Kole said before they left the house. "Be here tomorrow by seven o'clock."

Faye's feet began moving again with a new bounce in her step. The plan. That was what would keep her going. No matter how much turmoil she had within her, no matter how much fear she had broiling deep inside her gut—she would pull through with this plan. This was the only way she could ever hope to get justice for what the Government did to Terra.

"Find anything you might think is useful. It doesn't have to be much. If you have a camera, bring it. This is only reconnaissance. We don't know enough to go in there with a battle cry. We have to play this smart."

Play it smart. That meant that Faye couldn't run in there and attack for all she had. Under any normal circumstance that would have been okay with her. Faye was never one to do anything rash or stupid. She kept her head. But these people had murdered her sister. They'd taken Terra away from her. And for that they all deserved to die.

"We'll go in through the front doors," Alex had said, his arms crossed over his chest. "And let's pray that they don't have eyes on us. Since the cameras are down, I doubt they will. But we never know what's on the inside. So for Christ's sake, don't do anything stupid. Keep your heads low. Blend in. And split up. The buddy system isn't going to work on this one."

"But how will we keep in contact?" Errika had immediately shrieked. She'd grabbed onto Faye's arm, her jaw tight with concern. "What if something happens and we need help?"

That had been one of Faye's concerns, too. When Alex said that they had to split up, Faye wanted to laugh in his face. There was no way she was stepping into a building—one likely to be guarded heavily—without someone there with her. It was so foolish. But Alex had a point when he said, "If an official sees us in a group, isn't that going to be a bit skeptical?" So as long as she had a cell phone where she could call someone for help, then Faye could live with being by herself in the Government building. She didn't really have a choice.

Faye's eyes flicked behind her, to her sides, and then back ahead of her before she crossed the street. The quietness of the night did nothing but set her on edge. She realized how suspicious it probably looked for her to be out here at this time of night, and she wished that there was something she could do about it. But there was nothing. She and Errika hadn't gotten back to their side of the Gate until an hour before. And they had to play it up to Errika's mom, making it seem like everything was okay.

And now Faye had to play it up to her mother.

"So it's settled then," Kole had murmured, his eyes locking on Faye's. "Everyone understands the game plan?"

And everyone had nodded.

Faye brought a hand through her hair, letting out a long breath of air. She had to get home, say a few words to Mary, and then she had to get upstairs to her bedroom. Maybe then she'd be able to find more information through Terra. Maybe Terra had done what they did. Maybe she'd gone to the Government building—how else would she know everything?

There had to be something.

There had to be.

"Faye, where have you been?"

Faye felt her stomach drop as her eyes met her mother's. Mary's arms crossed over her chest, her eyes narrowed sternly. Faye had expected her mother to be agitated that she got home late—she'd told her that she'd be home an hour ago. But she hadn't expected her to be as angry as she was.

"M-mom," Faye stuttered in surprise. She gripped Terra's note-book tightly in her hand, praying that Mary wouldn't demand to see it. That would only tear the woman apart. And Faye did not want that to happen. "I'm sorry I'm late—"

"Where have you been, Faye?" Mary demanded again, her eyes flashing. "I've been worried sick about you."

"I've been at Errika's," Faye said softly, her eyes pleading with her mother's to just drop the subject. She needed to get upstairs. She needed to look through Terra's things. She needed to plan. She couldn't just stand here and deal with conflict. She couldn't. "I'm sorry, I meant to call—"

"You ran out of the house without telling me where you were going," her mother said, her voice cool. "I'm lenient with you, Faye, because you never do anything wrong. But we've always agreed that you would tell me when you're leaving. Instead, you made me frantic, calling around the house. I thought someone had taken you."

"I'm sorry." Faye's eyes burned. She never got in trouble with her mother, and didn't like the feeling of being spoken to like she was . . . well, Kat. "I really am. I was in a rush and completely forgot to tell you. I'm really sorry, Mom. I promise it will never happen again."

Mary stared at her for a long time. Faye bit her lip, silently praying that she would let this slip and give her another chance. It wasn't like she ever got in trouble—like her mother said, she never did anything wrong. But for her to just leave the house without telling her . . . it was a huge mistake.

Faye mentally slapped herself. The last time she left without telling her mother was the day she saw Terra's body. Mary had been too depressed to reprimand her about leaving the house by herself, but Faye could see the disapproval in her eyes. And now it was the only rule really held over Faye's head.

And she'd broken it.

"I'm really sorry, Mom," Faye whispered. "Really."

Mary sighed. "If you ever leave this house without telling me again ... you'll be grounded."

Faye smiled. "All right." She paused. "I'm going to go up to my room, okay?"

Faye gave her mother a quick hug before running up the stairs and into her bedroom. She didn't bother to kick off her shoes as she scurried over to the cardboard box, picking it up and hurrying over to her bed. She dropped it onto her comforter, breathing heavily. Anticipation slithered through her like poison. She didn't know what was worse. The fear of the unknown or the excitement of finally figuring things out.

She held her breath, opening the box and peering inside. All of Terra's things greeted her, flashing like stars. Faye knew that there was nothing else in the Geometry book. The boys, Errika, and she had gone over every page. They were just rants. Mostly her saying that the Government had to be stopped and that if someone wouldn't do something about it she would. There were also hints that she had done something about it, but the notebook ran about before any explanations were given.

It was safe to say that Terra had a lot of complaints about the Government.

Faye pulled out another notebook, this one labeled History. She was disappointed to find that this was actually history work--it proved so when she answered questions about the legend of the Gate with answers that schools would have wanted. Faye could sense Terra's sarcasm as she answered the questions, could practically feel her annoyance of having to write something down that wasn't true. And she empathized. She wasn't sure if she herself would be able to write something for history ever again.

Despite this, Faye flipped through the pages, unable to help herself. There was something about the way Terra wrote that captivated her. Maybe it was because Faye wanted to feel connected to her sister again. Or maybe it was the passion in which she wrote with. Faye read her essays for class without even glancing up from the paper. Even though each paper reeked with lies, Faye couldn't look away. She could almost believe the words written there.

Which, she supposed, had been the point.

Faye tossed the book to the side, pulling out a folder. These were filled with Terra's sketches, ones that Faye assumed to be fantasy worlds with fantasy creatures. She remembered trying to sneak a peek at these sketches when Terra drew them, wanting to know how well her older sister drew. Terra would always hide the pictures away, reminding Faye how important privacy was.

And now Faye knew why.

These weren't fantasy worlds at all. They were pictures of the other side, pictures of boys. Pictures of boys and girls together. Faye pulled a certain drawing toward her, drawn in in a way that she couldn't explain. It was a simple sketch—not much detail had been put in. A girl and a boy stood together, hand in hand as they stared out over a city. Faye's eyes drifted to the top of the drawing and read the words, The Gate keeps them apart—but not for long.

Faye closed her eyes for a moment before letting the drawing fall back into the folder. She pulled out another sheet of paper, sighing shakily. The amount of passion Terra had for this—it was unreal. To think that this whole time Terra knew—she knew—

Faye's thoughts cut short as her eyes reached the next paper. It wasn't a sketch like the others. It was an outline. No, not an outline. A blueprint. A blueprint of what?

The Government building.

Terra had either drawn or photocopied exactly what the inside of the Government building looked like. A complete layout of each room was there. There was the security room, the offices of Courtnie and Fortis (whoever that was). And then there were other rooms that Faye couldn't even make sense of.

But there was one thing that Faye was sure of. They were no longer going into the Government building blind. Terra had given them sight.

And for that, Faye could have kissed her. But with one look around the room, Faye felt a lump in her throat. Terra wasn't there to kiss.

"Is everyone here?"

Faye's eyes flicked around the room, pursing her lips. Kole stood beside her, his arm brushing hers. Seth and Terence stood close to one another, their expressions grave. Errika stood on Faye's other side, next to Alex who was playing leader. That was fine by Faye. He, unlike the rest of them, seemed to have the slightest idea as to what they were doing.

"I still can't believe Zander isn't coming," Seth muttered.

Zander backed out at the last minute, saying that he had to take care of his brother. Faye couldn't blame him. If Kat were a nicer person and if she didn't make Faye want to bite her head off, then she'd want to stay home and take care of her, too.

"Well, you better believe it," Alex said coolly. "We're one man down, so that means more ground we have to cover. Which means we have to be even more careful." He paused and gestured to his cell phone. "Does everyone have a copy of the blueprint."

Everyone nodded. Faye took a deep breath, her eyes sliding over to Kole. He smiled at her, and suddenly Faye felt at ease. Like they weren't about to go into the building that everyone feared. Like they weren't about to do something that could get them thrown in the prison wards for life—or worse. Like they weren't doing something really, really stupid.

"Now, remember which rooms you're covering," Alex said sternly, shoving his phone into his pocket. "And please, please, if there's any sign of danger, call someone and get your ass out of there. None of us are getting arrested today."

She felt Kole tense beside her. In an instant a rush of emotions threatened to consume her. Suddenly she wanted to grab his arm comfortingly, to assure him that everything would be all right. To hug him, even. She didn't know where these feelings were coming from, or even what they were, but they were terrifying.

Alex sighed, bringing a hand through his hair. "We've got flashlights, cameras, cell phones, and flash drives in case we come across computers, right?"

Everyone nodded.

"Can anyone think of anything else that we might be missing?"

"Can't we, like, bring a knife or something in order to protect ourselves?" Errika asked, cocking an eyebrow. "I mean, if I run into a guard who thinks they're going to put their grubby hands on me—"

"Having a weapon and being caught could have us put to death," Alex said immediately, shaking his head. "Fighting them would do nothing for us. So weaponry would defeat the point."

Errika sighed in defeat. Faye's eyebrows rose in surprise. Errika was never one to give up easily when she thought she was right. Even when the other person made sense. This was odd, Faye observed. Very, very odd.

"Is everyone ready?"

Faye nodded along with everyone else, feeling the anticipation grow. This was actually happening. They were actually going into the Government building. She couldn't believe it. She just couldn't believe it. She was going to the place that was at fault for all of this. She was going to the place that Terra despised.

She was going to the Government building.

Alex let out another deep sigh and put on a smile. "Well then," he said lightly, gesturing to the front door. "Let's go!"

CHAPTER 14

Faye was tense as she followed Errika and the boys through the woods, her feet making the underbrush crinkle beneath her feet.

Everything around her seemed so loud. Like if they did more than tiptoe their way toward the Government building, they would be found and shot. The animals skittering around the forest did nothing but set her on edge. She found herself constantly spinning around, praying that no official had found them.

And, luckily, no official had. For the past half hour of walking, everyone remained safe. Alex and Errika took the lead, standing the front of the group. It looked so natural for them to stand together, Faye couldn't help but notice. Like there was something that pulled the two together, intertwining and binding them. Faye didn't know what the bind was, but there certainly was one.

"How much longer until we get there?" Seth asked softly from in front of her, his eyes shooting over to Kole. Kole stood next to Faye, his arm nearly brushing hers. "Are we close?"

"We're getting closer," Kole said, shrugging. "I don't know how much longer, though."

Faye could feel it—that they were getting closer. The small hairs on her arms were sticking up, shivers running down her spine. The sense of something wrong was beginning to swim through her again, and in a moment Faye knew that the ice would be freezing her veins. But she would have to push past it—the ice. It was the only way that she would be able to make it through the Government building.

Faye didn't have many rooms to cover—at least, not as many as the others. Whether it was because they didn't think she was capable of going through as many rooms, or whether it was because they knew what effect the Government building had on her, Faye wasn't sure. But she didn't care. It made it less likely for her to screw up with fewer rooms.

"Are you going to be okay?" Kole whispered in her ear. "I know what the Government building did to you last time."

Faye gulped down her unease and nodded. "I don't have a choice," she replied. "They killed Terra."

And that was the only thing that kept her feet moving. The only thing that made her shake off her fears of being caught, of being murdered by the Government. The fact that they took her sister away from her. The fact that they would be something so demented, so vile, so cruel. Everyone had a right to know what their Government was doing to them. She would finish what Terra started.

No matter what. She would finish what her sister died for.

"Guys."

Faye looked up along with everyone else as Alex pointed forward, and her insides froze up immediately—so much that she couldn't breathe. She took deep breaths, struggling to get the air in as she stared down the Government building, willing the ice in her veins to melt. It had to melt. She had to go inside. She had to succeed. She had to. She had to.

"We're here," Alex breathed.

They were there.

She sifted through the video clips left by the cameras, her hand resting on her chin. So many images were captured on the cameras, so much surveillance to go through. But she didn't really care about any of that. All she cared about were the boy and the girl that met at the Gate.

The two met constantly, she'd come to know. And then the girl had gone onto the other side. When the girl and boy hugged, she almost squealed with excitement. The thought that the two genders were actually together—together—She just couldn't believe it.

She clicked onto a new clip, a small smile at the tip of her lips. The two had become so close to one another. She could see it so plainly. The way they walked next to each other, the way they spoke to each other with ease. The traces of fear from when they first met each other were gone completely. And she was glad. The closer they got, the more likely they would be to want to stop the Government from what it was doing.

There was strength in numbers.

She clicked onto the next clip, shocked to find a group of four boys and two girls walking together in the woods. The girl and boy from the previous clips were recognizable immediately, but the others? She felt her stomach curl in on itself in anticipation as she watched the group walk through the woods, wondering where they were going. They were caught on the cameras near the Government building. Did that mean—?

They disappeared from the camera's view. With a new found determination, she selected the next closest camera, the one right in front of the Government building. They couldn't be there, she thought. They had no idea where to find it—it wasn't possible.

She gasped as the group appeared in front of the Government building's yard, huddled together, their heads turning to make sure that no one was watching them. A boy stood out from the rest of them, holding up a piece of paper; the paper looked familiar, but she could not imagine why....

Suddenly the group was moving through the grass, toward the Government building's doors. Her eyes widened as she watched, unable to look away as the boy who stood out from the rest pulled the door open and gestured for everyone to go inside. One by one they disappeared inside the building. One by one they put in jeopardy everything the Government worked for.

Perfect.

Faye crept through the halls of the Government building, praying that an official wouldn't come and find her there. She'd been on her own for the past twenty minutes, slipping into rooms and taking pictures with her camera before moving on. Luckily, no one had seen her so far. She honestly didn't know what she would do if someone did.

She wondered how the others were doing. She hadn't gotten any calls, so that was a good sign. Or was it? What if they were trapped, unable to get to their cell phone but still needing help? What if they were being towed to the prisoner wards as she walked?

No. She had to stop thinking like this. Thinking like this would only cause panic, and panic was something that Faye could not afford.

She wouldn't panic. She wouldn't.

Faye immediately broke her promise to herself as she suddenly heard distant footsteps. She spun around, wielding her flashlight like a weapon, desperately trying to hide the camera around her neck. There was no use, however. It was a bulking thing. She inwardly cursed her mother for buying such fancy electronics.

A figure appeared and Faye felt her heart stop. She'd been found.

And she didn't have time to call for help.

Kole stared into the room, uncomprehending.

It was a room set up much like a classroom—exactly like a classroom, actually. Rows of desks with a projector in the front of the room. It wasn't playing anything at the moment, but Kole knew that soon it would be. On a chalkboard behind the projector were the words, Next class at ten o'clock in need handwriting. And, with one glance at his cell phone Kole knew that the next class would start in five minutes.

But why? Why would there be classrooms here? What was the point of that? There were classrooms in Cesve for the boys and girls to learn. None of it made any sense.

Then again, none of the Government made sense anymore.

Kole knew that he should have been moving away, running so that he could get to the next room he had to cover before anyone saw him. But something about the utter normalness of the room threw him off. He brought his hands up, camera in hand, about to take a picture when—

"Come on, this way!" a gruff voice sounded from the distance. Kole's eyes widened as the voice grew closer. "Hurry up, we haven't got all night!"

Kole felt his feet freeze as the voice grew closer and he heard a mass group of footsteps. There were definitely more than five people coming. Kole glanced toward the classroom and suddenly it clicked: There was a full class coming to learn.

Suddenly the group appeared. Kole braced himself, fear trickling down his spine as he watched the group come. Something about the people there ... it was depressing. The way their heads hung as though they'd lost hope; the way their feet dragged as though they hated the prospect of where they were going. Whatever was going on ... it wasn't good.

"You!"

Kole's eyes snapped upward as the man with the gruff voice regarded him. He was tall, muscular, and had a goatee. That was all Kole could bring himself to concentrate on. The fact that he was tall, muscular, and had a goatee. If he thought about the fact that the man in front of him worked for the Government, he would fall apart. And he couldn't afford to do that.

"Are you mute?" the Government worker demanded, sounding thoroughly annoyed.

"N-no," Kole stuttered out, struggling to keep his eyes from widening. He prayed that the man hadn't heard the stutter. Otherwise he was screwed.

"Wow, they warned me you were skittish but I didn't think you would be this skittish," the worker mused, bringing a hand to his goatee. Kole could see the group watch him curiously. The group, Kole couldn't help but notice, was made out of boys and girls.

"What?" Kole asked, his eyes widening now. What did the man mean by that? Had the Government told the man about him? If so—why not just grab him from the start?

"You're the person here to observe the class today, aren't you?" the worker demanded, his eyebrows furrowing.

Kole didn't know what possessed him to do what he did, but he found himself standing straighter and nodding. "Of course," he lied smoothly, unsure of where the sudden confidence was coming from. Maybe it was the intense fear of being found out and killed. Or maybe it was curiosity.

"Where's your notebook?"

"My what?"

The Government worker stared at him. "You need a notebook to take down notes, right?"

Kole shook his head, allowing himself to smile despite the ache that was beginning to sprout in his stomach. "I like to take pictures, if that's okay with you."

The worker shrugged dismissively, gesturing for Kole to move out of the way so he could get to the door. "Works for me," he said, opening the door. "Just make sure the flash is off, all right?"

Kole nodded, forcing the relief not to show as the class dragged their feet inside. It killed him to see the solemn expressions that everyone wore, and the fear that they all had in their eyes.

"Oh, thank goodness you're here!"

Faye blinked once. Twice. Three times. A woman stood in front of her, looking thoroughly unnerved. Her hands were shaking, Faye couldn't help but notice. What was this girl afraid of? And why was she speaking to Faye as though she knew her? "Excuse me?" Faye said softly.

"I've been looking all over for you!" the girl whispered frantically. She grabbed onto Faye's arm, her eyes widening. "Have you done what's needed to be done?"

Faye stared at her for a moment, uncomprehending. "Um, what?"

"Olyv, really!" the girl said briskly, shaking her head. "I asked you to get me the keys from Courtnie's office, remember?"

Faye didn't understand. Why did this girl think she was a girl named Olyv? Why was she talking about Courtnie's office? Who was this girl? "I'm sorry," she said softly, deciding to play along. "I'll get them now. Um, where is the office again?"

"You've been working here your whole life and you don't know where her office is?" the girl stared at her disbelievingly. "You have to be joking. Please be joking. I'm in a hurry."

"I'm joking," Faye said swiftly. "I'll go get the keys and bring them back to you."

The girl sighed deeply. "No, it's fine. Waiting here would take as long as you going to get them."

"Can I come with you anyway?" Faye asked quickly. She had to check out Courtnie's office anyway. Why not have a worker lead her there? "I'll guard the door while you grab them."

The girl nodded briskly. It wasn't a type of nod that said she was really okay with the idea of Faye tagging along, but a nod that said that she didn't have enough time on her hands to say no. Faye couldn't blame her, but she needed to get to Courtnie's office and take as many photographs as she could.

"What's your name?" Faye asked softly as they sped-walked their way through the halls. She knew it was odd—making small talk with a Government worker of all people. But she couldn't help it. Walking silently next to someone she didn't know unbearable.

"Olyv, we've been working together for over a year," the girl said, her eyebrows raised. "Are you okay?"

"Yeah," Faye said, shaking her head. She didn't know what to say. She didn't know who Olyv was or why this girl was mistaking her for her, but she had to work with it. She couldn't keep slipping up like this. "I had a lot to drink last night," she said softly. "Killer hangover, you know?"

Faye didn't know how she thought of the excuse, but she was going with it.

"You promised me you would stop going to the mixers!" the girl quipped, tossing Faye a reprimanding glance. "You know you always drink too much."

Faye sighed solemnly. "I know. I'm sorry. I promise I won't go anymore. But since I'm having a huge brain cramp, could you please tell me what your name is?"

"Miranda," the girl said, tossing Faye an unimpressed look. The shaking in her hands was gone now, replaced with the irritation at Faye's supposed drinking problem. This Olyv person must have gotten in a lot of trouble. She wasn't one to talk, though. She was the one who broke into the Government building with a group of people in order to figure out how to take the organization down. Faye couldn't help but think that was a little more disastrous than a drinking problem.

But of course she couldn't tell Miranda that.

"So what do you need from Courtnie's office?" Miranda asked quickly, her eyes darting everywhere. For a moment it seemed as though she wasn't really asking the question to Faye at all, but the walls in which they were speeding past. "Are you cleaning it again?"

Faye nodded. "Yes," she replied, just as swiftly as the question was asked. "You know how disorganized she is."

"You're telling me," Miranda said softly. Her eyes widened and the shaking returned as they reached a wide, rounded door. Faye knew immediately that this was Courtnie's office. Faye could feel the hairs prickling on her skin again. What if Courtnie was in there? Surely she'd be smart enough to notice that Faye wasn't Olyv, and that she was breaking into the Government building. Then she would be thrown in the prison wards—or killed.

"I have to hurry," Miranda whispered, pulling the door open and stepping inside. Faye followed her, her eyes wide. She was surprised to see just how disorganized the room was. Books were strewn across the floor, papers following their lead. It was like Courtnie had thrown a temper tantrum and hadn't bothered to pick the mess up. Faye wondered what that temper tantrum was about. And she wondered if this anger Courtnie obviously contained was going to be taken out on the prisoners here.

Something told her that yes, yes it would.

"Looks like Courtnie got angry," Miranda whispered, practically running for the desk that sat in the middle of the room. It was as messy as the rest of the room; everything was so chaotic. It was a wonder that nothing was broken. "Probably at the Miss again...."

"At the who?" Faye inquired, spinning to face Miranda. She was rifling through the drawers of Courtnie's desk, pulling out a ring of keys. There were so many, Faye thought with wide eyes. Why were there so many?

"No one," Miranda muttered, her tone final. Faye instantly knew that this girl was done speaking to Faye—or Olyv, she supposed. This girl was hiding something. And something told her that it was big.

Big enough for Faye to need to find out.

"Okay," she said softly, averting her gaze to the ground. She stood at the far corner of the room, her hands folded behind her back. If she were smart, she'd start cleaning up things—it would make her look less suspicious, right? But Faye couldn't bring herself to. All she could think about was this "Miss" and how Miranda spoke her name with a deep admiration. Like she followed her. It made Faye wonder—what was Miranda getting Courtnie's keys for? Was she stealing them to go meet the Miss? Who was the Miss? Was she someone a worker here? Or was she a captive in the prison wards? Or was she something else entirely?

It was impossible to know for sure.

"Thank you, Olyv," Miranda whispered, pushing the drawer shut and standing up straight. She struggled to smile, but Faye knew that it was difficult. She must have really been in a hurry. "Have fun cleaning."

With that, she hurried out of the room.

Faye paused for a moment, taking five or so pictures of Courtnie's office before glancing around. And then, after taking a deep breath, she sped out of the room, closing the door behind her. And, with spotting Miranda's figure, she crept after her, opening her cell phone and dialing Errika's number as she did.

"You are all here because you've committed treason," the Government worker snarled, standing in front of the desk as it sat in front of the projector screen. "You went into the Gate's territory knowing full well that it was against the law. And now you will learn what you can do to repay the debt."

Kole sat in the back row, his fingers snapping as he took photographs of the room. It was wide, so big that it could easily fit thirty students. Which was what it was doing now. All thirty of the seats were filled with boys and girls alike, their eyes concentrated on the teacher in front of them. They looked so tiny, Kole couldn't help but think. Tiny and afraid.

"You've been told that when you commit a transgression that you'll go to the prison wards," the teacher said, rubbing his goatee. "And you are—in the prison wards. But there is another thing that you have to do.

"And what is that? It is your responsibility to Cesve populated. What does that mean? It means that Cesve needs babies, people. And you're going to be responsible for making them."

Kole's eyes widened, pausing his photo taking to stare at the teacher. Making babies? How did one make a baby? Weren't they just purchased at the orphanage? He'd never really thought of how the babies came to be, or how he came to be. What was there to think about? It was just how things were.

Well, evidently, there was a lot to think about.

"As you can see, there are two different types of human beings in the room. One is the boy, one is the girl. Meet the beast on the other side of the Gate, my friends."

Kole watched as the boys and girls all turned to look at each other, their eyes wide. No wonder they seemed so afraid, Kole realized. They hadn't known what creature was standing next to them.

"Was it worth it?" the teacher demanded, cocking an eyebrow. "Sneaking away to the forest to see what this beast was? Are you proud of yourselves?

"I'm not here to reprimand you like children. I'm here to prepare you for the next step. You've all reached the age of twenty. This is the age where you have to start helping to populate Cesve.

"Now, before we get onto the lesson, I need to explain a couple of things to you...."

Kole blocked the teacher out as he began explaining the meaning of "he, his, him, and she, her, hers." He already knew all of this, and he didn't need a teacher to tell him. He didn't understand why the Government did this to people. Why bother separating them and then showing them the truth once behind bars? What was the point?

"I'm going to show you a video on reproduction," the teacher said, a knowing smirk on his face. "Don't ask me what reproduction is. It'll explain in the video."

Kole watched as the teacher moved to the desk and grabbed a remote, turning on the projector before moving to his laptop. He was probably getting the video ready to play, Kole thought. And Kole was going to sit there and learn about how babies were made just like everyone else.

Kole braced himself as the video screen appeared and the movie began. Did he even want to know about this? But did he really have a choice? He was beginning to regret his decision of pretending to be an observer. He could have just pretended he was lost.

"Reproduction: the natural process among organisms by which new individuals are generated and the species perpetuated. What does that mean? It means babies are made."

Kole's eyes locked on the screen with everyone else as the video continued on. It talked about the reproduction, how women had eggs that needed the sperm from men in order to fertilize. It talked about the period—apparently women bleed out of their private areas once a month?—and how when the woman was pregnant the period ceased. It was possible, but very highly unlikely for the period to come.

The most disturbing part was how the babies were made, though. Through something called—what was it?—sex? The video explained in much more detail than really necessary about how the man and woman had sex in order to transfer the sperm into the female. Kole just sat there, completely scarred.

And then they showed a segment of "relationships." Apparently it was people in "relationships" who had sex. Kole was introduced to the word girlfriend, boyfriend, couples, and marriage. The video explained how boys and girls who were in love became boyfriend, girlfriend, even married each other. Clips of couples walking hand in hand, clips of couples kissing. This was a different kind of kissing than Kole was used to. It wasn't a kiss on the head that father's usually gave their younger sons. No. This was a kiss on the lips.

When those scenes past, the only thing that Kole could think about was Faye. How it would be if he kissed her, if he held her hand while they walked. If he hugged her just to hug her—not just to say goodbye or to comfort her. To be her boyfriend as they called it.

He liked the idea more than he would like to admit.

Miranda hurried through the halls, her feet all but slamming on the tiled floors as she went. She wished she could be quieter, but she didn't have a choice. She needed to get to the prison wards and she had to get to the prison wards now.

If Olyv had just remembered the keys, she wouldn't be in this mess. She wouldn't be late. She wouldn't be letting the Miss down. She wouldn't have slipped up on saying "the Miss" to Olyv in the first place. Now she was probably going to have to explain something that she couldn't explain. The Miss swore her to secrecy a long time ago. No one but she and the other prisoners knew about the Miss's plan to take the Government down. And it was supposed to stay that way.

Finally, after what seemed like forever, she reached the prison wards. She quickly found the key she needed and plunged it into the keyhole, happy when it twisted and unlocked. She hurried into the prison, ignoring all of the cries and pleas from the women to let them go. There were less today—a good number of them had gone to the reproduction class. It was sick, Miranda thought. That they would teach them about reproduction and then make them go through artificial insemination. When the prisoners hit the age of twenty, they had to donate. Men had to donate sperm every five years, and women had to give birth every three to five years. They didn't want to have them donate all that often. If they did, too many siblings would be running around. As it was, there were some people who were best friends at the schools and were siblings—and they didn't even know it.

"Miss," Miranda called softly as she reached the last cell. She peered through the bars. "Miss?"

"Miranda!" the Miss exclaimed, hopping up from her cot and appearing at the face of the cell. "There you are. I thought Courtnie had kept you."

"No, this girl kept me busy," she explained. "She seemed a little lost, but that was because she has a drinking problem."

Miranda didn't know why she was explaining this to the Miss when there were more important things that needed to be done, but there she was. Babbling was a new habit that Miranda picked up on—one that she didn't quite enjoy but couldn't shake.

"A girl?" the Miss came to full attention, her fingers curling over the bars. "What did this girl look like?"

"Bright red hair, short, green eyes," Miranda answered. "She's just a girl who—"

"Miranda, I need you to listen to me," the Miss said swiftly. "There is a group of rebels in the building. Ones who know about boys and girls and who have talked to each other on each side of the Gate. That girl was one of them."

Miranda's eyes widened. A group of rebels—here? But how?

Then she realized. She'd helped to take the cameras down. And because the cameras were down, boys and girls were free to go over to the other side as they pleased.

"What?" she exclaimed. "But she looks exactly like—"

"You know what a twin is, don't you Miranda?" the Miss asked, her tone taking on a lighter tone but still managing to be more serious than anyone Miranda ever knew. "I know you've never seen one, but that's what you just saw. That is not that girl you thought it was. The girl you saw was a part of the rebel group."

"Wow," Miranda breathed. "Miss, what are we going to do?"

"I need you to hurry and make sure that they're okay. And if you see anyone that doesn't seem to belong, make sure that they don't do anything stupid. Make sure no one gets arrested."

Miranda nodded and immediately pried her hands away from the cell, rushing out of the prison wards, shutting the door tightly—or so she thought—behind her.

"I lost her!" Faye hissed into the phone, feeling despair trickle down her throat. "Errika, I lost her."

"Are you sure?" Errika breathed, her voice as soft as Faye's. Faye wondered where Errika was. Was she close to a group of people? Was Faye putting her in jeopardy by speaking to her? She prayed not. She wouldn't be able to handle putting her friend in any more danger than she already had. "You can't see her anywhere?"

Faye opened her mouth to reply, but suddenly a figure dashed out an adjacent hall, running in away from where Faye was standing. Faye stared, wide-eyed for a moment before realizing who it was: Miranda. She was sure of it. "Found her," Faye said brightly, happy that she wasn't as lost anymore. "I'm going to check out where she just ran from. I'll call you if I find anything."

"Okay. Be careful, Faye."

Faye hung up the phone and turned into the hall Miranda just ran from, stepping carefully. She was afraid that at any moment another Government worker was going to show up, this one not as friendly as Miranda was. This one would throw her away into a cell like she was nothing.

There was a door at the end of the hall. Faye glanced around her before hurrying over to it. It was crazy for her to be doing something like this. The door was probably locked. If it were so important, Miranda wouldn't have slipped up, right?

Wrong.

Faye felt surprise nip at her as she reached the door. It wasn't closed all the way. With a smile curling on her lips, Faye pulled the door open and stepped inside.

And was introduced screams.

Faye had to fight the urge to scream herself as she walked down the steel hallway, her stomach aching. So many people were screaming. So many. And all of them were girls. None of them were boys. It was when she saw the cells that she realized that this was the prison wards. But—why? Why would Miranda come to the prison wards? Was she visiting a prisoner? A mom? A sister? The Miss?

"Let us out!" girls screeched. "Let us out, please!"

But she couldn't let them out. She didn't have a key or the power to let everyone loose. All she could do was stare and curl her hands into fists. This was all so wrong—so wrong. These people did not deserve to be here. What was so wrong with wanting to know what was really out there? They had a right to know about boys, and boys had a right to know about girls. And that right had been taken away from them.

Faye came to stand in front of the last cell. Something about it called her to it, like it was whispering secrets into her ear. She felt her feet move her forward until she was standing right in front of the cell, her fingers curling on the bars.

Something moved inside the cell. Faye felt her stomach curl into itself as a girl stood up from their cot, moving toward the cell's door. And, as the girl crew closer, Faye felt her breathing stop altogether.

She took a step back, her hand going to her mouth. As she let it drop, her eyes widened and she had the sudden urge to hurl onto the floor. Her eyes locked on the door as she sputtered out one single word:

"Terra?"

CHAPTER 15

"Terra," Faye whispered again, taking another step back. She almost tripped on her own feet, all sense of balance lost. She couldn't think of anything—anything—but the girl in the cell. "Terra. Is it—is it really you?"

Faye watched as the girl's eyes widened and she wrapped her hands around the bars. "Faye," she whispered, so lowly that Faye almost couldn't hear her. If it weren't for her total concentration, the screams would have covered her words. "Oh my—Faye."

Faye fell forward, her hands curling on the bars. She couldn't believe it. She just couldn't believe it. Terra was standing right in front of her. Terra, who for the past seven years Faye thought to be dead.

Nothing made sense anymore.

"This can't be happening," Faye said, feeling dread curl within her stomach. "I saw your body—I saw it."

Terra shook her head. "No, Faye. You didn't. I'll explain everything later. For now, I need you to get the key from Miranda. Once I'm out we can get out of here, okay?"

She sounded exactly as she had seven years ago, Faye couldn't help but think . She looked and sounded exactly the same. It was like she hadn't aged at all. At all. It didn't make any sense, Faye's mind kept saying. No sense. No sense. No sense.

But it was happening.

Faye found herself nodding, and she was moving away from the cell when she heard a huge bang. She spun around, her eyes wide as Miranda came storming in, her arms flailing as she ran. Something had happened. Something had happened to her.

"Miss!" she hollered as she came barreling closer. She came to a stop in front of Faye, her eyes narrowing. "Olyv, what are you doing here? What are you doing here?"

Faye bit down the question as to why Miranda asked the question twice before trying to muster up a reply. "I'm—"

"Miranda, we've been over this," Terra said tiredly, dragging a hand down her face. "This is not Olyv. This is my sister, Faye."

Miranda froze. "You—you have a sister?"

"Yes." Terra paused. "Miranda, I need you to unlock my cell. Can you do that for me?"

Faye watched with surprise as Miranda nodded, pulling out the keys she'd taken from Courtnie's office. Was this the sole purpose of the keys? Visiting Terra inside her cell? How often had Miranda done this? How often over the past seven years had Miranda come to visit Terra while she was stuck at home mourning the loss of the sister who hadn't died. How often?

Miranda selected a key from the ring and moved forward, swiftly unlocking the cell. Faye stared as her sister strutted out of the cell, still as confident as she had been before Faye was tricked into thinking she committed suicide. "Faye," she said softly. "Oh my God, Faye."

Faye rushed into her sister's arms, squeezing her tightly as she was pulled closer. Terra held her just as tightly, her chin resting on Faye's head. Faye felt tears burn in her eyes as she hugged her sister. She knew thought she'd be able to do this ever again. And it killed her. But now? Now she felt like anything was possible. "I've missed you so much," she wept into Terra's shoulder.

"I've missed you too, hon. More than you know."

The girls pulled away and Terra held her out at arm's length. "You've grown up on me!" Terra said, smiling. "What happened to the little girl who was scared of the beast on the other side of the Gate?"

"I have different fears now." Faye's lips pricked into a smile.

Terra sighed, flashing another smile before letting her hands fall. "As amazing as it is to see you, we need to get out of here. Courtnie checks on me all the time, and if she catches us just standing here and chatting...."

Faye nodded. "Okay," she said softly. "Let's go."

Faye followed Terra through the Government building with a feeling that a huge weight had been thrown from her shoulders. For the first time in a long time she could breathe again. The ice shards that seemed to be permanently inserted into her skin had melted away, and everything seemed right again. In that moment, nothing could go wrong.

Well, unless they got caught by a Government official.

"I need to make a stop in Courtnie's office," Terra said softly, glancing at Faye from the corner of her eye. "Is that okay?"

Faye nodded. Everything was okay with her. Terra could have wanted to stand there and do nothing and Faye would have been all right with that. Just her being there—that was good enough for her. "Yeah," she said softly. "That's fine."

Terra smiled. "You've grown up strong, Faye," she said, tossing a proud look in her direction. "I am so proud of you, you know that?"

Faye stared at her, not responding. Strong? Ever since she thought Terra died, she'd felt anything but strong. She felt terrified and alone all the time. Like everything was in her way and there was no way to get past it. Like she didn't want to move on no matter how badly she needed to.

And then Kole had changed that.

"You don't believe me, do you?" Terra said, the smile not leaving her face. "Well. You don't have to. But I know better. Because I've seen you on the cameras."

Faye's mouth dropped. "You've seen me on the cameras?" she demanded, keeping her voice as low as possible. "But—I thought they were down—"

"Yeah, for Courtnie and Fortis." Terra snorted, flicking a hand through her hair. "They thought that just because they locked me up that they could stop me from bringing their government down. But they were wrong—obviously."

"How long have you been doing this?" Faye asked. "How long have you known about boys?"

"You know that night when you were crying in your room because you thought the beast was going to get you and I came in and told you that there was nothing to worry about?" Terra asked.

"Which time?" Faye asked, cocking an eyebrow. "You did that a lot."

"The first time." Terra winked. "I knew about boys since then."

Faye blinked at her. The first time Terra came into her room and reassured her about the beast on the other side of the gate was two years before Terra had "died." For that long she'd been plotting against the Government, carefully planning its demise? She couldn't imagine how hard it was to keep that secret from her family for that long. And to get thrown in jail because of it. ... "Wow," she said softly. She blinked back sudden tears as she murmured, "We really missed you, you know."

Terra sighed, and Faye could see the real despair in her eyes. She'd missed them as much as they'd missed her, Faye realized. And something in Faye seemed to crumble. How had it felt being confined in a cage for seven years with only your shattered thoughts for company? Faye didn't think she'd be able to take it. "I know," Terra replied softly. "You have no idea how bad I feel for making you two hurt the way I have. If I could turn it all around—"

"If you turned it all around then I would never have found out about what the Government is doing," Faye cut her sister off with a shake of the head. "I would have stayed scared my entire life and I wouldn't have Kat."

Terra brought an arm over her shoulder, squeezing her tightly. "I told you that you grew up strong, hon."

Faye was about to say something, but at that moment they reached Courtnie's office and Terra pushed the door open and stepped inside. Faye followed close behind, tossing nervous glances in all directions. Where was Courtnie, anyway? And where was this Fortis person? And where were all the workers? Was this place really that unguarded?

"Courtnie is probably trying to figure out how to fix the cameras," Terra mused, moving toward the laptop sitting on the desk. Faye's eyebrows creased. What was she doing? "That gives me plenty of time."

"What are you doing?" Faye asked as Terra took out what looked like a flash drive and stuck it into the laptop. "Are you sure—?"

"I'm copying all of the information from Courtnie's computer to mine," Terra replied. "And I'm sure it's safe. She doesn't have alarm systems on her laptop. She's too cocky for that."

Terra took a step back as the information copied itself, looking around. "Wow, is this what she does when she's pissed at me?" she asked, her eyebrows rising. "That's flattering."

Faye watched as her sister ambled around the room. She still had that confident bounce in her step, still had that bright look in her eyes like she knew something you didn't. She still carried herself like she was the most powerful human in the world. Nothing about her had changed. Nothing.

Faye knew she'd missed her sister, but she didn't realize just how much until this moment. She knew that just the thought of Terra killed her inside, but now seeing her ... it was like her entire heart had been ripped from her chest and thrown back inside. It was like her entire life had been redeemed. Like she'd gained another chance.

"Oh!" Terra exclaimed suddenly, clapping her hands in delight. "Faye, come here!"

Faye blinked and hurried over to where Terra was standing. There was a rack of movies in front of her—movies she didn't recognize. Terra was flipping through them like she'd seen them all, though Faye couldn't imagine how. She'd been in prison after all. "They're movies," Faye said blankly.

"Oh, my dear sister, I bet you have great grades in school." Terra winked. "Of course they're movies. But look at them."

Faye pulled one out and stared.

27 Dresses it read. Faye flipped it over and stared even more. There were both boys and girls there—together. And it seemed so right. So, so right. "They're together," she whispered. Her eyes locked with Terra's before she turned back to the movie. "Boys and girls. They're together."

Terra nodded. "They used to live together side by side." She sighed dreamily. "Romance, ah, I love it." She took the movie from Faye's hands and grinned. "We're watching this tonight. The guys might hate it, but you'll love it, I promise."

"Why would the guys hate it?" Faye asked, not understanding. If it were a movie with both boys and girls it would obviously be interesting, right?

"Because this is a chick flick," Terra said as though that made it obvious. Faye continued to stare. A chick flick? What the heck was a chick flick? Faye just didn't understand. "Boys hate chick flicks because they think they're girly. It's a thing that makes men stupid."

"What makes them girly?" Faye inquired. Girly? She'd never really imagined stuff not girl except for the boys themselves.

"The romance."

"What's romance?" Faye's eyes were wide. How did Terra know all this? It was one thing to know about boys, but all of this other information? Where did she get it?

Terra moved back to the desk, setting down the DVD and tapping her fingers on the desk's surface. "It's almost done," she announced, her eyes locked on the laptop. Her eyes flicked up at me and she smiled. "And romance is something that happens between boys and girls. It's love in a different way."

Love in a different way? What was that supposed to mean?

"You should probably call Errika and that boy," said Terra as she came to stand in front of her. "Courtnie and Fortis are sure to notice something is up soon. They visit my cell like all the time."

Faye nodded, pulling her phone out of her pocket and dialing Kole's number before bringing it to her ear. She knew she should call Errika first, but Kole had more people to call afterwards. Errika just needed to hurry over. This was the most efficient way.

"Faye?" Kole whispered. "Is everything okay?"

"We need to get out of here," Faye replied. "Everything is fine. Just call Alex and everyone else and hurry to our meeting spot."

"Okay."

Faye hung up the phone and quickly dialed up Errika's number. Errika picked up on the third ring. "Faye, you didn't call and I got worried."

"Sorry," Faye said softly, her eyes flicking to Terra as she pulled the flash drive out of the computer. "I got . . . distracted."

"By what?" Errika demanded. "Something happened. What is it?"

"You'll see when we meet. I can't risk you getting loud right now. Get out of the building and go to the meeting spot. I'll see you soon."

"All right—are you sure everything is okay?"

"Everything is fine," Faye assured her, smiling brightly. "It's more than fine. I promise."

That was all Errika needed because she hung up. Faye pocketed her phone and sighed. "Are we ready to go?" she asked, her attention turning back to Terra as she slipped the flash drive into her pocket. "Do you have everything?"

Terra made a small noise and hurried back to the desk, grabbing 27 Dresses and waving it in the air. "Can't forget my all-time favorite movie, now can I?" She laughed. "Now I'm ready. Come on, let's get out of here."

"How's Mom doing?" Terra murmured as she and Faye made their way down the desolate hall.

Faye's eyes widened as they flicked to her sister. Terra was staring straight ahead, expressionless. It was like she couldn't bring herself to feel the pain of how their mother reacted to her "death" and how she turned out. It was like she was shielding herself from Faye's reply. "Mom is fine," she assured her sister with a smile. "She adopted my sister Kat, and she's just as cheerful as she used to be."

Terra smiled, relief clear in her eyes. "That's good," she said softly. "That's good."

"It is good." Faye smiled. "She's the best mom anyone could ask for."

Terra blew air out through her teeth. "How did you two handle what happened?" she asked.

Faye paused before answering. Did she really want Terra to know the amount of heartbreak that she and her mother had been through since that day seven years ago? Did she really want Terra to know how close she came to hating her sister for leaving them the way she had? Did she really want Terra to know anything about the conflicted feelings she had inside? "It's been hard," she admitted. "Really hard. After a while we stopped crying and just hid the subject away. We didn't talk about it, but it was still there. All of your stuff is still in the attic. We couldn't get rid of it. Even though we never talked about you anymore, you were on our minds every single day." Faye sighed, feeling tears burn in her eyes. "Well, you were on mine at least."

Terra brought a hand through her hair. Whether that was what she wanted or expected to hear, I wasn't sure. But she didn't look shocked. "I'm sorry for what happened," she murmured. "And for the pain I've caused you two. You must have been so confused."

"They told us you killed yourself," Faye whispered, her eyes desperately trying to reach through Terra's, to find the answers. "The police women came to our house. Mom was crying. She told me to stay at the house with Errika, but I couldn't. I knew something was wrong, and I couldn't understand why you weren't there because you always were. So I followed them. And I—" Faye sucked in a shaky breath, wiping away a tear that was threatening to shed. "I saw your body. Well. I guess I didn't see your body. It must have been a dummy. A way to trick us into thinking you were dead—"

"It wasn't a dummy." Terra shared a sad glance with me. "She was a real girl. But she wasn't me."

"What do you—?"

Terra cut her off, slapping a hand over her mouth and pushing her against the wall. Faye watched with wide eyes as a group of people shuffled by in the hall ahead of them, their heads bent toward the ground. What they'd just endured, Faye wasn't sure. But it possibly couldn't be anything good. "They've just taken the health class," Terra whispered into her ear. "They're going to stay straight, back toward their cells. Which means that the guards are going to check cells soon—Courtnie's orders. Which means that they'll notice mine is empty."

Faye felt dread drip down her throat, into her stomach and spreading its way through her. What would happen when they found Terra's cell empty? What lengths would they go through to get her back? What would they—?

Faye's thoughts reached a stop as she spotted a person at the end of the line. He was snapping pictures and talking to the guard in charge of the group.

Kole.

"Isn't that the boy?" Terra asked, her hand still on top of Faye's mouth. It was like she was afraid Faye would scream. Faye couldn't blame her. The last time they'd seen each other, Faye had screamed at everything. Everything.

Faye nodded. Somehow he'd found a way to get passed the guards and even inside with them. How the hell had he managed that? She'd have to ask him later.

"Well, he must be on his way out," Terra spoke to herself. "He must be smart if he managed not to get caught by Victor."

Victor? Faye's eyes reached the Government worker, noticing his build and how intimidating he was. And apparently he wasn't stupid. How Kole managed not to get caught was beyond her, but that didn't matter. What mattered was that Kole was okay. Hopefully everyone else was, too.

"Oh my—oh my—oh my—"

Faye smiled as she stood next to Terra, watching Errika's reaction. They were the only three out here, but they wouldn't be for long. Soon Kole would be back, along with Terence, Seth, and Alex.

But, for now, the two girls had their own time with Terra. And that was good. Because they were in need of it.

"Hey, Errika," Terra said, her teeth gleaming as she smiled. "You went and grew up on me, too." She looked between Faye and Errika, making a noise of disapproval through her teeth. "You weren't supposed to do that, girls. You were supposed to stay my little seven-year-olds forever."

"You're—you're alive," Errika exclaimed as quietly as she could, throwing her arms in the air. "How is this—possible?"

"The Government likes to make things seem different than they are," Terra replied, her smile turning cool. "But I'll explain every-thing once we get out of here." She held open her arms. "Come here."

Errika threw her arms around Terra, squeezing her so tightly that Faye feared that Terra was going to burst. She wondered if she hugged her sister that hard, if not harder. Maybe she had. Either way Terra didn't seem to mind. In fact, she hugged back just as tightly.

"Who is this?"

Faye spun around, her face breaking into a bright smile as she spotted Kole. He was staring at Terra with guarded eyes, like he thought she was going to turn them in at any moment. Little did he know that that was the last thing she'd do. "Kole!" she exclaimed, throwing her arms around him. "You're okay. I saw you with that official dude, and I was worried you'd get caught."

"He thought I was a reporter on the class," Kole said softly, hug-ging her back for a moment before pulling away. He gestured with his head in Terra's direction. Terra and Errika were done hugging now and were watching Kole and Faye with lit up expressions on their faces. "Now who is this?"

"Kole," Faye murmured, taking a step back and taking ahold of Terra's hand. Terra held it tightly, shooting a smile in her direction. "This is Terra."

Kole blinked once, twice, three times. Something in his head didn't seem to be clicking, and Faye couldn't say that she blamed him. One minute she was saying that the Government murdered her sister because she knew too much and the next she was holding her hand and introducing them. He must have been so confused. "Terra?" he asked blankly.

Faye nodded. "You know how we thought the Government murdered her to shut her up? Well, we were wrong."

Kole blinked again. "But you saw her body—"

"It wasn't mine," Terra said, finality in her voice. "Their use of her body obviously did its purpose if it convinced all of you that it was me. But it wasn't. I've been locked away in the prison wards for the past seven years."

Kole opened his mouth to say something, but in that moment Alex, Terence, and Seth appeared, gawks on their faces. All at once they began demanding who Terra was and why she was with them when she could expose them to the Government. At that Terra laughed, pointing at them and shaking her finger between her giggles. Faye had to laugh, too. Terra, exposing them to the Government? Even if she didn't know about boys she wouldn't have done that. Not to Faye. Not to anyone.

"This is Terra," Kole explained to his friends and brother, holding up his hands. "Faye's sister."

"But—you told us she was dead, Faye—"

Kole's glare cut off Seth before he could start shooting accusa-
tions her way. Faye didn't doubt that he would turn it into a case
where she was plotting against them, waiting for them to make the
wrong move before turning them in to Courtnie without looking
back. He didn't like her much. "Obviously," Kole drawled, gesturing
from Faye to Terra, "there has been a misunderstanding that Terra
will clear up later. For now I think it's best if we get out of here."

Terra nodded, agreeing with him. "They'll notice I'm gone soon.
Really, really soon."

"Then we should probably get going."

It was Alex. He moved ahead of the group, gesturing toward the
forest. And just like that they were all leaving, careful not to make
too much noise to disrupt the utter silence around the Government
building.

And once they were far enough, they were running. Running
carelessly through the underbrush, not caring how loud they were.
It didn't matter. According to Terra the Government relied completely on the cameras to guard the forest from the people of
Cesve, and without them they were almost completely powerless.
The boys demanded to know how she knew that, and her answer
was simple: She'd been in the Government building for almost ten
years.

Finally, after what seemed like forever, they reached the Gate.
Seth, Terence, Alex, and Errika immediately started climbing, hasti-
ly trying to get as far away from the Government building as they
possibly could. Faye and Kole paused though, watching as Terra
looked the Gate up and down.

"Are you going to stay on this side?" Faye asked, breathless from
the amount of running they'd done.

Terra nodded. "It would be the smartest way. Courtnie thinks she knows me. She'd assume that I'd come on the boys side because she'd look on the girl's side. And she thinks that since I know she'd look on the boy's side that I'll just stay on the girl's side. So she won't look as hard for me over there."

Faye blinked, not sure if she understood what Terra meant or not. Terra grinned, shaking her head and wrapping her hands around the metal of the Gate. "Come on, Faye."

Faye gestured for Kole to follow before beginning her way up the Gate. For once the sense of fear that she would fall didn't come. It was like all of her fears fell away now that Terra was here. It was like she somehow knew that everything would be okay now that she knew Terra's body didn't end up deformed beyond repair. She wouldn't fall and end up like her. Because she was fine. She was strong, fiery, and alive.

She was alive.

And that was all that mattered. No matter what happened to her now, her sister was alive. She didn't leave her and her mom alone because she couldn't handle life anymore. No, she'd been trapped, wanting to come home to her. Missing her. This entire time Faye feared her sister didn't love her as much as she thought. But it was just the opposite.

"So where are we going?" Terra asked once everyone's feet were on the ground of the boy's side.

"My house," said Alex immediately, taking the authority role yet again. He glanced at Seth and said, "Seth, call Zander. Tell him this is an emergency. He can bring Zach if he wants. But we need him there. He has to hear what has to be said."

His eyes turned to Terra. "We want to hear Terra's story. All of it."

And then he turned, heading back toward civilization.

With one glance around the group, Faye and the others followed, silent as they continued toward the city beyond.

CHAPTER 16

C ourtnie stared at the open cell, uncomprehending. It was open. Open. And there was no one in it. Why was there no one in it? Where had she gone?

And just like that, after the question barely scraped her mind, Courtnie screamed. She screamed so loudly that the screams in the prison cells stopped and she was the only one left. They all stared at her from inside their cages, all secretly loved the emotions coursing through Courtnie's body. Courtnie slid to the ground, her eyes wide. She was gone. She was gone.

But—how?

"Fortis," Courtnie whispered. She didn't want to believe it, but what other choice did she have? Could Fortis have let her out? "Fortis."

Courtnie drew herself from the ground and glowered at the empty cell. It mocked her. Now that she was free there was no saying what she could do....

Ignoring the hateful stares all around her, Courtnie stormed out of the room, her hands curled into fists at her sides. Infuriation at a level that Courtnie didn't even think possible swam through her, threatening to drown her. All she could see was her hands around Fortis' throat, strangling him until his eyes were cool and lifeless. And then she'd go after her. She would find her and kill her like she should have when she first came to the prison wards.

Courtnie made her way through the halls, toward the boy's sector. It wasn't far away from the prison wards, so it didn't take that long. "Fortis!" Courtnie screeched as she entered the boy's sector. Fortis's office wasn't too far away now. "Fortis I know you're over here!"

Fortis appeared at the end of the hall, his eyes wide. Innocence dripped off of him, seeping into the floorboards and falling into the room below. But Courtnie knew that it was all a trick. He wasn't innocent. No. He was just as guilty as she was. "What's going on?" he demanded. "You weren't visiting her again were you?"

"Oh, you wouldn't want me to would you?" Courtnie seethed, her feet stomping on the floor as she made her way toward her brother. "You did this, you son of a—"

"Courtnie, stop," Fortis said softly grabbing ahold of her shoulders. In her anger Courtnie hadn't realized how close she'd come to her brother. She brought her fist up to punch him, but he caught it easily, bringing her hand back down to her side. "Now, what's going on?"

"You set her free," Courtnie hissed, throwing her fist up again. Fortis caught it again and threw it away from him. "You let her go, Fortis."

"Let who go?" Fortis demanded, his eyes wide.

"Oh don't act like you don't know," Courtnie barked, her nails digging into her palm now. She wanted to hit him so badly, but she knew that Fortis would only block her attack. "You let her go and now I'm going to kill you."

"Let who go?" Fortis shouted, his hands flying into the air. "Courtnie, I have no idea what you're talking—"

"Terra!" Courtnie screeched, the name like acid on her throat. She hated saying her name so much—so much. But there was nothing she could do about it now. "You let Terra free, you jackass! And now that's she's free she's going to ruin everything."

Fortis's mouth dropped, and for a moment Courtnie thought he was going to faint. But he didn't. Instead he closed his mouth and took a step back from her, his eyes threatening to fall out of their sockets as they bulged. "She's—she's gone?"

"Yes," Courtnie said icily, "she's gone."

"Courtnie." Fortis stared at her intently, and Courtnie could see legitimate shock in his eyes. He had no idea that any of this happened, Courtnie realized. He wasn't the one behind this. "I didn't let her out."

Courtnie suddenly felt sick to her stomach. "Then," she whispered, "who did?"

"We want the whole story."

Faye's eyes glided toward her sister as she sat on the shay lounge of Kole's living room. Terra seemed so at ease, she observed. How was it that she was able to enter an alien place and act as though it happened every day? Then again, maybe this place wasn't alien to Terra at all. Maybe she'd been on the boy's side numerous times, so many that she lost count.

But, still. When Faye first came to Kole's house she'd been beyond nervous. Terra acted as though she was sitting in her own living room. This was one of the many, many things that Faye admired about Terra. Her ability to go through everything without even blinking. To have so much strength.

"Don't skip over any details," Alex continued from his spot at the head of the room. He was standing, his arms crossed over his chest. He seemed to be taking a protective stance, as though he was trying to keep something safe. Faye wondered if this his big brotherly way of making sure Kole didn't get into any more trouble than he needed to be. Probably.

"Didn't plan on it," Terra said, her tone light. Her lips tilted into a smile as she regarded Alex. If he was trying to intimidate her, it definitely wasn't working. "Don't worry, you can trust me."

"We'll see about that," Seth muttered. He was seated on cushion furthest away from Faye, his hands curled into fists beside him. Terence and Zander sat next to him. Faye's eyes moved over to Kole, where he stood next to his brother. He caught her gaze and smiled. She smiled back.

Terra sighed deeply, rolling her eyes and standing up. She gestured for Alex and Kole to sit down, saying, "You might as well sit down. This is going to take a while."

Alex and Kole glanced at each other before shrugging, coming over to sit beside Faye and Errika on the couch. Kole perched next to Faye, his shoulders brushing hers as they crowded together on the shay lounge. Faye couldn't help but feel happy that Kole chose to sit by her instead of anyone else in the room. Her stomach did an odd flip at the thought.

"So, as you know, I'm Terra," Terra said, her hands shoved into her pockets. Faye would have been so nervous facing a group of people like she was, so pressured to say the right thing. But Terra didn't seem to care at all. "The girl who was supposed to be dead for the past seven years."

Faye stared at her sister as she spoke. She could not explain how amazing it felt to have her sister back in her life, to be given a second chance. No matter how many times she repeated it over and over in her mind, Faye still couldn't believe it. That after all this time Terra had been so close when she'd seemed so far away.

"This is what happened," Terra said.

"When I was in high school I met a girl named Daneigh. We looked exactly alike and we didn't know why. How was it possible to have someone look exactly like you? It just didn't make any sense. I immediately knew something was up. The whole 'beast on the other side of the Gate' always seemed like bullshit to me, but now I knew it was.

"Something was going on, and I was going to find out what. I told Daneigh that we needed to find out what the hell was going on because this just wasn't normal. It took a long time to convince her, but I did. She finally agreed to help me, and we started our plan to infiltrate the Government building.

"First we needed to get on the other side. There was no point in trying to get to the Government building if we couldn't even make it to the other side of the Gate without getting caught. Daneigh didn't think that we should try to go over the Gate, that we'd only get ourselves arrested. And that gave me an idea. If we got ourselves arrested then we'd be able to get inside the Government building without looking suspicious.

"Daneigh flat out told me no to that plan, and I understood why. It was risking too much to get arrested, to bank on getting away from the officers and back home without endangering ourselves at all. I had Faye and my mom to take care of, and she had her family to take care of. So that was out of the question.

"While we tried to think of another plan, we researched in libraries and talked to people we knew worked at the Government building. Of course we got nothing. The Government isn't stupid enough to leave information lying around, and the workers have to pledge secrecy if they're to stay at home while they work there. Only one or two workers get to work at home. And I've come to realize that they only get to work at home because they no absolutely nothing about what goes on inside. They've just been fed lies.

"Daneigh and I needed to do something, and we needed to do it fast. It wasn't going to be long before my mom was going to question how I was acting, or catch me and Daneigh together. So we decided that we were going to sneak onto the other side of the Gate.

"We did it at night, so the cameras couldn't track us. It took us hours because we moved slowly, carefully, so it would be less likely for the people watching the cameras to notice us. It obviously worked, because the next thing we knew we were on the other side and standing in a city nearly identical to our own.

"We walked around, looking for any answers that could be given to us. We found creatures that were much like us—boys. We instantly knew that the Government had screwed us all over, that they were planning something that definitely wasn't for the greater good of Cesve.

"We went to the Government building that same night.

"It was harder getting to the Government building than it was the other side. We had no idea where it was, let alone how to get there. So we just walked aimlessly, knowing that wherever we were going have to lead to somewhere.

"And it did. We got to the Government building and went inside. It was there were I first made the blueprints that you used in order to get through the building safely. I found a copy of them in Courtnie's office and traced them on a piece of printer paper. Daneigh kept a look out at the door, making sure that Courtnie didn't come and find us.

"We got caught by one of the workers—Miranda, Faye, you met her. She didn't suspect anything at all. She was never really the smartest person in the world. I doubt that she even remembers that night. She just looked between us and demanded to know if we were the new maids, and if we had to look like each other as a uniform. We told her that we were, and that was that. I finished tracing the blueprint and then we hurried out of the office. We did a little more looking around, using the blueprint, and then we left. While we wanted to bring the Government down quickly, it would be stupid to start a rebellion without thinking it through.

"So we formulated a plan. First, we would find a way to take down the cameras. And then, after that, more people would be able to go over to the other side and see the truth behind the Government's lies. And then we would take over the video broadcasts. Without their broadcasts and their cameras they were completely powerless.

"There was just one problem in our plan: We had no idea what to do. So, we needed to go back to the Government building. And we did. There we collected more information about how the cameras worked. We were there all night, sneaking around while the guards were gone. We found out exactly how to take the cameras and the voice broadcasts down. It wasn't hard at all. All that was needed was a virus, a transport, and a hacking.

"We were about to leave in the morning when we got caught again. This time it was by one of the guards, who were not as gullible as Miranda. He took us by our arms and dragged us to Courtnie, where she instantly recognized us. She had us sent to the prison wards.

"But we weren't going to have it that easy. Before Courtnie had us sent to the prison wards, she called in Fortis. He stared at us, his mouth slack with surprise. I can see it like it was yesterday. The utter disbelief that we were standing before him. Daneigh and I didn't understand at first, why he was staring at us like that, but then Courtnie explained—well in the way that she explains. Which means not at all.

"'I'd like you to meet your daughters, Fortis,' Courtnie had said, a smirk tilting on her lips. It was so triumphant, so filled with glee. I hadn't understood why. But now I realize that she'd warned Fortis about us from the beginning, tried to get him to keep us separated. He'd insisted that we both get to live a 'normal' life in Cesve. Live on the opposite sides of the city so that we'd be less likely to meet. Obviously Courtnie was glad that she'd proved him wrong.

"Daneigh demanded to know what Courtnie meant by us being his daughter, us being related at all. At the time we hadn't realized what we were, that they even existed. We hadn't known about the files on Courtnie's laptop with the lists of all of the true blood relatives in Cesve.

"It was then that we learned that we were siblings—twins actually. We shared the same blood, and Fortis was our father. Every girl has one—a father. And every boy has a mother. It was then that I learned that I was not blood related to anyone that I really considered family. My real family (besides Daneigh of course), was evil, plotting.

"And I was going to take them down.

"After Courtnie was done gloating, she gestured for the guards to take us away. It was then that I realized that we only had one hope of getting out. I curled over on myself, crying out in pain. I started hyperventilating, begging for them to stop the pain. Daneigh joined in a moment later, and soon enough we were both curled on the floor, pretending to be deathly sick when we weren't.

"Courtnie knew we were faking, but when we insisted that it must have been food poisoning, Fortis demanded that we get checked out by the hospital care unit they had downstairs. It was because he cared that we were able to get away. When the nurse went to go set us in a bed, Daneigh and I lashed out, knocking them out with the wooden visitor's chair next to one of the beds.

"And then we were running. We ran out of the building and through the woods, not caring if they noticed that we were leaving or not. We couldn't afford to go slow anymore. We ran, and for one night, we were safe.

"The next day guards showed up to our house while Faye and our mom were still sleeping. They were being so loud that I feared they were going to wake them up. So I went outside, and they tried to grab me. I got away, though, and then I was running again. This time I was hurrying for Daneigh's house. I needed to warn Daneigh, to give her a chance to run.

"But I was wrong to try and get to her. The guards were on my heels, and by the time I got to the house, they were trying to grab her, too. We were both running, and in the end we ended up by a cliff's edge. Stereotypical, cliché, whatever you want to call it, but that's how it was. We were trapped.

"I don't know what made Daneigh do it. But while we were standing there, watching the guards close in on us, she whispered, 'I won't go to the prison wards. I'm sorry, Terra.' And then she was gone. She threw herself off the cliff's edge, disappearing below.

"I screamed her name I don't know how many times. But even when the guard's got me, I screamed for them to help her, to save her before she hurt herself. I told them to let me go, that I had to go see if she was all right. It was ridiculous, of course—to do that. Daneigh was gone. And she wasn't coming back."

Terra sighed shakily, her story coming to a close as she wiped a hand across her face. Faye could see that telling it had pained her, and that she was trying very hard not to cry right now. The sudden want, the need to hug her right now almost consumed Faye whole. But Faye stayed where she was, unmoving. Terra wouldn't want her to hug her. Even when Faye was little and tried to console Terra when she was upset, Terra would push her away and smile, promising that everything was okay.

But nothing was really okay anymore, was it?

"So the body Faye saw," Errika murmured softly, her eyes wide. She, like the rest of them, could not believe what she'd just heard. "It was Daneigh's. Not yours."

Terra nodded, bringing a hand through her hair before letting it fall completely. "They hadn't expected Daneigh to do what she did, but they took advantage of it. They had Daneigh's family come first to see the body, and then they sent Mom over. There's no one in my grave in the graveyard. It's empty."

Faye gulped, her eyes watering. For so many years she'd visited Terra's grave, set flowers in front of it hoping that in some way Terra got them. But this whole time Terra hadn't been there, hadn't been watching over her. She'd been locked away, trapped and trying to get out.

Terra crossed her arms over her chest, and her eyes connected with Faye's. They were full of remorse, regret, and apology. She blamed herself for Daneigh's death, Faye realized. For the past seven years she'd thought that Daneigh would be alive if it hadn't been for her. "I continued on with the plan from the inside," Terra said softly. "I got Miranda to agree to help me—which wasn't that hard. She'd been told by Courtnie to come collect some of the prisoners for the health class, and that's when I got to her. She wanted to know my name, but I couldn't risk her accidentally telling anyone. Courtnie would have me killed on the spot.

"I had Miranda shut the cameras down with the file on my flash drive, and it gave me total control of the cameras. I saw Kole, and I saw Faye meet each other at the Gate's borders. I saw all of their visits, and I saw you guys coming to the building. I didn't know that it was Faye and Errika, though." Her lips tilted into a smile. "Ironic, isn't it, that my baby sister followed in my footsteps?"

Faye felt herself smile. For so many years she'd wanted to be like Terra, to succeed like she had. She'd spent so much time thinking about how different they were that she didn't see their similarities.

Terra sighed deeply. "That's my story," she said, her tone making it obvious that she was tired of the heavy atmosphere. The deepness of her story, of what happened to her and Daneigh weighed down on them all. Faye was surprised that she could breathe. "That's what happened. Now, please tell me that you have chips here. I haven't had a potato chip in seven years."

Faye snorted out a laugh as Terra turned to Alex, her eyes expectant. He stared at her in a way that told Faye that he thought Terra was kidding. But she wasn't. "Hello?" Terra asked, cocking an eyebrow. "Do you have chips or not?"

Alex blinked, and he cleared his throat. "Yeah," he mumbled, bringing a hand through his hair. His eyes held a distant fascination for her sister. Faye didn't know how she felt about that. "In the kitchen. This way."

Terra grinned as Alex led the way out of the room. She winked at Faye before saying in a sing-song voice, "Thank you!"

CHAPTER 17

"**T**his is my favorite part!" Terra squealed.

Faye smiled from her spot next to Kole on the couch. After a certain amount of demanding on Terra's part, a TV had been dragged down from Kole's room and into the sun room. According to Terra watching 27 Dresses was a rite of passage, and if they didn't do it now, they may never get the chance again. And that, according to Terra, was not okay.

Faye herself didn't quite understand the movie. Half of it went over her head, and there was no way to grasp it. Boys and girls were mingling together, talking and working together. Faye didn't understand. This woman apparently had—what was it?—a crush on her boss? What even was a crush? And why did she have it on a guy? And why were the woman's sister and the boss locking lips on the sofa? Faye didn't even know that happened let alone that it happened a lot. And then the woman started hanging out with this other guy while she planned something called a wedding? What in the world was a wedding, and why did guys and girls go through with it?

She just didn't understand.

According to Terra this was a movie about love. True love, actually. This was not a love that Faye understood at all. She grasped the concept of the love for family, but not crushes or "being in love" as the movie said. And when the woman and the guy were kissing—as Terra called it—in the back of a car.... Faye was just so confused.

As she watched the movie, Terra munched on her potato chips with a content smile on her face. She was sitting on the floor in front of Faye's spot, saying that she wanted to be as close to the movie as possible. Apparently this movie was her favorite, and she hadn't seen it in forever. How she'd seen it in the first place was beyond Faye, but she wasn't about to ask. She'd received enough information for the night.

The fact that Terra wasn't even really related to her hit Faye hard. She didn't know how she was handling it, but she was. She wasn't related to her mother, to Kat. She wasn't related to any of them. She could have—what was it?—a brother. She could be an only child. She had no idea who her mother was or her father. Faye still couldn't believe that she had a father. Just a little while ago she didn't know what father meant. Now apparently she had one.

"Why are they holding hands?" Errika asked, her eyebrows creased as she cut off Faye's turmoil-filled thoughts. "And why the hell would she let him kiss her like that? Terra what movie are you making us watch?"

Terra laughed, a light musical sound that filled the air. "Ah, maybe I should have made you all take the health class before we left," she mused. "You'd understand if you saw it."

From beside her, Faye felt Kole tense. She glanced over at him curiously. He had a distant look on his face, like he was remembering something terrible. Without even thinking about it, she touched his shoulder as though to comfort him. Kole's eyes flicked to her and then to her. They were wide, filled with wonder that Faye couldn't understand. "Kole?" Faye murmured. "Are you okay?"

Kole blinked again, as though he was forcing the wonder out of his expression. He shook his head in one swift motion before nodding. "Yeah," he mumbled. "I just went to the class she was talking about."

Faye stared at him. It was then that she remembered him walking with the group of those who'd finished the health class, a camera in his hand. She remembered wanting to ask him about it, but now she couldn't be bothered. Not with this movie on and Terra eating chips as though it was the most natural thing in the world. She felt too happy to try and figure things out now. That's why she wouldn't let herself wonder what a twin was and if Courtnie had figured out that Terra was gone yet. She wouldn't let herself think about anything that would cause her worry. Because this was a happy moment. And she wasn't about to ruin it by overthinking things.

"Ah, isn't that movie wonderful?" Terra asked as the ending credits came on. Apparently the woman figured out her boss wasn't the man for her and went with the other guy? I don't know, but I was cheering for that guy. Even though I didn't understand the plot at all, I hated the boss. He was annoying.

Faye stared at the television set, not really knowing if she enjoyed it or not. Something inside her felt oddly happy with how it turned out, but the other part of her wondered what the hell she'd just watched. She felt like Terra should have given her a little class before showing her something like that.

Alex stood up and stretched his arms out. "That was the most confusing movie I've ever seen. I didn't like it."

Terra rolled her eyes. "Not surprised."

Alex looked like he wanted to say something, but suddenly Kole was speaking. "In the beginning of the movie," he said softly. "Tess and the boss went dancing. Together."

Everyone turned to look at him. He had a strange look on his face, like he was piecing puzzle pieces together. His face gradually lit up until he seemed to finally understand. "Boys and girls dance together?" And then more to himself he continued, "I'd always known there was something wrong with the way people were dancing at the club...."

Terra gasped, hopping up and letting the bag of chips fall to the ground. Her eyes flicked between Kole and Faye as though she knew a secret that neither of them knew about themselves. Faye had the sudden urge to demand what that secret was, but she didn't ask it. "You two like each other," she observed, her eyebrows rising. "Aw, that's adorable! You two have to dance together."

Kole and Faye looked at each other before turning back to Terra. "What?" they asked blankly.

"Aw, this is so great! And none of you have ever danced together because of the stupid Government, ugh." Terra clapped her hands together. "I'm going to give you all dance lessons."

Everyone stared at Terra like she'd grown ten heads and announced that she was the beast on the other side of the Gate. Faye blinked, not saying anything. Errika, on the other hand, had no problem voicing her confusion. But that wasn't a surprise. She never did. "But we know how to dance," she said blankly. "They have dances at school you know."

"Yeah, but you don't know how to dance with other people do you?" Terra raised an eyebrow. "You don't know how to dance with a boy."

Everyone continued to stare at her as though she was insane. Faye blinked again, trying to comprehend what Terra was saying. Dancing with a boy? Was there really a specific way to do it? Faye glanced at Kole and bit her lip. And what did Terra mean by "you two like each other"? Of course she liked Kole, he was an amazing person. But did she mean the way the man and the woman liked each other in the movie? Faye's eyes flicked down to Kole's lips, and her stomach did a flip.

"Okay, Alex—that's your name right?" Terra cocked an eyebrow at Alex from where he sat. He stared at her, unblinking.

"Yes," he said, his own eyebrow raising. "What about it?"

"Get up." She smirked, making a motion with her hand. "Up. Now. Chop chop."

Faye had to resist the urge to laugh as Alex glanced around at everyone before getting up, his hands shoved into his pockets. Terra rolled her eyes, pulling his hands out of his pockets and holding onto them. She grinned at his unease, apparently finding humor in the discomfort. Faye watched with wide eyes, wondering what was going to happen next.

"Watch and learn," Terra drawled. "Now, Alex, put your hands on my waist."

"Uh. . . ."

Terra rolled her eyes again, bringing his hands down to her hips. They rested there, and Alex looked thoroughly uncomfortable. "My hips are not going to electrocute you, Alex, come on now." Terra winked. She glanced at everyone, her eyes bright. "Now, I'm going to put my arms around his neck. Okay ladies?"

Faye watched as Terra taught Alex how to dance. It was what Terra called a "slow dance." Apparently there were many different kinds, ones that Terra hadn't perfected herself but knew how to do. She didn't feel like teaching everyone, she told them. She did show them a dance that didn't really have a name. A sort of free-style dance where both moved together in their own melodies. Terra twisted around and danced in front of Alex, her hips swaying from side to side. Faye's eyes widened as Alex's hands went to her hips. It was as though he was acting on reflex.

"Ah, this just isn't as good without music," Terra mused, pursing her lips. "Does anyone have an iPod or something?"

Seth pulled an iPod out of his pocket and handed it to her. He looked like he didn't exactly want to give her his piece of technology, but he did it anyway. Faye wondered if he wanted to see what dancing was like with music. Faye knew she wanted to. It looked fascinating without it, so how did it look with it?

Terra took the iPod from Seth's hands, thanking him. Seth sat back, wide-eyed as Terra scrolled through his songs, a thoughtful look on her face. It was then Faye realized she'd never heard a boy sing before. What did it sound like? Was it as beautiful as some of the girls sang? Was it even better?

It was. Faye was practically hypnotized as Terra selected the song she wanted. His voice was angelic, something that Faye instantly would have purchased on her iTunes at home. She suddenly hated the Government even more. How dare they deprive them of such beauty? His voice, whoever he was, was amazing.

Alex and Terra went back to dancing, and it was completely magical. She'd never witnessed anything like it. Faye gaped at the scene before her, her fingers drumming on the side of the couch. She wanted to dance with them, to sway her hips back and forth like Terra did. She wanted in on this magic.

Terra's eyes met hers. "Faye, you and Kole should dance!" she called over the blasting music.

Faye's eyes widened. She glanced at Kole, questioning him with her eyes. She wanted to dance, and if she were to dance with anyone it would be Kole. He met her gaze and he smiled. "Do you want to dance?" he asked. When Faye nodded, he grinned and grabbed her hand, pulling her up.

Faye didn't know what overcame her, but suddenly they were dancing just like Alex and Terra, as though they'd known how to do it their entire lives. Faye's hips swayed back and forth, and she laughed as Kole danced with her, his movements smooth as though he'd been dancing his entire life. He laughed along with her, his hands going to her hips. She felt her skin burn from his touch, and she looked up at him, her eyes wide. What was going on? Was it natural for her stomach to act the way it was, for her skin to burn up? Her arms went around Kole's shoulders, and they began to burn, too.

Errika somehow convinced Terence to dance with her, and soon they were swaying back and forth, too. Seth and Zander watched from the sidelines. Seth seemed distantly amazed by the whole ordeal, but Zander seemed unfazed. It was like he wasn't really in the room, like he was miles away. Probably at his house, putting his brother to bed, reading him a story. That's what he said he was supposed to be doing. Faye felt bad for him. To have his whole life changed in a second because the Government took his father away. Her eyes widened. If only he'd gone to the Government building with them. Maybe he could have broken his father out, maybe they could have been reunited.

Faye let her concentration fall away from the two boys and concentrated on Kole. He consumed her. His eyes seemed especially bright. His hands were gentle as they held onto her hips, but that didn't matter. Everywhere he touched seemed to burn, to numb, to affect her. Faye didn't know what was going on, but she loved it. She didn't know why she loved it, but she did. It felt amazing.

If only they could dance all of their problems away, Faye thought. Then the world would be perfect.

Perfect.

"Faye, it's getting late."

Faye's eyes met Errika's and she sighed. Errika was right of course. It was nearing ten o'clock and they still had to get over the other side. Her eyes left Errika's and turned to her sister, where she stood with her arms crossed lightly over her chest. Tonight had been a dream. Getting her sister back after seven years of mourning, dancing with a boy. Not in all her life had she imagined this happening. "You're right," she murmured with a sigh. "We have to get back."

Terra frowned and nodded. Then she moved forward, wrapping her arms tightly around Faye. Faye hugged her just as tightly back, her head resting in the crook of her sister's neck. She didn't want to leave her here, to go home and pretend to be the same terrified girl that she'd become. She wanted to stay with Terra, with Kole and the others. Here she felt braver, like she actually had a purpose.

"I'll see you soon," Terra said with a smile as they pulled away. "I promise."

Faye smiled brightly. "Count on it," she replied. She gave her one last hug before stepping back and looking at Kole. She could still feel his arms around her as they danced, could still feel where his fingers had touched her skin. They'd stopped dancing an hour ago and Faye still felt as though they were swaying back and forth, their hips moving to the beat of the music.

She nodded to Kole before following Errika toward the door. They would be back soon, she knew that. They'd all agreed that they would go to Zander's house in order to upload the files from the flash drive. They couldn't do it at anyone else's house. Terence, Seth, Kole, and Alex were at risk of getting caught by their parents, and so were Errika and Faye. Zander was the only one who didn't have that problem. And even if it were a problem, his father wouldn't have minded. He'd tried to go to the Gate's borders after all.

Kole was right behind the two girls as they exited the house. As Errika started down the porch, and Faye moved to follow her, but Kole caught hold of her arm, pulling her back. Her eyebrows creased as she paused, turning to him. He was staring at her intently, like he was trying to figure something out. "Kole?" she asked, concern etching into her tone. "Are you all right?"

Kole didn't answer for a moment. His eyes searched her face. What he was looking for, Faye didn't know. But, as his hand cupped her cheek, her breath caught in her throat and she couldn't ask. She didn't know what he was doing, but she didn't care. She loved the feeling of his hand on her skin. It was so soft, so gentle. "That movie," he said hoarsely. "That movie kind of describes how I feel about you."

Faye's eyes widened as she took in what he said. She'd by lying if the movie didn't describe what she felt about him, but to hear him say the words out loud . . . she just couldn't believe it. How would they know if the movie described their feelings? How would they know if they were feeling really anything at all? The Government had deprived them of this knowledge, left them ignorant and clueless. "How do you know?" she whispered.

Kole smiled. "I have this feeling."

Faye continued to stare at Kole. She knew that Errika was waiting for her, was probably calling her name, but it didn't seem to matter. Kole was consuming her again, becoming all that she saw. She thought of the movie, of the way the man and the woman had held each other so close, their lips colliding. Her eyes found their way to his, and she wondered what that would feel like. She wanted to know so badly.

Faye swallowed. "It—it kind of describes how I feel about you, too," she confessed.

Kole's smile grew. And then his head was inching toward hers. Faye's breath caught as his lips grew closer. Her heart thrashed around in her chest, and for a moment she was terrified that she was about to have a heart attack. She let out a long breath of air just before Kole caught his lips with her own.

Faye couldn't describe what she felt as their lips touched. Her arms found their way around his neck, pulling him closer to her as their lips moved together. At first it was kind of awkward—neither of them really knew what to do. But then they both just let go.

Acted on instinct. Kole's free arm wrapped around her, pulling her closer to him.

Faye wondered if this was how the characters in the movie felt when they kissed each other. Did it feel this foreign, this utterly wonderful?

As soon as it began, it ended when they pulled away for air. "Wow," she breathed. She wanted to pull him back to her, to have their lips touching again. She wanted that incredible feeling back. But she knew that she couldn't. She had to get home before her mother worried. "That was—"

Kole pressed his lips against hers one last time before sighing. "Amazing," he finished. He pulled away completely, his arms falling to his side. "You should go," he murmured. "Errika's waiting."

Faye nodded, moving away from Kole as she dragged her feet down the porch, onto the walkway. She glanced back at Kole and smiled before coming to stand next to Errika. Her eyes were wide as she looked between Kole and Faye, her mouth agape. "Oh my—" She brought a hand to her mouth. "You better spill on every detail, girly. Walk with me. Now."

Faye laughed, looping her arm through Errika's as they began down the road, toward the forest, toward their home.

Faye was expecting to be reprimanded for coming home so late, but she wasn't. In fact the only reaction her mom had to her stepping through the door was calling, "Faye! Hurry, come here!"

Faye's eyebrows creased as she rushed into the living room, her eyes wide. Kat and her mom were sitting on the couch, holding each other's hands. Faye crept toward them, not knowing what to think. Why were they staring at her like that? Had they somehow found out about Terra? Had they found out that she'd been going over the Gate's borders?

Her mother nodded toward the television. Static consumed it, and Faye instantly knew that Courtnie was preparing to give a message to Cesve. She felt her stomach curl in on itself with rage. How dare Courtnie order them around? How dare she keep everyone in the dark? Everyone deserved to know the truth. Every girl and boy deserved to know what it felt like to hold someone in their arms, to kiss them the way that she and Kole had kissed not an hour before. But because of Courtnie and the rest of the Government, they couldn't.

Faye sighed, forcing herself to stop thinking angered thoughts before collapsing onto the free couch cushion. Her mother gripped her hand tightly as the static began to disappear and Courtnie's face appeared on the screen. Faye stared back at her, feeling like Courtnie was looking straight at her. Like she knew that Faye was the one who let Terra out. This was probably what this was about, Faye thought. The fact that Terra was missing. Of course they wouldn't say that outright—they weren't that stupid.

"Hello, Cesve," Courtnie murmured. Faye could see the distant, crazed look in Courtnie's eyes. It made her stomach do an uncomfortable flip. "This is an urgent message. A little while ago, made an edit on how far you could go into the forest before you reached the Gate's territory. Now we are doing it again."

Faye tensed. She prayed that her mother didn't notice, but from the look on Mary's face, she was sure that she had.

"Please understand that this is for the greater good of everyone," Courtnie continued. Her eyes bored into Faye as though she was ripping her apart. "I hereby decree that if anyone sets so much as a foot into the forest, they will be arrested. If anyone sees anyone going into the forest, they are to report it to the police immediately.

"Again, please understand that this is for the greater good."

The screen went black.

Faye hopped up, her hand falling out of her mother's grasp as she exclaimed, "She can't do that!"

Her mother stood up, grabbing onto her frantic daughter's shoulders. "Honey, I know that you and Errika enjoy the Campout, but this is the law. I'm sorry."

Faye's eyes met her mothers, her breaths coming out labored. If only her mother knew that she wasn't upset because of the Campout, that this was bigger than that—way bigger. If only her mother knew just how manipulative their leader was, how much she tortured people for no other reason than because she could. Faye wished that she could tell her mother everything.

But she couldn't.

Instead she sagged, forcing herself to pretend to calm down when inside she was anything but. She nodded. "Yeah," she mumbled. "It's the law."

Faye pulled away from her mother and stormed into her bedroom, pacing back and forth. How were she and Errika supposed to get back to the other side now? How were they supposed to discover just what Courtnie had on her computer? How were they supposed to take the Government down?

Before Faye could even think of what she was doing, she flipped open her cell phone and dialed Kole's number. She brought the phone to her ear, breathing deeply. Maybe Terra would have a plan. She always seemed to.

"Faye?"

"Did you see the broadcast?" she demanded, skipping the greeting, her voice tense. "Did you see it?"

"Yeah," Kole replied. "Fortis just clicked off. Seth, Terence, and Zander left right before it came on, so I'm not sure if they saw it yet. Alex is pissed off."

"And Terra?"

"She's laughing."

Faye fell back on her bed, closing her eyes. Of course Terra would find amusement in this. "She's making jokes, isn't she?" Faye drawled, wiping her face with the back of her hand. If only Terra were here making jokes. Maybe then Faye wouldn't feel so on edge.

"Yeah."

In the distance Faye could hear Terra's voice. Her heart skipped a beat. It was still so unreal that Terra was here and alive, that she was still cracking jokes instead of rotting in the ground. Faye opened her eyes, her gaze on her bedroom door. What if her mother walked in and heard her talking on the phone about Terra? What would happen then?

"What are we going to do?" Faye whispered.

Kole paused before answering. "Terra wants to talk to you."

"Kole—"

But Kole was gone, replaced with Terra. "Hello, Faye," she said brightly.

Faye let her gaze fall from her bedroom door before she stood up, her free hand shoved in her pocket. "Hey," she replied softly, her gaze on the floor.

Terra laughed. "Aw honey, relax. Courtnie won't be able to stop us with some stupid restriction law. I'll think of something I promise."

"Are you sure."

"Of course I'm sure." Terra snorted. "It won't be easy, but it's definitely possible. Leave the worrying to me, hon."

Faye cocked an eyebrow as she walked to her window, looking outside. It was almost completely pitch black outside except for the stars and street lights. Everything looked so normal, completely like it always had. It was the same street, the same city, the same people. And yet it looked completely different. Faye wasn't seeing it with the same eyes anymore.

"But you aren't worrying." Faye cocked an eyebrow. "So how am I supposed to leave the worrying to you?"

"Technicality," Terra said dismissively. "Now, why don't you tell me about that kiss you and Kole shared, yeah?"

Faye blinked. Out of all the things Terra wanted to talk about right now, it was her and Kole? "Uh...."

"Don't deny it! I looked out the window to see you leave and you were on the porch with Kole. Ah, my baby sister is growing up." Terra sighed dreamily. "This is great. So completely great."

"It was amazing," Faye admitted. "But don't we have other things to worry about right now? What if Courtnie and Fortis find you? What if—?"

Faye cut off as her bedroom door opened and Kat stepped in. Her stomach dropped as a smirk curled on her younger sister's face. This could not be good. She could hear Terra's laughter on the other line, and it only made her stomach drop more. "What do you want, Kat?" Faye demanded coolly, praying that Terra would hear her. She probably should have hung up the phone, but that would only be more suspicious.

"Who are you talking to?" Kat asked, cocking a blond eyebrow. Why she took a sudden interest in Faye's social life, she wasn't sure, but she didn't like it.

"Errika," Faye lied smoothly, rolling her eyes. "Why do you care?"

"You were just with Errika," Kat retorted. "So why would you be calling her?"

"Because the Government just took out our one thing that we enjoy doing, obviously," Faye snapped. "Go away, Kat."

"Wow, your little sister is feisty," Terra mused on the other line. Faye resisted the urge to laugh. If she did that would only bring more trouble.

"You've been disappearing a lot lately," Kat drawled, stepping further into the room. She fell onto Faye's bed, her eyes glinting nastily. Faye stared at her, not really knowing where Kat was going with all of this. If she knew something, she needed to spill it. But it wasn't like Faye could ask. If she did, and Kat didn't have information, she was screwed.

"Yeah, it's called a social life. Now get out of my room."

Kat rolled her eyes, hopping up from Faye's bed and sauntering toward the door. "You're up to something," she said lightly. "I know you are. And when I find out, you're so grounded."

With that, Kat left the room, the door shutting loudly behind her.

"Oh, the girl who likes getting the older sister grounded, nice," Terra drawled with a laugh. "She's funny, I like her."

"Of course you do." Faye dragged a hand down her face. "She's driving me nuts. She does random shit sometime just to get me going. A little while ago she brought down one of your boxes from the attic and put it on my bed. And then she was like, 'Oh hey Faye, I found this!' It's like she lives off my suffering or something."

Terra sighed. "She'll get over herself eventually. They all do."

"She better. Otherwise I'm going to have to kill her."

Terra snorted. "Yeah, like you'd kill someone." She paused. "Listen, I promise that we'll figure out a way to get past this stupid law, all right? Promise me you won't worry."

"But I—"

"Promise me."

Faye sighed deeply, bringing a hand through her hair. "Fine," she grumbled. "I promise."

"Good," Terra said lightly. "Good night, Faye! I'll see you soon."

Faye opened up her mouth to reply, but Terra had already hung up. She sighed again, shutting her phone and tossing it onto her bed. She struggled not to worry, not to concentrate on the fact that Courtnie had made it one-hundred times harder to get over to the other side. But it was hard. Despite Terra's orders, it was in Faye's nature to worry.

Faye fell back on her bed, closing her eyes again. Terra would find a way to get them through this, she knew that. All she had to do now was wait for the plan. She just hoped that it came soon, because something told Faye that they were running out of time.

CHAPTER 18

"What are we going to do when Dad gets back?"

Terra's eyes flicked in Alex's direction as he spoke quietly to Kole a few feet away. If he was trying to be secretive about the conversation, it wasn't working. Over the years Terra'd learned how to tune in on certain conversations, listen for certain sounds. It'd been crucial when listening out for the guards over the cries of the girls in the prison wards. Listening out for trouble had become instinct. So it was only natural for her to tune in now on the boys' conversation, listening to each nervous word.

"We could just hide her upstairs," Kole replied. "Dad never goes into our rooms. He respects our privacy, remember?"

"Yeah, but you've been disappearing a lot lately," Alex pointed out. "You do realize that he notices that, right?"

Kole sighed, crossing his arms over his chest. Terra knew that she was imposing on them, that she was creating quite a problem, but where else did she have to go? She couldn't just waltz into her old home like she'd never left. She couldn't do that to her mother. She'd rather have Mary believe her dead than put her in danger.

These boys knew about the Government, what they did. They put their own lives in danger just like she had. Her staying here would make no difference whatsoever.

Terra tilted her head to the side, concentrating on Kole instead of the conversation. She could see what Faye saw in him. A fit build with a kind looking face. Not only that, but she couldn't help but feel like he was the perfect fit for Faye. They had the same personalities, yet they were changing each other as well. Terra didn't know Kole all that well. In fact, all she knew about him was the footage from the cameras. But she could tell that through this whole ordeal he was changing. He and Faye had transformed into different, stronger people. And she knew that Alex could tell, too.

"Yes, I know he notices," Kole muttered. "I'm not stupid. But, Alex, what other choice do we have? I'm not throwing her out. She's Faye's sister."

Alex cast a glance in Terra's direction. Terra stared back unblinkingly, showing him that she knew exactly what they were talking about. His eyes widened, and he seemed utterly taken aback that she had no shame in showing that she was eavesdropping. What difference did it make if she knew or not, anyway? They were going to tell her in a few moments anyway.

"I understand that she's Faye's sister," Alex whispered. "And I understand that we can't just throw her out. But this is getting really dangerous, Kole. You heard the broadcast—"

"And Terra said we could find a way around it," Kole whispered back.

Terra felt her lips prick into a small smile. Kole put so much faith in her, she thought distantly. And why? Because Faye did. Faye would put her life in Terra's hands, and Kole would undoubtedly do the same. Terra probably should have felt a huge weight on her shoulders, but she didn't. All she could feel was the utter amazement that after all of these years Faye's love and trust never wavered. Even after she found out all Terra hid through the years, she still loved her more than really anything.

Terra didn't know what she'd do without Faye.

"But what if Terra can't find a way around it?" Alex visibly tensed. "What if they push us back against a wall and there's nowhere to run?"

"There's always a way to run," Kole said determinedly. "Even in the prison wards there are ways to sabotage."

"Not if the punishment is death, Kole." Alex's eyes seemed to plead with his brother to see, and Terra felt a tug on her heart. Their bond was strong, Alex's and Kole's. As strong as hers and Faye's. "What if they catch you and put you to death?"

"Then I die and you get pissed off," Kole said, cracking a small smile.

"I'm serious."

"I know." Kole sighed. "But we can't concentrate on the dangers, Alex. Not when we're doing what's right."

Alex sighed deeply, bringing a hand down his face and shaking his head. "I know that you're young and this is a huge adventure for you. And I know how deeply you care for Faye. I get it. And I encourage it. Hell, I think this is the best thing that could ever happen to us. But the second your life becomes threatened, we're done. Do you hear me? I am not going to let you die because of a girl."

Kole laughed softly. It wasn't a laugh with humor, no. It was a bitter laugh aimed toward this whole situation as a whole. "But

Alex, don't you get it? My life has been on the line this entire time. And I knew that. And I think it's worth it. And you must too because you haven't stopped me."

Alex froze, his eyes wide. It was like he was just realizing how much he and everyone had risked. "It didn't hit me until now," he admitted. "Kole, I'm just—"

"Worried, I know." Kole put a hand on Alex's shoulder. "But that doesn't change anything. Because right now what we have to concentrate on is hiding Terra, keeping all of this from Dad, and how to get the girls over the Gate without anyone noticing."

Terra stood up then, stepping toward the boys with a determined look in her eye. Kole and Alex both looked up as Terra moved forward. Apprehension was clear in Alex's eyes. "I promise that the second your father suspects there's someone else here, I'll leave," she said. "And he won't. Because I'm good at hiding. You may not think it because I ended up getting stuck in the prison wards, but I am. And," she added, a smirk pricking up on her lips, "I do have a plan on getting the girls over the Gate without anyone noticing. That is, if you're willing to hear it."

"If you had let me kill her right from the beginning this wouldn't be a problem."

Courtnie's fingernails dug into her palm as she glared her brother down. They stood in front of Terra's empty cell, one on either side of the door. Courtnie couldn't bear to be in touching distance of Fortis right now. If she was close enough, she'd probably tear his eyes out. This was his fault. His fault.

"If you didn't insist on keeping up with this pointless battle, none of this would be a problem." Fortis returned her glare. "You don't get it, do you Courtnie? All of these people here hate us because you're obsessed with a pointless cause."

"Don't turn this on me!" Courtnie practically shrieked. "This is about Terra escaping, not you losing sight on what's important."

"Me losing sight on what's important?" Fortis seethed. "Jesus, Courtnie—"

"Shut up," Courtnie snapped. "Just shut up."

What were they going to do? That was the question. It'd been Courtnie's idea to broadcast a message to Cesve stating no one was allowed in the woods. Terra was probably laughing her ass off right now, Courtnie thought bitterly. She was probably enjoying herself immensely, wherever she was. She could have been anywhere. Anywhere.

However, Terra escaping wasn't the only problem. Her escaping meant that she wasn't working alone. Who was helping her? Who aided this escape? Were they inside the building right now? Did they work here? It was impossible to tell at this point. Somehow Terra had managed to take control of all the cameras, even the security cameras in the building.

"I told you it was her fault the cameras were down," Courtnie hissed. "I told you she'd tampered with them. But no, Terra is innocent because she's your blood."

"I understand that you're upset, Courtnie—"

"Upset?" Courtnie spat. "I'm beyond upset, Fortis. You wish I was upset. No. I'm far past that."

"Well, whatever you are you have to get over it. Because that's not going to bring Terra back."

Courtnie smiled maliciously. "And she's not coming back. When I find her, I'm going to kill her. And you can't do anything to stop me."

Fortis opened his mouth to object, but Courtnie was already gone, spinning on her heel and storming out of the prison wards, back to her office.

"Are we sure this is going to work?" Faye whispered into her cell phone as she tiptoed down the stairs. It was almost pitch black, making it very hard to see as she navigated her way through the house. Under normal circumstances Faye wouldn't be out and about so late, but this was not a normal circumstance. No, now was the time that called for her to be out and about at two o'clock in the morning.

"I'm sure," Terra replied. "No one should be awake at this time of night, so no one will see you coming."

"But what if they are awake?" Faye asked softly.

She'd asked this question many times of course. It'd been three days since Terra and Kole called, telling her the plan. Errika and Faye insisted on waiting a couple of days before attempting, seeing how everyone's guards were bound to be up due to the broadcast. The people of Cesve weren't stupid. Everyone would know that Courtnie only broadcasted that because it was a measure she had to take. Three days didn't seem like a long enough wait, but Faye knew that they couldn't afford to wait any longer. Courtnie was obviously going to start searching for Terra sooner than later.

"They won't be," Terra assured Faye lightly. "And if they are—which they won't—just act like you're not going into the forest."

"Where would I be going?" Faye challenged. It wasn't to make it difficult for Terra. It was a legitimate question. She wasn't one to think of a good lie on the spot.

"You're going to the store because you're on your period and ran out of tampons."

Faye blinked. "It's quite alarming how fast you came up with that," she told her sister as she made it to the bottom of the stairs and headed toward the kitchen. She grimaced as she whacked her knee on something unknown, bending over and biting down on her lip to keep from swearing. She just hoped that no one heard that....

"Are you okay?" Terra asked, concern appearing in her tone. "What was that?"

"I banged into something," Faye muttered. "I'm fine—"

"Faye?"

Faye spun around, her eyes wide as they landed on Kat. Kat's hair was all out of place as though she hadn't cared enough to pull her hair back properly before finding out what the fuss was about. This shocked Faye more than it probably should have. Kat's appearance seemed to mean everything to her, yet she'd rushed down here like this was more important. She must have really wanted to catch Faye in her wrongdoings.

"Kat," Faye whispered harshly. "What are you doing up?"

Kat's expression hardened. "I could ask you the same question."

"Kat, I really can't afford to talk to you right now," Faye snapped. "Please, just go back to bed."

"And what, let you sneak out?" Kat snapped back. "Where are you going, Faye? Why are you sneaking around all the time now? What are you hiding?"

"Kat—"

"Faye, you have to hurry," Terra said softly. "We don't have much time to get you out of the forest on the other side before people start waking up for work."

Faye paused, inwardly groaning. Terra was right of course. Not only did Errika and Faye have to get to the Gate from their side without anyone noticing, but they also had to get to Kole's house without being noticed. She legitimately could not afford to stand here and have a conflict with Kat right now. "Kat," she muttered. "I need to go."

As Faye turned to leave, Kat grabbed onto her arm. "Nuh-uh," she hissed. "Where are you going, Faye?"

"Okay, I don't like this kid anymore," Terra said with an irritated voice. "We don't have time for this. Put me on speaker."

"But Ter—"

Faye's mouth snapped shut. Holy shit. Had she just slipped Terra's name? She'd ruined everything now.

"Ter?" Kat pulled away, letting out a gasp. "Do you mean Terra? Faye, she's dead."

Faye could hear Terra sigh. "Put me on speaker, Faye."

Faye bit her lip before doing as she was told, knowing that she was going to regret it immediately. What was Terra going to tell Kat? Kat couldn't have her life put in danger as well. Kat may have been annoying, but she wasn't that annoying.

"Kat?" Terra's voice came from the receiver. "Can you hear me?"

"Who are you?" Kat asked softly, fear clear in her voice. "And what are you and my sister up to?"

"Honey, I'm afraid that's none of your business," Terra said lightly. "Now I need you to do something for me. I need to you to walk your butt back upstairs to your bedroom, and I need you to go back to bed. Because it is quite important for Faye to leave now. And, while you're at it, don't tell your mother about this because there isn't really a need to. Faye will be back soon enough."

Faye felt her stomach tighten. The irritation was evident in Terra's voice, and she could all but imagine the annoyed expression on her face. Terra was never one to get irritated with Faye, so this was new. Even though the annoyance wasn't directed in her direction, it still made her uncomfortable.

"You're Terra, aren't you?" Kat whispered.

"Go to bed, Kat," Terra said, the light overtone leaving, replaced with pure agitation. "Now." Her voice directed at Faye now, she continued, "Faye, hon, please ignore your sister and hurry. We don't have much time."

Terra hung up.

Faye snapped her phone shut and placed it in her pocket. Her eyes collided with Kat's, and she knew that Kat had no doubt in her mind that that was Terra on the phone. "Don't tell anyone about what just happened," Faye said coolly. "Do you understand me?"

"I thought Terra was dead." Kat's voice trembled. "You and Mom said she was dead—"

"She is dead," Faye snapped meanly, her hands flying in the air. "Dammit, Kat, you're going to get me killed. I'm leaving, now."

Faye spun around and ran for the door, not at all caring about being quiet now. Kat had cost her precious time. Time that she did not have. And now she had to rush to Errika's house before it was too late. Otherwise they were doomed.

"Terra talked to Kat on the phone?" Errika hissed as they snuck through the night. "Is she crazy? That was such a bold move."

"Terra's bolder than anyone we know," Faye whispered. "Does it really surprise you that she did?"

Errika fell silent, her footsteps the only sound coming from her as they continued down the street. Their only source of light came from the assorted street lights. The stars and moon seemed to be blocked out by clouds, only making this seem so much more frightening than it was. Worried thoughts cluttered Faye's mind. What if Kat ran and woke up their mother? What if Kat told their mother that Terra was alive? That thought disturbed her most of all. If Kat told their mom that Terra was walking around, how would Mary survive that? To know that the past seven years had been a complete and utter lie?

"Kat knows it was Terra on the phone," Faye said.

"I don't doubt that."

"What if she tells my mom?" Faye demanded, shooting an anxious look in Errika's direction. "My mom will never survive that, Errika. You know that."

Errika glanced Faye's way, and Faye knew that Errika agreed with her. Losing Terra may have been unbearable, but finding out your daughter had a secret agenda and was arrested by the Government that'd been lying to everyone about everything would be worse. And having to explain how Faye found out Terra was alive.... She wouldn't be able to do it. That would put everyone's lives at risk. "She won't tell your mom," Errika said finally. "She's too afraid. If Terra can come back from the dead, what else can she do?"

Faye nodded, but she wasn't convinced. Kat could be really stupid.

She just prayed that she wasn't that stupid.

Courtnie typed away at her laptop, her eyes narrowed. She had no doubt in her mind that Terra had come in here and copied all of her files, no doubt in her mind at all. The fact that her copy of 27 Dresses only proved that. Over the years Fortis brought down the movies in hopes of winning Terra's affections. Though it never worked, she did enjoy watching the movies of both boys and girls together in harmony. A gross, utterly wrong harmony.

"Aha," she muttered, clicking onto her computer history and pulling it up. No one, not even Fortis, knew just how advanced her computer was. It was disguised as an ordinary laptop—no different from anyone else's. But, in reality, it had a high tech security system that could track every single action that was done on the computer.

Flash drive – copied all of information on device, the history read.

Courtnie sat back in her chair, her eyes narrowing even further. Where had Terra even gotten a flash drive? How had she managed to destroy things even from inside a cell? And how had she managed to convince someone to let her out of her cell without them being so terrified of being caught that they refused?

She clicked onto the Flash drive part of the history message, swiftly reading the information on it. Her computer could read all of the information on it, even when and where it was last used. The latest technology really had its perks.

Apparently there were enough gigabytes on the flash drive to hold the entire camera system, various viruses that could be injected into different software, and the entire contents of Court-nie's laptop (which held more data than any computer in Cesve). Courtnie read on, an evil smile growing with each word. Oh poor Terra, her mind cooed. That poor, mindless little girl. She had no idea about the power Courtnie held, had no idea that she could still track her even though she was long gone.

She had no idea about anything.

That was the best part. Terra might have thought she knew everything with her little smirks and her gaze that said she knew more than you did, but she didn't. And it was because of that that she was going to go down. Courtnie would bring her down. And she would enjoy it.

Courtnie's eyes landed on a certain piece of information and she grinned. I've got you, Terra Caldwell. I've got you.

"How much longer are you going to be, exactly?"

Kole barely looked at Zander as he crowded with everyone else around the computer screen. Terra moved swiftly through the files as she tried to find the one she was looking for. Part of Kole felt sorry that they were using Zander's place the way they were, but most of him couldn't be bothered to care. This was the only place they could go without any family members really discovering anything. Zachary wouldn't go on the computer even if he could. He was the type of boy who enjoyed going outside, not playing video games.

"Chill out, Zander," Terence muttered briskly as Terra paused to read over some information. Kole squinted, attempting to read what she was looking at. It looked like a list of people.

"Is that my name?" Faye asked suddenly. "What is this?"

Kole's eyes glided over to Faye. Her red hair seemed especially red today. Maybe it was the extra fire she seemed to hold lately. Or maybe it was the new way that Kole was looking at her. He wasn't just looking at her anymore. He was seeing her. He was seeing the greenness of her eyes, seeing the way her hair flowed down toward her hips. He was seeing her curves, the shape of her jaw as she spoke to Terra. He could see her now for what she was: utterly beautiful, utterly perfect.

"It's a list of everyone in Cesve," Terra replied. "It states the citizen's name, the father's name, the mother's name, and then any siblings they have."

"Who are my mom and dad?" Faye asked, her eyebrows creasing. "I mean—Mom is my mom, but—"

"I know what you mean, Faye." Terra gave her a half-smile. Her eyes held so much respect for Faye, Kole noticed. Terra was truly a great sister, he knew that. To be trapped in the prison wards and never lose sight of what was truly important ... that was amazing. If Kole had been trapped in there for so long, he would have been driven mad. But Terra didn't. She kept going, kept plotting and waiting for the moment when she could be reunited with Faye again. He respected her on so many levels and he barely knew her.

Terra paused as she read over Faye's information. "Your mother is a woman named Cecilia Banks, and your father is a man named Caleb Frost."

Kole froze before muttering a, "Frost?"

Everyone spun around to face him. Kole's eyes flicked to Alex swiftly before returning back to Terra's and Faye's. "My last name is Frost," he said. "Does that mean Faye and I are ... related?"

Terra laughed, shaking her head. "No, you're not related. You're not really related to your father, or to Alex. I'm guessing your father and Caleb are related, though. I've seen pictures of your dad and the eyes have a resemblance to Faye's."

Kole shook his head, not comprehending anything that Terra was saying. Well, he comprehended it a little, but not much. How could he not be related to Alex, to his father? They were his family, the only people that he was ever close to. It seemed utterly ridiculous that they weren't related.

"Do I have any blood-related siblings?" Faye asked.

Terra nodded. "Yes, you have a sister. Her name is Tannie."

Kole watched as Faye's eyes widened. She was remembering Tannie, he realized. She knew this girl, had interacted with this girl. What was that like—interacting with a sibling and having absolutely no idea you were related? Had that happened to Kole? Did he have a blood-related brother, a blood-related sister?

"That annoying girl from the Campout?" Errika exclaimed. She whistled through her teeth. "Wow, I'm sorry to hear that."

Terra snickered. "Why don't we see who you're related to, dear Errika?"

Terra scrolled through the information for a few moments before she stopped, her eyes widening. Kole leaned forward and his own eyes widened. What? "Oh my god," Terra whispered, awe and amusement clear in her voice. "Well, that totally makes sense."

"What?" Errika demanded immediately, pushing forward so that she could get a better look. "What is it?"

Kole turned to Alex. Of course, he thought. Of course. They looked so much alike; it made perfect sense....

"Errika, why don't you turn around and give your older brother a hug?" said Terra.

Errika spun around, her eyes locking on Alex. Alex seemed utterly confused for a moment, but then realization lit in his eyes. At first they just stared at each other, but then Errika rolled her eyes, grabbing Alex by the arm and pulling him to her, wrapping her arms around him. Kole almost laughed as Alex hesitated before hugging her back. This was his first time hugging a girl, he thought with more than a distant amusement.

"What exactly are we looking for?" Zander demanded again as the siblings drew apart. "Anything in particular? Or did you just steal all of Courtnie's information for the hell of it?"

"Zander, what's your problem?" Terence demanded, cocking an eyebrow. "You're usually chiller."

Zander glared. "It's almost four o'clock in the morning and Zachary could wake up at any minute and see us all crowding around the computer like a bunch of idiots. So excuse me if I'm a little rushed."

Kole stared at Zander. He'd changed a lot since his dad got tossed in the prison wards. He'd become more responsible, more cautious about what he did and when he did it. Zachary was all that really mattered to him now. Zachary's needs were what came first, not theirs. And Kole didn't blame him for that. If he were in Zander's position, he probably would act the same way, too.

"I took all of Courtnie's files because she's bound to have something that we can use," Terra said. "She's the head of the Government on the girl's side. She has all of the information on Cesve that she could possibly have."

"Is there any information on why we're separated?" Seth asked. He was acting strangely kind for someone who had a serious temper problem. He always seemed ticked off nowadays, but today he was perfectly fine. "Like, why they're doing this in the first place?"

Terra twisted around in her seat. Kole watched as her eyes flashed, and a deep anger bubbled inside of her. She hated the Government so much. Kole hated the Government, too, and with each day he despised it even more. But Terra? Her loathing was on a completely different level. Her hatred had time to settle, to simmer, to grow. "Oh, you guys didn't know?" she asked, her tone bitter. "The reason they keep us apart is to prevent what's going on between Faye and Kole."

Kole's eyes locked on Faye, and hers locked on his. He felt his fingers tingle, and his heart began to beat faster in his chest as he thought of his lips on hers, of kissing her on the porch. He wanted to kiss her again, wanted to hug her and hold her hand. But he couldn't do that right now. It wasn't the right time.

"What?" Terence demanded. "Is something bad happening to them?"

"No." Terra shook her head. "They're falling in love. And the Government doesn't want that to happen."

"Why?"

The question came from Zander. He had his arms crossed over his chest, his jaw working. His father was put away because of this. Kole knew that Zander was going to be pissed that the reason they kept the two genders apart was a completely idiotic one. Families were torn apart because the Government wanted to prevent love? Why?

"Because a long time ago," Terra explained, "the Government found that love was destructive." Her eyes locked on Kole. "Would you die for Faye?"

"Yes," Kole said without even thinking about it. And, as the words left his mouth, he realized they were true. He'd die for her in a heartbeat.

Terra nodded, a small smile curling on her lips. "Good," she said. It was like she expected him to say that. And, seeing how well she read people, he didn't doubt that she did. "And can you imagine your life without her? Can you imagine yourself with anyone else but her?"

Kole's eyes made their way to Faye again. "No," he whispered. He felt a pierce in his stomach at the thought of having a life without Faye in it. He'd known that feelings were brewing inside him, but he didn't know just what they were or how strong they were. The thought of losing Faye . . . it was worse than really anything he could imagine.

"Do you want to feel like this about anyone else?"

"No," Kole said immediately. "Of course not."

Faye smiled at him, and he smiled back. She felt the same way, her eyes and smile were telling him. She couldn't imagine a world without him in it, didn't want to. It was impossible, unbearable, out of the question. She wanted to be with him, and only him. He didn't really know what that meant, but he loved it.

"People back then felt the same way," Terra said with a nod. "And rightfully so, too. Love is a beautiful, powerful thing. But when people lost love, some people never recovered. In occasions such as a break up, a divorce, or a death, boys and girls alike went out of their mind. Many people killed themselves because of it. There was a time when so many people were killing themselves because of love that the Government decided to take action. Cesve was born. Volunteers built the Gate, and boys went one way while girls went another. Books were burned that had both boys and girls in it, movies, too. Every connection between boys and girls was broken.

"However, there was one problem: reproduction. In order for the human species to not run out, people still had to reproduce, to have babies. So, when lovers were trying to go over the Gate to see each other, the Government came up with a plan. Why not just arrest them and have them do the reproducing? No one had to know. And so it began. And now it's still continuing hundreds of years later."

Everyone was silent. Kole brought a hand through his hair, letting out a long breath of air. To think that these feelings stirring around inside him were the reason for why girls and boys were separated. It seemed utterly ridiculous—so completely stupid. It was one thing to try and prevent people from killing and hurting themselves, but to separate them completely?

He couldn't believe it.

"That's so stupid!" Errika exclaimed, her hands flying in the air. "Why did people just work out their problems instead of avoiding them to the point of this?"

"I don't know, Errika," Terra murmured. "Maybe if you were alive back then they would have."

Errika sighed. "Hell yeah they would have. Like I would have let them do something so incredibly stupid."

Kole couldn't help himself from laughing. Errika's face was turning red with anger as she threw her arms around and ranted. It got to the point where Faye had to shush her out of fear for waking Zachary up. At this Zander shot her a grateful look. Errika continued ranting, however, just at a lower decibel.

"It's getting really late." Faye glanced around, her eyes wide. "It's getting dangerous, staying here."

Terra nodded. She stood up, wrapping her arms around Faye quickly before holding her out at arm's length. "You go home and get some sleep. I'll call you if I get any information."

"I'm not putting you on speaker phone again," Faye told her, cracking a small smile.

Terra rolled her eyes. "That girl needs to get ahold of herself, honestly."

The two girls hugged again before pulling away completely. Terra gestured with her eyes for Kole to follow them out, and Kole complied immediately, falling into step beside Faye as she and Errika made their way for the door. Kole's hand slipped over Faye's as they exited the door and stepped onto the porch. Faye smiled brightly at him. He smiled brightly back.

"I don't understand how this could be a bad thing," Faye said, tilting her head to the side. "If anything, this is the best thing that could happen to anyone."

Kole brought a hand through her hair, his eyes devouring her face. He didn't understand it. "I don't know," he murmured. His hand came to rest on her cheek. "But we have it now, and that's all that matters, right?"

Faye nodded. Kole grinned before bringing his lips to hers in a kiss. Unlike last time, it wasn't awkward, wasn't completely confusing. It was perfect. As their lips moved together, and Faye's arms wrapped wrong Kole's neck, Kole felt as if nothing could ever get in his way.

"Kole," Faye muttered as they pulled away. Her eyes had darkened, a deep concern brewing within them. "I have a bad feeling."

Kole's hands, which had found their way to her waist, tightened their grip on her. "A bad feeling?" he asked. "About what?"

Faye shrugged. "I'm not sure, exactly. I just feel like something bad is going to happen. Something really bad."

Without really thinking about it, Kole brought Faye into an embrace. Her arms wrapped around him tightly, and he found himself bringing a hand through her hair. It was like his body knew what to do more than he did. "Everything is going to be fine," he assured her.

Faye pulled away. Her eyes drifted toward Errika where she was waiting at the bottom of the porch. Unlike last time, Errika seemed uneasy, as though she was actually afraid of getting caught. "Okay," she said softly. She tossed Kole a brief smile. "I'll see you soon."

And with that, Faye was gone, hurrying down the porch and to Errika, where they soon disappeared out of sight as they rushed down the road back toward home.

Kole sighed, bringing a hand through his hair. Faye had been right to feel the way she did. To feel like something was wrong, like something terrible was about to happen. Deep down, Kole felt it, too.

CHAPTER 19

Faye wasn't at all surprised to see Kat sitting on her bed when she arrived home.

Faye closed her bedroom door shut behind her as she crept into her bedroom, bringing a hand through her hair. Kat stared blankly at her with wide eyes. Faye wondered how long her sister had waited there, how long she'd sat there with her legs crossed over one another. Staring endlessly at a closed door. She should have felt bad that Kat waited here for so long, should have felt bad that her little sister was probably driving herself insane. However, it was rather difficult when the only reason Kat was like this was because she wanted to get Faye in trouble.

"You're back," Kat said tonelessly as Faye moved into the room.

Faye shrugged off her sweatshirt and threw it aimlessly onto the floor. She plopped onto her bed beside Kat, staring at the door for a moment before sighing. "You should have gone to bed."

Kat twisted around to face Faye with wide eyes. "Go to bed?" she whispered. "You expected me to go to bed after what happened?"

Faye's eyes scanned Kat slowly. She looked absolutely crazed as though she'd been locked in a padded cell for weeks. Her hair was all over the place, and whatever little mascara she'd had on fell in lines on her cheeks. Her clothes were all wrinkled as though she'd rolled around in an aimless fit to stay calm when she couldn't manage to think straight. And her eyes. They were wide, so wide. Wider than Faye had ever seen them.

Kat was frightening her to be honest.

"Nothing happened," Faye whispered.

Kat's eyes narrowed slightly, but they were still wider than usual. "You're bullshitting me," she snapped. Faye blinked. She'd never really heard her sister swear before. It was odd. "You have been for weeks. You think I don't know that you're not really going to Errika's when you sneak out? You may have Mom fooled, but you haven't fooled me. And your reaction to the last broadcast wasn't just because of the dumb Campout. It was bigger than that. Like you were the reason for it."

Faye didn't answer at first. What was she supposed to say? She couldn't keep lying to Kat; she obviously wasn't taking any of Faye's excuses anymore. But if she told her ... Kat's life would be at stake. "Look, I know that you think you're entitled to having all the information," Faye whispered. "But I'm not telling you because I want to keep you safe."

"I know." Kat sighed, wiping the back of her hand across her face. "I knew the second after you slipped on Terra's name. I knew this was bigger than any stupid excuse to get you grounded."

Faye stared at Kat for a long time. "This is the most understanding I think you've ever been. Ever."

Kat struggled to laugh but failed. "I just want to understand," she mumbled, her voice shaking. "I want to understand where you're going, why you're going there, and how Terra could be alive when you and Mom buried her." She closed her eyes for a moment before opening them. They shined with tears. "I just want to understand something big. Something more than hand-me-downs and the latest fashion. I want to do something important, too."

Faye nodded. She understood where Kat was coming from. For the first time she understood something Kat was saying. She understood. "I used to feel that way about Terra," Faye confessed. "I used to idolize her, to look up to her and wish that I could be so much more like her than I was. I wanted to be important, to be bright, to be loved by everyone the way she was. I wanted to be exactly like Terra because she succeeded in life where I didn't. She wasn't afraid of anything. I wanted to understand things like Terra did, to look at people like I knew more than they did and there was nothing they could do about it. But I couldn't because I was me."

Kat sighed shakily. "I've always wanted Mom to look at me the way she looks at you. I wanted to have my own clothes, to not feel like I was only here because Terra died. I can't help but feel like if Terra came back here Mom would give me up in a heartbeat. Terra will always come first to you guys. And I'll always come last."

Faye shook her head, wrapping her arms around Kat and pulling her to her. Kat collapsed in Faye's arms, weeping freely. "Kat, how could you ever think that?" Faye whispered. "You are just as much my sister was Terra is. And I would do everything in my power to keep you safe. Don't you get that's why I keep you in the dark?"

Kat nodded, continuing to sob into Faye's shirt. "I'm sorry," she cried. "I'm sorry for everything. I'm such a brat, and I'm a terrible person, and I know that I annoy you so much—"

Holding her out at arm's length, Faye stared Kat down with fierce determination. "You may annoy the hell out of me," Faye whispered. "And you may be a brat. But you are not a terrible person. And Mom and I do care about you. I may not show it that well, but that's because we're too busy arguing all the time. You know Mom loves you, don't you?"

Kat nodded, tears continuing to stream down her cheeks. "But I will never compare to Terra," she whispered. "I'll never be good enough."

Faye rolled her eyes, pulling Kat to her again. "Jeez, Kat," Faye mused, bringing a hand through her sister's hair. "No one can compare to Terra. Not even me."

With another shaky sigh Kat pulled away from Faye, wiping the tears from her eyes. She seemed so young, so vulnerable. And Faye's heart yearned to comfort her, to hug her again. It didn't happen often—Faye wanting to hug Kat—but it was happening now. For once Faye felt like she and Kat were on the same page.

"So Terra is alive," Kat said, her eyes searching Faye's face as though for the answer that she already had. "She didn't kill herself."

Faye sighed. "You already know the answer, and it would be a lot safer for me not to tell you." Faye smiled sadly. "Kat, just promise me something."

Kat nodded silently.

"If one day I don't come back home and the Government gives you some shit story about an accident, don't believe them. I won't have fallen; I won't have jumped off a cliff. If anyone killed me it was them. If I die it's because the Government did it, not anyone else."

"Do we really have to do this?"

Courtnie's eyes latched onto Fortis's for a single moment before returning to the task at hand. She slipped on her gloves, a smirk on her face. It was almost time, her inner voice sang. Almost time to bring this to an end. She was excited to say the least. Even Fortis couldn't bring her down now. "Of course," she said lightly. "Come on, Fortis. It'll all be over soon. Isn't that a good thing?"

Fortis frowned, his lips tugging downward. He, unlike her, made no move to dress up for the occasion. In fact, he hadn't even done his hair. It was like he'd just woken up from bed and had thrown on a random pair of clothes he'd found on his bedroom floor. A pair of jeans and a white shirt with a suited jacket and a pair of classy shoes. He dressed exactly like his mindset: torn and confused.

"I just don't think we should move in like this—"

"No, you don't think I should kill that little twit," Courtnie corrected. "Fortis, we've been over this. Stop looking at her like a daughter and see her for what she is: a traitor to everything the Government stands for. We need to put her down."

"You say it like she's an animal," Fortis grumbled. "She's a human being, Courtnie. And she is my daughter. Your daughter—"

"I'd kill Kat Caldwell in two seconds flat if she betrayed the Government. Daughter or not. See, Fortis, that's the difference between us. Our priorities are different. I don't have a relationship with Kat, nor do I really care about her. She's not my priority. My priority is Cesve as a whole."

"If you don't care about the people," Fortis murmured, "then how do you care about Cesve at all?"

"I care about the people as a whole!" Courtnie snapped venomously. "I do not care about each and every individual human being. I do not care about any of the Caldwells, nor do I care about any other family really. But I care about keeping their world safe. I care about keeping order for them. And your daughter, Fortis, has threatened that order. So now I'm going to take out the threat. Do you understand that?"

Fortis sighed, dragging a hand down his face. He hadn't been getting much sleep, Courtnie observed. In all truth she hadn't been getting much sleep either. She'd been staying up late at night searching for Terra, waiting for the right moment to tear her entire operation apart from the seams. And now that moment had come. And she wasn't about to let Fortis ruin that for her.

"I don't understand," Fortis drawled, "how someone so heartless could claim to care so much."

Courtnie stared at Fortis for a long time. He sounded resigned, as if he really didn't give a single damn how she reacted to his words. And she supposed he didn't. Maybe he'd become so torn up and defeated inside that he didn't care about anything. But of course he did care about something. Poor, poor Terra. Terra this, Terra that. Oh, please spare Terra's life. Well, she wasn't going to. They'd tried it Fortis's way.

It was Courtnie's turn now.

"Maybe your heart is clouding your judgment," Courtnie seethed. "Maybe you should try not caring so much. It would hurt less that way."

"It would, but life would then be pointless." Fortis smiled sadly. "You live a pointless life, Courtnie. You care about no one but yourself and help no one but yourself. If you continuously treat everyone the way you do, no one will miss you when you're gone."

"How can you stand here and say these things to your own sister?" Courtnie hissed. "You claim that I'm heartless, that I'm pointless, that I do nothing but destroy, that I'm cruel, that I'm everything except good, and yet you're the one who is verbally abusing me every second you get. How is that any better than me?"

Fortis's smile remained as he said. "You're only taking it as verbal abuse because you refuse to see the truth in it." He twisted around, facing away from Courtnie now as he readied himself to leave the room. "I will go with you to retrieve the girl, but after that I'm done with you and this place. I'll be leaving Cesve as quickly as possible."

Courtnie felt her stomach drop. "Where will you go, Fortis? You have no idea what's outside. There are no boats, no planes here. You haven't a single way of leaving unless you plan on swimming."

"I'd rather drown in the ocean than stay here with you."

With that, Fortis stormed out of the room, the door slamming shut behind him.

Terra smiled from the doorway of Kole's bedroom as Alex sat on the edge of it, whispering something to his brother that Terra couldn't hear. She could have easily tuned in on their conversation, but she didn't want to. No, this moment was not one to be intruded on. Terra could remember it like it was yesterday: talking to Faye like this, hugging her before she went to bed. Being with her all the time.

A lot of girls despised their sisters. They found them so irritating, so unbearable. But Terra never felt that way about Faye. Faye was one of the most important things in Terra's life. She always had been and always would be. Faye was more important to Terra than life itself. She longed to be with Faye now, with her mother. She missed them so much. So much, in fact, that Terra sometimes wished she'd never acted upon hers and Daneigh's similarities. If she hadn't pushed it ... none of this would have happened.

None of it.

Terra blinked, mentally shaking the thoughts away as Alex stood up from Kole's bed and moved toward her. She shifted to the side as though to allow him passage and he immediately squeezed by her whilst gesturing for her to follow him. Terra didn't hesitate to follow him down the hall and into his bedroom. What reason was there to? Besides, they'd decided that she would be sleeping in his room until they could find other arrangements.

"You really love your brother, don't you?" Terra murmured as she closed Alex's bedroom door shut. Her eyes flicked around as she took in her surroundings. His room was immaculate, completely free of any clutter whatsoever. A queen-size bed lay in the far corner of the room right in front of his window with a navy-blue comforter over the top. There was a desk at the opposite side of the room which was completely organized. Terra admired him for keeping his desk so organized. She'd never be able to do that.

Right next to the desk was a bookcase filled with books that Terra barely recognized. They were nothing worth reading, Terra knew that already. Most books in Cesve were terrible, completely missing one huge aspect: the other gender. Terra didn't blame anyone in Cesve for not noticing this, however. How could they? It wasn't their fault Courtnie and Fortis left them blinded.

"Yes, I do," Alex admitted, leaning against his bureau which rested beside his bed. He crossed his arms over his chest. "And you really love your sister, don't you?"

Terra's eyes raked Alex before answering. He was rather attractive with his fit build and piercing blue eyes. Shaggy dark brown hair fell over his head, making it look like he just rolled out of bed. He did look a lot like Errika. It was a wonder she didn't figure it out before reading the flash drive's information. "Yeah, I do," she replied finally. "A lot."

Alex tossed Terra a small smile. "Family is the most important thing in this world," he murmured. "And to think that they're not actually family."

"They may not be blood related," Terra murmured, "but they're still family. That will never change."

Alex sighed. "I'm just so worried about him, you know? He doesn't understand the depth of what he's doing."

Terra nodded, perching on Alex's bed. It was rather comfortable, she thought. She was almost sad she'd be sleeping on the floor. "You have a right to be worried," she told him. "I'm worried about Faye, too. I may not show it, but I am. She reminds me so much of me...." Terra sighed. "I didn't understand the depth of what I was doing, either. And I got my sister killed for it."

Alex shook his head. "You didn't force Daneigh to jump off that cliff, Terra. She made that choice on her own."

Terra stared straight ahead. But of course it was her fault. It always had been. That was one thing she could say she agreed with Courtnie on. Whenever Courtnie threw Daneigh in Terra's face, it was like Terra was there all over again watching in horror as her sister threw herself off the cliff's edge. If she hadn't gone running, if she'd just gone with the Government instead of trying to get to Daneigh first....

"I may not have forced her," Terra whispered, "but I made it so she had no other choice."

Alex sat down beside her. He had a thoughtful expression on his face, as though he was trying to pick the correct words to say. "She did have a choice, though. Because if there weren't another choice, you'd be dead, too."

"Daneigh and I may have looked identical, but we were very different people." Terra brought a hand through her hair. "She feared the prison wards more than she feared the beast on the other side. The thought of being locked up for the rest of her life terrified her more than you can possibly imagine. We all have fears. Mine is that I'll truly lose Faye, that I'll never be able to see her again. Losing my family scares me so much. Faye, well, she used to be frightened by the beast on the other side. She has different fears now, but she still has fears all the same. Daneigh was terrified of being locked up like a common animal. And that's why I tried to warn her before they could get her. I knew I was risking it by running to her, but...."

Alex knelt in front of her grabbing ahold of her shoulders. "You did not make Daneigh kill herself, Terra."

Terra looked away. She hated being comforted, hated being told that everything was okay. She always moved on in her own way, always figured things out for herself. She didn't even like Faye comforting her. Something about it made Terra feel weak, like she was still a child who couldn't defend herself against her problems. "I—"

"Faye has learned to face her fears, hasn't she?" Alex demanded, his expression determined. "She's moved past them. She met the 'creature' on the other side, even came on this side to hang out with them. Kole told me how she was terrified of falling but came over anyway, forcing herself to get over the fear and move on with her life. Faye decided not to let her fear control her. And do you let your fear control you? Obviously not. If you did, you wouldn't tolerate Faye coming over to this side. You would want to keep her in a little bubble of safety. Daneigh let her fear take over her and that is what controlled her. Not you, not the Government. In the end Daneigh chose not to get over her fear. And that was her choice, not yours."

Terra couldn't help but smile at Alex as he gripped her shoulders tightly. "What are you afraid of?" she murmured, suddenly curious.

Alex let his hands fall away from her shoulders as he deliberated. It was like he hadn't truly thought of his fears before. "I'm afraid of many things," he confessed. "I'm afraid of Kole getting hurt, I'm afraid of not understanding a situation. I'm afraid of the Government figuring out what we're doing and killing us all. And I guess I'm a little afraid of you."

Terra cocked an eyebrow. "Me? Flattering, really."

Alex laughed shortly. "Not afraid like the other things. An excited sort of scared I supposed. You're just ... different."

"Different?"

Alex nodded. "I can't put my finger on it, really. But as strange as it was to meet Faye for the first time, it was even stranger to meet you. Not just because Faye had just hypothesized that the

Government murdered you, but because you radiated power. You still do. It's like no one can truly hurt you no matter how hard they try."

Terra snickered, shaking her head. "I may radiate power, but that's only because I project confidence. And why? Because I'm pretty damn cocky. I probably wouldn't have made it as far as I did if I weren't so cocky. And maybe I would have made it further if I weren't so cocky. We'll never know, will we?"

Alex gave her a lopsided smile. "I suppose not."

"And the hero saved the two little boys from their cages and they were finally set free," Zander murmured as he read the last line of the kid's story. "The end."

Zachary murmured sleepily as Zander snapped the book shut and stood up. Though Zachary was surely old enough to go to sleep without bedtime stories, it soothed them both for Zander to read before Zachary went to bed. He wasn't quite sure why, but it made him feel more at ease to be by his brother's bedside. It was so mundane, so normal. Maybe that was why. With everything else going on, this felt like the only normal thing Zander truly had left.

"Zander," Zachary murmured sleepily. "I miss Dad."

Zander brought a hand through Zachary's hair and sighed. "I miss Dad, too. But we'll be okay. We've got each other."

Zachary nodded, his eyes slipping shut as he rolled over and fell into a light slumber. Zander stared at him for a short moment before moving toward the door and flicking off the light, closing the door shut behind him as he exited. He sighed deeply, bringing a hand through his hair as he trudged down the stairs. He missed his father so much. Life was so much easier when he was here. He was able to hang out with his friends without being worried that the sitter was mistreating his brother in any way. He was able to live life the way he wanted to. But now? Now he was practically a father himself.

Someone knocked on the door.

Zander's eyes narrowed as he wiped his hands on his jeans before sauntering toward the front door. Who could possibly be here at this hour? It surely wasn't Terence, Seth, Kole, Alex, or one of the girls. They'd all agreed to call before they stopped by. So would could it—

His question died before it even began as suddenly the door burst from its hinges and flew inward, mere inches from where Zander stood. Zander let out a cry of shock, falling backwards on his butt as he watched with wide eyes as the ones at fault stepped inside.

Fortis Caine sighed as he stepped into the house, a few guards behind him. There was a woman by his side—Courtnie Feather-strom he was guessing. She was probably the one who ruled the Government on the girl's side. At least, that's what he gathered from what Faye, Errika, and Terra said. And what else he gathered? She was a cruel, cruel human being.

"Zander Khadel," Courtnie drawled, taking a step forward. She seemed to be an especially good mood, Zander couldn't help but notice. "We're here to retrieve Terra Caldwell. Would you care to fetch her for me?"

"Tell me where she is."

Zander cried out in horror as the guards slapped Zachary again causing the little boy to scream in pain. He wanted to grab Zachary, to pull him out of the Government's hands, but he couldn't. He himself was strapped to a chair, blood falling in a line where Courtnie had sliced it with her knife. He was bruised, he was bloody, but he didn't care about that right now. All that mattered to him was Zachary's well-being.

"Let him go!" Zander croaked. "Please. He's just a little boy—"

"Then tell me where she is," Courtnie hissed. When Zander didn't answer, she rolled her eyes. "Honestly, boy, it's like you don't have a brain." She gestured to the guards and the man on Zachary's left side grinned maliciously. Zander watched, mortified as the guard pulled out a pocket knife. He tried to scream out, but when he started to, Courtnie slapped him upside the head and his scream died in his throat.

The knife swiped across Zachary's cheek and he screeched in pain. Tears dripped from the little boy's eyes. "Zander," he wept. "Zander, help me!"

"Your little brother is begging you, dear Zander Khadel. What are you going to do about it?"

"I don't know where she is," Zander rasped. "But I know who hid her."

From the corner of his eye he could see Fortis glaring at the far wall. He hadn't participated in any of the torturing this evening. He'd stayed back as Courtnie practically threw Zander up the stairs, stood back as the guards hauled Zachary out of bed and held him out as though to mock Zander as Courtnie tied him to the chair he'd just been sitting in just moments ago. Fortis didn't seem to want to participate at all. It was like he was against this. But, if he was, why wasn't he doing anything to stop it?

"Oh, goody!" Courtnie clapped her hands cheerfully. "More people to torture, this is just lovely. What are their names?"

Zander stared at Courtnie in disgust. How could she live with herself? Getting excited to torture people? What was wrong with her?

When Zander didn't answer fast enough, Courtnie gestured to the guards again. This time, they began twisting Zachary's arm, so much in fact that Zachary began to scream and cry in pain. "Stop!" Zander hissed. "I'll tell you, just let him go!"

Courtnie nodded and gestured to the guards again. All at once they let the little boy drop to the floor where he stayed there weeping in a small ball. "There, they let him go. But if you don't tell me, I'll just have them pick him up again." She smiled evilly. "Who has been hiding Terra Caldwell?"

For a short moment Zander was silent. He didn't want to do it—he truly didn't. But if he didn't tell Courtnie who was behind this, they were going to kill Zachary. Killing him was one thing, but killing Zachary was a completely different story. He would not stand to see his brother hurt. Zachary's safety was his responsibility. "It was Faye Caldwell," he whispered resignedly. "Faye Caldwell and Kole Frost. They hid her. They started this entire thing."

Courtnie laughed a loud, obnoxious laugh. "Thank you so much, Zander. You've been most helpful."

Zander chomped down on his cheek as Courtnie untied him from the chair. I'm sorry, Kole, his mind whispered. It was nothing personal. I had to save my brother.

CHAPTER 20

F aye wasn't sure how long she'd been trapped there.

Had it been hours, minutes, seconds? It was impossible to tell. All Faye knew at the moment was darkness. It was all around her, threatening to consume her. At the moment falling wasn't her greatest fear. No, it was the darkness. What was lurking inside it? What was waiting to snatch her before she had any time to react?

But of course she'd already been snatched up.

She'd barely gotten an hour of sleep before there came a banging on the door. Faye immediately knew that the Government had figured out what she did, had figured out everything. She didn't even have time to be afraid. No, instead she threw herself out of bed and ran down stairs. She couldn't afford for Kat or Mary to be woken up. Not for this.

Two guards greeted her as she pulled open the door. Without a word they grabbed ahold of her. Faye didn't even have time to think about running. They knew Terra was her sister, knew that Faye knew exactly what happened seven years ago. So they probably also knew that she'd make a run for it if she could. So they grabbed her as quickly as they could.

They didn't even close the door before hauling her off the porch and into one of the official Government cars. Faye wanted to yell for them to close the door, to make it at least seem like nothing happened, but she couldn't bring herself to. What was the point? Faye still wouldn't be in her bed when her family members woke up that morning. Faye would still be gone. They would have no idea why. The Government would make sure of that.

Well, Kat would know at least.

For some reason that comforted Faye as the Government workers peeled down the street. Kat would understand what happened to Faye. She would know that it wasn't an accident, that she didn't just run away. The Government took her because of what she found out. And that was that.

When she got to the Government building, Courtnie laughed in her face. She sneered, gloated, did every obnoxious thing that Faye could really imagine. She was completely smug as she ordered the guards to throw her in the holding cell. Apparently Faye needed to be questioned.

And so now here she sat, waiting. Waiting in complete darkness, wondering, fearing that the Government had gotten to Kole, too. The thought of them touching him with their grubby hands ... it mortified her. She didn't want to see him hurt. She didn't know what she would do if they hurt him. She wouldn't be able to stand it.

And did they find Terra? That was less probable than them getting ahold of Kole. If they'd found her, Faye wouldn't be waiting to be questioned. Faye would probably be in a cell right now with a life sentence. If she were receiving a life sentence right away, a police cruiser would have picked her up, and her mother would have been informed. But Courtnie couldn't do that—not without Faye revealing every single lie that she'd told all the girls of Cesve.

How did they find out, Faye wondered? How did they know that Faye had been sneaking over to the other side? They had no cameras, and no one saw her when she and Errika had gone the last time. If someone had seen her and Errika, Errika would be here, too. And Faye knew that she wasn't. She knew deep inside that Errika was safe and that was how she would stay.

Faye's eyes flicked upward as a creaking sound erupted in the seemingly everlasting silence. A door was opening, she realized. At first she was relieved that she wasn't trapped in a world of utterly nothing, but then she remembered why the door was opening. It was time to be questioned. And, when she refused to give them the answers she wanted, they were probably going to kill her.

"Faye Caldwell, is it?"

All at once Faye's word was drowned out by light. Faye squinted, struggling to see the woman standing in front of her. She knew who it was of course. She wasn't stupid. It was Courtnie Feather-strom. The woman who forced Faye to believe her sister was dead for seven years; the woman who put Faye through absolute hell. And she was here to wreak havoc once again. Because apparently that was all she was good at.

"You know my name," Faye croaked out, bringing a hand through her hair. Her voice was rusty with disuse. She must have been in this room longer than she thought.

"Yes of course I do," Courtnie said with a laugh. She placed her hand behind her back, much like how Faye's were placed.

However, there was one major difference between the two. While Courtnie had the freedom to move her arms at any time, Faye could not. Her hands were bound together with a thick rope that continuously chaffed her skin. Apparently this type of situation didn't call for handcuffs. "You're Terra Caldwell's little sister. I should have known that you would only cause me trouble."

Faye laughed bitterly. "Me cause you trouble? I thought it was the other way around."

"Oh, little Caldwell has an attitude, doesn't she?" Courtnie snickered. "Last time I knew you were a terrified little girl who didn't know how to do anything for herself. You were completely torn apart by Terra's death weren't you, little girl? You were afraid of everything. Everything."

Faye's jaw worked silently. Courtnie was throwing all of her weaknesses in her face as though to force Faye into the girl she used to be. But it wouldn't work. She'd changed, and there was no going back. And even if she could? She wouldn't.

"Oh, am I annoying you, Faye? Well, I would be a little more sympathetic but you happen to have caused me a lot of stress."

Faye cocked an eyebrow. "Oh yeah?" she murmured. "What's more stressful than thinking your sister is dead for seven years only to find out the Government who is supposed to be protecting you has hidden her away in the prison wards?"

Faye wasn't quite sure where this burst of bravery was coming from. Her hands weren't even shaking, nor was her voice. She was completely calm. Maybe it was the fact that she'd accepted that she was going to die today. Maybe it was her complete and utter loathing of the woman in front of her. Maybe it was both.

"Don't play smart with me, Caldwell," Courtnie snarled.

"Caldwell isn't even really my last name, is it?" Faye retorted. "You've lied to me about that too. You've lied to me and everyone about everything. I'm not playing it smart. I'm telling you the truth and you can't handle it."

Courtnie's hand slammed into the wall. Faye blinked in shock. Who knew that the collected woman on television was capable of so much violence? "Don't tell me what I can't handle!" she shrieked.

Faye almost smirked. She'd hit a soft spot. How many people had told her she couldn't handle something when she insisted she could? If this were any other person Faye would have felt sorry for her. But this was Courtnie. So she didn't give a damn. "Don't you deserve to know if you can't handle something?" she asked.

"Enough of these word games," Courtnie snapped.

Before Faye had any time to react, Courtnie was slapping her so hard across the face that her head jerked to the side. Faye chomped down on her tongue to keep from screaming. Blood pooled in her mouth. Ouch, her mind whispered.

"Tell me where your sister is," Courtnie hissed.

Faye smiled, and she could feel the blood staining her teeth as she said, "You mean that Olyv girl? She's probably drowning herself in alcohol the way your workers talk about her."

That earned her another slap. "Don't get sarcastic with me!" Courtnie yelled. "Tell me where Terra Caldwell is or I swear to God I will shoot you where you sit."

Faye watched with a resigned sort of horror as Courtnie pulled a pistol from her pocket. Faye almost sighed. She imagined the gun going off randomly while in Courtnie's pocket and almost laughed.

If only that had happened. Maybe then Courtnie would bleed out and die.

But she was hoping for too much.

"If you shoot me," Faye drawled, "you won't get any answers now will you?"

"You're so much like her," Courtnie spat. "And I hate her with every fiber of my being. If I could, I'd shoot her. So what makes you think I'll do any different to you?"

"I don't," Faye admitted. She leaned back against the wall and sighed. "But what makes you think I'll turn in my own sister?"

Courtnie smiled maliciously, and for the first time Faye felt extreme fear curl in her stomach. Courtnie was about to reveal something—something extremely important and life-threatening. She could feel it deep in her gut. "Because if you don't," Courtnie drawled, crouching in front of her. Faye scowled as Courtnie roughly grabbed ahold of her cheek and twisted her head to the right, where a television was beginning to flicker as it hung from the ceiling, "then he will die."

Faye's eyes widened and her stomach dropped as the television finally came into focus. And what did she see? She saw Kole.

Kole was in a room not much unlike hers. It was rundown and there was absolutely no furniture inside except for the small television hanging from the ceiling. His, unlike hers, was turned off. But the main difference? A man was there with Kole, and he was kicking him repeatedly in the side.

Faye let out gasp and felt her eyes begin to water. "Kole," she whispered.

"Tell me where the girl is," the Government worker hissed, kicking Kole for the umpteenth time. Kole hissed out in pain, but said nothing else. He would not give Terra's location to this man. He refused. He'd rather die.

It was supposed to be Fortis interrogating him, but the second they arrived to the Government building Fortis assigned one of the guards to take him in. Apparently Fortis had had enough of this place. Apparently he was leaving. Kole wished he could leave. He wished that he could take Faye, Alex, Terra, Errika, and the others and just leave. Let them live together in a way that they could be happy. No more sneaking around, no more pretending that the other gender didn't exist. Just live.

"Why don't you take a look at the TV, lover boy?"

Kole glared at the Government worker. The man didn't seem to care, for he simply grinned and nodded his head in the direction of the television set hanging on the wall. Kole didn't want to look—he really didn't want to. But something told him that if he didn't, he was going to regret it.

And as his eyes made contact with the screen, he realized why: It was Faye. She was bound like he was, and she didn't seem to be in much better shape. Kole watched with a growing horror as Courtnie reached over and slapped her across the face. Faye seemed to growl something at her and she received another slap in return.

"Let her go!" Kole hissed, glowering at the man in front of him. "Do whatever you want to me, but dammit let her go!"

The Government worker barked out a laugh before crouching in front of Kole and sneering. "Your little girlfriend isn't going to be around much longer if she doesn't give Courtnie what she wants," he told Kole triumphantly. "And you won't be here much longer if you don't give me what I want."

HENRY KELLY

Kole's eyes latched onto the television screen again, his mouth going dry. Anger tumbled around in his stomach, as did acidic fear. Courtnie was hurting her. She was hurting her. The pain was clear on Faye's face as she continued to get abused by her captor. Kole longed to save her, to rescue her from Courtnie's evil grasp. But he couldn't. He was just as trapped as she was.

"Hey!"

Kole growled as his captor slapped him upside the head. For a moment Kole's vision was nothing but stars. After a few moments, however, his vision was back to normal and he could see the man in front of him. He could see the annoyed expression on his captors face, could see his five o'clock shadow. He could see the angles of his jaw, the vein practically popping out of his skull as he glared Kole down. He could see the man clearly.

"Don't make me take away your TV privileges, kid," the guard snarled. Kole received another slap. "Now tell me where Terra Caldwell is."

"I don't know."

And it was true. The second they heard knocks on the door, Kole knew the Government had figured them out. He'd rushed to Alex's room and ordered Terra to hide somewhere where no one could find her. And then he'd raced downstairs before Alex could stop him. Alex tried so hard to keep the Government from taking him, Kole thought. He'd tried so damn hard. So hard, in fact, that the guard knocked him out.

Kole's stomach tightened. He prayed to God that his brother was okay. If Alex was in pain right now, he didn't know what he'd do.

"You're lying to me!" the guard hissed. Kole fought the urge to cry out as the guard punched him in the gut. "Stop lying to me. Where is she?"

"I don't know," Kole hissed back. "I'm telling you the truth."

"No you're not. And you'd better tell me soon because I have orders to shoot you in the head if you don't talk."

At first Kole thought the guard was saying this only to scare him. But then the Government worker pulled out a gun from his pocket and pointed it straight at his forehead. "So talk, Kole Frost. Or I'm going to shoot you in the head."

Kole remained silent.

"Errika," Kat whispered in an uneven voice. Her grip on Faye's cell phone was tight as she stood in Faye's empty bedroom. She felt completely numb, so completely empty. "Errika, something terrible has happened."

"Kat?" Errika mumbled sleepily. "Why do you have Faye's phone? What's going on?"

Kat sighed shakily. She'd felt like something was off when she woke up that morning. She felt like something was completely and utterly wrong as she made her way through the house only to find that no one was there. And, with each room that she entered, that feeling grew. It didn't help that she and Faye had shared a deep conversation just hours before and Faye practically warned her that the Government was going to be coming for her. So why wouldn't Kat be worried?

And when she stepped into Faye's bedroom to find her mother standing there weeping and Faye nowhere to be found, Kat knew.

"Faye's gone," Kat said, her voice thick. "The Government came and took her away."

Kat could hear their mother frantically calling people and pleading with them for information on where her little girl had gone. Kat felt sick to her stomach. Their mother had already gone through this once. The Government had already stolen one of her mother's children, and now the Government was doing it again. She couldn't imagine how her mother was feeling right now. It felt terrible enough losing Faye like this, but to lose two children?

"What do you mean the Government took her away?" Errika exclaimed. "Kat, what the hell happened?"

Errika sounded panicked. Fear was clear in her tone and Kat instantly knew that her sister's friend was ready to cry. "Faye came home last night and we talked," Kat said, wiping a tear that was making its way down her cheek. "She told me she was hiding everything from me to keep me safe, and I apologized for the way I've been acting. And then she told me to promise her if the Government came to our house and told us that there was an accident or that she killed herself not to believe them because it would be complete bullshit. She said that if she were to die, it would be the Government's fault." Kat was full-on crying now. "And I wake up this morning and she's gone, Errika! They took her, I know they did!"

"Kat, calm down," Errika murmured. Kat knew that Errika was trying to calm herself down more than her. "Everything is going to be—"

"Don't you dare say everything is going to be okay," Kat whispered harshly. "You know very well nothing is going to be okay. My mom already lost Terra. How do you think she's going to react when she loses another child?"

"I'm coming over there."

And with that, Errika hung up.

Kat pulled the phone away from her ear, staring at it. She felt tears burning in her eyes and all she wanted to do was throw herself on Faye's bed and weep until she had no more tears left. But she couldn't. And why was that? Because someone was knocking at the door, and Kat was pretty sure that Errika hadn't arrived in less than two seconds.

She crept downstairs and toward the front door, her eyes narrowed. Whoever was at the front door wasn't bringing good news. And it was probably completely bullshitted news at that.

There was a police woman at the door when Kat finally came to stand next to her mother. Apparently there'd been an "accident" and "a body may have been found." Mary was wailing freely, shaking her head and muttering, "Not again, oh god not again," over and over again.

Kat glowered. "I think it's best if you leave."

The police woman barely glanced Kat's way. "Miss Caldwell, I want you to know that it's not a definite yet, but it's a huge possibility—"

"There is no possibility!" Kat screeched. "Now get out of our house before I push you down the porch."

Her mother shot her an appalled look. "Kat—"

Kat's hands curled into fists. "Get out," she snarled. "Now."

The police woman smiled sadly at the two of them before sighing. "I'll be back later with more information."

"No you won't," Kat said simply. Before the police woman had any time to react, Kat was pushing her out onto the porch and slamming the door shut behind her. With one swift movement she locked the door and spun around, her eyes wide.

Her mother had her arms crossed over her chest as she glared Kat down. "That was rude, Kat," she snapped. "She was trying to help—"

Her mother cut off suddenly as a cry escaped her throat and she let her head fall into her hands. Kat watched as her mother's shoulders shook as she sobbed.

"Mom," Kat whispered, pulling her mother into her arms. Mary hugged her back tightly, holding onto her as though if she loosened her grip Kat would seep through her fingers and disappear. "Mom, I need to tell you something."

Her mother held her out at arm's length, her eyes searching. "What is it, Kat?"

Kat sighed shakily. "It's time you knew the truth."

"This would all end if you just told me where your sister was."

Faye hissed at Courtnie, backing against the wall. Her whole body ached. For hours she'd been put through various forms of torture and questioning, each more painful than the next. She'd been slapped, kicked, burned, cut, and even shot in the leg. Burns, bruises, and blood covered Faye's body, but she still remained undeterred. She would not give Courtnie what she wanted. She would not betray her sister. She was going to die; she knew that already. But she would not give in to the Government.

Faye shrieked as Courtnie sliced her knife across her cheek. A line of blood dripped down along her jaw and onto her neck, practically sizzling on the burn left there. The burn was from when Courtnie lit a match and brought it closer and closer, threatening to burn her if she didn't talk. And, naturally, Faye didn't. So she paid the price.

But none of this was as painful as watching Kole on the television screen. He was being tortured even worse than her—if that was possible. From the glimpses she'd caught on the screen she could see that Kole had a broken arm, a broken leg, and he seemed to be barely conscious at this point. But the Government worker wouldn't let him go.

"Let Kole go," Faye whispered. "He has nothing to do with this."

Courtnie snickered. "Tired of watching your boyfriend in pain? Of course I'm not going to let him go! He has just as much to do with this as you do. And he's going to be killed, too, if he doesn't fess up soon."

Faye glowered. "You're a monster," she seethed. "A heartless monster. How can you live with yourself?"

Courtnie answered by moving over to the TV and clicking a button. "Can you hear me, Nate?"

The Government worker looked up and Kole's eyes shifted toward the television. He nodded, but when he spoke, Faye could not hear anything.

"Turn on the speaker of the TV, would you?" Courtnie said lightly. "I think it's time the love birds heard each other's screams."

Faye froze. She knew that Courtnie was demented, but this? This was just sick. "Kole," she rasped as Nate, pressed the speaker on. "Kole, are you okay?"

Of course Kole wasn't okay. He was barely conscious, barely able to move. But Faye needed to ask him, needed to speak to him. This could very well be the last time they spoke to each other. With each moment that passed by, Faye thought it more true. She was going to die. She was going to die. She was going to die.

Kole struggled to nod. "Are you okay?" he asked softly.

Faye nodded, tears in her eyes. "Be strong," she called to him.

Kole nodded. He opened his mouth to say something, but suddenly his words were cut short as Nate grabbed ahold of him by his hair and threw him against the wall. Faye let out a gasp as Kole cried out in agony. "Stop hurting him!" Faye shrieked. "Please—"

Suddenly Courtnie was in front of her, a lit match in her hand. Faye screeched as Courtnie brought the match toward her skin, burning her. She could hear Kole begging for them to stop hurting her, to just let her go, but all Courtnie did was laugh. Faye could feel tears burning in her eyes, but she refused to shed them. She would not give Courtnie that satisfaction.

"Are your tongues loosened?" Courtnie asked, looking between Faye and the television set. "Where is Terra Caldwell?"

"I love you, Faye," Kole called huskily, his teeth grinding with pain.

Faye sighed shakily. "I love you, too."

"We did not turn these speakers on so you could confess your love to one another!" Courtnie snapped. "Tell me where Terra Caldwell is or Kole will die with you watching."

Faye watched in horror as Nate grabbed Kole by the collar of his shirt and held him up. She could see the pain Kole was in, and all she wanted to do was help him. She could give a false location, but that would do no good. Courtnie would instantly know she was lying. Faye was sure of it. The only way to get out of this was by telling the truth. But she couldn't do that. Not with Terra's life at stake.

But if she didn't tell, Kole would die.

"Don't tell her, Faye," Kole ordered, his eyes reaching for hers. Faye met his gaze, her eyes wide. "They'll kill us both anyway. Don't tell her. Promise me you won't tell her."

Faye bit her lip. Blood covered them, but she took no notice. Her entire mouth was covered in blood. It made no difference to her anymore. Not with the amount of torment she'd gone through so far. She nodded her head and Kole sagged back as though relieved. Relieved that this situation was almost over. Relieved that the torture was going to end.

Faye felt as though she'd betrayed him, too.

Courtnie sighed deeply. She seemed thoroughly agitated, as though she couldn't believe they weren't giving in. But they wouldn't. They wouldn't give Courtnie the satisfaction. Neither of them would. They'd both accepted their fates. "If you want to play it that way, fine," she drawled.

Faye let out a cry as Courtnie grabbed her roughly by her shirt and hauled her off the floor. The shirt scratched her burns, digging into them like a knife. In that moment white flashed before Faye's eyes and she feared she was going to pass out from the pain.

Courtnie's hands gripped the sides of Faye's face tightly as she steered it in the direction of the television screen. Faye stared. Kole was in so much agony. She wanted to take it all away, to make him feel better again. Just yesterday they were fine. They were kissing on porches and smiling at each other. Now? Now they were waiting for death to come. Faye was actually starting to welcome it.

"Do it, Nate," Courtnie ordered.

"No!" Faye cried as Nate pressed his gun against Kole's head. She yearned to turn away, to close her eyes, but she couldn't. It was as if her eyes were permanently open, as if it were impossible for her to ever close them again. "Please, no, no, no, no, no—"

Faye screeched louder than she'd ever screamed before as a gun shot rang out and Nate dropped Kole's lifeless body on the floor. Courtnie threw Faye away from her and she slid on the floor, landing in a heap. Faye cried freely now, her tears mixing in with the blood on her face. Kole was dead. Kole was dead.

And she was next.

"You killed him!" Faye shrieked. "You killed him, you son of a—"

"I didn't kill him," Courtnie spat. "You did. You refused to speak. You knew the punishment and you took it anyway. And now he is dead. It hurts, doesn't it?"

Faye's eyes dragged toward the television screen. Kole was still lying there, unnaturally still. Faye began breathing rapidly as she struggled not to go into a complete meltdown. Kole was dead, Kole was dead, Kole was dead, Kole was dead, Kole was dead. This wasn't some mind trick played by the Government like they'd pulled with Terra. Kole wasn't secretly locked up in a cell somewhere while his twin died in his stead.

Kole was dead.

And she was next.

"You and your damned government killed him," Faye hissed. "If it weren't for you none of this would be happening. We could all be happy."

"You were happy," Courtnie told her, grabbing onto her hair and pulling. Faye cried out. "You were happy when your life was only with the girls. And then you went onto the boys' side because your damn sister managed to take control of the cameras. Ever since then your life has been falling apart. Don't you get it? The two genders together is nothing but destructive."

"You're pretty fricken delusional," Faye muttered. "You twist everything to make it look like what you stand for is right, but really it's the most twisted up shit ever."

Courtnie hissed through her teeth and Faye's insides felt cold. For a moment all the ice that'd thawed since Terra's return froze again, and she almost went completely numb. For a moment almost all of the pain was completely gone and she barely even noticed when Courtnie slapped her across the face.

"I've had about enough of you," Courtnie snarled, bringing out her pistol again. She'd pocketed it earlier to burn her with matches. Every moment Faye was tortured, she silently prayed that the gun would implode on Courtnie. But it never did. "Tell me where Terra Caldwell is or I'm going to shoot you right here, right now."

Faye laughed without humor. "You just killed Kole. Do you really think I give a damn whether you shoot me or not?" She smirked. "Go ahead. Shoot me. I won't be in any pain anymore, and you won't have the answers you want. So do it. Do it."

With a growl, Courtnie aimed the gun at Faye's forehead. Faye suddenly felt at piece as Courtnie cocked the gun and got ready to shoot. In a moment it'll all be over, she thought. There will be no more pain, and maybe you'll be with Kole again. It'll all be—

"Any last words?" Courtnie drawled.

Faye spat on Courtnie's feet. "Screw you and your government," she said.

In her mind she said her last words to everyone she loved. To her mom, to Terra, to Kat, to Errika, to all the boys that she'd met. She whispered apologies to them for not being there for them and she silently wished that Courtnie would never get to them. She was about to whisper a final "I love you" in her head when Courtnie laughed maliciously and fired the gun, shooting a bullet straight into Faye's head.

Epilogue

The freezing wind blew through the night and pierced her skin, but Terra didn't feel it. She didn't feel anything, not even the gun in her hand as she gripped it so tightly that her knuckles turned white. What did it matter anyway? What did it matter if she felt the pain of the metal, the pain of the wind? What did it matter?

"Terra!" Errika shrieked into the phone. "Something awful has happened."

"What" Terra demanded. "What happened?"

Of course Terra had already known what happened before Errika called. She could feel it deep inside her. She could feel the sudden loss, like a chunk of her had been ripped right out of her and thrown out of her reach. She knew that Faye was dead. She knew it.

"Faye is gone," Errika whispered. "The Government picked her up."

Terra had shut the phone and chucked it across the room, letting out a mangled cry of despair. She'd fallen to the ground and curled herself into a ball, all her strength over the years seeming to diminish in a single moment. Faye was gone, her mind repeated over and over again. She was gone. Terra hadn't even been able to say goodbye. She hadn't been able to hug her, to kiss her on the head like she'd done when Faye was a little girl.

The Government took her little sister away from her.

And why? Why did they take Faye away from her? Because someone gave her name to them.

Terra's grip tightened on the gun and her pace sped up. Zander, her mind screamed. Zander did this. It's his fault!

Terra's feet slapped against the pavement, clouds of air appearing in front of her with each breath she took. It was hard to breathe, as it had been since the moment she knew her sister died. Terra was honestly surprised she was operating at all. When Alex found her earlier that night, she hadn't even been able to speak. Not really, anyway.

"Terra," Alex whispered, his eyes wide from his doorway.

Terra tried to open her mouth, to tell him the simple words "my sister's dead" but she couldn't. She couldn't without him realizing that his brother was dead, that he would never see Kole again either. There was one thing Terra was certain of: if Faye was dead, Kole was dead too. Both of their fears had been released into the open.

She'd always been so sure that she would make it through this all right. Terra had worried about Faye's well-being, but she'd never truly imagined losing her like this. Terra wasn't going to let it happen. She wasn't going to allow a sleaze like Courtnie ruin her life like this.

But she had.

Terra turned down the street of Zander Khadel's house, her feet moving faster and faster. With each step she took her anger and despair seemed to grow. She wondered how much pain her little sister was in before she died. Courtnie was never one to hold back on the torture. When Terra was first placed in the prison wards she was tortured for days on end. Then Fortis found out about it and he put a stop to it. But he only stopped her because Terra was his daughter. Faye wouldn't have that same privilege.

Guilt stabbed her in the gut and Terra almost fell over. She should have been there. She should have saved Faye and Kole from the fates that they received. They should be alive right now, not in what she could only assume as a bloody mess on the holding cells' floors.

"Terra," Alex murmured, pulling Terra into his arms. For the first time her hate for comfort was completely forgotten and Terra wrapped her arms around him, hugging him tightly. "Terra, I'm so sorry."

Terra wept for a very long time. This was the first time she'd really cried in years—ever since Daneigh died. Though she cared about Daneigh deeply, the pain of this loss hurt so much more than Terra could even imagine. How was she supposed to move on from this? How could anyone move on from this? "Who did it?" she whispered harshly, pushing Alex away from her and standing up. "Dammit, who did this?"

Alex stood up. His face was red from fallen tears, and she knew that he was already aware of Kole's murder. "I—"

A deep inner rage whirled within Terra as she glared Alex down. She was more infuriated than she'd ever been at anyone. This even topped her hatred for Courtnie and Fortis. This was so much worse than anything else Terra had ever felt before.

"You know who did this," Terra snapped. "Someone had to give the Government names, Alex. Who did it? Who got my sister killed?"

Alex had looked so frightened, Terra thought dully. Of her, of the situation as a whole. But, in the end, he'd given her the name: Zander. The Government had come to Zander's house and he'd told them the two names necessary to get him out of this alive. He hadn't given Terence's name, not Seth's, not Alex's, not hers. He'd only given up Faye and Kole. Tolerable collateral damage.

She was going to kill him.

"I'm going to kill him!" she shrieked, pounding toward the door. She already had a gun in her hand. It hadn't been hard to find. It was in their father's office, in a drawer where he thought his sons wouldn't look. But Terra had.

"Terra, please think about this!" Alex pleaded. "I know it hurts—God, I know it hurts. But killing Zander won't ease that pain any."

"I don't give a damn if it eases the pain," Terra hissed. "He deserves to die."

And with that Terra stormed out of the house, slamming the door shut behind her.

Terra was at Zander's house now. Her face contorted with anger as she stomped up the steps and began pounding on the door. Every time she hit the door with her hand she imagined Courtnie slapping Faye, inflicting pain just because she could. Terra's stomach throbbed, ached with the want for Faye to come back home.

But she wouldn't. Never again.

And it was because of the boy who lived in this house.

The door opened and Seth's face appeared. His eyes widened in fear as he caught the murderous expression on Terra's face. "Terra," he whispered. "Oh god, you know."

"Damn right I know," Terra snapped. She shoved Seth mercilessly aside and stepped into the house. "Where is he?"

Zander appeared, a remorseful expression on his face as he spotted Terra in the doorway. How dare he feel sad? How dare he feel anything when this was all his fault? "You," Terra spat. All at once she was rushing forward, grabbing Zander by his neck and pinning him against the wall. Zander wriggled, the terror clear in his eyes. Terra didn't care, though. She wanted him to be afraid. She wanted it so bad. "Give me one good reason why I shouldn't kill you right here, right now!" she screamed, resting the gun against his temple.

"I'm sorry," he whispered.

"You're sorry?" she continued to scream. Terra pulled him forward just to slam him against the wall again, somewhat satisfied when he grimaced in pain. "You had my sister killed! You gave her up to the Government. She was only seventeen!" Terra's eyes burned with tears as she slammed him into the wall for the third time. "You deserve to die for this."

Terra could feel Seth's eyes on her as she cocked the gun. Let him watch the traitor die, she thought. Let him watch. She didn't care. She didn't care. Nothing in the world mattered to her anymore. Her entire world seemed to go black now that Faye wasn't in it. What was the point to any of this?

"Terra!"

Terra shrieked as a pair of strong arms gripped her shoulders and pulled her away from Zander. Terra lashed out, kicking and scratching at the person pulling her away. She didn't attempt to shoot them, though. No. It wasn't their fault this was happening. It was Zander's fault. Zander's and Courtnie's. "Let me go!" she hissed. "I'm going to kill him!"

"No, you're not."

Suddenly Terra was twisted around and Terence's face appeared in front of her. She could see the pain of losing his best friend in his eyes, and she suddenly ached for Errika. How was Errika feeling right now? How was she handling this? Someone had to go comfort her.

But who could comfort her in a time like this?

"How can you stand here and protect him like this?" Terra demanded, shoving Terence away from her. "He had your best friend killed!"

"We know," Seth muttered, coming to stand next to Terence. The loss was clear in his face, too. Though he and Kole had never really gotten along (as Kole put it), they were still good friends. "And don't you think that making him live with the guilt is a better punishment than taking all of his pain away?"

Terra twisted around and shot a look that could kill in Zander's direction. He was still up against the wall, a mournful expression on his face. "Why did you do it?" Terra demanded coolly. "To save your own skin? Didn't want to die in order to protect your friends?"

Zander met Terra's gaze. "They were torturing my little brother," he told her. "I wasn't going to let my little brother die for a problem that wasn't his."

Though his intentions weren't awful, Terra couldn't bring herself to accept them. "You can live with your guilt," she said, injecting as much venom into her words as she possibly could. She stepped away from Terence and Seth and stopped right in front of Zander, just mere inches from where he stood. "I pray to God that this tortures you. I hope you go insane with guilt and that you can't sleep another night because of nightmares. I hope you hate yourself for what you did. And I hope you are haunted by this until the day you die."

She hadn't yelled the words, hadn't even really spoken in a raised voice. She'd concentrated on the violence in the words, not the way they were projected. It seemed to work because Zander's eyes widened with each word, and turmoil seemed to spread without them as she continued on. Terra smiled icily and then she punched him, satisfied at the ache in her hand. What was a little pain in her hand when she got to see blood coming from Zander's nose?

"I'm going to go finish this," Terra muttered, moving away from Zander now and heading toward the door. "I'm going to go finish this once and for all."

"But isn't it already finished?" Seth asked. "They killed Kole and Faye. Zander said they agreed to let him and Zachary go as long as he gave information. No one knows we're involved."

Terra's gaze hardened. "You think this is over? It's not. I'm still here, aren't I? And Courtnie is going to keep killing until she finds me. So I'm going to go end this."

"You're going to turn yourself in?"

Terra shook her head and she almost laughed. "You really think I'd let Faye die in vain? No. I'm going to kill Courtnie. I'm going to kill her, and then this will all be over."

Terence grabbed ahold of Terra's shoulder. She paused for a moment, resisting the urge to slap him. He was wasting valuable time. "Do you really think that's possible?" he asked softly.

"Of course it's possible." Terra shook Terence's hand off and she pulled open the front door. "But if you don't want me to kill Courtnie I could always kill Zander instead."

She spun around, cocking an eyebrow at Terence as she waited for him to argue with her. If he tested her too much she was going to shoot him. All she wanted to do was lash out. Losing Faye was destroying her inside and out.

"Goodbye," she said.

And then she was gone, disappearing out the front door.

Finding Courtnie's bedroom wasn't hard at all.

Terra hadn't needed to fight any guards, hadn't needed to hide from anyone. The halls remained deserted as the whole building slept. Why Courtnie was stupid enough to let the guards sleep during the night, Terra didn't know. And she didn't care. All it did was make less work for her.

Terra pushed open Courtnie's bedroom door and stepped inside. She wasn't at all surprised to see how elegant the place was. It was the bedroom fit for a spoiled little princess. Tiled flooring, floral wallpaper, canopy bed that took up more room than really necessary. A huge closer with more clothes than Terra had ever seen before. A huge dresser and a makeup stand. It was the kind of room that Terra would hate to have.

Moving toward Courtnie's bed now, Terra felt hate roll around inside her. She thought she hated Courtnie when she was locked up, but this was hate. Every fiber of her being told her to shoot the gun, to end it right now. Terra wanted to make Courtnie pay for what she did. Courtnie had to die.

Courtnie was completely oblivious, slumbering away as Terra hopped onto the bed and placed her legs on either side of her. It grossed Terra out to be in such close distance to Courtnie, but she couldn't have Courtnie fighting back. With one slick motion Terra pointed the gun at Courtnie before slapping her upside the head with her freehand. "Wake up," she snarled.

Courtnie jolted, but Terra didn't move. She simple smirked evilly as Courtnie awoke. Her eyes latched onto Terra and she let out a gasp. "What the hell are you doing here?" she demanded. Her eyes migrated toward the gun in Terra's hand. A smirk curled on her lips. "I see you heard about Faye then, I presume."

Terra cried out angrily and jabbed Courtnie in the throat with her arm. Courtnie made a choking noise, bringing a hand to her throat as she watched Terra through slits. "Don't you dare talk about Faye like that," Terra hissed. "She was a better person than you'll ever be."

"I bet you hate yourself, don't you?" Courtnie drawled breathlessly, letting her hand fall. She wasn't making any move to escape, nor did Terra expect her to. She was too cocky, too sure she was going to get out of this just fine. But she wouldn't. Not this time. "First Daneigh and now Faye. How many sisters are you going to have killed, dear Terra Caldwell? How many more people are going to die for you? You've already got three people who died in your name. And yet you continue to act against me as though you'll actually win."

Terra lashed out, scratching Courtnie across the face. Blood streaked in lines. "No one else is going to die for me," she hissed. "Because I'm going to kill you. Right now."

Courtnie grinned. Before Terra had any time to react, Courtnie was pushing her. Terra flew off the bed and onto the floor. Terra almost rolled her eyes. Did Courtnie really think that Terra still couldn't kill her from this distance? She knew how to work a gun.

"Your sister screamed as I tortured her," Courtnie cooed. "She begged and she screamed. She screamed as I cut into her skin, screamed as I burned her with open flames. She screamed. And screamed. And screamed."

Terra felt her stomach tighten and she rolled over before standing up, pointing the gun and shooting Courtnie in the arm. "Shut up!" she shrieked. "Shut up, shut up, shut up!"

"Aw, does that hurt you, Terra Caldwell? Do you not appreciate hearing how much pain your sister was in before she died? Before I shot her in the head?"

Terra glared. Courtnie didn't seem to notice the gunshot wound at all as she taunted and prodded at Terra, endlessly torturing her with her words. Usually Terra wouldn't let Courtnie get to her like this, but she was still reeling with the loss of a loved one. She wanted Faye back so damn much.

"Enough," Terra said coldly after ten minutes of Courtnie mocking her. "I'm done with you, Courtnie Featherstrom."

Courtnie's eyes widened as Terra aimed the gun and shot her cleanly at the top of the head.

Terra watched blankly as Courtnie fell to the ground. All of her problems were over; she knew that. Courtnie could no longer go after anyone else she cared about, could no longer torture people endlessly. Now everyone in the prison wards could be free. Now boys and girls could truly have the opportunity to live in harmony together.

But she still lost Faye.

Terra dropped the gun on Courtnie's bed and left the room, her hands at her sides. She thought she was going to leave immediately, but she found herself walking into Courtnie's office, her eyes barely sweeping around her surroundings before she sauntered over to Courtnie's chair and sat down. She pressed the application on Courtnie's laptop that was for the broadcasts.

Suddenly the video application appeared. Terra hurried to adjust the privacy settings. There were three options. Girls, Boys, and all.

Terra clicked on all.

Suddenly a popup appeared, asking if she was sure she wanted to broadcast to all. Terra told the machine that she did, and then a video feed popped up. Terra instantly knew that all of Cesve could see her.

Terra's grip on the chair was tight as she regarded the video feed in front of her. "Hello, Cesve," she said. "I think it's time we all have a little chat."

9 781944 260224